W9-BRX-538

THE
SILVER SHIP
AND THE SEA

TOR BOOKS BY BRENDA COOPER

The Silver Ship and the Sea
Reading the Wind
Building Harlequin's Moon (with Larry Niven)

THE
SILVER SHIP
AND SEA
THE

BRENDA COOPER

A TOM DOHERTY ASSOCIATES BOOK
NEW YORK

This is a work of fiction. All of the characters, organizations, and events portrayed in this novel are either products of the author's imagination or are used fictitiously.

THE SILVER SHIP AND THE SEA

Copyright © 2007 by Brenda Cooper

A Tor Book
Published by Tom Doherty Associates, LLC
175 Fifth Avenue
New York, NY 10010

www.tor-forge.com

Tor® is a registered trademark of Tom Doherty Associates, LLC.

ISBN-13: 978-0-7653-5509-6
ISBN-10: 0-7653-5509-4

First Edition: March 2007
First Mass Market Edition: July 2008

Printed in the United States of America

0 9 8 7 6 5 4 3 2 1

To my father,
David Cooper,

and my son,
David Cooper

ACKNOWLEDGMENTS

This is my first solo novel. It seems appropriate to thank the people who taught me what I needed to know to write it. Steven Barnes taught me how to set goals and become a writer. Larry Niven took a chance and collaborated with me on our joint novel, *Building Harlequin's Moon,* and on many short stories. Joseph Green inspired my early career in his classes at Lower Columbia College and while racing J boats on the Columbia River. Caroline Wood taught me to live with my characters. Glen Hiemstra spent years helping me learn to think like a futurist, which is a wonderful skill for any science fiction writer. Kristine Kathryn Rusch and Dean Wesley Smith taught numerous useful workshops about both the business and craft of writing.

I am grateful to the Fairwood Writers, who suffered through the first draft and helped it become a much better story. They are Renee Stern, John Pitts, Darragh Metzger, Erin Tidwell, David Silas, and others who came and went throughout the process.

I owe immeasurable thanks to my partner, Toni Cramer, and to Toni's daughter, Katie. They have almost always been patient with my regular disappearances from family life to hide and write.

My father, David Cooper, read the entire final first draft and made excellent comments. My son, also David Cooper, always helps with the bits about fires.

I am very grateful to Bob Gleason, Eric Raab, and Tom Doherty of Tor Books for taking a chance on this book, and to Eleanor Wood, my very capable agent.

THE
SILVER SHIP
AND
THE SEA

PROLOG

FROM THE STORY OF CHELO LEE, DATED JULY 17, YEAR 222,
FREMONT STANDARD, AS BROUGHT TO THE ACADEMY OF
NEW WORLD HISTORIANS

Fremont was discovered in the year zero. Zero always begins the marking of a new planet's time, as if it did not exist before humans found it.

My story did not begin until after year zero, but I feel I should begin with discovery. With zero. Which is, in a way, full of infinite possibilities. Five bright metallic probes swooped in from Inhabited Space, circled my wild planet, and then, one by one, plunged to the surface. Three landed in oceans, reporting salt and brine and signs of life. One disappeared entirely; possibly swallowed by the molten Fire River that issues from the mouth of the volcano Blaze, the hot soul of the continent Islandia. The fifth probe landed in Green Valley, where we live today. It reported that humans could breathe the air and that carbon-based life existed abundantly on Fremont.

And so, a hundred years later, the thousand colonists came. All original humans, they came from a planet much like Fremont, much like Earth, called Deerfly after the shape of one of its seas, like a deer with wings. The shape of that sea is painted on the outside of the thousand colonists' ship, *Traveler.*

They parked *Traveler* in orbit, taking seven small planet-hoppers to the surface, shuttling up and down for months with people and supplies. Being careful. Even so, Fremont's predators began killing them even before they all made it to the surface. For Fremont was joyous, riotous, very alive, and very wild. The probes mapped a moment in time: a snapshot, not a movie. If more had found our valleys, had found the two livable continents (Islandia and Jini), had found the wide grass plains, the colonists might have been better prepared.

Fremont rumbles and moves and shifts. Its blood flows across the surface in red-orange rivers and slides into its waters, sending steam hissing and spewing to honor the marriage of water and fire. Fremont's grasses and plants and animals are sharp-edged and sharp-toothed. Edible, but only once their defenses are breached.

New colonies often fail. Fremont's almost did.

After a full hundred years, Fremont hosted only fifteen hundred people, now third and fourth and fifth generation, ragged and hungry and tired. About two hundred were wanderers, called roamers, scientists who traveled the continent of Jini, where Fremont's one city, Artistos, nestles between the Lace Forest and the Grass Plains. The roamers planted and tended a continental network of information feeds, and documented the beauty and danger of Fremont. They fought to gain the knowledge and experience needed for the colony to survive. Everyone else lived in Artistos. Behind fences.

Artistos's planners designed for five thousand. The houses, of course, were not all built. The guild building and meeting rooms went up, surrounding the town's true center, Commons Park. The park was kept up, the town maintained, the granaries filled, as well as possible, by stubborn hardworking people.

The colonists' stubbornness nearly doomed them. They claimed true humanity, refused to be augmented, to improve their physical nature, to better match Fremont. Their spiritual natures were also stubborn; they did not give up when many others might have done so.

Two unexpected ships landed on the Grass Plains in the year 200, bearing my parents and others like them. *New Making* and *Journey* were smaller and more flexible than *Traveler,* so they flew down and landed in the open field next to Artistos's spaceport, searing the ground black and bending the yellow-green whip grass flat. A mere three hundred people, but three hundred *altered*. Modified for intelligence, for strength, for quickness, for long life. My early education on Fremont taught me they were arrogant, but since they were my own people, I prefer to imagine they didn't understand what they flew into. Surely they had the skills to survive, had they only understood the battleground.

The seeds of the war lie buried in history, history from long before either group came here, but we now call it the Altered War, the Ten Years War, and all of us hope that no one else comes to make another one. Most say it started over scarce food supplies, or over demands from the *altered* that the original humans follow their footsteps. Others whisper that it started over bad advice given intentionally to the newcomers.

I don't care. I do not know why it became war. Why couldn't we all live here? After all, we believe both Jini and Islandia are habitable, even though no human lives on Islandia yet. Never mind, for it does not matter.

However it began, in the end fewer than a hundred *altered* survived to flee Fremont, taking the *Journey*. Half of the first colonists were dead. One *altered* still lived: Jenna—blind in one eye, one arm lost, but fast as a paw-cat. Jenna ran, climbed, hunted, and outfoxed everyone who tried to kill her.

And us. The only *altered,* as far as we know, born on Fremont.

There are six of us. Children of the dead. We were adopted, mostly separated. Alicia and Liam, both three years old, went to two groups of roamers. Four of us went to Artistos. My brother and I remained together, adopted by Artistos's leaders, Therese and Steven, as a sign of the end of the war. Kayleen went to the popular, and barren, biologist, Paloma. Bryan became part of a large household in the builders guild, who have never liked him much. I was five at the time and Joseph two. Kayleen and Bryan were both four. So I was the oldest. The responsible one.

My new mother, Therese, once told me the *altered* hoped our unique talents would help them gain a future, help them save themselves. The words she used were, "They made you for this place." My first parents must have been made for Fremont as well, but made for the snapshot the probe sent back, not for the real place. We did not grow up in time to do whatever they made us for. They are, of course, gone. Or dead. Their ship, the *New Making,* stands upright where it landed. The ground surrounding the ship is still mostly bare and black in a circle as wide as the ship is tall. Wider than twenty of us lying down. It reminds us of our heritage. It remains locked, inaccessible.

It is twelve years since the end of the Altered War, but it has not been twelve years of peace. The first colonists returned to an enemy that had harried their flank, and in some ways had become their ally, as they fought the *altered.* They returned to the struggle to survive Fremont.

I barely remember my first parents. They floated in and out of our lives like smoke, coming to our tents late at night, exhausted, then leaving again at daybreak. I do remember Chiaro, one of the last *altered* to be killed. She raised us. She was our teacher. To this day, although the pain has shrunk to a small stone in my belly, I miss Chiaro. Therese told me once that Chiaro saved us, bartered her own life for the six of us, claiming that we would someday be helpful.

Therese and Steven treat me well enough, and I respect them. At first, they were our captors more than our parents. It was only when we became old enough to work alongside them, old enough to begin learning our abilities, how to offer them carefully and subtly, that they began to treat us with respect and, perhaps, as family. My brother Joseph loves them, I think. He has no memory of our first parents. He has little memory of the first few years we lived in Artistos. He does not recall being watched carefully, as if he would turn and bite the hands that brought him breakfast. He does not remember the time before Artistos began to appreciate our abilities, to begrudgingly allow us to participate in the life of the colony.

And why not appreciate us?

I am very strong, and think well about spatial relationships, about trajectories, about trends, about interactions between people. Those skills let me become quietly important, useful without being easily noticed. Joseph, like me, has no external physical enhancements, although he, too, is strong and fast with keen senses. His extraordinary gift is built deep inside him. He absorbs and synthesizes and directs data, balancing multiple streams in his brain, accepting many inputs, seeing multiple current moments, and correlating information. He is so earnest in his desire to please that most love him. And why not?

We all need each other to survive.

1

OUR SECOND LOSS

❧

Let me start with a nearly perfect dawn on Fremont. Morning light dappled my legs with patterns made by the broad leaves of the tent tree I sat beneath. The Lace River ran smoothly fifteen meters below me. Two of our seven moons shone above me: Faith, large and round, followed by her smaller companion, Hope; both pale in the bright daylight. As round as the moons, but near at hand and small, the redberry bush fruit had swollen into sticky orbs the size of my thumbnail. My fingers were stained red. I sat, twirling a stick idly in my hands, thinking about the summer, which had been easier than most, about the good harvest being tucked into the granaries and the storage bins. My hands moved of their own accord, restless because the peace made me restless.

Footsteps on the path behind me announced my little brother Joseph, just old enough for light fuzzy down to ghost along his chin and a slight widening of the shoulders to emphasize his thin frame. He grinned widely as he sat down next to me, and then took the stick from my hands.

"Here, Chelo, let me show you." He reached up and plucked

a wide green diamond-shaped leaf from a low branch of the
tent tree. He folded the leaf, then made a crack in the top of
the dry stick and wedged the leaf into the crack. "See?" He
twisted the stick, fast, so the black mottling of the whitish bark
blurred to gray, his palms flat. He smiled, impish, his dark
eyes dancing. His hands flew open and the stick rose, impos-
sibly, higher than our heads, whirring like night-crickets.
Leaf and stick separated. The leaf fluttered down onto my
head and I laughed with him.

"Come on, sis, let's go." He stood, shifting on his feet, full
of restless energy. He was nearly my height, black-haired
and black-eyed like me, and fast and strong, like all six of us
altered. In Joseph, speed and strength showed in long wiry
limbs and well-defined muscles. Neither he nor I displayed
obvious physical differences; we didn't have Bryan's size or
Kayleen's long feet and extra-strong toes.

Green Valley spread below us as I followed Joseph down
the packed-dirt path to the science guild hall. Artistos nestled against the Lace Forest. The Lace River, behind us now
as we walked, bordered Artistos to the north, cliffs marched
up and away to the east, cleared land gave way to thick forest to the south. Another cliff face bounded the valley, falling
westward to the Grass Plains that themselves ended in the
sea. The town itself spread neatly out from the largest open
space, Commons Park, and thin strips of green parkway ran
beside the river, buffering Artistos and making space for
fishing and gathering and walking. The two cliffs, up and
down, the High Road and the sea road, forced the town's
small industrial base north, across the river, and barns and
fields bellied up to wide tent trees and tall thick-trunked
near-elm of the forest in the south. Dense thorny underbrush
made the forest a true barrier. All the land we needed so far
had been long cleared, although each spring we fought the
forest to maintain the boundary.

Nearly everyone lived as close to Commons Park and the
guild halls as they could, so the edges of Artistos were
empty. Still, Joseph and I passed small groups of people hurrying to cross the river and start work.

We began to walk faster. If we were last, Nava would be

mad. We already angered her just by being ourselves, by being born at all. We couldn't help that, but we could be on
time. Our jobs were simple. For us. Joseph would slip open
to the data nets, feeling the subtle messages carried on the
air from the networks; his blood, bone, and then brain vibrat-
ing with and understanding the myriad stories of hundreds of
pinpoint wireless data nodes that surround Artistos. Today,
he would monitor a repair team heading past the perimeter to
fix and replace failing network nodes. Meshed with satellite
data and images from *Traveler,* Artistos depended on the
wireless network to track movements of large animals, identify weather, gather seismic data, and provide a host of other
information. The data network served as warning, science,
and reassurance all at once.

I would be Joseph's help, bringing him water, asking him
questions from the others and relaying answers, recording as
much as I could in my pad for us to talk about later. I would
make sure he ate.

We crossed Park Street, heading for the science guild hall.
Garmin and Klia and May walked toward us. They were all
roughly our age, and in a hurry; at risk of being late for work
across the river in the industrial complex. Klia looked up
and saw us, and elbowed Garmin, who glanced our way and
grasped Klia's and May's hands, pulling them toward the
other side of the street, away from us.

"Good morning, Garmin!" I called, my voice as loud and
cheery as I could make it be.

Garmin glared at me, just for a moment, and I expected
him to say something mean. But he only turned and whispered to Klia, who watched the ground. I heard the words,
". . . darn mutants. They shouldn't be allowed out."

I was mutant enough to hear his whispered words, but not
rude enough to reply. Joseph scowled, but he, too, ignored
them.

May watched the park intently, as if she expected something scary to pop out of the grass and frighten her. Or as if
she just didn't want to look at us. If we'd passed May alone,
she might have nodded politely, maybe even have said hello.
In groups, almost none of the kids our age were even that po-

lite. Joseph and I glanced at each other and walked faster, getting distance between us and Garmin. We didn't look back until we ducked into the science guild door.

The main room of the science guild hall was large enough for five hundred people. Offices, labs, and meeting rooms lined two sides of the building. The walls were wood from the Lace Forest, the roof tiles made of molded riverbank clay. The builders guild makes us glass windows, hauling sand up from the beaches and across the Grass Plains after the fall burn, when the grass is low enough for safe travel. Guild members set the thick windows loosely in clever slides designed to survive the frequent small earthquakes that plague Fremont.

When we arrived, Nava, Tom, and Paloma waited for us in the monitoring room. Nava frowned when we came in, her green eyes an icy contrast to her red hair. "You're late."

We weren't late, we were just last. I ignored her, accustomed to her coldness, her resentment of every use the colony made of our skills. Her husband Tom, a dark-haired, stocky, and round-faced gentle bear of a man, greeted us more warmly, smiling and handing us glasses of apple juice. We drank, and I ushered Joseph to the soft blue chair Steven designed so he could lie curled in his favorite monitoring position, hands and feet drawn up into a ball. It was more like a little round bed than a chair, although Joseph could sit up in it when he liked. He almost never did.

Paloma stood in the far corner of the oblong room, her back to us, poring over logs from the night before. "*Traveler,*" she said to no one in particular, "reported two small chondrite asteroids last night. One burned up on entry and the other landed in the ocean."

Tom grunted. "Could have been big ones. Gianna said we'll be in the storm for months. It's the worst on record."

"Let's just hope all the big ones miss us," Paloma muttered, her words almost a prayer. Only when she completed the logs did she look over and smile at us. She was Kayleen's adoptive mother, and she treated us, and our gifts, our alterations, as normal. I loved her for it. Even Steven and Therese, who stood up for us, did not treat us as if we were like them. Paloma grinned. "They're leaving. Are you ready?"

Joseph drained his apple juice, handed the glass to me, and leaned in to take my hand. "Blood, bone, and brain," he murmured, reciting the words he and Kayleen used to trigger the changes in their consciousness that hooked them into the data nets. "Take care of me, sis." He smiled, falling away from me, his eyes closed, his face relaxing, slack, as if he were sleeping, as if he were dreaming a good dream. He loved nothing more, then, than to feel and hear his body sing with data.

Today's repair team included our adoptive parents, Steven and Therese, who led the colony. They rarely left Artistos's boundaries, tethered by their responsibilities. Perhaps it was the easy summer, the comparative rest, that drew them out.

All together, there were ten, a large group, mostly because they planned to hunt for djuri. Djuri flesh is soft and almost sweet, tender, a treat when you are accustomed only to goats and chickens. Djuri herds often come near us in winter, but they stay higher in summer, and today the team took the High Road. We all hoped for a feast.

The team was tied to us by four of the increasingly rare earsets that allowed people any distance apart to talk, using the satellite network and ground-based wireless nodes to beam clear voice anywhere inside the wireless net. I'd been allowed to use one twice on trips to the Grass Plains with Therese and Paloma to catalog species, and they tickled my ear inside. We could not make new ones here yet; every one we lost reduced our communications ability. Joseph though, Joseph could hear the earsets without needing one himself. He couldn't speak, but he could hear.

I looked at Joseph. His body had softened, as if sleeping, and he breathed easily. By now he held at least three data streams in parallel, his agile brain watching them all, interpreting the varied messages from outer pods, the relentless pings of the boundary, and the voice streams from the expedition members, probably laughing and happy to be out, moving easily with their hebras' fast, rolling gait.

The boundary bells rang friendly exit as the expedition passed beyond the near data nets, the walls, the hard-won relative safety of Artistos. I wished I were with them, feeling a breeze cooling my sweat, hearing birdsong. Being in danger. I turned my face to the window to hide my longing and watched the long fronds of the twintrees in the park across the street and the play of five children throwing hoops on the fine grass.

Twintrees were native, but the grass, tightly controlled, came from Deerfly. Children could fall on it without being scratched. Commons Park was the softest place on Fremont.

We waited. Joseph would speak anything we needed to know, talking through the repair process while Paloma and Tom watched on their own monitors, a step removed from Joseph's intimate data immersion.

Never one to waste time, Paloma analyzed crop yields, periodically wiping her long blond hair from her face as she took notes. Tom and Nava argued quietly in the corner.

Joseph spoke. "They're starting up the High Road."

Paloma stretched and went out. I watched through the window as she shimmied up one twined trunk of a twintree set, and pulled down a shirtfront full of bittersweet fruit. She came back in and handed me two fruits, round balls the size of my fist, crowned with small thorns. I set one aside for Joseph, and started carefully peeling the bitter rind of my own. The salt-and-sour smell of the rind filled the long narrow room.

Joseph narrated the trip. "Pod 42A. Test and replace." I wrote, my own recording of the journey, kept for Joseph to remember, to supplement the dry electronic recording of events. "Knitting pod data." Freed from its thick skin, twintree fruit is small and yellowish. I popped mine into my mouth, whole, and bit down, savoring the sweetness as he continued. "Complete. Moving up toward pod 58B." Monitoring was a rhythm. He spoke, I wrote, he spoke, I wrote, I teased him up from his trance to drink water, to eat, he fell back into data and spoke and I wrote.

An hour passed. Two.

"Djuri herd!"

I repeated his words loudly, smelling grilled djuri meat already. Tom and Nava drifted closer to us.

Excitement painted the edges of Joseph's voice. "Gi Lin counts ten, Therese counts twenty."

I laughed. The pessimist and the optimist. I would bet on fifteen. Djuri are small animals, human-sized, long-eared and four-legged, horned; thin runners that blend into thickets. I imagined them in a band of trees, dappled with light. There would be a cliff, a stream, the trees, the broad High Road, and then a steep falling away to the Lace River below. The expedition would break into two groups, one ahead, one behind, and drive them together to stun them. Most would escape, but not all.

Alarm crept into Joseph's voice, feeding data back to the expedition. "Paw-cat above you. In-line between pod 97A and B." He'd have caught the size and shape of movement only. Enough. The cats had their own data signature, in the way they moved fast and low and the heat of their strong bodies. The nets almost never made mistakes identifying them. Paw-cats loved djuri as much as we did. I pictured the High Road in my head. The cat would be in the rocks, hard to spot. Joseph breathed a relieved sigh. "Steven and Mary see it. Circling to run it off."

"Are there more?" Tom asked.

"Probably."

Which meant he hadn't identified more.

Suddenly Joseph tensed, then he called, "Quake," and then, moments after the words registered, the quake bell rang in Artistos, once, for medium danger. The window rattled in its clever cage, Joseph shook in his chair, my own chair bumped below me like a live thing, and Tom and Nava and Paloma grabbed for each other.

Then the quake was gone.

We laughed, the nervous relieved laughter of fright.

"Six point five," Joseph said, then called to the expedition, "Are you all right?" He began narrating. "Gi Lin and Therese report everyone accounted for. The hebras are nervous. Steven lost sight of the cat, thinks it went up, away from them. Therese says the djuri have gathered in a knot, the does in the middle, says she's never seen that. They'll try and take some now, while they're frightened. Gi Lin can't make his hebra move. It's—" His face screwed up suddenly, and he yelled, "The rocks. Falling. Run. Quake. Run!" He reached for me blindly, his eyes shut, his hand clamping down on mine, hard and tight. His eyes opened, dark whorls filled with horror. I pulled him in, close to me, looking for a safe place to go.

The only sound I heard for the space of four heartbeats was his ragged breathing.

The quake bell clanged over and over and over: *danger, danger, danger.* Joseph screamed. The window shattered outward, tiles fell, the ground bucked under my feet, throwing me on top of Joseph. My ears were full of the bell, of Joseph's scream, of Nava and Tom and Paloma yelling, of the dull thud of tiles crashing onto the street and landing on the shattered glass. Alarm bells rang from the hospital, the school, the guild halls, the water plant. The ground shivered a last time and went still.

I gathered Joseph to me, holding him, rocking him, tears streaming down my face. Why wasn't he talking to Therese and Steven? To Gi Lin? To me? "Joseph, can you hear them? Are they okay?"

He'd lost control. Joseph never lost control monitoring. But if he felt them all die? What if they died? Fear touched my voice as I called, "Joseph?"

He hung slack in my arms, as if he were someplace far away, as if he were crushed by the rock fall that devastated our team. A scream filled me, wanting to burst out my throat, and I kept it in, fighting it, fighting for control. Joseph needed me.

Nava's voice behind me, demanding answers I didn't have. "What happened to them? What does he see?"

I held Joseph close to me, not looking at her. "He doesn't see anything," I snapped. Couldn't she see his pain? We needed to be in the open, away from the shattered window, the damaged guild hall, away from Nava's bad grace. I tugged on Joseph. "Wake up, wake up. Now. Come on." He didn't respond. His eyes stayed closed and narrow. His skin felt cool, as if he himself were not there in my arms at all.

Tom came up behind me, gently moving me aside, separating me from my brother. He knelt by Joseph, who must have sensed my absence; he struggled and kicked, lashing out wildly. Tom pinned Joseph's legs, picked him up, and started toward the door. He looked over his shoulder and caught my eyes. "Follow me." He spoke into his earset, his voice high and worried, "Report out. Anyone. Anyone."

I followed Tom out and across to the park, thinking of Joseph. Only of Joseph. I couldn't think of Therese or Steven or Gi Lin yet, of the silence that answered Tom's repeated pleas. I focused on Joseph, limp in Tom's arms, his eyes closed, his face over Tom's shoulder completely white.

Soft grass tickled my ankles. Tom settled Joseph so his head rested in my lap. I stroked his shoulder, the side of his face, trying to pull him back from wherever he had gone.

The sounds of the colony accounting for itself flowed around us. Nava, taking charge, using the deep sonorous gather-tones of the central bell, pulling the townspeople to meet at the amphitheater behind me. Children crying. People calling for their loved ones. Dogs barking.

The guild halls and houses ringing the park nearly all showed damage, but they all stood. Water from a broken underground pipe gushed up through the tight-packed stones on the street between me and the school.

Kayleen and Bryan found us, Bryan's eyebrows drawn together in worry. Fear brightened Kayleen's blue eyes. Like Joseph, Kayleen could tap data streams, although two or three at a time, not the unlimited number that Joseph seemed able to juggle. "He's in shock." She reached a hand out and touched his cheek, her dark hair falling over her face. "How connected was he? What's the last thing he said?"

I told them the story. Bryan sat across from Joseph, watching his face. Kayleen sat next to me, chewing on her lip, uncharacteristically quiet. She was at least as disturbed as me. It bothered me that she had no answers, no suggestions.

Townspeople poured around us, streaming to the roll call bell, discussing damage in loud, worried tones. Hilario's handsome dark face was covered in blood, his arms and hands bathed in it, as if something had opened a fountain of blood in his skull. Gianna limped. One group carried a prone form on a stretcher toward the hospital.

It all felt unreal. We were used to death and danger on Fremont, but by ones and twos, nothing so widespread.

The bell called for us, too. Bryan picked Joseph up, carrying him like a baby, and Kayleen and I followed, holding hands. We settled at the top of the amphitheater, Joseph lying on the grass, his head pillowed on my thigh. Bryan sat on my other side, sometimes taking my hand. Our feet dangled over the edge of the wall. Above us, a large twintree leaned over the amphitheater. It was usually full of kids scampering up and down its broad branches, picking fruit and scaring their parents into high-pitched calls for care, but today only two small boys seemed brave enough to climb it.

We looked down into a ring of granite steps falling gently downslope to a stage. Built in the first hundred years, when the colonists were more hopeful, the open amphitheater could hold two thousand easily; fewer than eleven hundred lived in Artistos today. Empty seats surrounded any gathering held there.

There was no gathering today, rather a stream reporting in and being sent back out in small knots to check streets, record damage, find wounded, do all of the hundreds of things that needed to be done. Nava and the other three Town Council members assigned work and recorded information. Tom ran errands for them. Hope surged in me as the boundary bell rang until I recognized the exit tone: riders being sent to check on the expedition.

Paloma took Kayleen to check on the hebras and goats, but Bryan stayed with us, silent and protective. So he was beside me when Nava charged up the aisle toward us, standing over us like some red-haired warrior, her hands dirty, her shoulder-length hair hanging in damp red strings around her face, her green eyes boring into mine. "Has he said anything else? Does he know if any of them are alive?"

"He seems to be in shock," I said, as evenly as I could.

"Well, your job, both of you, is to fix him. We need him back on the data nets."

The ground chose that instant to shiver and jerk again, enough to jolt more tiles from the guild hall roofs onto the ground, to cause a child to scream. "I have to go," she said. "Get him working." Nava jogged away from us.

Bryan whispered under his breath, "He's not a machine," and I heard the anger in him. Bryan's strong, polite outer nature shielded him against rude treatment from his adoptive family, who never forgot his *altered* strength or forgave his extraordinary patience and intelligence. Patience, however, is not forgiveness. It is merely patience. Bryan's anger burned deep. Now, it lit his blue eyes, tightened the line of his jaw, and flushed his skin. He pushed his brown hair from his face with one large hand and stared out across town, his gaze apparently fixed on the horizon. Bryan was always sweet and patient with us, but like the big sheepdog that helped Stile with the hebras, I knew he could be dangerous to anyone who threatened me or Kayleen or Joseph.

For now, Nava and I both wanted Joseph to heal. We just had different reasons.

Bryan got up, smiled softly at us, and walked down the hill. He came back a few moments later, carrying a blanket, a canteen, and a hunk of bread. He covered Joseph carefully with the blanket and handed me the water and half the bread. My shocked body welcomed the water, but I simply held the bread in my lap, unable to take a bite. I stroked Joseph's head.

Dusk had driven the twintree shadows nearly the length of the park when the boundary bell rang again: entrance. I looked up, my heart leaping with hope and confounded by dread all at once. Bryan must have seen my feelings in my eyes, because he said, "Go, I'll watch Joseph." I kissed them both on the forehead, and ran down the street toward the river. They'd be coming in from the north. I could intercept them at Little Lace Park. If there were any dead, the searchers would have to pass through the park to take the bodies to the other side of the river for preparation. I'd pass anyone bringing the living to the hospital. I ran all out, blood pumping through my limbs, my fingers, my toes, my heart driven to find out, now. I passed four groups of people before I ran up on Paloma, her blond hair flying. She turned toward me, her blue eyes startled, and put a hand out, yelling, "Chelo!"

It took great effort to slow my steps, to bridle the energy that burned in me and obey her, to go no faster than her pace, draw no more attention. But I did it.

Kayleen and Tom and about ten other people had beaten us to converge on the riders in the park. The long graceful necks of two hebras poked above the human heads, nearly silhouettes in the evening light. Tom struggled with a bundle strapped to the back of the nearest hebra. I ran up to him. Tom narrowed his eyes and looked as if he were going to send me away, but Paloma and Kayleen stood beside me. He sighed, and swallowed, and continued with his work. It seemed to take forever.

The burdened hebra turned its bearded head, watching Tom carefully, its wide-set dark eyes curious. Cold settled inside my stomach. The body lowered and the shroud opened to reveal Gi Lin, one side of his face flattened, the other perfect. Kayleen and Paloma and I nearly crushed each other's hands from sorrow and disbelief.

The other hebra was similarly burdened. Just as Tom loosened the ropes, a hand flopped out. Steven's hand. His left little finger was missing, an accident from the last days of the war. It is one thing to be certain of something, and another to have knowledge of it driven into you with the harsh stake of reality. I landed on my knees on the stony grass of the park, and Kayleen and Paloma knelt on each side of me. Someone keened. When I found my breath again, I pushed myself back to standing. Behind me, Paloma asked, "Any word of the others?"

Ken, one of the men who'd gone to retrieve the bodies, answered her. His words were choppy, uneven, as if he still had trouble admitting their truth. "Rocks fell almost all the way across the road. Hard to pass at all, but if someone was on the upward side, they could get to us. We saw a dead hebra off the cliff, but there are rocks there, too, rocks crossed the road." He swallowed. "We did see Therese's body, but there's a rock too big to move covering most of her. We'll have to go back later."

I stumbled into Paloma's arms as the second expected blow became real.

Tom came up, putting his arm over my shoulder. "Go on, Chelo, take care of Joseph. You can't stay in the park all night. Your house came up safe in the survey. Go there. We'll check on you tomorrow." He glanced at Paloma and Kayleen, his eyes demanding rather than asking. "Can you take her back? Settle her and Joseph in? Then meet me at the amphitheater—I'll be there in an hour."

We walked back, clutching each other's hands, stumbling through nearly complete darkness. Only one weak moon, Plowman, added to the starlight. The town's evening lights hadn't come on. We stumbled through the dark to find Joseph and Bryan where I had left them. Bryan carried Joseph, and the five of us shuffled carefully home, crunching shards of glass and ceramic roof tile under our feet.

Kayleen and Paloma helped me tuck Joseph in. Bryan made me a cup of mint and redberry tea. After they left, I tried to drink the tea, but it tasted bitter. I wandered about, restless, picking up cups and pictures that had fallen, sweeping the shards of a broken potted plant into the trash.

Steven and Therese should walk in any minute. I knew better, yet I looked up for them over and over.

I pulled my bedding into Joseph's room and lay down on the floor. False crickets chirped outside the window and the occasional call of a night bird sounded from up above the house in the beginning of the Lower Lace Forest.

The night passed slowly. What if Joseph didn't get better? What would happen to us now? Who would take us in?

2

MOURNING

Light falling in the window woke me. I blinked. Where was
Therese? She usually woke us up. I remembered, and wanted
to fall back asleep until Therese woke me. But she wouldn't,
ever again. My back was stiff from sleeping huddled on
the hard floor of Joseph's room and he lay, hurt, above
me. Joseph stirred, as if waking in sync with me. "Are you
awake?" I whispered.

"Yes."

I sat up and gazed at him. He was on his back, looking up
at the ceiling, his face white. "How do you feel?"

Joseph's eyes met mine, but looked right through me. It
made me shiver. "Like fire burned me inside out," he murmured, his voice cracking. "I heard them, their voices, their
cries. Steven calling out for Therese, Mary yelling for Jonas,
but of course, he wasn't with them. I was afraid with them,
as if the rocks were falling on *me*. I heard their pain, heard
them wink away, one by one. Therese was one of the first,
and I heard Steven yell for her, then I heard him scream." He
looked up at the ceiling. "I couldn't help them." Tears glistened in the corners of his eyes. "I . . . I felt it here, felt the
quake rock my body, but I'd already felt it up the hill and
they were dying, so my attention stuck there, with them."

His voice was shaky, and I wanted to hold him, but I
didn't want anything physical to break his thoughts. His pain
was too deep for me to touch away. When he fell silent a moment, I whispered, "Do you remember sitting in the park?"

"I sensed you all, you and Kayleen and Bryan, and Tom once. Bryan stayed with us." Finally, he looked at me. "Is everyone else okay?"

Okay? Of course not. But I nodded and fetched him a glass of water. His lips looked dry and chapped and his eyes were the wrong shade of black, like thunderclouds about to pour rain and fire. I watched him take a long, slow drink. Only when he handed me back the empty glass did I say, "No one died here. Denise broke her wrist and Hilario's face got banged up by a falling roof tile. Gianna hurt her ankle. I heard the hospital was full, but they released most people. We were lucky."

"Were we?"

A knock at the door saved me from answering. I dragged myself from Joseph's side. Something as normal as answering the door seemed impossible, like walking through waves. As I pushed the door open, the widening crack spilled light and birdsong into the short hallway. The happy normal sounds scraped at my confused grief; I wanted the world to be silent and respectful.

Bryan stood just outside, his bulk filling much of the doorway. He folded me into his arms. He whispered into my hair. "I'm so sorry. I would have come sooner, but I couldn't." I didn't answer, just stood in his arms, drawing strength from his bulk, his steadiness. After a minute, he asked, "How's Joseph?"

"He's awake. Come in." I stepped back and Bryan passed me, heading for Joseph's room. The empty place he left in the doorway filled with Kayleen, damp from a shower, but not fresh; her eyes drooped and she moved slowly. "Sorry I just couldn't come earlier. Nava made me and Mom run tests on the data nets until after midnight." She pulled out a kitchen chair, sat down with a thump, and started combing her hair with her fingers, watching me. "You don't look like you slept. You look exhausted. Just a minute, I'll find us some breakfast. How's Joseph?"

Seeing her lifted my spirits a tiny bit. "He's . . . he's hurting."

Kayleen headed for Joseph's room, still trying to untangle

her hair. I followed her, so the four of us crowded into the small square room. There was only one chair, which Bryan filled, so Kayleen sat on my rumpled bedding and I perched on the narrow bed by Joseph, who had turned back to the wall.

Bryan's voice was low and even. ". . . need to talk. I know you don't want to, I know it's not a good time yet, but Kayleen and I are worried. We need to come up with a plan for you two."

I blinked, startled. That was my job. I hadn't been doing it. I didn't want to do it, not yet. I put a hand on Joseph's shoulder. "He's right. We need to plan." There would be too much to do to let anyone grieve long. Nava wasn't one to wait on emotions, and certainly not on ours. The town couldn't wait. A fresh wave of loss washed through me. Therese and Steven. "We'll probably all be called to work today."

Joseph groaned and whispered, "I can't."

"We'll be okay." I rubbed his shoulders lightly. "We'll manage. They need us, and I'm sure we can do something easy."

Joseph burrowed into the pillow. "How come you're always so positive?" he mumbled.

Bryan twisted his hands in his lap. "She's made that way. Now, come get some breakfast. You need to eat."

Joseph pulled the covers tighter. "I'm not hungry."

"Do I have to carry you?" Bryan asked. He glanced at Kayleen and me. "You two, go on. Get something easy for him to eat. We'll be in."

I smiled at Bryan. "Thanks for being here."

Kayleen found four small red apples in a basket on the counter. I dug goat milk out of the refrigerator and a few thick slices of bread, which we'd have to eat dry since the butter container had fallen from the counter in the quake and lay in greasy shards under the corner of the cabinets. We finished just as Bryan and Joseph came down the hallway and settled into chairs. Joseph's hands shook in his lap and he didn't reach for any of the food. I understood, but took a slice of apple, hoping to coax him into eating.

Kayleen drummed her fingers on the table. "So, Bryan told you we've been talking. You're almost an adult, Chelo. You will be in a year. Surely you can make a case for living by yourselves now. It would solve the problem of where you're going to go. There are plenty of empty houses."

We'd daydreamed about the four of us living together when we grew up. Why not now? Who'd want us, anyway? I could be completely responsible for Joseph, protect him. A small sliver of hope rose inside me.

Kayleen continued, her words rushing out like cool spring wind. "And maybe we can live there, too. I *know* Paloma would let me, at least sometimes. We could practice together without having to go outside. Joseph and I could explore the data fields more, maybe I could learn to handle more than two data streams." She leaned forward, her blue eyes bright with her idea. "We could have our long talks and not worry about being interrupted. Bryan's family can't stand him. I bet they'd let him go."

Bryan looked less willing to believe in good fortune. "Will Town Council let us?"

"Not if Nava is in charge." I mused out loud, my head clicking through possibilities slowly. "She'd never allow it. She likes us where she can watch us. They let us be friends, but remember, they split four of us across three guilds on purpose, and gave two to the roamers, to keep us separate." But what would the colony really do about leadership? Grief kept my head from forming questions as easily as usual.

Bryan added, "Nava runs the logistics guild. Exactly the skills we'll need to rebuild the town."

Kayleen held a slice of apple near Joseph's hand. "I know you don't want to eat. But you need to. Please?"

Joseph ignored her, as if he *couldn't* respond. I watched with growing alarm. He was never rude, never silent, never all the things he was that moment.

After a moment, Kayleen set the apple down and asked him, "Hey, what do you think about us living together?"

His voice shook. "I'm not going."

"Where?" she asked.

"Back into the data streams. I can't go there."

I bit back an immediate reply. He had to. He'd discovered his talent when he was six. I could still see it clearly—it was the first moment it really sank in that we were more powerful, in some ways, than even the adults around us.

I was watching him in the playground at the park. His attention drifted, so he didn't notice the ball as I threw it to him. Then he stiffened and his eyes widened so he looked puzzled and excited and scared all at once. He said, "Something's trying to come in."

"What?" I asked him.

"Demons." His eyes rolled in his head and he sat down, going completely still, frightening me. It was as if he'd died right there, gone so far away that I might as well not have been there. A full minute later the boundary bell rang the high sharp tones for animal intrusion. It was a pack of demon dogs; fast four-legged animals with sharp teeth. Gi Lin and Steven scared the pack off, but from that day forward, Joseph's primary play was listening to the vast wireless networks that surrounded us. I was deaf to them, but Kayleen quickly learned to join him in data-play.

How to deal with Joseph's fear? He fought commands; I'd circle back to his data connection later. "What about living together?"

"Who has to approve it?" Bryan asked me.

"Probably Nava. I suppose we could petition Town Council. Their attention won't be available to us until the mess is cleaned up. I'll watch for a good opening."

Kayleen waved the apple in front of Joseph again, and he grunted and pushed himself to standing. His knees buckled and he crumpled, limp, his arms splayed across the floor, his cheek turned to one side. He moaned softly.

I felt as weak as Joseph, scared for him all over again, like in the park.

Bryan scooped him off the floor, and carried him back to bed. I followed, my breath catching in my throat. Joseph looked small and vulnerable in Bryan's arms. Had something serious broken in him? How would we know?

Kayleen brought the apples and a glass of water and set them on Joseph's bedside table. As Bryan covered him with a blanket, Joseph looked gratefully at him. Yesterday morning, or any other morning, Joseph would have turned beet-red at being carried.

Bryan smiled down at him. "Go on, little brother, sleep. We'll try to decide what to do."

Joseph nodded and rolled on his side, looking away from us at the blank wall beside his bed.

The three of us headed back to our interrupted breakfast. "Why can't he stand?" Bryan asked the question before I got it out of my mouth.

Kayleen finished her milk and set the glass down. "Sometimes, when I try to handle too much data, it exhausts me, like it wears out my nervous system. Joseph was seriously immersed, right? Then jerked out? It might take a day or two before his body does what he wants it to."

Another knock on the door.

I went to answer it, followed by Kayleen and Bryan.

Nava stood there. Her hair was wet from a shower and she wore clean coveralls and a light shirt. Dark circles spread under her eyes. "Good," she said, "you're all here." She paused, then drew herself up. "I know you're hurting, but so are we all. We lost two greenhouses, one storeroom is missing its roof, and only half the houses we've checked so far are safe to live in." Nava stopped and looked at us, as if gauging our reactions. "Gianna thinks there's a storm coming. I'm going to need you all this morning. I'll need everyone." She looked down, her fists balled by her side.

A deep need to be moving, doing, seemed to shoot out from Nava, as if she were a comet about to explode against some solid object. I wanted her to leave. She was looking at me. "I know you feel bad, we all do. We just"—she shrugged—"there's no time."

"Of course," I said. "The three of us will come and help. But Joseph's asleep; he's exhausted, he can hardly walk. He needs to rest."

Nava frowned, as if she wanted to contradict me, but nodded. "Should I send over a doctor?"

Joseph would hate that. "I think he just needs rest. Please, I want to work nearby, where I can check on him."

"I'll do what I can." She glanced at Kayleen. "That means we'll need you to work with Paloma. Be at the amphitheater in twenty minutes. All three of you."

"All right," Kayleen piped up from behind me. "We'll be there."

Nava turned quickly on her heel, heading for the neighbors' house.

"She is *not* happy about Joseph being out of the nets," Kayleen said, shaking her head.

Bryan grunted. "She could have at least asked how you were before telling you what to do."

We finished breakfast. None of it had any flavor.

The gather-bell rang. I checked on Joseph while the other two picked up the kitchen. He breathed softly and evenly, clearly asleep, although soft little whimpering sounds rose from deep in his throat. I kissed his smooth cheek and straightened the blankets around him.

We held hands as we walked over to the park. The air felt heavy and damp, pregnant with electricity and rain. Only the early crops had been harvested; the third hay cutting, the squash, and the second crop of beans were still in the fields. Some of what we'd already harvested had probably been damaged, and rain might damage more. We never got our disasters in ones. Always twos or threes or fours.

The crowd gathering at the amphitheater talked quietly, looking somber. Family groups walked together, parents holding children's hands. I often helped at the elementary school, and some of the children waved at us, but most adults ignored us. We sat near the top, like yesterday, Bryan and Kayleen on either side of me.

I felt a hand on my shoulder. Startled, I looked up into Jenna's single steel-gray eye. Her mangled face was weathered, her skin dark from living outside. Her breath smelled like twintree fruit. She said, "Take care of your little brother. His pain is huge." She didn't wait for a reply but let go of my shoulder, backing up, sitting by herself in a shadowed corner. She never came into town, never responded to the gather-bell. I hoped she would be all right in the crowd.

"What's she doing here?" Kayleen whispered.

I shook my head. "I don't know. How does she know about Joseph?"

Jenna lived outside of town but inside the boundaries. People chased her when I was a little girl, as if she were some kind of animal, trying to kill her. She outfoxed them; she killed a few paw-cats and caught two of the long yellow snakes, which she brought, one by one as she made her kills, into the middle of the park and left for people to find. We modeled our own acceptance on hers. Being useful.

Jenna was the only adult example we had of what we might become, even if she was broken and barely tolerated and hard to talk to. Jenna was wary of everyone, even us. Still, we'd puzzled out some of our abilities by watching her. She had Bryan's strength, although she was tall and wiry, less boxy, and she ran like Kayleen, fast and agile.

Kayleen chewed on her lower lip. "Do you think anyone besides us ever talks to her, or she to them? Does she have any friends at all?"

Down on the stage, Nava cleared her throat into the microphone. The crowd quieted. "Good morning. I believe everyone knows most of the news, but I will repeat it officially for the record.

"The earthquake yesterday registered nine point five, the second worst in our history." She swept her gaze across the whole of the amphitheater. "First, to acknowledge our losses. Ten people, including Therese and Steven, died in a rock fall on the High Road above us." Nava hesitated, and it seemed that her grief and the crowd's grief and the knot in my stomach all bound together into something palpable, something with weight. I blinked, trying not to cry. Bryan squeezed my hand and Kayleen put an arm across my shoulders, steadying me. Nava continued. "We will mourn them together. Tomorrow night. They were our leaders, and would have wanted us to ensure our safety first. We will do that.

"We've started assessing damage. Nearly everything can be fixed; what cannot be fixed can be replaced. We made lists of tasks." Nava pointed to a table with lists set out on it.

"Some of you have been preassigned based on skills. Others may choose spots to fill in. We need to work hard, even in our grief and pain. We need to beat the storm. Let us work together today, and eat together tonight, and work again tomorrow, and then we will mourn our dead."

The crowd moved down, subdued, and began checking and completing lists, then drifted across the park or across streets or toward warehouses to begin the work. We were almost the last in line. I looked behind me for Jenna, but she had disappeared.

On the lists, Kayleen's name was coupled with Paloma's, to keep helping with data readings, assessing the overall damage to the network. Bryan's assignment was to help repair hebra barns. My name had been scratched out of the list of people moving things from the damaged storehouse and written into the child-care list. So Nava *had* made sure I'd be near enough to check on Joseph. I closed my eyes, weak and swaying. Briefly grateful to Nava.

There were nearly sixty children between two and about ten years old, and four of us to manage them all. The kids were uncommonly subdued, moving in quiet groups, holding hands, whispering to each other, crying easily. We started in the park, to keep the buildings free for inspection and repairs. Heat and damp and wind drove us to the bowl of the amphitheater to organize tag games for the bigger kids. I sang songs with the littler ones, wiped noses, and comforted.

Three hours passed before I dug myself free to check on Joseph. The sky brooded above me as I walked home, the clouds a sickly yellow-green that blocked so much light it looked like early evening.

It was just past lunch.

Joseph sat up in his bed, back against the wall, his legs curled up to his chest, echoing one of the postures he used for data communing. Dried tear tracks showed on his cheeks. He offered a slight smile when I came in the door. "How do you feel?" I asked.

"Like you look."

I smiled at that. "I've got child-care duty. Want to come help me with the kids?"

He looked down for a moment before meeting my eyes. "I got up to get water. I was so weak I almost fell again. Nothing hurts. I want to stay here, sleep."

I frowned. "Jenna suggested we watch out for you. But that's all she said."

"She came to town?" Joseph's eyes widened.

"To the meeting this morning. No one stopped her."

"Wow. Why me? Didn't she ask about us all?"

I shook my head. "Just you. But she could see *us*, after all. It's going to storm something fierce." During the last big storm, Joseph and I had stood outside in the lashing rain, leaning into the wind, laughing at the sheer power of it. "Are you sure you can't go out?"

He nodded.

"The funeral is tomorrow evening. Will you go with me?"

He nodded, looking miserable, and I knelt over him and hugged him. "I love you, little brother. We'll get through this." Against my better judgment, I added, "Maybe they will let us stay by ourselves."

He was quiet for a minute. "Do you really think so?"

I was always honest with him. "No, not really. Not if Nava's in charge."

"She'll probably figure out the worst possible place for us, or split us up."

"It won't be that bad. She needs us functional, especially you." I looked around. Because we'd been Therese and Steven's, we lived in the town leader's house. "We'll have to move somewhere. If they don't let us stay alone, maybe we can hook up with Paloma and Kayleen. Look, I've got to go."

He smiled up at me, a sad smile, an expression I'd never seen on his face before. "Bye. See you tonight. I'll try to at least make it to the kitchen table by then."

"I'll hold you to that." I hugged him briefly, and left.

I returned just in time for the first thunder to shake us all into cowering, to paint fear on the children's faces all over again. We gathered them from the corners of the amphitheater and started marching them to the street, needing cover. We were across the street from the science guild hall when the rain slammed down like a wall, making it hard to even see the children it soaked. We counted noses inside the hall to make sure everyone was accounted for. Within a few minutes, dripping and worn-out parents started coming in to claim their tired children.

Full dark descended before Kayleen found me in the nearly empty guild hall. "Gosh I'm exhausted." Her fingers twisted through her hair, combing the damp locks, just like at the breakfast table this morning.

I laughed. Even tired, Kayleen couldn't be completely still. "Well, try managing sixty scared kids through a thunderstorm. They were as edgy as a trapped uncut male hebra, and they whined."

"You like kids," she teased.

"Sometimes." I sighed and looked around. Only three children and one adult remained. They didn't need me anymore. I reached for my coat. "Come on, let's go. I want to check on Joseph. I was home a few hours ago, and he was talking, but he's still weak."

"Nava wants to see us. She's going to your house."

"You didn't ask her about us living by ourselves, did you?"

Kayleen grinned at me. "Of course not. She thinks I'm next to useless, at least most of the time. I bet she just wants to check on Joseph and see if he 'works' again. She made *me* work pretty hard today."

"How is the net?"

We stepped out into the driving rain, heads down, walking fast. Kayleen's big feet made extra splashes in the growing puddles. We were soaked in moments. She said, "The immediate perimeter is weaved all right, but the outside is mostly silent. Only a few nodes seem to be working. With so many quiet nodes, the farthest ones may not be able to reach us. There are big holes. Mom and Nava think the quake wasn't even centered here." She pointed up at the sky. "Satellite data has been pretty sketchy between clouds and electrical interference from the storm, but we had clear pictures yesterday. There's damage all up and down the High Road, and some of the paths by the lakes look blocked, too."

We stepped carefully to avoid wide streams filling the low spots in the streets. "So did you hear from the roamers?"

"No. We're hoping it's just the bad data net."

"Surely they're all right. They'd have been outside." I said it as much to reassure myself. "We'll hear from them soon."

I had to jog to keep up with Kayleen, even tired as she was. As we stopped to take our mud-covered shoes off, I was grateful to be home. When I pushed the door open, I expected to see Joseph. Instead, Nava sat at our kitchen table like she owned the place, scribbling notes on her pad and talking into her radio. She didn't look up. "Hi, Chelo. I checked on Joseph and he refused to come out." She frowned. "He wants to hear what I have to say. I need you to dig him up."

I grimaced. "I'll try. Let me change clothes."

She glanced up long enough to see how wet I was, but even then she hesitated, as if giving me a few moments went against her core self. She nodded, then spoke to Kayleen, "I have a message for you to take to Paloma."

"But—"

Nava held out a folded note. "Go home and get dry. We'll see you at the group dinner. Fifteen minutes."

Kayleen took the note, gave me a stricken look, then turned and went back into the storm.

It took ten minutes to find dry clothes and convince Joseph, who emerged grumbling and shaky from his bed, that he had to listen to Nava. It wasn't like Nava couldn't have just gone to Joseph's room to say whatever she needed to say.

Once we sat down, she ignored us until she finished writing. Then she looked up at Joseph. "It's good to see you can move, after all." Her gaze switched to me. "Council met this afternoon during the worst of the storm. They elected me to run Artistos for the next six months; they'll decide again after that. Tom and I are to move in here."

So we would have to move. Maybe Paloma would take us in. Or Gianna. Gianna was nice to us.

Nava cleared her throat and shifted in her chair. "We're to take over your guardianship. You'll live with us, here."

I glanced at Joseph. His face was impassive, but I knew him well enough to read the set of his body. Even sick and shocky, he stiffened at *this* news.

I took a deep breath. This was too fast. "I was hoping we could live by ourselves. There's plenty of housing, and we'd be out of your way. Wouldn't it be better for you to have the whole house?"

Nava looked at me evenly, her jaw set. "You still need to be watched. Lyssa suggested you will do better in your own home."

I clamped my jaw shut, holding back. This was not the moment to take her on. It showed in every part of her stiff body language. If we had to live with her, this would be a good time to say thank you, but I just couldn't make myself do it.

She pushed herself up from the table. "Coming to dinner?"

I shook my head. "No, I think Joseph's too weak. I'll fix him something here."

"Suit yourself." She left, leaving her papers on the table.

The storm pounded the roof with a fury wind all night. Hot hard rain drummed against the leaves outside my window, a backdrop to difficult dreams of Therese and Steven lost in a sea of stones.

I woke to a clear dawn. A light breeze carried the scent of mud and water in through chinks in the windowsills.

That day, I took care of children again. I struggled to find a way to feel good about living with Nava while I managed a team of nine- and ten-year-old children, picking up soaked and shattered tiles and stacking them in wagons. Maybe living with us would change Nava's mind. Knowing the enemy would help us. We could earn her trust. I didn't believe any of it, except that Tom would be good for Joseph. Maybe. All I really knew about Tom was that he was kinder to us than Nava, polite. But he wasn't like Paloma, not a champion. He hadn't really seemed to notice us much. Just after lunch, Gianna limped up to us, smiling softly at me.

Pain and exhaustion marred her thin face. "We heard from the roamers. Both bands. They're all right"—she pushed back her long hair—"except that Gene Wolk died in the quake. But we were afraid we'd lost more."

Gene used to carve all of us children little wooden trees and people. "I . . . I'll miss him," I stammered.

One more death to add to the list, one more face I'd never see again. At least Alicia and Liam were okay. "Are you okay?" Gianna asked.

I nodded. "As okay as anyone right now. Joseph's having a hard time."

"I'd heard that. I hope he's better soon." She smiled softly at me and limped away.

When the end-of-shift bell finally rang, my head hurt from thinking too hard and my shoulders and back blazed with pain from stacking tiles.

That evening, Joseph could walk without falling down. It hurt; he pinched his lips tightly closed and his eyes watered. We dressed carefully for the funeral in deep blue shirts, the formal color of Deerfly, and now of Fremont. It used to be the color of ship's uniforms on *Traveler*. I brushed his black hair back from his eyes, but his face was still white and dark circles pooled under his eyes. He managed a small smile. I held him close and whispered, "I love you."

He whispered back, "I love you, too. Let's go. I'll make it."

As we walked, a deep red-gold sunset softened the wide wooden planks of the Lace River Bridge and sent light motes dancing along the top of the tiny wavelets as water rounded rocks.

People gave us room, walking around us, uncomfortable with our grief, weighted down with their own. We crossed the narrow Stream Bridge and took the muddy path toward the orchard. As we passed the smelter and woodshop, the path lights snapped on, making our way past the edges of the orchards easier. By the time we arrived at the funeral clearing, beads of sweat stood out on Joseph's forehead.

I had been to funerals before, we all had. This was different, it was my people, my guardians, and I hated every step. I was grateful that almost no one spoke to us, and grateful that they came. About half the crowd wore the formal deep blue. Others clearly came directly from work; dirt streaked their faces, their clothes were damp and their feet muddy. Hilario came, his head bandaged, led by his tiny blond sweetheart Isadora.

Gianna stood as greeter, dressed in formal blues, handing each of us who had lost a direct family member a white ribbon to tie around our upper arm. She hugged us as she gave us our ribbons, her eyes red from tears. "I'm so sorry," she murmured in my ear. "I believe in you and your brother, and I know you have it hard sometimes, especially now. I'll help you if I can."

I held her back, squeezing her hard, wanting to hold on, but the next person stood in line and I turned away from her to help Joseph tie on his ribbon.

There must have been nearly a hundred ribbons; parents, brothers and sisters, life partners, and children. Everyone with a ribbon stood in the first circle around the wooden pyres. Jonas, Mary's husband, stood near us, his face a mask of stoic calm except for the tears trailing down his cheeks.

The wood looked dry; it must have been stacked since the storm. A team had been up the High Road and returned with three more bodies, all they could find, or reach. Therese, Mary, and Rob. The bodies were draped in long blue shrouds. Someone had thrown yellow flowers on top of Therese's shroud. It was a gift that the faces of the dead were covered. I wanted to remember them all alive and active and smiling.

Five tall pyres clustered together, and around them, five cones of wood for the missing dead; we would honor everyone.

Full dark fell. We turned, facing outward, watching the living watch us. "This is your remaining family. They embrace you in your grief," Nava intoned from somewhere to our right. Electric light came from behind the crowd, so we saw silhouettes, rows and rows of them, then bright lights, and behind them, green trees dotted with red fruit. The light evening wind blew toward me, and I smelled apples and the fiery metallic scent of the smelter, which could not be shut down for something as simple as a funeral. Not when the colony was in crisis.

Nava continued. "We are gathered to mourn the passing of our leaders, of Steven and Therese, and of eight other brave souls. Gi Lin . . . Mary . . . Rob . . . Hans . . . AnnaLisa . . . Barnil . . . Thang . . . Jackson." As Nava spoke each name, a moment of silence trailed behind the name before she began the next.

When the list was complete, she said, "We will miss them all. This is the largest funeral since the war."

I swallowed, uneasy. We reminded Nava of the war. It was a dim childhood memory to us, but many adults still felt losses from the war sharply; loved ones killed by our original parents, by our real people—and they hated us for it, as if we had pulled triggers. Some passed their fears to their children, and so Garmin and a few others hated us. The war was our unwelcome shadow and I didn't want it here, not at this funeral.

But as Nava continued, she said, "We should take this as a reminder that we are at war with Fremont. We will stand together in our fight, and we will win. We will rebuild all that has been broken in Artistos, and we will go forward and rebuild the families that are broken."

In the short silence she left then, I thought of her new leadership. Was there anything except politics in her assumption of care for me and my brother? I thought not. We were symbols of Therese and Steven's life. The previous leaders had us so Nava would have us. White-hot anger threatened to rise up alongside my grief, but I pushed it down. This was not the time.

Tiny fires sprang to life; ten funeral torches. Tom carried one to me, a stick as long as my arm with a flame burning at its top. His face seemed to dance and sway in the firelight. "Light the pyre behind you for Therese and Steven, who loved you both well." He switched his gaze from me to Joseph. "Stand with your sister. Use the fire to cleanse and purify your grief."

Joseph nodded, his eyes fixed on the fist-sized fire, his hand clutching mine. We stood until all of the torches were delivered.

Drums sounded.

The signal.

Joseph and I stepped forward together, and I lowered my hand, touching the bright torch to the corner of stacked wood nearest me. Flame leaped from the torch to the dry wood, rising fast, and I handed the end of the burning brand to Joseph. He hesitated a moment, then with a low moan, he clenched his teeth and tossed the entire torch up high, near Steven's covered body. Heat drove us back, step by step, until we touched the crowd. I felt Bryan's arms around me, looked to see Kayleen cradling Joseph.

Flames licked hungrily at the bodies, rising against the dark sky until they blotted the stars from view. I made myself watch even though it hurt to see. The peculiar smell of burning flesh filled the air. The crowd murmured behind us, a jumbled weave of singing, babies crying, wails of pain, and the drums. Joseph and I were silent, watching the flames leap and dance until they blurred behind my tears. We stood that way, the four of us together, staring at the fire for hours, until it finally burned to red-hot ashes.

3

JENNA AND THE PAW-CAT

As first light poured in the windows the next day, I answered a knock on the door. Stile stood awkwardly, holding two small red-clay urns filled with ashes from the fire. His eyes held a hint of cool appraisal as he handed them to me, one arm moving freely and the other one jerking and slow, a war wound. "I'm sorry," he mumbled.

"Thank you."

He nodded, turned, and walked quickly away without looking back.

Joseph and I tied our white ribbons around the stout necks of the urns. I set them on the windowsill in my room.

Someday, we would return our parents' ashes to Fremont's soil. For now, the containers were dour reminders of our loss.

That afternoon, Nava and Tom moved armloads of their personal things into the house, into Steven and Therese's old room. They felt wrong in the house; too taut, too driven, too cold. They provided for our needs, but the sole focus of conversation was recovery from the earthquake. I was glad they left early and returned late, overseeing the rebuilding from dawn to long after dusk. When they were home, we stayed in our rooms whenever we could.

Joseph pleaded sick and stayed home for days, even though he now walked normally and no longer slept all day. Still sullen, he napped in his room, or took short walks, avoiding the daily life of Artistos. He continued to shun the data networks.

I missed Joseph's laughter as much as I missed Steven's teasing and Therese's gentle smile.

On the morning of the third day after the funeral, Joseph and I were having a light breakfast before I went to work. Just as we were finishing, Nava came in and sat down across from Joseph. She had pulled her hair tight behind her head and her green eyes looked determined and intense. "Joseph, you need to work today. We need you." She took a long sip of her habitual morning tea. "You can choose to work with Paloma and Kayleen on the data networks, or you can accept whatever other assignment I give you."

Joseph met her eyes and said evenly, "What else would you have me do?"

She leaned toward him, her mouth drawn tight. Her words came out clipped and short. "Artistos's safety depends on the early warning system you helped us develop. It is your *duty* to maintain it."

I held my breath, waiting for his response.

His eyes stayed on hers as he said, "I can't do it. I won't."

She let out a short exasperated sigh. "Consider yourself reassigned to the builders guild until you change your mind. There's a crew working on the water reclamation plant this morning."

I grimaced inwardly, but stayed out of the conversation.

Force never worked well with Joseph; he needed time and patience.

Bryan had the most strength, but we were all stronger than original humans. Joseph threw himself into the manual labor, working hard, perhaps burning away his losses in sweat.

But he did not love it. His eyes never danced at the idea of work. He no longer drew diagrams of networks in his spare time or touched nodes purely because he could. Fixing sewers gave him a physical outlet for his loss, but it was not fun for him.

To placate Nava some, I partnered with Kayleen and Paloma myself as they struggled to fix the data networks without leaving Artistos. Much of the work wasn't Kayleen's at all, but Paloma's, using standard data readers. I knew the rhythms of repairing nets from being beside Joseph when he did the same things; this felt like working with the blind and the half blind. Joseph was that much better.

The boundary had two parts; a physical gated wall that guarded Artistos on every side except the cliffs and parts of the river, and a companion string of wireless devices, a virtual fence that sent information to the boundary bell. The wireless boundary ran along the top of every wall, every gate, and crossed every river and stream, making an uneven circle of comparative safety around Artistos. Data pods sensed heat and motion and size and read ID tags, so the bell knew to ring differently for paw-cat, for hebra herd, for human entrance and exit. Everyone except Jenna had an ident chip that alerted the boundary to our passage in and out.

Nearly two weeks after the quake, the four of us sat silently at breakfast. The bell rang for a paw-cat. It took me a second to recognize the tones; it had been two years since a paw-cat came to town. Nava and Tom pushed up from the table and ran outside. Joseph and I glanced at each other, then followed, watching over our shoulders nervously as we headed for the park.

Tom and Nava and seven or eight others were huddled in conversation when we came up to them. A handful of other adults were approaching. I overheard snippets of talk.

". . . east boundary . . . hebras? . . . armory for stunners . . . children inside."

Tom stood and pointed toward the edge of the park, a slight, wry smile touching his lips. Jenna stood next to a twintree, the dead cat hanging limply down her back. Its body, nose to rump, streamed from her head to her calves, and its tail hung over her shoulder, draping down the front of her. It must have weighed seventy kilos, yet she seemed only lightly burdened. She came up to the group of us and dropped the body on the grass.

Jenna stood at least a head taller than anyone else in the circle. Her gray hair was tied in a long rough braid behind her back, and her green hemp work clothes dripped with the cat's blood. She was magnificent.

It felt good to see her strong, to know she and I were of the same people, that I was more like her than the colonists. Oh, I didn't envy her loneliness, but her sense of power and grace, of competence; those called to me. Even with her mangled face and single pale eye, she radiated pride, accomplishment, and control. She pointed at the cat. "I found this by the hebra barns. It came in gate five. It was alone."

She turned abruptly and left, jogging away in long ground-eating strides, and Tom alone had the presence of mind to call out, "Thank you."

The next morning Paloma and Kayleen and I painstakingly tested gate five's digital reflexes, checking the mesh of the signals by moving through it and recording when it responded and when it didn't.

Just past noon, Paloma stood up, sweat dripping down her face. "I'm thirsty. Will you two be okay here while I go get us water and a snack?"

We nodded. We had protected ourselves by setting up a secondary data fence in a half circle outside the gate, but we looked around often, remembering the cat.

I nearly screamed when Jenna appeared in front of me. This was twice in two weeks she had sought me out. We often went months without seeing her except at a distance.

She held her one hand up for silence. "Your brother is not riding the data networks."

I blinked at her, confused. "No. He is afraid."

She cocked her head, looking at me appraisingly. "He saw death. So? Fear will stop him, and stop us all, from our destiny. You need him, all of you. Tell him."

Too many people were telling me to fix Joseph. Nava and Jenna both wanting us to perform, wanting Joseph for their own ends, acting as if I didn't want him to heal more than anything. "He is not listening to me about returning to his old duties. Perhaps he will listen if you talk to him."

Kayleen stepped nearer, cautiously, as if she were afraid Jenna would spook.

Jenna shook her head. "He has not been where I can tell him. I cannot walk safely through town. You are his sister. He is a key, and he must heal. And you are the vehicle that can help him, only you."

Jenna wasn't given to long conversation, but this was more cryptic than usual. "A key? To what?" Kayleen asked.

Jenna put her finger to her lips and nodded toward the gate. Of course. Data pods could send conversation to another node in our defenses, even record it. Probably everyone was busy, but you never knew who listened to what. Then Jenna said, "Artistos needs Joseph to make the data network strong." She nodded vigorously as she said this, as if I should be getting more from her words than I was.

I glanced at Kayleen, but she looked as puzzled as I felt.

"Paloma comes. Heal Joseph." Jenna faded quietly into the sharp thick underbrush.

"Thanks for killing the paw-cat," I said to her retreating back. I knew she heard. Her hearing was as *altered* as ours.

"What did she mean?" Kayleen asked. "A key?"

"I'm not sure."

Paloma rounded the corner toward us, bringing Kayleen and I welcome bottles of cold water. Her presence stilled our conversation for the moment.

4

THE SILVER SHIP AND THE SEA

Tom and Nava were already at the breakfast table when Joseph and I got up on the first free morning after eighteen days of straight dawn-to-dusk hard labor. Sunlight streamed in the kitchen window, promising a bright fall day. I sat down, reaching for a plate of toast and goat cheese. Tom's eyes sparkled, as if he had some great secret. He smiled at me. "I thought we'd go out and spread your parents' ashes. Get out of town for the day, take a ride. Interested?"

Nava's lips turned down in a fine hard line. "I need you here. We haven't ridden the whole perimeter since the quake."

"Paloma has." Tom frowned. "We declared today a personal day. This is something personal that needs to be done."

Nava stood abruptly and started taking plates to the kitchen.

Tom nodded at Nava's back, his mouth as thin a line as hers, then he turned to me and I watched the hard line of his jaw relax as he smiled. "Do you want to go?"

I had other plans. I needed time with Bryan and Kayleen, time to assess choices, to figure out how to heal my brother. As soon as Nava declared it a free day, we'd planned to get together. But Tom clearly wanted us to go. A private but ceremonial mourning for Therese and Steven might be just what Joseph needed. I glanced at Nava's stiff back as she stacked dishes in the sink. "Sure, I'd like to go."

Joseph twisted his hands in his lap, and then looked over at me. "I'm ready. I mean, I'm ready to scatter the ashes."

"Where would you like to take them?" Tom asked.

Joseph answered, "To the sea. Therese liked it there." It startled me that he didn't choose the mountains, Steven's favorite haunt. Perhaps he wasn't ready to see the High Road yet.

"All right," I said. "They'd want to be together, and Steven would have been willing to go to the sea to be with her." A hard lump rose in my throat.

Tom brightened at our answers. "I thought you'd pick the water." He spoke up, for Nava's benefit. "We can check on the spaceport as we go. Make the trip useful. Let's saddle up some hebras."

Nava turned toward him, her green eyes cool. "I think you should take more people. The plains aren't safe."

He returned her look, cool for cool. "We'll be okay."

She frowned at him, but didn't say anything else.

Joseph and I dressed carefully, wearing long, loose pants we could tie around our ankles through the Grass Plains, and light coats against the sea breeze over thin shirts designed for the hot plains. We tied the funeral urns to our belts using the white ribbons and packed water and food. I left a note for Kayleen and Bryan.

Joseph and I jogged to keep up with Tom, passing fresh-cut hay fields. Tom carried a light pack and wore his stunner on his belt for easy access. The Grass Plains were full of both predators and prey, and we wanted to be neither today. The air felt cool. An early-morning nip signified summer's true end.

My spirits rose as we neared the hebra barn. I hadn't been far outside the boundaries since before the earthquake. The roamers would be in soon. We would see Liam and Alicia. Maybe it would be okay.

The barn, almost entirely rebuilt, smelled more like new wood than hebra sweat and hay. The hebras stamped restlessly in their stalls after the morning feeding, peering at us through the open top halves of the stall doors and making low whickering noises.

Steven had once described hebras to me as a strange combination of horses and camels and giraffes with beards. He'd used pictures of the three animals. He started with a camel, and pasted half a giraffe's neck onto it, then changed the ears to look like a floppy version of horse ears, removed the hump, made the hooves more like horse hooves, and drew a long curly beard.

The wooden barn held about twenty hebras, but I had a favorite. Jinks had the only white coat, with a dark tip on her tail and dark beard. I kissed her long soft nose, slid the face harness over her head, and pulled her out to a hitch while Tom and Joseph chose mounts. They both picked mottled brown animals that matched the dirt on the plains and the color of the late-fall grass. Joseph bridled his own favorite, Legs, who was taller than Jinks by almost a foot, and a faster runner. Tom chose a steady mount named Sugar Wheat, named for the way her tail looked like the flower of the most common grass on the plains.

Hebra saddles have high backs to provide support for the riders against the tall animal's rolling gait. To climb up, I lowered a rope with loops tied into it from the saddle, took three steps up this loop ladder, then flung my right leg up and over Jinks's neck, since the back of the saddle was too high to clear the other way. Once on Jinks, my feet hung as high as my head when I stood. She twisted her head all the way around to look on me, her eyes level with mine, nickering softly. Perhaps she wanted out as much as I did.

Joseph brightened visibly as he climbed on Legs; it was the first genuine smile I'd seen on him since the earthquake. He led the way. We rode east, through the stubble of the cornfields, then turned south and passed under the huge wood and metal hoist used to lift heavy goods from the plains to Aristos. We crossed the boundary, the bell tinkling three times as it read our idents, and pulled up at the edge of the cliff.

The single paved road between the cliff and the spaceport cut the sea of greens and browns and reds like a wide river. Thick swaths of short grass on both sides of the road showed where we harvested hebra feed for winter. The Lace River bordered the plains to our left, and to our right, far away, the dark greens of forest marched uphill. Across the plains, the ocean glittered like a bright blue sparkling line between the ground and the light blue sky. Tom pointed below us, near the base of the cliff. "Look—wild hebras."

A medium-sized herd, maybe ten hebras. They grazed below us, visible as long thin backs and tails cutting their way slowly through the hebra-belly-height grass. Two scout hebras patrolled the edges of the herd, heads up.

We wound single file down steep switchbacks, leaning back, our saddles creaking under us. Two huge plains eagles swirled lazily on warming air currents, spiraling up from below us to hang in the air above the cliff.

When we reached the road, Joseph stayed ahead and Tom and I rode side by side. I glanced over at Tom. "He's enjoying himself. It was a good idea to come out here."

Tom looked pleased. "He looks better than he has in days. Nava's fit to be tied that he isn't on the data nets. We need to get the outer perimeter working before winter sets in."

"I know," I said simply. Everyone needed Joseph fixed. But not today. I wanted to be left alone today, to ride, to bury our parents in the sea.

Tom sat easily in his saddle, his stocky body balancing nicely on Sugar Wheat. "I hoped getting away would help him let go of his anger and get back to work."

I gave him the same answer I gave Jenna. "I'm not sure he's angry. I think he's scared."

Ahead of us, Joseph pushed his hebra into a slow canter and we followed, our mounts' split hooves tapping on the hard-packed dirt path. "Anger and fear are related, Chelo. He's lost a lot. Maybe he's angry with himself."

"He needs time. Can't we give him more time?"

"You've been working on the data nets. You know how long it takes us to fix them without him."

"What happens if Joseph just quits the data nets?" I didn't tell Tom that Joseph had sworn never to go back. After all, I knew he had to. Somehow.

"If it were up to me? Nothing. He could join the culture guild for all I care. But there are rules that bind us together, bind each of us to do our best."

There was an implicit threat there, as well as a truth. "I know."

We rode silently through grass tall enough to hide me standing if I weren't astride. It felt like riding through parted water, making it difficult to see clearly or far. Only the wide road let us pass easily; the ride between the spaceport and the ocean would be harder. The feathered tips of the grass were bone dry, but the stalks were damp and still green. Later, as winter approached, lightning would catch the plains on fire, a bright flash feeding on the grass, preparing the seed to open in spring. Fire kept the plains monocultured; no trees grew here. Just yellow grass, tall grass, sharp grass, silver grass, whip grass, and insects, rodents, hebras, snakes, and paw-cats.

It took an hour to reach the spaceport. Four square kilometers of concrete buffered the buildings from the annual fires, and in the center, two small houses, three hangars, and a well. Sugar Wheat bugled, and Legs stopped, waiting. We caught up to Joseph and rode three abreast to the water. I dismounted and brushed dust and dead moths from the metal trough, then pulled on the pump, hoping the station still worked. Clear water filled the long shallow half pipe. The hebras plunged their noses into it, drinking in soft little slurps, making satisfied low noises in their throats. We drank, too, clear water from near the spigot, and chewed dry salty djuri jerky and tore hunks of bread from a single shared loaf.

We rode around the concrete pad, recording damage. Two long cracks had severed one corner. One crack was half a meter wide. If it wasn't repaired before spring, grass would grow through next season, pushing up the concrete.

Most importantly, the three remaining shuttles from *Traveler* nestled safely in one of the hangars. The colony still used them to check on *Traveler* at least once a year. Tom was one of the ten trained pilots. Even though they looked fine, he walked carefully around each shuttle, touching them, running his hands along the outsides.

Next we checked the keeper's cabin. No one lived there except for hunting trips, or support crew for shuttle launchings, the last of which had been almost a year ago. The cabin looked sound from the outside. Inside, we found a crack in the stovepipe, and broken cups and plates.

While Tom picked up plates, I took Jinks out to the *New Making,* which stood upright, like a perfectly round fat silver stick with a pointed top. It rested on its own small concrete pad, a hundred meters from the spaceport proper. Jinks's hooves crunched across the dead zone, a circle around the pad the ship rested on that grew only short stubbled grass, even after twenty-two years.

New Making loomed above me, twenty times my height. The metal skin of the ship gleamed, also a mystery after so much time, so much rain and storm and fire. There was no obvious break in the ship's skin for a door. I put one hand on the urn of ashes at my belt, suddenly feeling twice bereft. Therese and Steven had conquered my first parents, yet I had cared for all of them. I didn't understand the war, didn't understand the Fremontian need to be "pure" human. Why not want to be stronger and faster like we were? *New Making* reminded me that Joseph and I were different, and made me ache sharply for my first parents, and for Chiaro, who cared for us while they fought for us.

New Making's past affected the way people treated us now, fed into the dark undercurrents of the colony's fear, and made many people watch the sky regularly. The future was harder to read than the present. Would the *altered* ever return for us? Even if my parents lived, would I recognize them now, twelve years later? Was the *New Making* merely a reminder, or would we figure out how to open her someday? How to pry loose her secrets? I imagined clues about who we were, all captive inside the unassailable silver shell of the ship.

Did Jenna know how to get in?

Joseph brought Legs next to me, and said, "It makes me feel like we lost something before we were old enough to know it." His soft voice trailed off for a moment, and then he looked over at me and said, "I guess we're no good at keeping parents, huh?" Tears filled his eyes, but didn't spill down his cheeks.

"It wasn't our fault. Either time," I said firmly. I put my hand on the little urn at my side, and Joseph did the same. My heart hurt for him. For me, too. I missed Therese and

Steven. It had been such an uphill battle to get them to accept us that it never really registered when it wasn't a fight anymore.

Now we had to do it all over again.

The thought struck me silent as we left the spaceport.

Tom rode ahead of us, scanning the grass for signs of paw-cat or hebra herds. Perhaps he would be a good guardian, but Nava? Nava would never have taken time to bring us out here.

I shook my head to clear worries and breathed in the grass and the heat and the sun and the dust. My focus should be on Joseph. I started one of the songs Therese sang when she worked outside, one she'd written to celebrate the things she loved about Fremont; the huge blue flowers that adorned the twintrees every spring, the colorful birds with strong beaks and talons for clawing seeds free from near-elm, the pleasant shade of the bright green tent trees. By the time I reached the first chorus, Joseph joined with me, and as we neared the ocean we had worked through every song we knew, even some of the bawdy drinking songs we weren't supposed to sing at our age. A fitting funeral procession.

Tom turned in his saddle and smiled at us, although he didn't join us singing. A sharp warm wind blew inland, carrying the scents and sounds of the sea. The rhythmic roll of waves accompanied the lyrics.

Tom led us down the steep trail to the wide beaches. At the bottom, the hebras stamped their feet in the sand, uncomfortable with the change in footing. Joseph leaned forward and sent Legs galloping down the beach. I followed, Jinks falling farther behind with every step. The wind pulled my hair back and the waves filled my ears. Near the end of the crescent beach, Joseph pulled Legs to a stop and stared at the busy water, waiting for me to catch up.

We urged the hebras into the edge of the surf together, close enough for Joseph and me to hold hands, until the water reached the hebras' knees and they moved apart a little, uneasy as foamy breakers tickled their bellies. I loosened the urn from my belt and held it up to the sky, yelling into the white noise of the sea. "For you, Therese and Steven, for your care of us, your care of Artistos, of Fremont. We wish you good journey."

Joseph's voice joined mine, strong and sure. "Thank you. We will miss you forever, and think of you always."

Both urns dangled over the water. The hebras danced under us, and the sun shone on the waves. As one, we uncorked the urns and turned them upside down, pouring the ashes into the water. A wave mingled them together. We stayed until the water absorbed the last trace of the ashes. We threw the urns as far out as we could.

A black sea-hunter swooped down from the sky and picked one of the urns up in its huge claws, then dropped it, cawing in disgust. I laughed at its confusion. We turned our hebras around and walked them quietly back to where Tom waited at the bottom of the path.

He looked at each of us in turn, balancing easily on his mount, as if he belonged here near the wild sea rather than working in Artistos. "When my mom died, I scattered her ashes in Little Lace Lake. She used to take me there to picnic, the whole Lace Forest spread around us, and just the two of us to explore it. It wasn't, perhaps, very safe. But I always felt alive there with her. It felt good to leave her there."

I nodded. "Thank you."

Joseph said, "Perhaps it will always feel special to be here now."

This was a kind thing for Tom to do, to help us get here, and to know we needed our own private moment to wish them well. As we wound up the steep trail single file, I felt lighter, as if the urn had weighed far more than it truly did. My throat was raw from singing our way to the sea, but still I hummed softly to Jinks, grateful to her for carrying me here.

Once we reached straight solid path, Joseph moved Legs into a slow gallop and I followed, Tom behind us this time. The sun warmed my back. Jinks's thick hide began to darken with sweat. I thought perhaps we should slow down, but Joseph was too far ahead to hear me yell, and I didn't want to be separated from him. Jinks strained, trying to keep up with Legs, but we continued to lose ground. Tom was just behind us and I heard him yell, "Slow down, I'm passing."

The grass suddenly parted in front and to the left of Joseph. Legs reared and leaped right, away from the path, screaming. Jinks's head flew up. The tawny coat of a paw-cat, tall as a man, flashed across the path. I stood in the stir-rups, looking for its pack mates.

A second wave of disturbed grass approached Joseph from behind.

Jinks jerked to a halt, throwing me onto her long neck. She swiveled her head quickly, her eyes passing over me, searching the grass. I urged her forward, after Joseph, clamping my legs tightly around her middle. She reared up, but she came down running, obeying. I blessed her under my breath.

Tom and Sugar Wheat shot past us, running full out, Tom urging Sugar Wheat on. His hand was on his stunner. It wouldn't do much good here; the cats would be hard targets racing through the tall thick grass.

I clung to the saddle and looked for Joseph. Legs's head, Joseph's bobbing ahead and behind, raced through the grass, parallel to the path but twenty meters off. Joseph struggled to pull the frightened hebra back to the path where they stood a better chance of outrunning the paw-cats. Hebras are faster than paw-cats, but the advantage means more in the open. The Grass Plains hide rocks and depressions and small streams that can trip and slow the big beasts. Tom was following the first paw-cat's grass track, still far behind.

Jinks and I pounded down the path, drawing parallel to where Joseph and Tom raced through the grass.

Jinks darted left with a scream that almost drowned the paw-cat roar that filled my ears. I glimpsed a big female ten meters ahead of us. Jinks wheeled and we were in the grass, too. I held my breath, not wanting to draw Tom's attention from Joseph. My hands shook with fear. Jinks was their nat-ural prey. Paw-cats didn't eat humans, but they killed us if we were in the way. The cat was huge, and every movement it made was the graceful flow of impending death.

I couldn't look behind, just hold tightly to Jinks, leaning forward, urging her on. Jinks wasn't fast for a hebra, but the cat's next roar sounded farther away. Jinks veered to avoid a pile of rocks, then stumbled as her foot caught.

The cat gained on us.

I tried to turn Jinks to regain the path, but she fought me and I let her flee, trusting her. She jerked and turned, twisting away from a second cat, heading back for the rocks. She chose well; we raced past the first cat, still going the other way. It snarled and whirled, huge paw slashing. Pain like an electric shock flared through my right leg, and then we were past it, gone.

We raced away.

Jinks's breath sounded labored and she slowed under me. I looked back, but couldn't spot the cats behind us. I heard them though, close behind.

Rocks loomed in front of us again, maybe the same, maybe different: two or three large rocks and many smaller ones making a three-foot-tall hill. Jinks gathered herself to jump. I knew, even as we left the ground, that it was too high, that I was too heavy. Her right foreleg caught on the top stone. She twisted, screaming, and I glimpsed one of her eyes flashing with fear as I tumbled over, clearing the rocks, sharp grass sawing at me.

Jinks screamed again, fear and then pain, and I knew at least one of the cats was on her.

I scrambled away. I'd be too low, I'd be lost in the grass and Tom and Joseph wouldn't see me. The cats; the cats would find me.

I glanced back.

Nothing.

Which way was the path?

I ran, parting the grass, ignoring the sharp grass tips flailing my cheeks, my arms. The grass thinned in front of me and a smaller patch of rocks rose a meter and a half above the ground. A view. I leaped for the top, looking frantically around.

I'd been paralleling the path.

A cat's scream from behind announced the kill, calling the pack to fresh meat.

I couldn't see Joseph, but Tom stood in his saddle on Sugar Wheat, looking around, not far ahead of me. I waved my arms, and Tom's head snapped around. A feral smile filled his face as he and Sugar Wheat barreled toward me. Tom leaned way down, holding out an arm. I grabbed it and he swung me up, hard, throwing me across the front of his saddle. The wide, low saddle bump dug into my side and I struggled to sit, managed a sideways position where I was in front of Tom, but between him and the saddle bump. "Joseph?" I called up to Tom.

"He's safe." Tom held me on with one hand, but every stride pushed breath from me, and it was all I could do to stay on, to breathe, and to not scream from the pain. The slash in my leg hurt. Joseph and Legs swung in noisily from the side, both breathing hard. Joseph's white face searched mine. "Chelo—are you okay? What happened?"

Talking and breathing and bouncing, I managed, "They . . . got . . . Jinks." I saw again the last look she'd given me, the fear in her eyes as she fell.

Legs and Sugar Wheat slowed. Moments later their hooves clattered on pavement. Safety. The cats were probably satisfied with one kill anyway, but the open expanse of pavement discouraged cats as well as grass. Paw-cats hated being in the open, being seen.

Tom stopped and climbed down, and I turned to sit properly in the saddle, gasping for breath. My side hurt from bumping up and down against the saddle, the claw mark in my leg screamed fire, and every bare spot of exposed skin was grass-cut. I couldn't stop picturing poor Jinks, feeding paw-cats somewhere behind me.

Sweat streaked both hebras, and a long shallow slash curved down Legs's flank, dripping blood. Joseph dismounted, too, and he and Tom walked together, leading Legs and Sugar Wheat. I wasn't sure if I could walk at all yet, so I stayed up. My own leg dripped blood, matching Legs's flank. Legs let out a long tremulous call and turned to look directly behind him. I swear he looked sad. "Do you think they know about Jinks?" I asked.

Joseph said, "Sure. They're herd animals. They know about death, and when they've lost a family member."

Tom reached a hand up to pat Legs on the neck. "And smart. Hebras are smarter than most animals in our databases. Not like us, but most of the animals from Deerfly didn't communicate as well with each other, or us, as hebras seem to."

We reached the watering station, and I slid off Sugar Wheat and sat on the warm concrete while they gave the hebras water. Joseph came over and helped me stand. "Are you all right?"

I nodded, testing my ability to walk by taking a few steps. I nearly fell. My right leg hurt, but it worked correctly, responded to my commands.

"I'm sorry," Joseph said.

"Me, too." I thought about the cats feeding on Jinks. Poor beautiful Jinks.

"That I wasn't there to help you."

Oh. "You were just ahead. If Tom hadn't gotten there first, you would have been there." My dry mouth had trouble forming words clearly, and I reached for my water bag and drew a mouthful.

Joseph turned to look at Tom, who stood by the water trough, rubbing Sugar Wheat's nose. "I'm glad he was here. Maybe he will be all right for us."

I smiled at that. "Maybe he will. He's been good this trip."

"He stunned at least one of the cats chasing me. It was close. That's how Legs got scratched."

"At least we're all okay, everyone but Jinks. They started after you."

He looked at me with a sudden tenderness in his eyes. "I couldn't have stood losing you, too."

"I know. We have to keep each other safe." I hugged him, hard, and then pulled back, looking into his eyes. They were clear and sharp, very alive. "Let's go clean up."

Joseph helped me wash my cuts and the wide claw slash, while Tom cleaned up Legs's flank. We stayed at the spaceport for an hour, calming the hebras, calming ourselves. The wide road back from here was safer than the narrow road from the sea, but the spaceport was safer yet. Finally, the sun's fall toward the horizon pushed us toward home. We needed to beat the dark.

I rode back to Artistos behind Joseph. I'd always been afraid something would happen to me, leaving Joseph to fend for himself. I held him tightly, glad we rode together. Two of us in a saddle meant for one was a close, cramped fit. I scanned the grass for signs of danger. We saw nothing worse than small birds and rodents and, once, a thin grass snake slithering across the path. Our shadows were long in front of us as we started up the switchbacks toward home.

The boundary bell sounded sweet as we passed inside, and we stopped and looked back. The sky was sun-painted: orange and gold with a hint of deep red. The darkening plains looked like water again from this height.

We arrived home an hour later, after rubbing down the hebras and tending Legs's cut. Destiny, the largest of our seven moons, shone full enough to light the river path as we straggled home from the barns.

Surprisingly, we found Nava at the stove, stirring a pot of stew. The warm kitchen smelled like onion and pepper and djuri meat. She glanced up as we came in. "Stile caught two djuri and brought us meat. I thought it would be good to have a meal together." I couldn't remember her ever cooking anything elaborate. It felt good to be greeted with warm homemade food. She narrowed her eyes and frowned at me. "You're walking wrong. What happened?"

Tom spoke up. "We lost Chelo's hebra to a paw-cat."

Nava arched an eyebrow. "It looks like you almost lost Chelo."

I collapsed into a chair, suddenly feeling dizzy, as if all the adrenaline had leaked from my body into the warmth of the kitchen. My hands shook. "Bruises, and a scratch. Tom saved me from worse."

Nava glanced over at Tom. Her voice sounded strained, slightly angry. "I told you to take more people with you. You could have gotten them killed."

Nice of her to appreciate that we didn't die.

Tom ignored her barb and set the table. We ate quietly. The stew tasted wonderful, but I could only manage a few bites. After dinner, Joseph helped me clean up with hot water, which stung so much I danced. He frowned at me when he was done. "Should I use some medi-tape?"

"No. Let it breathe."

"All right. But have Paloma look at it tomorrow."

I climbed into bed, sighing as the soft mattress cradled my sore body, and instantly drifted off.

Some time later, pain from the bruises in my side jolted me awake. My stomach growled, and the spicy taste of the stew filled my empty mouth. I watched Destiny's trail of light across my wall for a long while, trying to will myself back to sleep. Finally, I pushed up and limped out my door. I heard Tom and Nava moving around the kitchen even though the night was half gone. Nava's voice carried to me before I reached the doorway; I paused to listen. "You have to succeed soon. We need to finish fixing our security and I just can't afford the resources to do it the slow way."

Tom kept his voice low and I had to strain to hear his answer. "We managed before we had Joseph's skills. He's hurting, Nava, he felt his parents' death."

"They weren't his parents," she snapped.

"He thinks so. They thought so, too. Why did you agree to take them if you didn't intend to be a parent? They need protection."

"Hmmm . . . like going out onto the Grass Plains and almost getting killed?" A pot banged against the sink. "It's more likely we'll need protection from them. They're growing up, getting stronger. What will we do with them as adults?"

I barely breathed.

"What do we need protection from?" Tom asked. "They trust us, they help."

Nava's voice was pitched low, but firm. "You know how strong they are. How much they can do. Look at that wild woman in the woods. Can you imagine what damage five of her—or seven—could cause?"

Tom laughed softly. "And you think they're just going to

rise up some night and revolt? Seven of them against all of us? They need the colony, and the colony needs them."

I heard dishes in the sink. I'd have to go in or go back soon.

Tom continued. "Try building bridges with them. Jenna hasn't done any harm since just after the rest of them took off. She's helped us."

"Tom, she killed my father."

I hadn't known that. Tom's voice was pitched very low as he said, "But Chelo and Joseph didn't. Besides, you know it probably *wasn't* Jenna."

"If it wasn't her, it was one of her kind."

I heard footsteps coming toward the door, and rushed quietly back to my room, my hunger forgotten.

5

THE ROAMERS' RETURN

I didn't get back to the science guild the next day either. Everyone worked together to protect the harvest and finish repairing damaged buildings, fences, barns, and pipes. So I dragged through bagging flour at the mill, my leg stiff, my head running over and over the conversation I'd overheard the night before. No wonder Nava had such a terrible time with us. I knew the emptiness of losing a father. Twice over. But how did that change the rift between her and me? Between Nava and all of us? The long day brought me no answers, just hands sticky with sweat and flour.

As soon as the end-of-shift bell rang, instead of walking home across the river to Artistos, I went behind the mill and crossed to the open space behind the wood shop and the smelter. The freight yard had already emptied out. The buildings were squat and utilitarian, metal or stone with no decoration.

The data networks ensure little privacy exists in Artistos, but we had adopted the freight yard as a relatively quiet place to meet. Here, the data net and warning bells nestled far out in the edge of forest, to avoid false alarms triggered by the normal activities of loading and unloading ore and cut wood, of moving materials, and so on.

Raw trunks of golden brown near-elm lay neatly stacked to dry along one fence. Large bins of reddish iron ore and black coal stood near the smelter. I walked across the open space, and pushed through the low branches of a tent tree on the far side, left standing for a shady lunch spot. Three long flat benches with no backs sat halfway between the trunk and the curtain of diamond-shaped foliage.

Minutes later, Bryan parted the long branches, stepping over and squeezing my side so hard I yelped. "Watch out— I'm bruised." I laughed up at him, wrinkling my nose. "You smell like the hebra barns."

He smiled down at me, but his soft brown eyes looked worried. "I heard about Jinks. And I saw Legs's gash. Are you all right?"

"A little shaky."

I stepped back and rolled up my pants leg. He looked me over, his eyes widening as he noticed the many tiny grass-cuts and then the tip of the long cat scratch. "You look pretty beat-up."

"It will heal." And it would. We *altered* healed fast.

"So how's Joseph? Was he hurt yesterday?"

I pursed my lips, seeing the darkness that haunted Joseph's eyes, the way it lifted just when he climbed on Legs. "Actually, until the paw-cat attack, we had a pretty good day." We sat side by side on one of the benches, close, but not touching. "Tom was with us, and he was kind to us both. And later, when the paw-cats nearly ate us, he may very well have saved us both." I shivered, remembering. "But Nava got mad at him for it afterward."

He raised an eyebrow. "For saving you?"

I sighed. "Not exactly. I think she's depending on Tom to get Joseph back to work, and I suspect a paw-cat encounter didn't seem like just the thing to convince Joseph to overcome his fears."

"Ahhhh . . ." He stared up at the top of the tree. Points of sunlight fell between the leaves and danced on his cheeks. "And what do you think will?"

I shook my head. "Did I tell you Kayleen and I saw Jenna a few days ago? She told me to heal Joseph because he's the *key*. But she didn't suggest what he's the key to."

Bryan looked thoughtful. "It must have something to do with the way he reads data." We'd often wondered why we six had been designed with the particular gifts we had. Stories of the war told us many of our parents appeared more *altered* than we were. There were tales of marksmen who could kill from great distances, of whole camps able to outrun and outhide and outshoot the original humans. One story told of two men with six arms each, another of a human who ran on all fours and used both hands and feet as weapons. Campfire stories, but they made us wonder why we seemed so normal.

Bryan paced, looking a bit like a paw-cat himself. "She probably meant the key to figuring something out. She uses riddles to goad us into learning new things. Remember how she tricked Kayleen into trying to beat Joseph at data stream games?"

As if on cue, Kayleen stepped through the low-hanging branches. Bits of hay stuck in her hair and mud and hay caked the sides of her long shoes. Her feet were outgrowing them again. Eric, the shoemaker, would tease her about having to make a new shoe last already. No one on Fremont had feet as long or agile as Kayleen's.

She stretched. "What a day. Mom made me count everything in two whole harvest sheds, and all the while people were bringing things in and rearranging everything. I had to count the corn bushels twice to get it right." She flopped down on a bench without taking a breath or pausing. "I had to climb both hay shelters, too—the hebra grass hay and the timothy. I heard about your adventure—I'm glad you're okay. Did you hear the roamers are on their way? I brought some twintree fruit and water. And you two look cozy. Where's Joseph?"

Before I could respond, Joseph answered her last question himself by following her in. "Hi. Chelo, how's your scratch? I brought some salve."

"Thanks." My cheeks flushed red as I stripped out of my shoes and pants, leaving only my underwear and a shirt barely long enough to cover them. Kayleen blinked and said, "Wow. That's no scratch. You can walk with that slice in your leg?"

Joseph spread Paloma's plant oil ointment over the cut, his fingers gentle against my torn skin. The salve sent fiery tingles deep into my leg, and I bit my lip against the pain, not wanting to cry out. It was hard enough to be the center of so much attention.

Bryan looked politely away while I struggled carefully back into my pants. "Well, no running for you today. Did you and Joseph figure out this key business yet?"

I sighed. "I haven't told him about it yet. I didn't want to mix it in with yesterday's trip."

Joseph flashed me a disgusted glance and I said, "Well, I was going to tell you. I just . . . I thought you've been getting enough pressure. The way Nava's always on you." I sighed and sat down carefully, looking Joseph in the eyes. "Jenna surprised me and Kayleen the day we were working gate five, trying to remesh the data nodes, right after the paw-cat came in. She told us to get you back in the data nets, that you're 'the key.' She was really insistent, and seemed to think we should know what she meant. She didn't say anything else useful."

Joseph lay down on one of the benches, staring up at the roof of the tent tree. His lips tightened in a stubborn frown. "I don't ever want to go back to riding the data nets."

I took a twintree fruit from Kayleen's stretched-out hand. "I know. But we need your help. Kayleen just can't do it all herself."

"Artistos did fine before we got here."

"Tom said the same thing, but he also said we all pull together." That was a colony rule. And ours, as well. Anyone violating the rule earned sharp tongues and difficult tasks from whichever guildsmaster they served. "The nets have been much stronger since you started helping. Your work matters."

Joseph kept his eyes on the graceful belled canopy of the tent tree. His jaws were locked tight. He was silent a long time, and then when he spoke his voice was soft and halting. "I know. But I don't think I can anyway. Not now. I can't relax enough." He turned toward me. "I used to hear the data all the time, and I haven't been able to since . . ."

"Could your system be burned out?" Kayleen asked. "Sometimes when I try three flows, I go deaf to the net for a while. Did such a big flow of data hurt you? Maybe you just need time."

Joseph turned to her and put a hand out for a piece of twintree fruit. "Thanks. I don't hear the nets, feel them, like I used to. I don't want to." He tossed the fruit carefully from hand to hand, like a ball, yelping once when a sticker penetrated the fleshy pad of his ring finger. "Don't you understand? I couldn't help them. Any of them. I heard them die and there was nothing I could do." Tears glistened in the edges of his eyes, and he swiped the back of his free hand across them and turned his face away from all of us, gazing up at the green diamond leaves.

A minute passed before Bryan spoke into the quiet. "They would have known that. They knew you loved them. But what would Steven and Therese want you to do? They spent every waking hour worrying about everyone's safety and needs, and now Tom and Nava are doing the same." He paused, his brow furrowed. "Nava's hard, I know, but you can adjust. I've had to. The Smiths resent me, but I still do what I need to do. And they do, too. It's just harder."

Joseph pulled the outer rind off in one strong twist of his wrist. The sour-sweet smell of fruit permeated the still air. "I like the kind of work I'm doing. It feels good to see something physical get done, to lay a pipe, and see water going through it. I feel better."

It was a lie. He hardly ever smiled anymore. He just worked, and came home, and went to his room.

Kayleen practically spoke for me. "All right. I think Jenna meant something important. You're the strongest one of us in the nets. I can't do what you do. And Jenna doesn't seem to be able to either. I don't think she can feel data at all. She's like Chelo. She has other gifts."

Bryan said, "We don't know that. We only know what we can observe, and what she tells us. Which isn't much."

I frowned, picturing Jenna standing with the dead paw-cat strung over her shoulder like a flour sack. "The first year we lived here, they hunted her. They would have killed her if they could have. I was only five, but I remember how much they hated her. Who knows what she hides, or why?"

The entrance bells chimed. Kayleen glanced at us, then proclaimed, "The roamers!"

Grins split all of our faces. Liam and Alicia. Story Night and then Trading Day. The deep tones of the gather-bell rang next, calling us to town.

Joseph and Kayleen jogged back ahead of us. Bryan stayed with me, walking by my side. I appreciated the kindness; my leg truly wasn't up to anything more than a slow walk. He linked an arm with mine, supporting me, and the pleasure of walking with him made up for not being in town before the roamers reached the science guild hall.

As we crossed the Lace River, the sun touched the roamers' wagons in Little Lace Park, illuminating bright yellows and oranges, colors chosen to show in satellite photos against the greens and grays of Fremont, so we could visually track them. The wagons looked like gaudy flowers from this distance. I stopped briefly, leaning on the bridge rail, watching the painted wagons, the tethered hebras, the few brightly dressed roamers who were still closing up, hurrying to town like we were.

By the time we reached the guild hall, we had to press in through a crowd. Culture guild servers passed among us. Old Chub and his wife, Kiki, bent but still moving, slowly carried trays of roasted djuri, leavened bread, and fresh corn. Chayla, who lost a hand in the war, balancing trays of slim glasses filled with the traditional wheat beer of Story Night. We were offered all the food we could fill our plates with, and one glass of beer each. Long rectangular tables filled the hall. Someone had brought in shiny green red-berry leaves and lacy cream-colored saw grass tufts to dec-orate each table. I spotted Kayleen and Joseph protecting two empty seats for us near the front. Holding our plates and glasses carefully in the jostling crowd, we made our way up to them.

As we started eating, I leaned in to Kayleen. "Have you seen Alicia or Liam?"

She pointed to the stage. "Liam's been moving around backstage, but he hasn't stopped long enough for me to get his attention." The roamers were the colony's eyes and ears, wandering the continent for two things: scientific exploration, and foraging. The colony grew Earth- and Deerfly-based food. The roamers had learned, sometimes the hard way, which na-tive foods humans could eat, like twintree fruits, and which would make us sick or give us fevers. They studied native plants and animals. Every year, they brought back djuri meat and dried nuts and seeds and fruit that they traded for corn, wheat, hay, chickens, and goats.

They also brought back stories. The whole town came, hungry for the feast and the knowledge.

The leaders of both bands of roamers milled about the stage, bright and gaudy in their best ceremonial dress, wearing red necklaces for the East Band and gold ones for the West Band. The bands' names had nothing to do with directions; I'd heard they were based on two universities back on Deerfly (we only had one university here, run by the science guild in the cold hall every winter, the lessons culled from databases and roamer papers).

Before we finished half our meal, I spotted Alicia sitting with her adoptive parents, Bella and Michael, at a table on the far side of the room from us. She saw me, but looked away, avoiding my eyes. Her long dark hair lay in tangles across her shoulders and she wore thin, old clothes.

I forced my attention back to my food, wishing I could just walk up and talk to her. Her family treated her like a prisoner of war. She joined community events, but they kept her by their side. Our contact with her had always been limited.

Liam had it better, maybe better than we did. Although we didn't know much about his gifts, he had a reputation for inventing useful tools, and seemed well respected. He had been adopted by Akashi and Mayah, the leaders of the West Band. Akashi kept him busy, so maybe he just didn't have time to sit with us.

One of the old women who ran the culture guild clapped for people to clear tables. I tipped my glass and finished the last of the beer, enjoying the warm feeling the rare treat left in my stomach. The babble of conversation in the room trailed off. People shifted chairs to find the best view of the stage. Children up to about ten years old settled on the floor in front of the stage, giggling and whispering among themselves.

Akashi walked up to a microphone at the end of the stage. He was tall and slightly bent in around the shoulders, probably fifty or more years old, and his gray hair hung in a long braid behind him. He wore a red and black performer's costume, with white and tan beads and shells sewn into the shoulders and along the hem of his loose pants. His dark skin showed the kiss of sun and wind over an olive complexion. His dark eyes sparkled with warm pleasure. Even the children quieted as he cleared his throat.

"I suppose the first thing you want to hear is the earthquake. I will tell only our story. The East Band will tell their own in its turn." He paused, looking around the room, gathering attention with his intense gaze. "The day shone bright and sunny, the heat making us sweaty and sleepy and content. We were pulling our wagons through the high summer pastures. Luckily, we rode on a wide flat trail." He paused. "The ground rumbled, then stopped." His hands, parallel to the floor, demonstrated the shifting earth and then stilled, opening up. "We breathed a sigh of relief. Then, as if a giant hand squeezed the rocks and path under us, everything twisted and jerked all at once. Our children cried. The hebras who pulled our wagons threw their heads up and pranced. Two took off running, and the wagon they pulled fell." He pantomimed with his hands, drawing a fast line across the air in front of him and then showing a sudden stop and a sideways jerk. "One of our favorites, Twisted Beard, broke a leg, and had to be killed."

The look of pain that flashed briefly across his face reminded me of Jinks.

"Twisted Beard's partner, Rocky, kicked so hard in her traces she bruised a leg and we had to lead her by hand for five days. We were scared. We lost much of our data, including direct access to you, and we were afraid for two days that we would find Artistos leveled. The data networks remain shredded. The gaping holes left us feeling vulnerable until we could return here."

Bryan and I shared a quick glance. I looked over at Joseph, but he was studying his feet intently.

Up on the stage, Akashi continued, his voice filled with solemn notes and sadness. "The hard part was getting here. We would have returned a week ago, except we had to move rocks off of the High Road to make a wagon track." Now he looked down at the ground. "We are sorry for your losses, but grateful that Artistos is now returned largely to itself, and that most of you are here with us."

The crowd murmured and shifted, a kind of quiet agreement.

Akashi brightened. "But of course, that is not all that happened to us. We bring you stories of three new beasts and one new flower, and we bring you wagons laden with meat and dried berries and herbs. Trading of our bounty for yours begins at dawn. But first, let us relay the gifts of our stories." He looked down at the children just below him. "And which story would you like first? The dragon, the snake, the bird, or the flower?"

The smallest boy, Jali, threw his hand up in the air.

Akashi nodded at him.

Jali drew himself up as tall as his little five-year-old body could go, and said, "Dragon please," in an awed voice.

Akashi laughed. "So you shall have the dragon first."

The roamers loved to tease us, we who lived behind our boundaries, while they wandered the wilds of Jini, open to tooth and claw, relying on themselves and each other even more than we did. They loved jokes. We leaned forward in our chairs, eager to hear about dragons. Much here was named after similar items from other human experiences, but of course, Fremont's native life was truly different. Near-elm was not elm. Dragons would not be dragons.

Akashi began with dragons, however. "Many of you have heard the old myths of Earth. How winged and fanged lizards with whirling eyes, bright red or blue scales, and bellies of fire protected treasure hoards from greedy humans. You might even think that Fremont itself is like a fine dragon, with a belly of fire that bursts forth from her string of volcanoes. You might wonder, lying abed after any earthquake, if it is the stomach of Fremont rumbling, digesting its fire, perhaps causing the very ground to twist and turn in discomfort."

A small boy cried, then ran back to his mother.

Akashi leaned back, affecting a relaxed pose. "Well, and there were other dragons on Earth—insects with long bodies like broken twigs and even longer wings called dragonflies. And dragonfish on Deerfly; red and blue eels with fins like wings and faces like pictures of dragons from Earth." Now he smiled. "So what kind of dragon might we have found here?"

The room was quiet. Even the children had fallen still and silent.

Akashi gestured toward the back, and Liam came forward through a curtain, pulling a cage behind him. Liam was tall like us, strong, but not as broad as Bryan. A shock of blond hair hung over dark eyes, and a long blond braid twisted like a white rope against his nut-brown skin. The cage, covered with a yellow-gold cloth, was as tall as Liam, and long enough he could have stretched out inside it.

Some of the children on the floor crowded the stage and others scooted away. We were close, and we stayed put.

Akashi scanned the crowd, a master storyteller drawing a few moments of waiting toward forever. Finally, he gestured to Liam, who whisked away the red cloth with a flourish. "Behold the dragonbirds."

Two birds filled the cage. Really. Filled that huge cage. The brightest and most colorful birds I had ever seen, as if all the red and green of the Lace Forest in fall had been concentrated in two near-mythical beings. They stood as tall as Bryan, as thin as Kayleen. Their heads shimmered blue and green, and each one had bright red circles in the green fluffy ruffs around long necks. A few red circles adorned each wing. Their bellies were redberry-leaf green, and their tails a multitude of lighter greens shading to dark gray-brown. Instead of perching like most birds, they stood upright on two tall thin legs.

Akashi spoke. "And now Liam will show you how we missed them."

On cue, Liam came out pulling yet another contraption behind him: a planter with redberry bushes almost as tall as he was. He pulled the planter right behind the cage, and the birds disappeared. I blinked. Squinting, I finally made out the birds. They now looked exactly like redberry bushes, except a bit brighter.

Light applause broke out, and a woman's voice from somewhere behind me asked, "How did you find them?"

One of the children asked, "Where do they live?"

"Have you seen more?" another child asked.

Kayleen piped up. "Why do you call them dragons?"

Liam caught my eyes and grinned. Akashi held up his arms to forestall more questions. "Liam saw them first." Liam beamed while Akashi continued. "They live at the edges of a lake we named Dragon Lake, at the top of Small Fish Mountain. Yes, there were more. Once we learned to flush them by moving and calling out, we counted at least fifteen pairs. Like twintrees, they seem to always be paired, and to stay close to each other. They live at the very edges of the lake, their feet in water, right where the water plants give way to the redberries. We have not seen them before. And we call them dragons because of the red, like fire, that flames around their necks and colors their breasts."

Eric's five-year-old daughter Sudie asked, "Why did you bring them here? Won't they miss their families?"

Akashi smiled at Sudie. "Excellent question. We brought them to show you of course, so you can learn about Fremont."

Sudie looked appeased and settled back, staring happily at the bright birds.

Akashi kept his eyes on her. "We will take them back as soon as we leave here, so they can winter wherever their kind do. For that very reason, we will be here just a few days. But now, before we show you the snake or the flower, we will yield to the East." He gestured toward Ruth, who led the East Band, and then he himself pulled back the dragonbirds, leaning into the job, making a show of it, while Liam pulled the redberry bushes quietly and easily from the stage.

Ruth was tall and thin, slightly younger than Akashi, with a full head of dark hair streaked with gray and a narrow face. She walked purposefully to the stage, and began right away, without Akashi's showmanship. Her voice was tight and slow, as if she were struggling to control her emotions. "This was a difficult summer for us. We started off well, but early on we lost one of our own, my nephew Varay."

The crowd murmured. We had heard about Gene, but not Varay. I remembered him vaguely, a young man, about Alicia's and Liam's age, with huge dark eyes that always seemed to watch us curiously.

"Varay fell from a cliff. His death saddened us."

Ruth stood quietly, letting the crowd feel the death, the sorrow. Just as the silence seemed almost too much to bear, she continued. "And then we lost Gene Wolk in the earthquake. We were not in the open, but just coming down-trail from Silver Spring and starting to cross a clearing. The last wagons were still on the hill trail, which is steep. Gene was in the rear. We barely felt the first earthquake, but the second one washed the trail from under Gene's wagon, and the wagon tumbled into a ravine, killing him."

Roamers did die, of course, nearly every season. It was more dangerous to be out there than inside the data nets and walls of Artistos. Story Night told of the deaths, but never dwelt on them. The roamers mourned their own, in their own way.

So Ruth moved us along past the natural sadness of death and displayed a new tea her group made from a combination of grasses that turned out to be good for unsettled stomachs, and three new insects, all of which bit or stung. Nothing the

East Band had to offer rivaled the dragonbirds; new animals larger than a hand were rare finds now that humans had explored Fremont for two hundred years.

Akashi returned to tell the rest of the West Band's story. They had captured a large carrion-eating bird named a blaze flier we'd seen drawings of but never caught before. Although only half the wingspan of the dragonbirds, it squawked angrily in its cage and the smaller children drew back from it. Akashi looked at the frightened little ones, and in a very soft gentle voice he said, "Do not be afraid of knowledge." He paused. "The blaze flier is caged, and inside the cage, it is not your enemy. It lives near Rage Mountain and feeds on dead things killed by the confluence of mountain blood and seawater. We will let it go where it can find its way home, and it will not trouble you here. This bird is squawking because it fears you." He paused for a full beat, then continued. "It is best to always remember that lack of knowledge will kill you faster than gathering knowledge."

At that, a few of the little ones came closer again, and looked more carefully at the bird.

Once all of the displays were over, the families with young children left and the rest of us stayed, snacking on late-summer berries in goat milk. Liam came down to our table and sat with us for a few moments, looking pleased with himself. He smiled at me, his eyes sparkling. "Will I see you at trading tomorrow?"

The day after the roamers' return was always a holiday in Artistos. For the first time in weeks, I looked forward to something. "I will find you." Then I remembered myself and looked at the others. "We all will. And if you come across Alicia, will you tell her we hope to see her, too?"

A frown marred Liam's beautiful face for a moment, and his brows drew tightly together. "I'll look for a chance. But she is well kept, as if just talking to me would poison her obedience."

"Would it?" I asked.

He laughed. "Perhaps. But I will look for her." With that,

he turned and vaulted back onto the stage, returning to his band.

On the walk home, Joseph glanced at me and asked, "Which one do you prefer, Liam or Bryan?"

I didn't have an answer to give him. I loved them both. But someday I would have to choose a mate. If we lived that long. Another *altered*. Only we would live so long, and how could I bear someone with half my senses, half my speed, half my strength?

6

TRADING DAY

As I woke, the usual excitement of Trading Day filled my chest. Not loss, not Joseph, just Trading Day. A day of stories and chatter with friends, of Liam.

A sudden heavy feeling pushed me back into bed. For the first time in years, I had nothing to trade. An image of Therese filled my head. She knelt at the edge of the boundary, near the Lace Forest, humming softly, sun dappling her skin, her long fingers picking fragrant herbs for the soap we had planned to make for today's trading. We were going to make straw baskets to carry our soap in, and decorate them with the yellow and red flowers of late fall. We had started gathering herbs to scent our soap a week before the earthquake.

I shook my head, trying to clear the image. It didn't matter anyway. I couldn't imagine doing it without her.

I got up and splashed cold water on my face. The house was quiet; Nava and Tom had probably left already.

I looked around my room. What could I possibly trade? Unusual rocks and dried leaves lay scattered on my one shelf. Nothing there. The walls had pictures Joseph or I had drawn, mostly scenes from around Artistos, not artistic enough to have trading value. Hanging in my closet, I spotted clothes I had outgrown. Those would have to do. The pants would be long for almost anyone, but could be shortened. I folded three shirts and two pairs of pants carefully into a light backpack and went to wake up Joseph.

Trading Day happened twice each year: fall and spring. In spring, the roamers brought homemade materials dyed with redberries or sun-chalices or black-root or simply the pale olive of natural hemp. Spring meant polished rock and clay-bead jewelry and small clever paintings, hand-carved wooden flutes decorated with blue or green or red feathers; beautiful things that could be made in small spaces with simple tools, patience, and no industrial base. We mostly traded pots and forks and knives and nails and wheels; practical things that came from our smelter or our woodshop.

Sophia designed loose hand-embroidered shirts the roamers loved; Eric made leather pouches to match his shoes and boots; and Therese and I had twice made goats-milk soap, scenting it with herb and flower oils.

Today, for fall trading, Artistos would offer apples, hay, grain, squash, beans, and tomatoes in exchange for game and gathered fruits from the forests. The roamers would choose food and milk goats from this year's herds. Art and jewelry and clothing would still change hands, but the bulk of goods traded in fall made the rain and cool of winter easier.

I found Joseph filling his pockets with small wooden animals he had carved, some before the earthquake, and some after.

Joseph and I walked to the park, taking it slow since my leg had tightened up overnight. A cool breeze blew lightly against my cheeks, and songbirds chattered from the trees by the path.

Paloma called out, "Good morning," from behind us. We stopped and turned. Kayleen and Paloma jogged to catch us. Paloma was dressed in neatly pressed official green hemp work clothes. Kayleen grinned at me, dressed in green work pants and a hand-embroidered white blouse with blue flowers that matched her eyes. She'd tamed her unruly hair in three wooden clips. "The dragonbirds were wonderful. I heard the East Band caught a whole herd of djuri. Mom said I can help her with the colony trading. Didn't Liam look good?"

Joseph laughed. "Chelo thinks so." I aimed a playful swat at his head as payment for the jibe. Truthfully, I was so pleased he felt well enough to tease me that I didn't mind, even though my face grew hot at the mention of Liam's name.

Kayleen kept right on talking. "He's beautiful. He grew a lot this year, and Akashi certainly favors him."

I laughed. She was like the early-morning greeting-birds that chirped outside my window each dawn, except she talked all day. She balanced my tendency to be quiet. "That's a good thing, Kayleen."

Paloma broke in, sounding worried. "I overheard someone from the East Band saying Liam shouldn't be given so much privilege."

"Well, he's earned it," Kayleen said.

Paloma nodded in agreement. "That's true, but it may still cause him troubles."

Joseph scowled, his earlier happiness vanishing. He sounded almost petulant. "I hate it that they treat Alicia so badly. There's nothing wrong with her."

"Of course there isn't." Paloma brushed a stray wisp of long blond hair from her freckled face. "But Ruth lost her husband and brother in the war, and her pain and anger colors how the East Band treats Alicia. They see their leader keep a close eye on her, and they treat her the same way. Akashi genuinely likes Liam, and values his skills. Leadership makes a difference."

Well, I thought, sure it does. Therese and Steven accepted us, and that mattered.

Kayleen looked disgusted. "Alicia didn't start the war.

And neither did we. Some people seem to know that, and they treat us all right. But then there's Nava and Lucius and Jack and Ruth . . ."

Paloma interrupted her. "For some, it's about the war. For others, it's about the ways you are different. We've had this conversation. The only way for you to change people's minds is to be as useful to the colony as you can. It's worked here; Artistos treats you well."

Joseph's mouth set in a sharp scowl. "Some people treat us well."

Kayleen frowned, then said, "Well, Liam earned Akashi's trust. He's so competent. I bet no one else could have found the dragonbirds." Before I had to hear too much about how beautiful Liam was, we reached the edge of the park. Kayleen and Paloma headed off to the main tables where the official trading of common goods would take all morning. Joseph and I paused to look around, to see where to start.

The wagons were pulled into two loose circles, one for each band. Paintings or carved wood decorated each one. The long, thin wagons were designed to be drawn by two hebras each. Today, most had tables set in front with whatever goods were available for personal trade.

Half the town appeared to have beaten us here. Children raced, laughing, while their parents and older siblings examined goods and caught up on news. Dogs barked. Joseph and I walked slowly through the park, looking for Mayah and Akashi's distinctive wagon.

We found it at the far edge of the West Band's circle. The base color was bright yellow. Almost all of the wagons were personalized, but I loved this one most of all. It had a large picture of the spaceship *Traveler* painted on one side and a picture of Fremont on the other. Akashi had altered the real layout of the world so the two continents were visible against the large bright blue ocean. Jini was a yellow and green disk, a topographic display showing the mountains rising right in the middle. A single red dot showed Rage Mountain on the southern coast. The perpetual steam where the mountain's fiery lava met the ocean had been captured as a tiny white cloud. Islandia sported the same colors as Jini, although Islandia was long and thin with edges along one side that looked like teeth. Blaze was represented by a long thin slash of red, as if a giant's knife had cut through the ocean and the blood of Fremont welled out.

No one stood outside the wagon, and a bright golden cloth covered the trading table. I waited in front and considered knocking on the door, when Akashi came around from the back of the wagon. As he saw us, his smile warmed his eyes, making me smile back without thinking. This close, I could see the wrinkles around his mouth and on the backs of his hands. "Good morning, Chelo, Joseph." His face grew more serious. "I'm terribly sorry for the loss of your parents."

"Thank you." I felt a little nervous. Akashi seemed to have so much energy and power, so much influence over the roamers, and yet he always treated us kindly. And he had been a friend of Steven's. What he thought about me and Joseph mattered. "Thank you. We miss them very much. We're looking for Liam."

"My son asked me to watch for you. Go on in." His word, "son," touched my heart with pride and longing. Therese had treated me like a daughter in some ways, but she had never called me one.

We climbed up three wooden steps and pushed open the gold-painted door. Inside, past a small kitchen, the central core of the wagon was a comfortable-looking rectangular room with cabinets lining the top of the walls and soft bench seats that must double as beds along both long sides.

Liam sat on the far bench, his hair falling gently against his face, his braid covering his heart. He looked up and a wide smile lightened his face. "I see *you* found *me*." He held a fat wooden flute between his knees, and was tying a bright feather that could only have come from a dragonbird onto the flute with a long thin sinew. He tugged the knot tight and held the flute out to me. "I made it for you."

Surprise stunned me into silence. I sat down opposite Liam and took the flute in shaking hands, running my fingers along its smooth surface. I'd never had such a fine instrument of my own. It felt lighter than it looked, and yet also solid and comforting in my hand. Just holding it brought pleasure.

Liam watched my face, and his grin widened, pleased by my reaction. "Go on, play it."

I brought the flute to my mouth and blew. A single low, soft note floated through the air, sad and haunting. My fingers fumbled at the holes along the top as I worked out how to change notes. The flute had at least a full octave range.

Liam glowed with pride. "I'll help you more later." He reached into the cabinet above his head and produced a wooden drum with a red-and-gold-painted leather head just two hand spans across, and twice as tall. "And this is for you, Joseph."

Joseph tapped on the drum. Even with Joseph's soft touch, the small wagon filled with a deep, full beat. Loose items rattled on the shelves.

I smiled at Liam. He gazed back at me, his eyes hopeful. My cheeks burned and I dropped my eyes. "Thank you. It's beautiful. Both are beautiful." I held the flute on my lap, fingering the bright feather. It was as long as my hand, less than half as long as the flute, and thinner than my little finger. The deep green shaft faded to black at the base. "But I don't have anything for you." There was no tradition of us trading gifts, and in fact, we did not know Liam well, not really. The roamers usually only spent a few days in town, twice a year. It seemed like an extravagant gesture on his part, like an offering of some part of himself.

"Akashi suggested it. After the earthquake, in those few days we were wondering how you all fared here. He said you are my family more than he is."

I looked up at him, trying to read his expression. "Do you think that?" I asked. Liam had always been polite, and courteous, but he seemed bound more to Akashi and Mayah and the band than to us.

Liam shrugged. "No one in the band is like me. Akashi says I have surpassed him, and that I should find out more about what you know."

Joseph reached into his pocket and took out a carving of a hebra. It stood on four legs in his palm, and its head was turned backward, as if looking behind it. "I made this. I'd like you to have it." He glanced at me, a tender smile briefly touching his face. "It's from both of us."

Liam held the little beast up and admired it. "That's good work. Thank you; I am honored."

Joseph seemed pleased with Liam's acceptance of his gift, and also with the drum, which he held loosely in his lap, running his fingers along the edge of the head. I was proud of him; it had been exactly the right gesture. If only I had something personal to give Liam from me. I offered words. "I have always thought of you and Alicia as family."

"Thank you," Liam said simply, and turned to put the carved hebra on a shelf.

Alicia. It felt important to find her. "Did you see Alicia last night?"

Liam's face darkened. "Not up close. I asked Walter, a friend of mine in the East Band, about her. He said Alicia is a freak. She mutters to herself all day and hardly ever talks to anyone. He seemed angry with her, and he never gets mad at anyone. He promised to tell her we want to talk to her."

Joseph spoke up. "Well, she won't find us here. And I'm hungry."

"All right. Let me get Kayleen's gift." Liam picked up a small wooden box with a dragonbird carved in the top. He let me hold it while he found a brain-tanned djuri leather pouch. "Do you think she'll like it?" he asked.

The detail on the miniature dragonbird showed individual tiny feathers, and the ruff around its neck had been tinted red. The lid fit closely. The wood had been polished as smooth as my flute. "It's beautiful. I'm sure she'll love it."

We left our gifts inside the wagon and walked outside, squinting into the bright morning sun. Akashi stood deep in conversation with two children, but he looked up to wave as we passed him. I waited until we were out of earshot, then leaned close to Liam. "You are very lucky."

He glanced behind him and smiled softly. "I know."

Liam led us toward the crowded central tables. There, the three of us stood awkwardly, looking for Kayleen or Bryan or Alicia. Joseph spotted Kayleen helping Paloma count out hay chits, and we moved as close to her as we could, waiting for her to look up. Kayleen's fingers flew as she grouped the chits in tens, pushing them toward Paloma, who finished each deal with a smile and a handshake. Finally, she looked up and beamed at Liam. Then she noticed me standing next to him, and a slight frown flitted across her face before she erased it. She whispered to Paloma, then walked over to us, brushing her hair into place with her long fingers. She stood looking at Liam, grinning widely, tongue-tied for once.

"Have you seen Alicia?" I asked.

Kayleen shook her head. "I haven't seen Bryan either."

"Can you help us find them?" Liam asked.

Kayleen bit her lip and gestured at the long line of people standing by Paloma's table. "We're busy. Paloma asked if one of you could stay and help." She looked hopefully at Liam.

"I'll do it," Joseph said. "We can listen for news."

Disappointment flickered in Kayleen's eyes. It wasn't lost on me that Liam made her blush, but I suddenly wondered if Joseph liked Kayleen. Maybe it was the excitement of Trading Day, or the uneasiness of so many recent losses, or just being around Liam, and sensing the changes in him this season. Whatever it was, I often felt awkward now, and new tensions ran like tiny morning winds between us.

Kayleen flicked her gaze from me to Liam. "You seem worried about Alicia. Is there something specific we should find out?"

Liam frowned. "We stopped once with the East Band after the quake, and she didn't speak to me at all; she stayed in her wagon. I glimpsed her from a distance a few times. She looked sad. I haven't seen her up close this trip, but she usually *is* out Trading Days. Also, my friend Walter seemed angry at her. I didn't get to talk to him long, though. We were all too busy setting up."

Kayleen nodded. "Will you come back in an hour? We might be done by then."

"Sure." Liam held out his gift. "For you."

Kayleen eagerly opened the pouch and lifted the box out. It glowed warmly in the sunlight. A wide grin lightened the sharp angles of her face and brought a glow to her dark eyes. "Did you make it?"

He smiled and his cheeks reddened. "Yes."

She opened the box lid, and lifted out a little tiny red feather from a dragonbird ruff. Her eyes shone. "Will you take us to see the dragonbirds later?" she asked.

Liam laughed. "If there's time."

Kayleen carefully returned the feather and closed the lid. She reached forward and hugged Liam, planting a kiss on his cheek.

Why hadn't I thought of that when he handed me the flute?

"Come on, Joseph, we've got to go." Kayleen carefully tucked the bag with Liam's gift under her arm, and hurried back to Paloma, Joseph trailing behind her.

I turned away from watching Kayleen to find Liam watching me appraisingly. "Joseph is so distant. I'm sorry about your parents, but it seems"—Liam looked at the ground—"Joseph seems even worse than he should."

What to say? I didn't want his pity, but maybe he could help me with Joseph. "It is harder. Nava doesn't like us, but I think Tom does. Joseph has been pretending to be normal, not *altered*, and eating himself up from the inside over it. He hardly ever laughs anymore. I worry about him; we all worry about him." I shrugged, not wanting him to pity us. "Let me know if you have any ideas."

"I'm sorry." I thought for a moment he was going to fold me in his arms, but he straightened. "Come on. We should be looking for Alicia."

As I followed Liam toward the East Band wagons, I watched his broad back, the proud way he carried his head.

We knew which wagon Alicia belonged to, but I also knew from experience that we couldn't just walk up and talk to her. Her adoptive parents, Michael and Bella, disapproved of us, finding reasons Alicia wasn't around or wasn't available. They were dour people, with two children, besides Alicia, who were allowed a few more freedoms, but still well guarded. Michael and Bella kept a big sable and black dog named Lucky who watched over the entrance to their wagon, growling softly at anyone who came too near.

As we walked fully into the circle of wagons, Liam leaned into me and suggested, "Shall we browse the tables? We can watch for her, and see what we overhear."

I still carried my pack of outgrown clothes. Maybe I could trade for a gift for Liam to thank him for the flute. I pointed to the first table on the right. An older man stood behind it, looking down and rearranging a display of small handmade mirrors. His mouth began breaking into a welcoming smile. Then he recognized us. A mask fell over his features. The sudden change in his demeanor stopped me, but Liam kept right on walking up to the table. He picked up a round clay wall decoration with a mirror in the center and small polished blue and green stones around the edges. His voice was neutral and even as he greeted the man. "Hello, Klauss, how are you? Did the season treat you well?"

I came up beside Liam. He handed me the mirror and I admired the smooth stones. Klauss's words were clipped. "A hard year for us."

His eyes followed the mirror as if he wanted to take it from my hands. Roamers were usually happy to discuss trades. As a test, I slid my pack from my back and started to open it.

Klauss narrowed his eyes. "Trading values are high this year."

I glanced at his wagon to identify his specialty. A painting of blue water falling through gray rocks adorned the side, and actual pebbles had been fastened to the edges of the roof. A geologist. I took a deep breath, trying not to show the sharp anger rising up in me. No adult in Artistos had treated us so blatantly badly in years. Some ignored us, some watched us, some grew quiet when we approached. But only the kids were rude. I ran my hands along the tiny inset stones by the mirror. "You've found some beautiful stones this year."

He looked me directly in the eye and said, "I found some very pretty ones along the High Road."

Liam's hand, suddenly a warm weight in the middle of my back, kept me from lunging forward across the table. I backed up into Liam, smelling the clean salt of his sweat, feeling taut stomach muscles. I zipped my bag, my hands shaking. No roamer had ever been hostile on Trading Day. Ever. But I was here to look for Alicia. That was more important than understanding Klauss.

I swallowed hard and turned, and Liam turned with me, his hand on my shoulder a silent offer of support.

Eric the shoemaker, his daughter Sudie on his hip, laughed and joked with a pair of middle-aged women at the next table, which was heaped with dried herbs separated into bundles and tied with hemp twine. We stood off to the side, waiting to be acknowledged, but after the shoemaker left, the women sat down and talked between themselves instead of looking up and offering us goods. I pulled Liam to the side. "What is going on here? How were you treated last night?"

His brow furrowed with anger, his face reddened. "I don't know. I mean I don't know what this is about. I didn't notice it last night, but my focus was on the dragonbirds and helping Mom and Dad. I didn't really talk to anyone from this band last night except Walter, and that was just for a moment."

I looked around, trying to decide where to go next. A young woman with two long dark braids sitting behind a table covered with hand-carved barrettes and buttons motioned us over with a small furtive hand signal. Liam and I drifted toward her, now wary of any East Band member who *wanted* to talk to us.

As we got close she handed me a barrette. Her voice was pitched low. "Look interested in this." She leaned in to pin the barrette in my hair. "Alicia is down by the river," she whispered. "Hurry; she will not be able to stay away for long. Her guardians are already looking for her." She drew back, then leaned in close again. "Alicia is my friend, and asked me to watch for any of you. Go to her." She unpinned the barrette, shaking her head. "Perhaps you'll return later? I'll look for a nice barrette for you then, after you find Alicia."

So she was a trader at heart. And perhaps a friend. I wanted to ask what drove her band members to such mistrust, but she waved us away. "Go, but go quietly."

I caught her gaze with mine, holding it briefly. "Thank you," I mouthed.

I glanced at Liam. He nodded, a small smile playing around his lips. So he had heard her.

We turned and walked back out of the band's circle. I imagined a sigh of relief as we left. The East Band had always been less friendly to us than the West, but they had always been at least polite, and some had been openly welcoming.

But Therese had always been by my side before. Now we were alone.

Liam and I edged along the park, following a path that wound just above where the cliffs fell down to the Lace River, walking slowly to avoid drawing attention. The sound of the river became louder until we neared the bridge where the cliffs faded into a low riverbank. We scrambled down the bank, clutching at redberry bushes and nearly losing our footing twice.

Alicia stood on the gravel at the edge of the water, her back to us, her long dark hair hanging in thick waves down her back, obscuring her slender form. Bryan faced her, deep in conversation. His big hands cupped her shoulders, his blue eyes stared at her face, full of concern. Alicia looked up as we neared them, tears streaming down her cheeks.

"What happened?" Liam asked, his face as concerned as Bryan's.

She sucked in a deep breath, gulping back tears. "Ruth is telling people I murdered Varay."

Murder? The word set me reeling. There had been no murder on Fremont in my lifetime, as far as I knew. Except for the war. I swayed, momentarily dizzy. Was this why people treated us so badly?

Liam looked hard at her, as if weighing her words. "Alicia, tell me what happened."

She took another deep trembling breath and wiped at her violet eyes, deeply bruised from her tears, and perhaps lack of sleep. "He died a few days before the earthquake. Varay and I were friends. Ruth hated that. He was her nephew, and she struggled to keep him away from me. But we didn't let her keep us apart. We met whenever we could, making it look like an accident." She stopped to wipe at her eyes again. "That day, Ruth sent me to search for herbs, and Varay was waiting for me just out of camp. He was apprenticed to Clell the biologist, who sent him to look for a particular small brown bird which nests in cliff sides. Since the herbs Ruth sent me to find grow in the cliffs, too, Varay and I went together." She stopped again, staring out over the water, her lips drawn tight.

"He lost his footing halfway up. I was above him, and so there was nothing I could do except watch him fall. He hit his head." She shuddered and drew her arms tight around her torso. "I climbed down as fast as I could, and carried him back to the band, but by the time we got there, he had died in my arms."

"That wasn't murder." Poor Alicia.

"No. But I was so hurt and lost, and so unhappy we had not thought to rope together, that after I brought Varay's body back, and told people what happened, I kept to myself." She swallowed and fresh tears tumbled down her cheeks. "I was so sad."

I remembered the soap Therese and I were going to make, and how it hurt not to see her or Steven or Gi Lin or the others. "I understand," I said softly.

"Then the quake came, and we were all busy, but afterward, once we had fixed everything we could and buried Varay and Gene, I just couldn't stand to talk to anyone, and Ruth glared at me whenever I saw her, so I kept to myself. Only more and more people started avoiding me, people that used to be at least polite."

She looked down at the ground, as if searching for something. "Most of the older members of the band distrust me, but the kids my age . . . I thought they were my friends. They stopped talking to me, and I thought it was respect for my grief. Then three days ago, Sky told me Ruth was saying that I killed Varay. That I used my strength to pitch him from the cliff. That since I was so strong and so fast, I could have saved him if I wanted to, so since I didn't, I murdered him."

The idea that our strengths could so doom us even when we tried to help made me shiver even in the heat.

She looked pleadingly at me and Liam. "I would have saved him if I could have."

Bryan answered her. "Of course you would have." After an awkward moment of silence, he asked, "But she hasn't accused you formally?"

"She knows that would mean Nava and Tom for judges."

Of course. Ruth herself would judge events in her own band, but if she were accused or accuser, then she would have to submit to the leadership of Artistos. And even though Nava didn't like us, she saw uses for us. Without proof, which Ruth didn't seem to have, Nava wouldn't find her guilty.

"It's not fair to accuse you with rumors. You'll never get a trial, never get to clear yourself. She has to be stopped." I had no idea how, but we had to deal with this. Now. While the roamers were in town.

Bryan asked, "How was the death entered in the records?"

Alicia shook her head. "I don't know. Not as murder. If she'd entered it that way she would have had to accuse me. That's the rule."

"Maybe she just wants to ruin your honor," Liam said. "Let me talk to Akashi about it."

"And Paloma," Bryan said.

"Ruth has always hated me," Alicia said. "The war is never over for her, and I am its symbol. She will hate me until the day she dies. Or I do." She looked around our small circle. "I hate the war. I hate these people for starting it, and I hate my parents for leaving me here, and I just . . ." Her shoulders heaved and she sobbed, breaking off her words. I stepped toward her, put a hand on her near shoulder, and she suddenly reached for me and buried her head against my chest, sobbing.

I glanced up at Bryan and Liam. They came in and joined us, so the three of us encircled Alicia, holding her, being there. The things she'd just said lived inside me as small thoughts every day, and it felt like Alicia's tears touched us all, drew us all together.

After a while, her crying subsided and she stepped away from me. We gave her room, widening our little circle. She looked carefully at each of us, reaching out a hand to stroke my hair, to touch Bryan's broad shoulder, Liam's cheek. "I have to go before Bella comes looking for me."

Liam asked, "Can you meet us later, just before dark? Back here?"

She nodded. "I'll try. I should be able to get away during the feast. I won't be able to stay long."

Bryan folded her in his arms and held her a long time before letting her go. She came briefly by turns into Liam's arms and then mine. She smelled like herbs and water and she felt sad and small.

As we watched her scramble up the shallow bank and disappear over the top, I swore not to let her down.

7

SEARCHING FOR HELP

After Alicia scrambled away, the rest of us stood quietly on the riverbank. Murder. She couldn't have done it, but clearly the East Band believed it. Some of them. My head whirled with implications. We'd worked so hard to earn Artistos's trust; could we lose it over this? Would Nava stand up for us, for Alicia? Tom? Garmin and a lot of the kids our age teased us, even threw things sometimes, and tried to tempt us into fights. Wei-Wei was a Town Council member, and her eyes always avoided ours even though she was polite. I could name many people who might believe us capable of . . . something. But murder? If it were some other accuser . . . but Ruth? Ruth was a Council member, and the leader of her band.

It took a few moments for the cool river breeze to bring me back to the present, back to my friends. I grabbed Bryan's hand, and Liam's, and the three of us looked at each other.

Bryan's eyes were dark and smoky, as if the deep fires of anger that ran under his placid surface licked at his core. I touched his hand, briefly, hoping to soothe him. "We'll figure it out. Let's go find Kayleen and Joseph. Maybe they've heard something."

Bryan took off, bolting halfway up the bank before Liam and I gathered ourselves enough to follow him. Bryan stayed ahead of us all along the path, setting a fast pace toward the trading tables. Liam held my hand, supporting me, and still we barely managed to keep up with Bryan. My stiff leg screamed.

If only I knew what to do. Get help. This was too big for us, alone.

We found Kayleen and Joseph still helping Paloma. The line had dwindled away to nearly nothing, as had the piles of hay chits on the table. Paloma noticed us first, and leaned down to Kayleen, whispering in her ear and pointing at us, then scooping Joseph's and Kayleen's chits toward herself. Kayleen grabbed her gift pouch, and practically ran toward us, Joseph trailing after. Her eyes flashed anger. "We have to talk," she said.

I looked around, spotted a quiet place under a tree, and gestured to the others. "Let's sit here."

Kayleen started talking before we were even settled. "Some people wouldn't let us help them. They wanted Mom to count their chits, as if Joseph and I couldn't count to ten. Mom stood up for us. She said if they wanted help, they could let us help them." She leaned into us, her voice incredulous. "One guy actually walked away. Like he wasn't planning on feeding his goats if he had to take his chits from an *altered*."

Joseph added, "From the East Band. All the rude people were Easters, although not all of *them* were mean. Akashi's people treated us okay."

Kayleen glanced at Liam. "What does it mean? Did you find Alicia? We didn't see her, but I heard people talking about her. It sounds like she's in trouble. Do you know what happened?"

Liam sat very still, his jaw set, his eyes scanning the crowd. Trading was winding down, most people now sitting like us, in small groups, or walking home. Gianna passed us, waving and smiling. A family I recognized from the East Band made a wide circle to avoid us. Liam watched for at least five minutes before he answered Kayleen. "Ruth," he said. "Ruth never wanted Alicia in her band. She asked us to take Alicia four summers ago, but Akashi refused, said the decisions about mixing us up in the community were made for good reason, and Ruth should learn to get along with Alicia. Last summer, Akashi told me he was sorry. He'll want to hear about this murder accusation."

"Murder?" Kayleen's eyes widened. "Alicia murdered someone?"

"Of course not," Bryan said, grimacing. "Alicia didn't do it. But Ruth is spreading rumors about it, saying she killed him."

"Who?" Joseph asked.

I repeated Alicia's own story as best as I could. It seemed to become more real in the telling, and near the end, tears splashed onto my hands and my voice shook. Alicia must feel so alone.

Kayleen and Joseph both grew as quiet as the rest of us. After a while, they looked over at me, and Joseph asked, "What should we do?"

Bryan fidgeted. I glanced at Liam. He knew the roamers better than I did. But he waited for me to answer.

A breeze blew from town, carrying the smells of the Trading Day feast: roasting whole djuri and kid goat, and corn cooking on coals. "We need help."

Liam nodded. "I know."

I scanned their faces. Joseph and Kayleen nodded at me.

Bryan's jaw was clenched. "I don't want help. I want people to leave us alone."

I ignored him and spoke to Kayleen. "Find Paloma, and ask her to sit with us at the feast. Tell her what's going on. We're usually together at group meals, no one will think anything of it. We can ask if she'll help us with the Town Council. They won't listen to us."

Kayleen nodded, and stood, brushing dirt and grass from her pants. She waited to see what else I'd say.

"Bryan, will you go with Kayleen? You were there when Alicia told her story."

Bryan shrugged. "Sure, I'd be happy to."

I asked Liam, "Can you see if Akashi will meet us, too? Fill him in?"

And last, Joseph. What would be easy? "Go on, go with Liam. You can get my flute and your drum, so we'll have them at home."

There was a barrette waiting for me to claim it before trading stopped completely.

I walked between the tables this time, not bothering to stop. I did glare at Klauss when I walked by. He looked up briefly and then looked away again, a flick of his eyes that looked, just for a second, like fear. I shivered. Fear of us was worse than anger at us.

I didn't see Alicia anywhere.

May and Klia stood by Sky's booth, chattering and laughing. When they saw me, May glanced at me, and looked like she was about to say hello, but Klia pulled her away before I got to Sky's table.

Sky smiled broadly as I walked up, showing even, white teeth. She reached into her pocket, pulling out a pretty near-elm barrette carved in the long, thin shape of a summer-fish. "I thought this one might look good in your hair." She handed me a brush and held up a mirror. She glanced around, then lowered her voice. "Alicia ran through here about an hour ago, looking like she'd been crying. Did you find her?"

I nodded. "She told us Ruth thinks she killed Varay. But she couldn't have."

Sky watched me for a minute, as if appraising whether or not I was trustworthy. Then she smiled and angled the mirror just right. "Of course Alicia didn't kill Varay. The barrette looks good on you."

I clasped it in my hair and cocked my head. The light wood showed well against my dark hair. "All I have is clothes to trade."

"Let me see."

Sky pursed her lips and tugged at her long braids, watching carefully as I pulled out my old clothes. They'd be adequate trade for the barrette. More than adequate. As Sky held each shirt and extra-long pair of pants up to examine them, I thought about Alicia's ragged clothes. "Sky? Will you take all of these, and set aside an outfit for Alicia? You can keep the rest. I have one more favor to ask, too."

She rubbed her chin contemplatively, eyeing the pile of clothes. It was worth ten barrettes. But she was a roamer, a trader. She'd take it. Sure enough, she nodded, then she turned and picked out two small blue hair clips and handed them to me. "It's too much. Take these, too." She smiled broadly. "The blue will set off the gold flecks in your eyes."

She set her mirror down on the table and tucked my old clothes into a basket on the ground. "Alicia will appreciate the clothes." Her smile faded into a puzzled frown. "But what is the favor? I have not yet agreed to grant it, you know."

I leaned forward and lowered my voice. "We're going to meet Akashi and Paloma tonight, just after we get our food. Will you meet with us, too? Tell them what's going on?"

"Ruth won't like it."

"But you'll come? Just for a few minutes—just tell them what you told me. I want them to hear it from you."

She hesitated. I couldn't blame her. She lived in Ruth's band. She swallowed hard before nodding. "I won't stay long. Just long enough to tell my story."

"Thanks. We'll find a place on the grass, a little away from people. Hiding in the open." I tucked the blue barrettes into my pocket. "We won't keep you long."

Her wide-set brown eyes were wary, as if she still didn't

trust me completely. "I will be there. What Ruth is doing to Alicia is wrong. I saw how Alicia looked at Varay. She didn't kill him; she couldn't have. I saw her pain when she brought his body back, sat with her on two long nights afterward."

"Thank you." I zipped my nearly empty pack and threw it over my shoulder, walking as quickly as I could to more friendly territory in the West Band circle of wagons.

The culture guild always started preparing the Trading Day feast just after dawn. Long tables had been dragged from the guild halls to the park and were now being filled with steaming djuri and goat, rows of hot fresh corn, and bowls overflowing with mixed vegetables and fresh-baked bread. The crowd felt festive, happy, sated with conversation and trading. In a way, the feast celebrated the work we'd done, all of Artistos, to harvest in spite of the quake and storm, in spite of our losses and our aching hearts.

I walked aimlessly through the slowly growing crowd. The dread in the pit of my stomach every time I thought about Alicia, or Ruth, made me uncomfortable, out of step with almost everyone I passed. I declined an offered beer, taking water instead.

The culture guild served the feast when the sun still had a full hour before it would even kiss the treetops. A slight breeze hung thick with food smells and sweat and conversation. Families and groups of teenagers gathered in knots, eating together on bright blankets spread under the twin-trees.

Joseph and Bryan came up to me, and Joseph handed me my flute. I held it briefly to my chest, embracing it, feeling the smoothness of its surface under my fingers before tucking it into my bag.

As Joseph and Bryan and I filled our plates, I watched for Alicia. Surely they would let her come to the feast.

No sign.

She'd promised to meet us down by the river at dusk. Hopefully, she could keep her word.

Bryan pointed to a spot outside of the biggest crowds, on a

low hill where we could talk without being overheard. Kayleen and Liam joined us a few minutes later, Liam carrying his plate and hers, while Kayleen balanced a stack of old blankets, which she spread out in a patchwork of red, green, and blue.

Akashi and Paloma walked slowly up the hill, Akashi taller by a head, leaning down to hear something Paloma said. Akashi was dressed more simply than yesterday, in a gold-and-white belted top over black pants. Paloma wore a simple off-white shift. As they sat down, I looked for Sky or Alicia, but didn't see either of them.

Akashi drew his brows together and drummed his fingers, as if unsure where to start. "Paloma told me how Joseph and Kayleen were treated today."

Liam cleared his throat. "The East Band was rude to Chelo and me, too. Or at least most of them. But the real problem is Alicia's trouble."

I stood up, watching for Sky in the crowd.

Akashi looked at each of us in turn, as if trying to read a truth in our faces. "And you are convinced she did not kill Varay?"

Bryan nodded. "Of course she didn't."

Akashi kept his voice low and gentle, and I remembered that he led a band, and must therefore act as judge from time to time. "She has been treated poorly. That might give her reason to be angry, and thus to hurt." He glanced at Liam. "Is she as strong as you are?"

Liam shrugged. "Probably. We are all about the same, except Bryan, who is stronger. It doesn't matter whether or not she could have done it, she didn't do it. I'm sure."

Akashi nodded. "Very well. You are a good judge of character."

I spotted Sky by her dark braid and the dark freckles that stood against her light skin, and waved my hand briefly over my head. She started toward us. "Akashi, Paloma, Sky is coming."

"I know Sky." Akashi smiled briefly, looking up at me, his face serious. "The young carver. I trust her. She is bright and brave."

I smiled briefly at Akashi's way of making everything seem to be part of a story. As Sky neared us, she glanced nervously behind her, as if looking for shadows. She folded down into our circle gracefully, sitting with her legs crossed, her plate on her lap. She moved her braids behind her shoulder with a flick of her head, keeping the unruly tips of hair away from her food. We'd all seen each other every Trading Day. But here, she sat with every *altered* on Fremont except her friend Alicia. It seemed to make her feel more nervous than she had been with just me and Liam, or just me, at her booth. I smiled at her, trying to help her feel comfortable. "Thank you, Sky. We won't keep you long. Can you tell us what you know about Alicia's situation?"

She cleared her throat and took a drink of her beer. "First, let me tell you about Alicia. She is lost there, she is Ruth's bad dog. She is perhaps unaware of it, but since Varay's death . . ." She looked up. "You know about that, and about the accusations?"

"Yes," Kayleen said.

"Since the accusations, the band split. There are some, like me, maybe one in ten, who believe in her, who consider her a friend. And maybe half believe Ruth when she says that all of you are trouble, and you will bring death to us."

She paused, perhaps to let us absorb her words.

"The rest are not sure. Alicia is scared. She avoids most band members, which doesn't help her. Very few of us know Alicia well. Since Varay's death, she's been withdrawn. She cries a lot, and sometimes she talks to herself. She's grieving, and she has no one to really help her except me and a few other people our age. But she is not guilty." She paused again, and took another sip of beer. Her plate sat untouched in front of her. "Varay and Alicia were sweet on each other, although I don't know if they did anything about that or not. They were old enough, but Alicia told me Ruth forbid her to touch him."

I filed that thought away for the future. We had talked about it, of course, but we did not know if our *alterations* would breed true. There would be—implications—of us breeding, depending on what such unions produced. The thousand colonists came here to have a place to stay genetically unchanged, and their descendants mistrusted us because we were changed. The war was, at its core, about that very same thing.

Sky continued. "Since Ruth hasn't accused her formally, I don't think she will. She can't judge Alicia as band leader, not when she also serves as accuser. Ruth won't want anyone else to get involved." Sky folded her hands over her torso. It made her look small. "I watch out for Alicia as closely as I can. I won't be surprised if one day I wake up and she's simply not there, or if I wake up and there's been an accident."

Akashi frowned, but once more his voice was gentle. "Do you know what you are saying?"

Sky nodded, looking miserable.

Paloma broke in, "But do you have any proof that Alicia didn't kill Varay? That she couldn't have?"

Sky sighed. "Alicia loved him. I know that. But they were together when he died, with no witnesses. Besides, if she killed him, why would she carry his body back, crying the whole way? Why? When no one knew they were together? She could have just walked away."

Akashi smiled at her, and put a hand on her shoulder. "Do you know anything else that might help us?"

She shook her head. "Just that Alicia is a good person, and my friend."

Akashi smiled. "She is very lucky to know you. Thank you, and feel free to come visit anytime." He leaned closer to her. "If you get any information, you can tell any of us."

"Okay." Sky stood, and took her plate, still full, down the hill away from us. I watched her walk, alone, until she was out of my direct line of sight. Alicia was lucky to have such a friend. Sky must be an adult to have her own trading table, but this was probably her first year.

We had no friends near our age except each other. Sky made me think we should have tried to make some.

"So what do you think?" I asked, looking from Paloma to Akashi. "Town Council won't listen to us. Ruth won't."

Paloma turned her hands over and over in her lap, letting a long silence fall before she answered. "Well, we don't *know* if Sky's fears are justified, but I believe her. She is there, after all. What if I do nothing, and Alicia doesn't come back next spring? We need to bring these accusations into the open." She glanced at Akashi. "And I don't think Akashi should do it, since he and Ruth have to work together on so many levels to make the two bands work."

Akashi showed no reaction, but Liam nodded. "That's right."

"Will Town Council investigate a direct complaint from the girl?" Akashi asked.

Paloma frowned. "I think so."

Akashi put a hand up, as if it were Story Night and he was asking us to be quiet. "Investigating Ruth? Making her angry may not be a good tactic. An investigation will put Alicia at risk, too. If the story I have heard is right, Alicia has no alibi. If she did not do it, then Ruth has no proof. That makes a standoff, and I do not know who would win a standoff."

I broke in. "But if there's no investigation, and they take Alicia away with them, I'll be worried all winter that she'll be killed. We *have* to force it. This isn't just about Alicia, it's about all of us. We want the Council to talk to us, too."

Akashi steepled his hands, his dark eyes looking out over the heads of the feasting crowd. "She could die either way. I have only seen one investigation where the penalty was death, and that was years ago, for aiding the enemy during the war. I do not think this colony would kill a child, and Alicia is still legally a child. Yet she is the child of the enemy, and many of us are frightened of you all."

I shivered. People died on Fremont. In all of my life, all that I remembered, it was from accidents like the earthquake, or paw-cats, or the bite of a yellow-snake. It hadn't occurred to me to worry that the people we worked with and ate with could kill us. Might kill us.

Paloma cleared her throat. "Someone needs to talk to Alicia. We can't decide any of this for her."

Akashi nodded. "Of course. An inquiry could harm her more than mere rumors. In fact, it's perhaps best if Alicia herself lodges the complaint. Then she can call who she wants for witnesses."

I liked that idea, and thought Alicia might like it, too.

"We'll talk to Alicia when we see her later on." Then I had another thought. "But Nava will be one of the judges, and she doesn't like us."

Paloma glanced at me. "Nava will choose to be fair. Don't underestimate her."

"Well," Akashi said, "I think that's up to you to find out, Chelo. Liam said Alicia promised to meet you down by the river soon. Why not ask Alicia how she wants to handle this, and then go by your house and talk to Tom and Nava if Alicia wants to act?"

The stakes made me dizzy. "All right." I glanced at Joseph. "Will you help? I might want to have a witness for this conversation."

All the color had faded from Joseph's face. "Of course."

Akashi stood. "Now, I'm sorry, but I have to go. I have some business to attend to." He started walking down the hill. Unlike Sky, he didn't remain alone. By the time he got partway down the hill, a half-dozen people had converged on him.

Paloma said, "I always thought you would face new challenges as you got older, and smarter." She paused. "And stronger."

The implications weren't lost on me, and I knew Paloma was thinking much the same. If Alicia was found guilty with no actual proof, then we all faced the same risks. If we got involved, and Alicia won, we would have the permanent enmity of the leader of the East Band. That was the best of the two outcomes. I didn't like either.

Bryan stood and held his hand out for my plate. "It's almost time to meet Alicia." We worked together, gathering up plates and blankets, then stood in an awkward circle.

Paloma swept her steady gaze across us all, her eyes fastening on us one by one, holding us, saving me for last. She sounded pleased and somewhat shaky as she said, "I'm glad you asked for advice. I hope we can help." Noticing that imperturbable Paloma was shaken by this did nothing for the roiling worries dancing in my gut and head.

I led the five of us back toward the river, slowly, trying to seem like we were on a casual errand.

We got to the riverbank before Alicia was supposed to

show. Bryan picked up a large, flat rock and skipped it nearly to the other side of the river. We had stopped throwing stones in view of anyone except ourselves years ago, after we saw the looks on the adults' faces when we outskipped them. We saw no one, so we threw, our stones making whirring noises as they spun in the air, skipping hard and fast over the surface of the water, sometimes going so far we actually didn't see them finally sink under the water. Instead of competing, we just threw, and threw again, grunting with the slight effort of every toss, watching the stones and the river rings without conversation. Even Kayleen was quiet.

The sky slowly darkened.

Eventually, we could only see the first two or three skips of each stone. "What if she can't come?" Joseph asked.

"I don't know," I said. "I didn't see her at the feast, not at all. We'll need to go home, eventually. Although I don't know what to say to Tom and Nava if I don't talk to Alicia first."

Bryan still held a stone in his right hand. He flung it hard, and we listened to seven tiny splashes. "I'll stay. No one will really notice if I'm home."

"I'll sit with you," Liam told him.

I pulled them both to me, smelling the tangy sharpness of Bryan's anger on his bare slippery bicep, and the wood shavings embedded in Liam's shirt. Liam's braid tickled my nose. "You two are fantastic. Tell us if you find her," I whispered.

Kayleen and Joseph and I walked reluctantly home. It worried me that Alicia hadn't been at the feast or made it to the river to see us. But surely no one would hurt her in Artistos. I couldn't help but feel like all the hatred we had been slowly pushing underground by doing well, by helping, had somehow been watered and fed this year, and that it was sprouting up for us, and everyone on Fremont, to look at. But how could hatred grow anything but thorns?

When Joseph and I got home, I wrapped the flute inside a soft cloth that Therese had made me, and set it on the windowsill where Steven's and Therese's urns had once rested. It fit perfectly.

I found Tom seated in the common room, making notes. No sign of Nava, so she was probably still at the feast. I wanted to wait until Bryan could tell me whether Alicia came to the river, but the two-day deadline until the roamers left loomed. I took a deep breath and pulled Joseph after me into the common room. "Tom, can we talk to you?"

He nodded and set his slate down. "Sure. What do you need?"

I sat down on the chair closest to Tom, and Joseph sat across the room from us, in near shadow, ready to witness. He'd let me do most of the talking. "If I ask you some questions, can you promise not to talk to Nava unless we say it's okay?"

Tom cleared his throat and took a moment to answer. "I'm willing to agree to tell you before I talk to Nava, but not to ask you."

It was a fair enough answer. "All right." My hands twisted together like live things in my lap, and I forced them quiet. Destiny's light came in the window above Joseph, so Tom's face was lit by two sources: the moon and the lamp on the wooden table between us. "First, this isn't about us, but what if one of us, of the *altered*, was accused of a crime? Would the same laws apply to us that apply to everyone else?"

Tom leaned forward in his chair, new intensity in his eyes, which he fastened directly on me as he spoke slowly. "What crime?"

"I'm not ready to talk about it yet."

He leaned back, chewing on his lip, taking a moment to answer. "I can see this will be a serious conversation. I'm going to get a glass of water. Chelo? Joseph?"

Joseph stood up. "I'll get them."

"Thank you."

While we waited for Joseph, I watched Tom carefully, wondering how he would treat this conversation. He looked out the window, tapping his foot silently in the air, chewing his lower lip. He would be involved in the investigation, if there was one, alongside Nava and the rest of the Town Council.

Joseph returned with three glasses balanced carefully, handed us each one, and then sat back down.

Tom took a long drink of water. "I think the same laws would apply to you or me or anyone. The agreements that formed our colony talk about how citizens are treated. I don't know what got written down about your adoption by the community." He paused, brows drawn together, lips tight. "I doubt it says citizen."

"I know," I said. "Therese told me once. It said 'prisoner of war.'"

Tom frowned.

Joseph spoke up from his perch across the room. "But we *are* citizens. We live here, we work here, we do things to help the colony. We even go to school."

"I agree. But there are five Council, seven including me and Nava."

I pictured Jenna, her seamed face folded around her missing eye. She was certainly not considered a citizen. A problem, a helper, a mystery, but not a member of the community.

Tom continued. "We expect you to take your rightful roles here, and be part of the community. It follows that you should be judged by the community's standards." He frowned. "Can you tell me why you're asking?"

I bit my lip. What could I say safely? "A roamer is accusing Alicia of something she didn't do. Not formally, but she's telling people, and it's making trouble for Alicia."

"The roamers usually do their own policing. Is there some reason they can't take care of it?"

"I'm not sure they would be fair." I swallowed and tamed my hands again. "Ruth seems to be involved."

"Well, Alicia should start there anyway."

I wasn't telling him enough for him to understand, but what else could I say? I hadn't talked to Alicia yet.

The front door banged open, and I heard Bryan's voice, and Liam's, out of breath as if they'd been running. "Chelo, Joseph?"

All three of us stood. Liam held the door open, and Bryan followed him in, carrying Alicia in his arms the way one would carry a small child. Her hair obscured her face. Fresh bruises purpled her arms. Anger and worry warred across Bryan's face.

"Take her to my room," I said. "What happened?" Had she been beaten?

We trailed after Bryan, surrounding the bed as he laid Alicia carefully on it. She wore only loose shorts and a hemp top that was too big for her and belted tight with a rope. Her feet were bare. Both arms, one cheek, and one of her knees were bruised and banged up. Pain clouded her violet eyes. She pushed herself up to a sitting position on the bed, her back against the wall, her arms wrapped around her knees.

"What happened?" Tom demanded.

Bryan cleared his throat. "She was supposed to meet us at the river. When she didn't come, we decided to go look for her. We found her locked in her—her parents'," he spit the word out, "her guardians' wagon. She was banging herself up trying to get out, like a bird in a cage, and we were afraid she'd hurt herself. So we tied up the dog and gave her a little help getting out of the locked door." He raised an eyebrow and grinned a little. "It doesn't lock anymore. Bella and Michael must have known she talked to us."

Tom sat down on the edge of the bed, near Alicia, not touching her. "Talked to you about what?"

Alicia raked a lock of hair out of her face, her voice shaking. "Ruth is telling people I killed Varay. But I didn't. Bella locked me up, but I'm sure Ruth told her to. They told me to stay in the wagon today, earlier, before I saw you guys at the river, but I sneaked out." She looked over at us. "I had to tell someone what was going on."

Tom's eyes trailed over her, his frown deepening. "Who gave you the bruises?"

Alicia looked down at her arms, as if seeing them for the first time. "I guess . . . I guess some are from Bella pushing me into the wagon, but I gave myself the others, struggling to get out. I tried to break down the door, even though the dog was there. I just couldn't quite do it." She glanced over at Bryan and Liam, suddenly flashing a brief smile. "I was so glad to get out. Thank you."

I frowned. It wouldn't do for us to get caught breaking into locked wagons. "Did anyone see you two?"

Liam shrugged. "Probably, but I don't know who. Bella and Michael weren't home. We weren't worried about being seen. We were angry."

"Your anger is scary." Tom's brows furrowed. "You just used your strength, your extra strength, and broke the lock off the door?"

Bryan nodded. "What else were we supposed to do?"

"Well, for one, you could have come and gotten me or Nava. It doesn't seem right that Alicia was locked up, but you should have gotten help. It would have looked better for us to go inquire."

Bryan and Liam didn't respond. They didn't know Tom. Even Joseph and I only knew him a little, and I didn't know how much to trust him. Just that he had been all right so far. On the plus side, there was a glint of approval in his eyes despite his scolding.

Alicia broke in. "Can I stay here tonight?"

Tom chewed on his bottom lip. "They say you killed someone? Tonight? Who?"

"No. Before the earthquake. Varay. Ruth's telling the whole band I killed him, although she's never accused me directly." Tears glistened in her eyes. "I'm afraid."

The door opened and I heard Nava's swift footsteps coming down the hall. "Hello?" She poked her head in the door and her eyes widened at the sight of six of us crowded into the tiny room. Then she noticed Alicia. "What are you doing here?" She stepped closer to Alicia, bending over the girl. Her voice softened. "How did you get hurt?"

Tom took her elbow. "Let's go to the kitchen. I'll fill you in." He glanced at Bryan and Liam. "And I think you two should go home. Quietly. Let us figure out what to do."

Bryan looked at him evenly. "I'd much rather stay. Someone needs to watch over Alicia."

"Go home." Tom's tone suggested he wanted no argument. "I don't know what we're going to do, but having all of you here won't make us look impartial."

Liam tugged gently on Bryan's arm. Bryan stood unyielding, and I held my breath, willing him to obey Tom. Liam glanced at me, and said, "Akashi will be looking for me. He'll want to know."

Bryan didn't move.

Liam tugged again. "Come with me. Akashi can use your insights as well as mine."

Bryan shook Liam's hand from his arm and knelt briefly by my bed, next to Alicia, and whispered something to her. Then he stood and nodded at Liam, and Nava and Tom stepped back from the doorway, letting them out. Bryan's shoulders and neck muscles stood out, tight with anger. Liam's steps were confident and sure, his head up.

Joseph looked at the empty place in the doorway. He'd been quiet, but his eyes held some of the same anger Bryan could barely hide anymore. Anger filled my body, too, but none of us could afford to act on it. Not now.

Nava paced, her mouth a tight line. "Would someone please tell me what's going on here?"

Alicia sat up straighter and pushed the hair from her face again. It was like a live thing, accustomed to hiding her, and she had to work to keep her face free. Red and black rimmed her eyes. "Let *me* tell you. Don't leave and talk about me."

Nava sat down on the end of the bed, not touching Alicia, watching her closely. Tom and Joseph and I all stood in a little half circle behind Nava. I wondered if Alicia knew that Nava didn't like us, and didn't trust us, but I saw no way to warn her.

Alicia began again at the beginning, telling her story much like she had told us earlier, down at the river, adding only that she had been locked in the wagon as soon as she returned and not allowed to go to the feast. She didn't cry this time, and anger laced her face and even her words from time to time.

Both Nava and Alicia needed to hear about our earlier meeting. I broke in as soon as Alicia's story was complete. "We talked to Paloma and Akashi about the rumors. They thought Alicia should take the initiative, and accuse Ruth of telling people a lie. Get it talked about here, where the Town Council can deal with it instead of Ruth, who can't judge the situation since she started it." I glanced at Alicia, making sure I had her attention. I did. "They suggested Alicia bring a formal complaint against Ruth for the rumors. But the problem is, there's no proof one way or the other, so Alicia could be judged guilty either way."

Nava chewed her lip. "If it's going to come to the Town Council, I'll have to judge it, and I'll have to be impartial. That means you can't stay here." She glanced at me. "Chelo, can you see if she can go to Paloma's?"

Joseph surprised me by speaking up. "I'll go."

Nava nodded. "Thank you."

Joseph left quickly, the door opening and closing noisily behind him.

Nava asked Alicia, "What do you want?"

Alicia leaned forward, squared her shoulders, and took a long, trembling breath. She spoke clearly and firmly. "I don't want to go back to the band, or to Bella and Michael. I want to go with Akashi's band. I want to clear my name. I want to be treated like normal. I didn't ask to be different, or to be here. I can't help being myself."

Nava shook her head slightly, frowning. "I can't promise you anything at this point, except to find you shelter for the evening in town. Does anyone know you're here?"

"Probably. People were watching."

Nava glanced over at Tom.

He seemed to understand her wordless look, because he immediately said, "I'll go tell the East Band that Alicia's here."

Nava stood. "Chelo, come with me to the kitchen. I need a cup of tea." It was a command. She left, heading for the kitchen.

"I'll be right there," I called after her. I glanced at Alicia, and she gave a little nod, telling me she would be all right. I went to my clothes drawer and pulled out a clean pair of pants and a clean off-white shirt that would look nice against the long dark fall of her hair. "Here—maybe cleaning up will help you feel better." I pointed toward the bathroom. "Take a shower."

She smiled for the first time that evening. "Thank you." I watched her stand and walk unsteadily toward the bathroom, then I headed for the kitchen, which already smelled like mint and redberry tea.

Nava sat at the table, one cup of hot tea in front of her, one in front of an empty seat across the table. She gestured to the empty chair. "Your friends should not have brought Alicia here."

I took my time, sipping tea slowly, thinking before answering. "They brought Alicia to me."

"I will have to judge this problem."

"Alicia didn't murder Varay; she loved him. I'm sure Ruth hated that. She hates Alicia." And then I ventured into unsafe territory. "Look, Ruth's family died in the war. She lost her husband, and her father." I let that lie for a second, let Nava draw her own conclusions, perhaps remember her own father who died in the same war. "And now, Ruth's nephew died. She can't accept that it's an accident. It's easier to blame the same enemy who killed the rest of her family."

Nava laughed, and wry amusement danced in her eyes. "Chelo, I spent two summers with the East Band. Ruth is not that simple."

"Sorry." Ruth had led the band as long as I remembered. I twirled my cup in my hand, searching for the right thing to say next. "Please, Nava. If there is an inquiry tomorrow, please be open. Our parents were at war with you, but not us. We understand that we all have to work together."

She arched an eyebrow. "Do you?"

I knew she was talking about Joseph, and how he wouldn't do what she wanted. "Nava, I know we need you."

Nava frowned.

"And, Nava, you need us."

"Not to repair sewers."

I laughed, and it seemed to break her mood some.

One side of her mouth curled up briefly into a smile and she sighed exaggeratedly. "No one has lodged a formal complaint yet. I half expect the first complaint to be against

Bryan and Liam for breaking down a wagon door. If anyone lodges any complaints at all, against anyone, I will do what seems right when I've heard both sides, and when the Council has deliberated." She stood and set her cup in the sink. "And now, I'm going to bed.

"Good night."

Joseph came in with Kayleen and Paloma, who took Alicia with them. We all scattered to our own rooms, as if there were nothing to talk about. I sat on my bed, picking at a drop of Alicia's blood on the coverlet. I pulled the flute down, and practiced, playing as softly as I could, calming myself with the low sweet notes.

DECISIONS

Sunshine and birdsong streamed in my window. I lay in bed, stretching stiff muscles and trying to clear my muzzy sleep-ridden head of images of Jinks and the paw-cat and Ruth and Alicia that had filled my dreams.

Poor Alicia, living with so much hostility every day. Nava's businesslike coldness paled in comparison. Alicia's predicament endangered us, too. Therese and Steven would have blocked questions about our rights. Now that they were gone, I could see the shelter they gave us clearly.

I rolled out of bed, dressed, and went to the small bathroom, splashing cold water on my face from the sink and running a brush through my tangled hair.

The scent of warm tea wafted down the hallway and low

voices sounded in the kitchen. When I pushed open the kitchen door, I stopped short. Ruth and Nava sat together at the kitchen table, laughing. Nava's red hair and Ruth's black-streaked-with-gray hair almost mingled, their heads were so close together. Nava looked—brighter—than I had seen her for weeks; comfortable.

They looked up and saw me. Their laughter stilled.

Nava pushed back from the table and began to clear the dishes. "Ruth?" she said over her shoulder, her tone cautious. "You've met Chelo?"

We had met, briefly, more than once. She had never been polite. I waited for her response, keeping my face neutral, being careful not to show my rising anger.

Ruth's cold look belied the laughter I'd just heard, and the wrinkles around her eyes were slashed dark shadows. Her gaze slid across me and past, almost as if I weren't there, landing again on Nava. "Yes, I've met Chelo. Look, I'm going back now. Thanks for breakfast." She rose, carefully pushing the chair back against the table, and turned and left, without a single direct look at me. As she passed it felt like a cold wind brushed my skin.

A small red bird hopped on the sill outside the kitchen window, then noticed Nava in the window, and flew away. Nava started washing dishes. She spoke to me, her back still turned. "Chelo? There's some tea left in the pot."

What had she and Ruth been laughing about? I poured myself a cup of tea, took a bracing sniff of the minty steam, and forced my voice to stay light. "I didn't mean to sleep so late. When did Ruth get here?"

"Ruth stayed on the couch last night. She came home with Tom, late, demanding to know what authority we have to hold Alicia."

"What did you tell her?"

"That Alicia came here of her own free will and it didn't have anything to do with my wishes at all." Nava turned toward me, her brows drawn together. She didn't like me questioning her; it showed in the sharp set of her jaw and a red tinge on her neck and cheeks.

But she didn't look angry, just frustrated. And I had to

know what was happening. "Did Ruth know Alicia was locked up? That she escaped?"

Nava finished rinsing dishes and picked up the drying towel. I sipped my tea, waiting. After a long silence, she said, "I don't know. She didn't say."

I went to stand by her at the sink, looking out the window at the brightening morning. "Is that all Ruth wanted?" I reached a hand for a dry plate, and put it away. "Did she bring up Varay's death? Did Alicia decide to bring a complaint to the Council?"

"I don't know what Alicia decided. No one has come to tell me." Nava handed me the last clean dry cup and set her damp towel down. "I'm going to see the Council. It's a work day for you, today."

So much for finding out what else Ruth wanted. I watched Nava's back as she strode from the room.

Joseph trailed in, rubbing at his eyes. "Where's Tom?"

"He was gone when I woke up. He left a note on the counter—he's gone to see Paloma and Alicia."

We ate quickly. I told him about seeing Ruth, and he grimaced, but didn't comment. Silence had become easier for him than speech lately. As if everything we said was something he didn't want to hear. "Nava told me we have to work today."

"Figures." He glanced at the kitchen clock.

"We have a half an hour." I grinned, glanced at the dishes we'd just dirtied, and laughed. They could wait. "That's enough time to go to Paloma's."

He grinned at me, the clouds momentarily lifting from his expression. "You're on."

We jogged down the path to town and up the street to Paloma's. Joseph reached the doorway at least ten steps ahead of me.

Kayleen and Paloma lived in a four-house; four families each had a single wall of private rooms, and shared a central garden and common space. Joseph reached around the dried herb wreath that nearly covered the wooden door and knocked.

Kayleen opened the door. The rich scents of mint and

wild mountain-fern and redberry and basil spilled out the open door from Paloma's spare room, where she dried herbs and leaves for tea and salves, like the one Joseph had brought me for my leg.

"Oh, I'm glad you're here." The circles under Kayleen's eyes were nearly as deep as Alicia's had been the night before, and her voice was scratchy. But she smiled at us. "Come on in. Alicia dragged Paloma to lodge a complaint with Town Council. Alicia was really shaky, but she meant it. You should've seen the look in her eyes. Paloma made me stay here, just go to work. Have you seen Bryan this morning?"

I laughed. "Good morning. And no, I haven't seen Bryan. But Ruth was at the house when I woke up, talking to Nava. She spent the night at our house. They seem like old friends."

Kayleen's eyes rounded. She leaned in, as if there was someone to overhear us. "Did you hear them? Do you know what they talked about?"

"No, I was asleep. But they were laughing this morning."

Kayleen frowned. "I don't trust them. Do you want some juice?"

"Can't. I have to get to the mill, so I better start now. Will you come tell me if anything happens?"

Kayleen nodded. "Sure. I'll just wander over—no one will care." Her smile took the sarcastic sting out of her words. "Seriously, I will if I can. I'm with Gianna today, so maybe I can get away."

We waved good-bye, and Joseph and I headed off to our respective duties. As I crossed the bridge, I glanced at the roamers' wagons. They seemed darker and less cheerful than just two days before.

At the mill, I sealed bags of flour and marked them with the date, then stacked them to distribute before the roamers left. I watched out the window every time I passed it, imagining that every person crossing the bridge was coming to tell me the Town Council wanted me.

There seemed to be an infinite number of bags of flour.

The shift ended with no word. I scrubbed the flour from

my hands and face and bolted back across the bridge, running almost as fast as I could, displaying my speed to anyone who cared to watch, reminding them I was *altered*. I didn't care.

Liam sat on the grass just past the end of the bridge. Maybe he knew what was going on. He stood as he heard my pelting footsteps; surely he was waiting just for me. As I neared him, I slowed to a fast walk and he fell in step beside me, talking quickly. "They've been arguing all day. I wasn't there, but Akashi told me what happened. Ruth tried to keep the Town Council out of it. She started saying it was nothing, not important, and when that didn't work, she claimed it was her business and not Artistos's." He grimaced. "I guess Nava wanted to agree, had two Councilors on her side, and all she needed was one more for a majority." He glanced sideways at me and grinned, his eyes flashing excitement. A little storyteller's flourish. His voice rose. "Then Akashi stepped in and said 'roamer business and town business are the same.' He said the only reason we have separate justice systems is because we're physically separate and right now we aren't, and becoming two completely separate cultures would undo us. The vote switched back and Nava only had Ruth on her side."

I laughed, picturing Nava's face. She could almost always keep her voice controlled, but her skin betrayed her emotions like a spoiled child, flashing the reds of her anger and stress. She'd done it just this morning in the kitchen. "What happens next?"

"They're going to have the whole investigation out in the open, in the amphitheater. Tonight. Ruth's fit to be tied, but she said that way we'd all know how dangerous Alicia is."

I clenched my fists. "Alicia's not dangerous."

Liam shrugged, as if the notion weren't even worth considering. "Everyone who wants to can come. Since I wasn't working today, I got there as soon as I knew and saved us seats near the front. I left to find you as soon as the others came. Paloma will join us. Akashi is on the Council, since it affects the roamer bands as well."

"Is Ruth?"

Liam sounded disgusted. "Yes."

We jogged along the edge of the park. I spotted Gianna and Sophia walking together, talking, and farther away, two couples with kids in tow heading for the amphitheater. The sun's rays slanted through the park, elongating the twintree shadows. Even though it was still early, it would be dark within the hour.

I sat between Paloma and Liam. Past Paloma, Kayleen and then Bryan and Joseph sat in a row. Alicia sat on the far end, a little apart from Joseph. She glanced over as we came in, looking like a caged bird. But her eyes glowed with intent, as if perhaps she were a thin and hungry bird of prey. Gianna slid onto the bench next to Alicia, acknowledging us with a slight smile before turning to watch the dais.

Meetings were rare, and usually only the affected people went, and maybe their families.

People streamed into the amphitheater, grouping and knotting into bands and family groups. More than half the adults in Artistos were here, and a few of the children. May and Klia and other teenagers sat together in small crowds, none close to us. I spotted Sky four rows above us, sitting with two of her band mates. She smiled briefly, and gave me a little nod, then turned back to her friends.

This was how Artistos resolved community issues; witnessed consent among the Town Council. Anyone who demanded a voice could speak.

I never had.

Nava would lead. Councilors would ask questions, then they'd talk among themselves before deciding. It could take hours.

Noise of many conversations swirled about. Above us, the damaged or old men and women of the culture guild bustled about, setting cold water and leftovers from yesterday's feast on tables near the top.

On the stage, Town Council sat at two long banquet tables. Nava and Tom were in the middle, Akashi and Ruth on the two ends. In between Nava and Akashi, Lyssa and Wei-Wei sat together. I focused on the two of them. Lyssa was tall and blond, with light blue eyes and small hands that fluttered around her face. Therese had complained repeatedly that Lyssa always chose for the accused, no matter what the proof. Lyssa saw herself as the savior of the downtrodden. She would see Alicia that way, especially once she noticed the bruises.

Wei-Wei, however, would almost certainly vote against Alicia. A short dark-haired and brown-skinned woman with almond eyes, Wei-Wei tended to be quiet and thoughtful, but strict. I knew of at least two incidences where she'd recommended weeks of hard work for teenagers caught bending the rules, even mildly. She was notoriously hard on the few adults who tended to drunkenness. And worse, distrust flecked Wei-Wei's dark eyes every time she passed us in town.

I was pretty sure Tom was for Alicia, and Nava against, but remembered Paloma's suggestion that I was selling Nava short.

That left Hunter, who sat between Tom and Ruth. Hunter's gray hair hung wispy and thin along the sides of his wrinkled face. Age and injury had twisted his fingers into claws, but he sat tall. He had led Artistos's defense in the war, becoming the town hero. I had no idea how he would approach this problem, and had to content myself with his reputation for fairness.

Next to Akashi, one empty chair sat to the side of the table.

Nava cleared her throat into the microphone. "Please quiet down. We will begin in one minute."

I looked behind me once again. Jenna sat in the top row, above the crowd. Shadow already filled most of the amphitheater, but Jenna sat high, in a beam of sunshine. She wore a cloak of paw-cat fur edged with yellow-snake skin around her shoulders, even though it was not cold. She gazed placidly down at the Council. Ever since the earthquake, she seemed to be watching town business more closely. I shook Liam's shoulder, pointing. "That's Jenna."

"I know." He turned, his eyes following my finger, and smiled. "She's amazing."

He sounded confident rather than curious. He was a roamer, only in town ten days or so a year. Jenna never attended

Story Night or Trading Day. "Have you heard stories about her?"

"She comes and talks to me and Akashi a few times every year."

Jenna visited the roamers? Talked to Akashi and Liam? When and why? What did she say? I wanted to ask, but Nava cleared her throat into the microphone again, and I bit back my questions and turned toward the dais. The lights came on, illuminating the Town Council's features, shining on us.

"Good evening." Nava smiled softly. "I presume the turnout means that news has flown through our community along all of the usual informal channels." She left a beat of silence before continuing. "Still, I'm glad to see everyone. It will help dispel any incorrect rumors." The crowd laughed softly, a bit nervously.

"We are meeting to address a formal complaint, and a request, both filed by Alicia Gupta of the East Band." She looked directly at me, then scanned the rest of the crowd, her gaze quieting any lingering conversations. She frowned as she spotted Jenna, but said nothing. She gestured to Gianna, who stood and took Alicia's hand, pulling her up onto the dais. Alicia glanced over her shoulder at us, fear and resolve burning in her violet eyes, then turned and walked up the steps.

Nava said, "Alicia has lodged a complaint against Ruth. Ruth sits here as a valued member of our Council and a leader in her own right, and she will have her say, but will not vote."

At least that was something. I shifted in my seat, uncomfortable.

Alicia reached the top of the steps and turned, the purple and black bruises on her face sharp against her white skin. The crowd murmured. Alicia sat in the extra chair, on the end near Akashi, watching them, her face impassive. I could hardly imagine what it must be like to sit there with everyone watching her. She was still and calm and moved only to breathe and turn her face toward Nava.

Ruth leaned forward to speak, but Nava put a hand up. "Let us hear from the girl first." She turned toward Alicia. "Alicia, please state your complaint."

The crowd quieted as if, as one, they leaned toward Alicia to listen to her. Alicia spoke slowly, her voice carrying well. "As you heard on Story Night, there was a death in the East Band, a young man named Varay. He was my friend, one of my few friends in the band." She licked her lips and glanced briefly at Ruth.

Ruth watched us, not Alicia. The naked animosity in her gaze made me want to look away. I held her eyes for a long moment before turning to watch Alicia continue with her story. "Varay fell to his death, and I was with him. It was . . . it was the most awful experience of my life, to watch him fall, knowing I was above him, and could do nothing." Her voice trembled, softened, and it seemed like everyone there leaned forward slightly, quietly. "To see him dead, to carry back his broken body, wishing with every step that he was still alive.

"A few days later, I began to hear something disturbing from my few other friends in the band. They told me that Ruth was telling people I killed Varay. At first, I believed this must be a rumor, but when I heard it over and over, it began to feel, to sound, like a truth." Her hands clasped the edge of the chair, her knuckles white. "People in the band began treating me worse than before, turning my daily life from something tolerable to something"—she paused, as if struggling for the right words—"hard and painful. I have been accused, but never openly. I have no idea how to clear my name, because only Varay and I were there. . . ." A tear slid down her cheek and she stopped for a second, clearly struggling for control. "Only he and I know that his death was an accident, and he cannot speak about it. Since I cannot clear my name, I wish to be removed from the East Band."

Liam's hand stole into mine, warm and comforting, strong.

Nava asked, "How did you get the bruises?"

"Bella and Michael locked me in the wagon. Some of these came from them." Her hands rose to her bruised face. "Others I gave myself, trying to get out." Her hands returned to her knees.

The crowd's murmur rose and fell again. We had a jail, but

it had lain unused since I was about ten. We did not lock each other up.

Nava asked, "Is there more you want to say?"

Alicia looked quietly in front of her. "Not now."

Ruth stood, her posture demanding attention. Nava nodded at her.

"First, I think we need to be clear about Alicia's status. She was given into my care as a prisoner of war, not as a family member, or a band member. As such, we have treated her extraordinarily well. A prisoner of war is not entitled to a hearing, but only reasonably good treatment." She sat down again. "There is no reason for me to respond to her accusations. This Council should reject her claims."

Tom leaned forward. "Alicia came by our house briefly last night. After her visit, I looked up the meeting record from the day we took the six children left behind into our care. Ruth is correct. The term in the records is 'prisoner of war.'" He stopped a moment, glanced at Nava, and took a drink of water. "But we are a body of community law. Our charter and original ideals demand flexibility in response to the actual, current situation. That's how a successful colony responds. We are not, after all, treating any of the other five *children* like prisoners." He stopped and glanced directly at Ruth. "In fact, we rely on them to help us in a number of tasks."

I thanked him silently for his words, and turned to look at the crowd, watching their varied reactions. Some nodded, some leaned into neighbors and whispered, others sat, still, their faces unreadable. A few looked hostile, but it was hard to tell toward whom. My eyes scraped past Garmin's, and he scowled hostilely at us.

I turned back to Tom, to find his eyes briefly on me, then on Paloma. He smiled faintly, then began again, his voice strong. "It is true that our ancestors fled inhabited space because they had no desire to be changed in any way, because the core and center of our beliefs is that we are best off as original humans. But these six"—he glanced down at us, his tense expression relaxing some—"did not choose to be *altered*. To reject their humanity for it is similar to rejecting a child for having a birth defect. But we don't do that. We take the injured and broken—the different—and give them work."

I smiled, hoping Tom could see my approval.

Wei-Wei spoke, her voice hard and clipped. "Our people came here to find a place where all humans could be on equal ground, where money or privilege or better science did not separate us. Where we could be free of the power of those who chose long lives and health over their very humanity." She glanced at me, at us, and I saw fear behind the anger in her words. "The very existence of these children here threatens our peace, and to grant them full rights threatens it even more."

A few people clapped, and I wanted to turn and see who, but Nava held her hand up to forestall the crowd's reaction, and looked at the tall blond woman who sat beside her. "Lyssa, what do you think?"

"Both points have merit. We do not need to make a decision about how to treat these six as adults for"—her brow furrowed—"almost a year. Today, we only need to decide if Alicia has the right to lodge a complaint against Ruth. I say that she does. Not because of who she is, or isn't." She spread her hands wide in front of her, taking in the crowd with them. "Because we are fair and we should not let anyone be so bruised and persecuted without being able to speak up for themselves."

Nava nodded. "Akashi?"

Akashi looked over at us, smiling, his eyes catching Liam's. "My son is due his full measure of rights. So are his peers."

"Hunter?"

I watched him closely. His damaged hands rested on the table and he spoke slowly, deliberately. His voice was soft with age, but still carried the authority of a leader. "Lyssa is fundamentally correct. Ruth raises an issue that does not need to be answered now, to veil a question that does. Allow Alicia to make her complaint, and hear Ruth out. We should keep our deliberation focused on Alicia's complaint." He stopped and sipped water. "Separately, we must finish planning for the time when the *altered* will be adults. That question is something to debate this winter, to explore slowly, to resolve in spring when the bands return. There are issues of security I want to discuss."

Up on the dais, Nava's face and neck flushed red.

So everyone, except Ruth and Nava, was willing to at least address Alicia's challenges. But only Tom and Akashi, so far, supported full rights. Next to me, Paloma shifted and licked her lips. Liam withdrew his hand and leaned forward, chewing his bottom lip. I felt the absence of his touch, and wanted to reach for him, but sat back instead, watching.

Ruth crossed her arms in front of her chest and leaned back in her chair, sharing a glance with Nava. "Very well," she said gruffly, "I withdraw my objection to discussing Alicia's complaint. But it is spurious. She is, in fact, sullen and difficult, and Bella and Michael and I have gone out of our way to treat her fairly while still treating her as Hunter requested when we took her in: as potentially dangerous. Nothing said here has changed that. I would not turn my back on this girl.

"As to whether or not she killed my nephew? He was a brilliant climber, and would not have simply fallen to his death. As I said, she is sullen and sometimes angry. Perhaps he said something she resented, and she pushed him. It would be easy for any of them, one on one, to kill any of us."

Paloma drew her breath in sharply, Liam stiffened next to me, and even though I couldn't see him, I felt Bryan's anger rise. Alicia sat still, bone still, as if Ruth's words had slapped all sound from her.

I couldn't sit still. I stood, looking at Nava, drawing her eyes. "Chelo?" she said. "What do you want?"

Alicia's exoneration. To be seen as human. "May I address the Council?"

She hesitated. "Certainly. Come stand here, so the crowd can hear you."

I walked up to the dais, blinking in surprise that I was allowed to talk, my feet unsteady, unsure of what I was actually going to say, but knowing I couldn't stand there and let Ruth treat Alicia, treat us all, so poorly. I stood beside Alicia's chair, my right hand on her shoulder. The crowd seemed bigger, almost like a single living thing. At first no words came. Alicia put a hand briefly on my arm, and smiled up at me. I swallowed, and started, hoping for the right tone. "Yesterday, Trading Day, a festival for all of us, Liam and I both felt shut out by many East Band members, and we didn't understand why. We, the four of us who live in Artistos, Bryan and Joseph and Kayleen and I, have tried to be part of this colony. I believe Alicia and Liam have both made the same choices." After a moment of silence, I added, "It is the only choice we can make."

The crowd murmured, and I looked out across them, trying to read their mood. Many nodded; others looked unsure, and a few hostile. I glanced up, half expecting Jenna to be gone, surprised to see she had actually moved down three steps, and was watching me closely. She nodded, nearly imperceptible, and an approving smile flashed briefly across her features.

I continued. "Allow us to participate in the discussion about us. Regarding Ruth's accusations, I believe Alicia is innocent." I glanced at Ruth, wanting to take her on directly, to treat her as openly rudely as she had treated Alicia, but I was scared to. My citizenship status was in question and I was not yet a legal adult. "In the meantime, surely Alicia can stay in Artistos." Swallowing hard, hoping I had said enough to matter, I started back to my seat.

Nava called my name. "Chelo. Stay a moment."

I stopped, and looked at her. She regarded me thoughtfully. "Chelo, you say that you work for the good of the colony?"

I nodded, wary.

"All of you."

I glanced at Joseph, suddenly sure I knew where this was going. After him. But what could I say? I swallowed. "All of us."

She turned to the crowd. "Many issues raised today clearly require long discussion, and can be resolved later." She glanced at Tom, drew her brows together, and turned directly to me and Alicia. "There is a possible compromise."

Next to me, Alicia nodded. I didn't like this, yet the weight of the entire community's eyes on me trapped me into silence. "I'll listen."

"Much of our data network remains earthquake-damaged." She pursed her lips, as if suddenly aware of the need to gain the other Councilors' approval. She looked up and down the table, waiting for heads to nod.

Hunter waved his clawed right hand impatiently. "Go on."

"I'd like you and Joseph and Kayleen"—she paused, looking at Tom briefly—"and Tom and Paloma to go on a trip to fix the network. I want Joseph's help." Nava glanced at Joseph and then at Alicia. "And if you will do that, Alicia may go with you."

That would get Alicia out of the East Band, at least until they returned in spring. If Joseph agreed.

"And while you are gone, we will continue this conversation."

No! But Nava had me backed into a corner. I swept a glance across the dais. A small smile played on Ruth's face. Lyssa nodded. Wei-Wei frowned. Confusion and curiosity played across Tom's face as he watched Nava closely, as if unsure of what she had just said. Hunter's face was unreadable, Akashi's wary.

I turned around and glanced up. Jenna stood, silent, watching us.

Nava turned to Joseph. "Will you go and fix the nets?"

My gaze slid down to Joseph. He stood, looking around, as if caught between needing to save Alicia and fear of the data nets. "Don't," I whispered under my breath. "Not yet." If he gave in too easily, I'd lose any chance to negotiate for more. Joseph would want to be noble for Alicia. I glanced at Paloma. Surely she'd see it, she'd stop him, but Joseph chose that moment to speak. "I will go." He spoke clearly. He didn't even sound reluctant.

I bit my tongue. I could have argued for Bryan and Liam to go with us. We needed a voice here, but did it have to be Bryan, the angriest one of us? Was that part of Nava's plan? And what if Joseph couldn't fix the nets?

The other Councilors quickly agreed.

Tom nodded with everyone else, although he shot another puzzled look at his wife. Perhaps he was unsure why she was sending him away. I thought I knew; Tom supported us, and had done so publicly during this discussion. If he weren't here, and Paloma was gone as well, then our two biggest supporters would be with us, excluded from the discussion. And more practically, Tom was the only adult besides Paloma whom Joseph trusted. Nava would know that, too. I did not like this.

But it was decided.

Nava and Ruth had outmaneuvered us.

Ruth probably didn't mind being rid of Alicia, and she'd never had to even defend herself against Alicia's accusations. She didn't seem to have expected to. Perhaps she and Nava had plotted our absence in the kitchen this morning. We would be gone, Tom and Paloma, who stood up for us, would be gone, and so would Akashi. The only bright spot was that Ruth, too, would be gone.

Left behind, there would be only Hunter, Nava, Wei-Wei, and Lyssa. And Lyssa was not truly a champion. She was a devil's advocate; the best she'd do is mitigate.

On the way out, I noticed Jenna sitting, watching me, her cloak now on her lap and her chin on her hand.

I hesitated. People would notice if I sat beside her, but the power of her coming, and staying, was so strong I sat beside her anyway. Everyone already knew Jenna and I were alike; they'd spent all night being reminded of our differences from them. Jenna smelled like cat hide and the Lace Forest. She smiled briefly when I sat down next to her, although her gaze stayed on the dais. In a soft voice, she said, "I will help you." She and I sat together in the dark, watching others begin to drift up and away. Joseph, Liam, Bryan, Kayleen, and Alicia came up the stairs. Jenna faded away into the background before they reached me, wrapped in her own silence. The others, joining me, watched her leave with expressions varying from puzzlement to avid curiosity. Liam's mouth quirked up, nearly a smile. He watched the place she disappeared into, as if he were not surprised at all that she had been there.

9

PREPARATION

We hardly saw Alicia the next day. At Paloma's insistence, she spent the morning in the infirmary and that afternoon, Paloma took her to retrieve her gear from Bella and Michael.

I fretted all day. I nursed anger over breakfast while Nava and Tom made lists of supplies, kept the anger while Joseph and Kayleen and I gathered dried djuri meat, water bottles, and large saddlebags designed to fit over the backs and rumps of pack hebras from various storehouses. I hated the idea of Council talking about us while we were gone. Nava had outmaneuvered us, but she had also, ultimately, been clever, and had crafted a solution that removed Alicia from the East Band without making Ruth, an important leader, and Nava's friend, lose face. By midafternoon, my anger with Ruth still burned brightly, but Nava, I grudgingly conceded, had done the right thing for the colony, if not for us.

We each had some room for personal gear. I took the flute, packing it carefully inside a roll of clothes, all three barrettes, and some precious handmade paper and pens with colored dipping ink.

Joseph hardly spoke except to clarify instructions. His mood felt as black as mine. An hour before dinner, I grew impatient enough with both Joseph and myself that I fled to look for Bryan. I had been watching for him all day, expecting him to find us, but he didn't. Last night, he had simply left as soon as the meeting was over, his shoulders tense, his jaw clenched.

It took a half an hour to find Bryan out beyond the hebra barns, barely inside the boundaries. He was standing near the edge of the cliff, looking toward the sea and the Grass Plains. As I walked up near him I noticed the smell and shine of sweat. "You've been running."

He put a big, heavy arm across my shoulder and drew me toward him. "I want to go with you." His arms shook, and his cheek rested on the top of my head.

I missed him already, missed him even though he was holding me that instant. The four of us had never been separated more than a day or two, for errands near Artistos. We'd never left town farther than the Grass Plains or partway up the High Road.

I bit my lip. Bryan wanted to make his own choices so badly. When he got angry, I was the one who calmed him, listened to him, the one who held his hand or watched him pace. Who would do that for him with me gone? I clung to him, trembling and afraid for him. After a while, I choked out, "I want you to be with us, too. But you know one of us must be here to hear what's said while we're gone."

"Nava wouldn't want me out of her sight. I scare her."

Because of his strength. Because everyone could see his strength in his wide biceps and broad back and height. "Promise you'll be careful? Don't make anyone angry, or get angry, no matter what they say? Promise me you'll talk to someone if you need help? Gianna is fair, Lyssa, Eric . . . try for us?"

"I wish you were staying."

"Joseph needs me."

He held me tighter, and his arms trembled a little. "Perhaps I need you, too. I'll miss you terribly. All of you, but you especially, Chelo."

Tears rolled down my cheeks, and Bryan kissed my forehead and my sobs deepened as if a flood of pain and anger was coming out of me, falling from me, falling into Bryan's strength. And I was always the even one, the one who didn't cry, who helped everyone else. Me and Bryan, and we helped each other.

After my tears dried, we walked back, arm in arm, silent. Words would have been extra burdens.

Nava had cooked a whole chicken, which she served with fresh bread and steamed yellow beans, all things Tom loved. Surprisingly, I cleaned my plate. Throughout dinner, I watched Nava, seeking clues. She maintained a cheerful and empty face, speaking cheerful and empty chatter. I needed to talk to her, to convince her to wait for our return before she made up her mind. As soon as the dinner dishes were neatly dried and stacked, I asked her, "Nava, will you take a walk with me?"

She smiled, almost as if she expected the invitation, and held the door open. We stepped out into a cool, misty evening. Two moons, Wishstone and Plowman, hung in the sky above us, appearing near each other through an accident of orbits, even though Plowman was farther away by half, and smaller. Night birds sang, and small animals rustled through the low grasses and shrubs near the path. I led us to River Walk Park, not entirely sure what to say. Nava seemed willing to let me take my time.

As we reached the river, it dawned on me where I had to start, although it was hard to swallow my frustration enough to sound sincere. "Nava, thank you for helping Alicia."

Nava walked quickly, her hands in her pockets, her head down. "I believe Ruth. Not necessarily about Varay—she can't know how he died—but that Alicia is wild and dangerous. It seemed right to buy time."

"It will help."

"Time will help more if you use it, if you actually repair a good portion of the nets. That will make a difference, and to do that, you'll need Joseph."

"I know." The first red-gold fall leaves bobbed by on the quiet river. "He knows it, too. I bet that's why he's been so sullen all day."

She laughed at that, quietly.

"Why don't you trust us?" I asked her. "We've done everything we can to follow the rules, to be helpful."

"I am only a little worried about who you are now. But I

am worried about your future. And ours. How will six *altered* adults affect us? We came here to avoid what you are, to make sure we will never become what you will become. It presents a rather difficult problem."

"Have I ever done anything you don't like?"

"Not you. As far as I can tell, you are the most balanced, the least dangerous. But you do not remember the wars, the deaths, or the loss. Alicia could have killed Varay. That frightens us."

"Alicia didn't kill Varay." I realized I'd raised my voice, and bit my lip to keep myself from saying any more.

Nava's voice was soft but icy. "Neither you nor I have any proof of that." She sighed, softening her tone. "But at least she will be under Tom's and Paloma's watchful eyes."

"I *have* talked to her. She could not have done this. She's heartbroken."

"Alicia is angry. I see it sometimes in Bryan as well. I do not see it in you, or Liam, or Kayleen. Joseph is angry, too."

I bridled. "Joseph is fine!" I was wrong. "He will be fine."

We walked quietly for a few minutes. We were already halfway down the river walk, and I had not convinced her of anything. "So we're stronger and faster. Yet the six of us would not survive without the colony, without you and all the others. There are enough of you to control us. So why are you so scared?"

"We don't know who you are. You don't even know who you are, not really. Look at Jenna. She doesn't interact directly with us, yet as a single, damaged, genetically *altered* adult, she protects all of our borders. Rather well. We never forget, however, that she is not human. We don't know how many of us she killed during the war. She is still alive because we don't know that, because none of us saw her kill anyone."

I didn't say that I thought she was alive because no one had been able to kill her.

Nava continued. "But if she can kill paw-cats and yellow-snakes and drive away demon dogs so easily, what could she do to us? Jenna will outlive us all. You will outlive us all. How do we know what she plans? What her plans for you are?"

That hit a nerve. "She, too, needs the colony to survive. You aren't giving us enough of a chance."

Nava sighed heavily, and took a seat on a bench. "Sit down, let me tell you a story."

I settled on the opposite side of the bench, stretching my legs, listening to the water, the distant, faint sounds of people moving about Artistos.

Nava took a deep breath. "I was your age when the *altered* landed. At first, we were just wary of each other. It took time for worries to become war. I remember my parents arguing endlessly at night. We were here first. We wouldn't leave, and besides, we couldn't. *Traveler* hasn't the fuel for another interstellar journey, and besides, already no one knew how to fly her. We could barely manage to keep the skills to take the shuttles up and down.

"We might have accepted it if they had even simply gone to Islandia, had left us in peace on Jini."

She looked out over the river. Her voice lacked its usual hard edge. "I was born here. My parents were born here. Their parents were born here, but had grown up on the living stories of people who were not. We chose Fremont for humans, true humans. You know what we care about. Living and dying as family, accepting who we are instead of trying to change it. Growing to our natural potential without adding machinery or changing our faces, our lives, or our deaths." She seemed to drift in the story, talking to herself as much as to me. "The stories passed from Deerfly warned us of the dangers of anything different. Original humans no longer controlled their own destiny, no longer led, no longer had a voice that mattered. The world out there"—she waved her hands at the sky—"is perilous. So we came here. Then the things we left behind followed us."

She shifted, stretching her arms in front of her, cracking her knuckles. "Those were the stories I grew up on. But they were only stories until your people landed. I don't think we really believed them. And there were not many *altered,* around three hundred, but they wanted control, demanded to stay with us, told us they would help us.

"We didn't want help.

"They wouldn't leave. It started at their camp, outside of Artistos. Two of my friend's big brothers, my brother, and a few other young men confronted the *altered*. One *altered,* and all but one of the young men died. My brother died. And the *altered* that killed him didn't use weapons. He used his bare hands."

Her voice was higher now, more strained. "My father was a gentle man. He loved to make things. He helped build the walls, the hebra barns, the water plant. When he came home after working all day, sweaty and tired, he read to us and he carved toys for the littler children. The night the war started, he came home crying. I had never seen him cry. He gathered Mom and me in his arms and held us, and told us he'd be gone for a while, and we must stay inside the walls, and we must be quiet."

A moon-moth fluttered near Nava's face, and she brushed it away, careful not to let it bite her. "For the next three years, he came home when he could. He grew thin. His eyes had changed, or what was in them had changed. Anger and fear and hatred . . ."

She paused, ran her hands through her hair. The darkness obscured her features, softened them, and she gulped air, hard, and then gripped the edge of the bench and leaned forward. "He came for funerals. He almost never spent the night in the house."

I thought of my own parents, of Chiaro caring for us because they were out fighting the same war, of how seldom I had seen them.

"And then one night, someone brought his body home. My mother cried for days. I just remember being numb, not believing it, expecting him to walk in any day." She paused. "So many were gone by then. The first five years of the war we lost over three hundred people, and they lost fewer than a hundred. For years, I expected everyone on Fremont to die." She stopped, looking down at her hands, as if they held some secret.

"Two weeks after my father's death, my mother came to me and told me Hunter had decided we all had to fight. Mom said we would all die, but that was better than living anymore anyway. We packed up that night and left town for the hills. Hunter was brilliant, and brave, and still we lost people. My mother got her wish and died."

I reached toward her, almost brushed her shoulder with my fingertips. She flinched and scooted away, then mumbled, "Sorry." But she didn't scoot back, or make any move to touch me in return.

"The years after she died are a blur. I was terribly alone, and because I was fast, I carried messages from camp to camp, helped plan strategy." Her voice regained some of its edge, became harder. "I wanted every one of the *altered* to die. I remember the day the *Journey* left. Stile and Eric and I were on the High Road, heading back into Artistos, which had by then been nearly abandoned. We heard the low-pitched rumble of the ship, saw it rise up from the Grass Plains, and we cheered. We yelled and screamed and jumped and shook our fists in the air, and then we ran back here, back home. The *altered* were gone!"

I knew the next part, so I said it. "But we were here."

Nava looked over at me. "We almost killed you all. Akashi argued against it, and we were sick of killing, and we were tired."

I wondered if she wished they *had* killed us. If she had suggested they kill us. She would not have held power then, not like she did now, but what had she argued for?

"And now, well, we died easily at the hands of your people. But there are only six of you. Seven, if you count Jenna." She stood, pacing up and down, and then sat down again, tapping her feet. "Already, our data nets are stronger because of Joseph. Liam has shown leadership in his band, and Akashi tried to set him up as heir apparent. All that before you are even adults." She spread her arms wide, a gesture of amazement. "We don't want you to lead us. Now, we can tell you what to do, and you comply. But you will not be that way in ten years, in twenty." She paused and swallowed. "In a hundred years."

"We will not harm you."

Now she sounded bitter, a little imperious, as if she had let down her guard and was now putting her usual personality back on. "Harm comes in many forms."

"And what would you do with us, if you could?" I asked.

"I would send you away. Figure out how that damned left-over ship works, and send you away."

It was, I thought, better than saying she would kill us even now. She couldn't know how often I'd wanted to leave, how often I made games in my head of flying off and finding my own people.

She stood and started back, walking fast. I kept up, and as we reached the end of Commons Park, I asked, "So what exactly do you need from us on this trip? What will tell you we've succeeded?"

"Fix the data networks, and spend some time with Alicia, figure out how broken she really is."

"If I do that, will you protect our rights? We've earned them."

"You, Chelo, you're the leader. Earn your keep. Quit protecting Joseph and make him fulfill his potential. We need the networks back."

I knew what she needed, but I didn't know how to give it to her. Nor could I tell what Nava might give me in return, except that it sounded like it wasn't enough.

UP THE HIGH ROAD

Joseph and I rose early the next morning and walked through thin morning mist to the hebra barn, following Tom. Kayleen and Paloma and Alicia were already there, nearly geared up. Kayleen and Alicia worked together to tie a saddlebag on one of the pack hebras. I stopped, suddenly struck by their similarities. They were the same height, just slightly shorter than me, and their matching light skin and dark hair made them a remarkable mirror image unless you counted the difference between Kayleen's river-blue eyes and Alicia's violet ones. Or—I glanced down—the difference in the length of their feet. I suppressed a giggle. Kayleen's feet did look funny, but she was the only one in Artistos capable of shinnying up pongaberry trees without ropes.

Kayleen glanced over at me, a slight grin touching her face and lighting her eyes. "Hey sleepyhead, you missed the East Band. They trundled off at sunup."

So Nava had not said good-bye to Ruth. "Well then, I didn't miss much, did I?" I glanced at Alicia's startled eyes and rethought my flippancy. "It will be easier for us not to say good-bye to them."

Alicia laughed, a strangled soft sound. "I do not care if I ever see them again." As she climbed up on a stool to tie saddlebags on her near-black hebra, Ink, she added, "Except Sky."

I found the hebra Tom had helped me pick out yesterday. Yellows and dry browns slashed Stripes's dun coat. She watched my approach curiously, her deep brown eyes telegraphing intelligent appraisal. She was young, slightly fractious, as tall as Legs; I looked forward to finding out if she was as fast. She twisted her head back as I saddled her, nuzzling my shoulder, apparently approving of me. Everywhere I went, she watched carefully, as if she wanted to know my soul. I kissed her nose, missing Jinks momentarily.

We finally managed to tie every lace, adjust every face harness and lead line. We mounted up and let ourselves out of the corral. Two extra hebras trailed behind Paloma as pack animals. Joseph rode Legs again, and Tom had chosen Sugar Wheat. As the six of us wound through town, heading for the park, Hunter walked toward us. He stopped to watch us approach, an appraising look in his light green eyes. As we came within easy earshot, he called up to Tom, "Be careful out there. Be sure you all stay safe."

Tom nodded. "I will, sir."

Hunter walked up to Stripes, and put a twisted hand on my foot, which was almost shoulder high to him with me mounted. This close, I could make out at least two scars on his wrinkled visage. "And you, take good care of your brother." Not a question; a command.

I swallowed hard. Hunter had rarely spoken to me, nothing but polite greetings in passing or direct questions. "I intend for us all to get home safely, sir."

He smiled then. "Perhaps you'll do, after all. Show me, Chelo. No acting up out there. I want to hear that you four"—he swept his gaze across us all—"do exactly what Paloma and Tom tell you. No more, no less." This time, his eyes stopped on Joseph. "Do you understand?"

Joseph looked down and mumbled assent, and Tom added, "We will be careful, all of us," and lightly kicked Sugar Wheat into a walk. I looked back at Hunter as we rode away, feeling like I'd been given military orders, like failure would bring punishment. The man radiated quiet power and secrets. I shivered.

At Little Lace Park, we met up with the chaos of a roamer band preparing to leave for the winter. People from Artistos hovered around the wagons. Dogs barked, children called, goats bleated in protest as their owners tied them behind wagons. Hebras snorted and stamped in their wagon traces, as if to say, "All right, let's go. We're harnessed already." Klia held hands with a young roamer, her dark hair and dark eyes flashing with laughter, then smothered by a kiss. A few places, town parents stood watching their roamer children prepare to leave for another full season.

Akashi, mounted, flitted from wagon to wagon, calling out questions, sometimes stopping to suggest an adjustment. Once, he scooped a toddler from under the belly of a fractious hebra and deposited it in its young mother's startled lap with a barking order to keep track of her child. So he didn't always keep his temper.

He stopped by us, briefly. He wore simple loose brown pants and a gray shirt. He looked more formidable in those than in his ceremonial clothes, perhaps simply because I had never seen him dressed like one of us. "You should ride near the front. The wagons will slow significantly near the top, and you needn't wait for us." He reached down to pet his excited young hebra. "I'll send Liam along with you until the place where we part."

Kayleen blurted out, "Can't he stay with us? Until we're done?"

Akashi fixed her eyes with his, then turned his gaze on mine. "He has responsibilities to our band." A small smile escaped his lips. "But perhaps we will all meet on the trail. Who knows?" Then a tall young man called for him. Akashi smiled at Tom and Paloma, and nodded. "Good travel." He turned and disappeared into the melee of near-readiness.

Nava found us there, and checked over everything we had with us twice. Once, I saw her stopped, watching me, her head cocked to the side and her lips pursed. At the last minute, after we'd mounted, she came and stood close to me and looked up, her face neutral, except for her eyes, which were uncharacteristically warm. "Good luck, Chelo. Take care of Joseph and Alicia. Obey Tom."

There was no touch between us, but it felt as if a genuine parting occurred. It dawned on me that we had never touched. Last night, we had come close. She did not feel touchable this morning, either. It was food for thought as we started out near the front of the band.

The caravan took off in a cacophony of creaks and hoofbeats and final called good-byes. Liam's mother, Mayah, waved at him as she started the lead wagon off. A few long noisy minutes later, the dragonbirds and blaze fliers screeched in fear as the wagons their cages were lashed to started off.

Close to town, the High Road rose slowly upward, cutting through the lower reaches of the cool shadowy Lace Forest. Joseph's face was nearly as drawn and white as it had been the first few days after the earthquake, and his eyes looked dull, as if he weren't looking out of them, but rather inside somewhere. He had looked more like himself the last few weeks, even at breakfast. What part of the trip gouged the laughter from him again? Perhaps it was one thing for him to stand up in the amphitheater and proclaim he'd go with us, and another altogether for him to face the data networks. Or perhaps it was simply going up the High Road, passing the place our parents died. I swallowed hard, suddenly scared, and reached down to stroke Stripes's long neck, seeking calm in the touch.

After about an hour of riding up through the thick Lower Lace Forest, we burst into the open. To our left, cliffs a few feet taller than our heads followed one side of the road, a gray wall lined with wild mountain-fern and blooming yellow fox lilies and tiny sprays of purple cliff-hugger. To our right, Artistos spread below us, a checkerboard of color from the edge of the cliffs below us to the next cliff, which in turn fell down to the Grass Plains, sun-kissed and glowing yellow-green in the midmorning light. Beyond the plains, the sea enclosed the entire western edge of Jini in hot electric-blue.

Sun glinted off the fat silver spire that was the *New Making*. In my head, I saw it rising up away from the plains, trailing smoke and fire, heading to Inhabited Space, to a place we'd find our people. Heading home. *New Making* was a distant dream, a tease, a painful reminder of our difference, a promise that might never be kept. I tore my eyes away from the ship. My focus needed to be on the here and now. I had no idea how I could meet Hunter's and Nava's and Akashi's expectations. I glanced again at Joseph, chewing my lip. It was not all up to me.

The roamers' wagons creaked and complained as we wound up a steep grade. Drivers called back and forth to each other. Two or three hunting dogs kept quiet watchful pace, running up and down beside the caravan, skillfully avoiding the hebras' sharp hooves. The cliffs towered far above us, throwing shadows across the wide road, and a thin line of trees hugged the cliff base, fed by a largely unseen stream.

Liam caught up with us, looking from one to the other as if checking our feelings. His voice was soft but firm as he said, "The rock fall is two bends ahead." We pushed in front of the wagons, so we could move through alone.

Liam rode near me, his face quiet and composed. As if the mantle of Akashi's calm was falling onto him now that he was on the road, roaming. Alicia flanked Joseph. Tom and Paloma and Kayleen came up behind us, and so we rode four and three abreast, Joseph and I surrounded by our friends. Paloma started a song, and Liam joined, then Alicia, and we wound our way up the narrow twisted trail to the rocks that had killed our family. All of the joy of traveling left me then, and a deep heaviness filled the places it had been.

The rocks were so large it seemed they must have been there for years, always been there, except for the deep raw gouges in the ground behind them. The dark and jagged cliff face next to us looked like an open wound compared to the normal monotonous grays of the cliffs. Periodically we had to pick our way past dirty webbed root balls as tall as the hebras' heads, or jagged trunks of trees the rock fall had pulled across the road. To find a path wide enough, we followed the East Band's wagon prints, which doubled almost sideways twice.

Liam led us. Joseph closed his eyes and swayed, and Tom rode up next to him, watching him quietly. At least twice, I thought Joseph would slide from Legs's back. He slumped, and wobbled, and had no color. Legs's head twisted back from time to time, as if he, too, worried about Joseph. I wondered what specific memories assaulted him.

Tears dripped down Kayleen's cheeks.

I tried to focus only on my friends, my brother, on Stripes's ears, tried not to see the gray-brown rocks. Near the end, I too closed my eyes, trusting Stripes to follow Liam. Then I felt her pace quicken, and looked.

Before me, the trail wound properly, barely disturbed. We kicked the hebras into a slow gallop. The litter of rocks was spaced out, fist-sized, and the hebras avoided them easily. Joseph held his own, leaning forward over Legs's tall withers, one hand on the saddle bump in front of him. Legs's cat-scar showed clearly, a dark moon-sliver shape against his grass-colored coat. Tom kept Sugar Wheat near Legs, his eyes on Joseph.

As we put distance between us and the rock fall, my mood

lightened. We were away. Tasked, about to be tested, but absent from Artistos and accompanied only by the two original humans who liked us best of anyone. Sure, Paloma and Tom were our keepers. As Nava's husband, Tom would report back on us. Still, if I had to choose, only Gianna might have been better support than Tom. Besides, Tom was strong and knew how to use his stunner. We might need that skill. In spite of the fact that Nava thought they were good choices, I was glad these two were our keepers. However we solved our problems, we did not have to hide ourselves. Much.

We rode until we could no longer hear the sounds of the wagons, until it was just us and our hebras and the pack hebras stringing behind Paloma. The ride became my focus, as if being on Stripes's back emptied me of both the sorrow of the rocks and the pleasure of our new freedom. We slowed only when the trail became too steep for the animals to make speed, winding back and forth up the last hill before the two lakes. The sun beat down on us. The long pull up the switchbacks felt like a long rocking dream, one hebra footfall in front of the other.

"How do they get the wagons up this?" I asked Liam.

He laughed. "With difficulty. There's worse later. The people will walk this section, leading the hebras. There are places on this trip where they'll even have to unload the wagons."

At the top, in a large clearing beaten down by wagon tracks and hoofprints, we stopped for a last long look over Artistos and the plains, waiting for the wagons to catch up. Trails wound up the mountains in three directions. Here we would split off from the roamers and head for the lakes and the shattered data network around them, while the roamers took a separate path to continue their work and eventually reach their wintering grounds on the other side of the mountains. The straightest path showed the tracks of the East Band; beaten dirt, muddled hoofprints, and thin steady wagon tracks.

The road intersected another stream by the clearing. We dismounted to rest, watering the hebras and snapping lead lines to their leather face harnesses to let them graze. Tom and Paloma wandered off a little ways, heads together, and the five of us, all the *altered* here, sat on a long rock shelf by the slowly running water. I wondered briefly how Bryan was doing and sent him a silent wish to fare well.

Kayleen wiped at her face, clearing the tear tracks, and looked at Liam. "I wish you could go with us."

"I know. But Akashi needs me. Besides, I have to return the dragonbirds. We all take care of our own finds. And Akashi wouldn't change Nava's orders."

I remembered Liam's comment about Jenna. "Liam, where does Jenna meet with you?"

He shrugged. "Where she wants. Always this side of the mountains. She believes she needs to stay close to protect you."

"We hardly see her," Joseph said.

Alicia brushed a strand of dark hair from her face. "We never do. She is mostly a story to me."

Liam laughed. "Well, she's no fool. She knows Akashi will not hurt her. Ruth might be a different story."

Alicia threw her long hair over her shoulder. The purple bruise on her face still stood out, but her eyes glowed with more energy than I had ever seen in them. "I'm happy not to be with my band."

"Is that enough for you?" I asked. "Being away from them?"

She looked down for a moment. "No. Bella was mean, but she only did what Ruth told her. Michael did what they both said. But Ruth . . . I want Ruth to be punished, to feel like she's dangerous and must be watched, to feel like she made me feel." She twisted her dark hair around her thin fingers. "But this is more than I had hoped for. Maybe I had lost all my hope." She paused. "I didn't expect anyone to stand up for us, except maybe Akashi. But Tom stood up for me, too. I hardly know him."

Liam watched her carefully, a small frown marring his features. "Most people don't hate us, Alicia. Paloma and Akashi, for example, are pleased we can do the things we do. And I'm glad you are away from the Easters." He glanced at me. "It was more than Akashi hoped for as well." His eyes flicked to Joseph. "However, it *is* clearly a test. I wish I *could* go with you."

We sat quietly. I watched Liam, trying to remember every nuance: his long hands resting carefully in his lap, the bronze of his skin as the sun shone down on it, the way the light illuminated some strands in his dark blond hair so they looked almost white, the ridges and valleys of his biceps and shoulders. I didn't want him to go.

Tom and Paloma walked back to us. We ate apples and drank water, mostly quiet. Stripes came over and sniffed the apples. She raised her lip, exposing her teeth. I laughed. "No. Apples are *not* good for you. Earth food gives hebras bellyaches." She gave me a baleful glare before turning back to the grass at her feet.

I pointed to a thin dark slash on a rock near us. "What made that?"

Liam looked at me curiously. "Us. That's from an *altered*'s weapon. You'll see many signs of the war out here."

I realized I *had* seen slashes like that in the rock on the trip up. I just hadn't recognized them. Nothing I knew of could do that to rock.

Joseph walked over to the rock and ran his fingers across the smooth spot. "It feels melted."

"It is melted," Alicia said.

Liam nodded. "You'll see a lot of those where there were major battles. Look carefully around the lake."

I didn't want to piece the war together; I wanted it to go away. Fat chance. We were born in the middle of it, and had never been free of it.

The roamers' wagons began to struggle up the long path below us, and we watched them, waiting. I was in no hurry for them to reach us, for us to separate into our own small group. The West wagons, and the roamers' knowledge, seemed like friendship and support. I glanced at Alicia. Surely she knew much of the country we would travel.

Liam stood behind me for a moment, curling his arms around me, hands resting on my stomach. My head just fit below his shoulder. Even two years ago I had been the tallest, but Liam and Bryan had both grown past me the last year. Liam leaned down and whispered, "Good luck," and kissed my cheek softly. His lips felt like hot feathers, nearly burning my skin. My voice choked up, and came out halting as I said, "You, too. Take care this winter."

He hugged Kayleen as well, kissing her on top of the head. She wound her arms around him so he had to step back and pull them away gently, laughing. He turned to Alicia, who kept a little distance from him, but held out her hand. He took it and smiled at her. "Good luck to you, too. Good journey."

She smiled softly. "Thank Akashi for me."

"I will." He turned to Joseph. "Have fun. Take care of these three troublemakers."

Joseph only nodded, as if he still couldn't quite talk after the trip up the High Road.

Tom and Paloma had already mounted, and the rest of us followed suit. Liam began to ride back down to his band. He turned around at the last minute, just before rounding the first switchback, and smiled broadly and waved once at us.

We waved back and followed Paloma down the smallest of the three paths, toward Little Lace Lake. Tom took the rear.

We rode for nearly a half hour, occasionally pushing through undergrowth attempting to take back the path. A stream gurgled nearby, sometimes visible. We crossed it twice, the hebras' hooves splashing on the damp rocks, kicking cool water up onto my feet. The narrow path forced us single file. I watched Stripes's ears and how carefully she carried her head, looking around on all sides, sniffing the air. It reminded me that paw-cats and demon dogs and wild orries and yellow-snakes lived in the forest here.

We crested the rounded hump of a steep hill, and Tom called to us to all stop. The lake below us was a great circle of deep blue, lighter around the edges, surrounded by multiple shades of green. Thick forest met the bank on both sides below us. On the opposite bank, folded low hills rose to the crater's edge, dotted with small stands of trees. The sun hung directly overhead, so no shadows fell on the lake. The water looked smooth and cool and inviting. "All of this is a meteor crater."

I swallowed, trying to imagine something so large. The lake would take days to ride around; the rock that made it must have been as big as a mountain.

"What would happen if something that big hit us now?" Kayleen asked.

"We would all die," Paloma said.

"We're in a meteor shower now," Kayleen said, her eyes wide.

Paloma smiled. "This was the size of a small moon. Nothing Gianna has tracked in this shower is as big as the stone that made this lake. But some may be big enough to worry about; Gianna is watching closely."

We wound down, still single file. Near the lake, the trail forked. Paloma stopped, looked both ways, then shrugged. "We need to go all the way around anyway." She turned her hebra right, and after no more than twenty minutes, we rounded a corner and saw a rusty metal data spike, a tall pole with a small rounded data pod strapped to the top with rope. Nearby, a cabin occupied the center of a clearing. A metal corral sat beside it, and behind, a wide stream flowed slightly downhill toward the lake.

Paloma eyed the rough-hewn cabin. It looked smaller than any house in Artistos, but big enough for more than one room. "I was here once, a long time ago." She seemed to be lost momentarily, in memories, and for the first time I wondered what she had done in the war. "It will be tight, but we'll all fit, and it will be easier than camping out tonight. At least there's running water." I looked down, and barely made out a pipe sticking up by the corral and another heading into the cabin. "This is one of the locations marked for us to fix—L4S." She glanced at Tom. He nodded at her, his face tight and drawn, and I suspected he, too, had memories of this place. Paloma dismounted and led her hebra toward the corral.

Tom and Alicia scanned the cabin for spiders and biting blackbugs, Joseph and Kayleen took care of the hebras and tack, and I helped Paloma set up the perimeter bells—a series of tiny wireless pods programmed to detect intrusion, identify the intruders, and make sounds like its much bigger cousin that surrounded Artistos. We set the perimeter at the edge of the forest, claiming the entire clearing, including part of the inbound trail and the data spike, as ours. We tested the invisible fencing by walking through it, hearing the chime of exit and entrance bells. The perimeter made us safer, although nothing guaranteed safety on Fremont. We found the others gathered in the clearing on some stumps and cut-up logs set outside the cabin for seats.

Tom squinted at a small square data monitor in his hands. I couldn't see it from where I sat, but knew it would have a readout of the data pod diagnostics, if the pod was healthy enough to broadcast. I arrived in time to catch the end of a question he was asking Kayleen. ". . . feel anything from the pod?"

Kayleen closed her eyes and went still, and after a moment she said, "Yes, it's—"

"Don't tell me. Yet." Tom cut her off. "Joseph? What about you?"

Joseph looked around, as if hunting for somewhere to escape to. His feet tapped the ground, his hands twisted in his lap. He wouldn't be able to connect to anything while he fidgeted so much. Finally, he slowed and stopped and closed his eyes. His hands were still, but clenched so tight the muscles in his forearms stood out. He shook his head.

No one spoke. I silently urged him to say something, to engage.

Tom's voice was gentle. "Humor me. Talk to me. Tell me what process you go through to connect."

Joseph opened his eyes. "I'm sorry. I can't feel anything."

"What would you have felt, before?"

Joseph was quiet so long I thought he wasn't going to answer. "It . . . it used to almost always be there. The whole web, something I felt, like heat or rain. Background noise. And to go deeper, I would stop and focus only on the data. It's like picking up threads, one by one, until you have all you can hold. And as I picked up threads, the rest of the world disappeared, bit by bit, until it seemed like I wasn't in my body anymore."

Paloma glanced at me, a thoughtful look on her face. "And

Chelo helped you? Is that why she sat beside you all the time, so you felt safe enough to let the rest of the world go?"

Joseph's hands twisted and twined again, sharp fast little movements. "Only . . . only when I went really deep. Following one thread didn't mean losing the world, or two threads, or three. But to handle as much as possible, to fade out completely, it mattered if Chelo was there."

Tom nodded. "Okay. But for one thread, that was easy? Not so threatening?"

Joseph nodded, looking miserable.

Paloma asked Kayleen, "Okay, so how many threads do you feel here?"

Kayleen closed her eyes, bending her head down so her hair obscured her face. "Just now, only one. But that was all I was looking for. The diagnostic thread. If there's a bunch of stuff—say weather data and intrusion detection and seismographic data, that comes out like separate threads." She closed her eyes and went still for a moment, checking back into the data networks. "I don't feel anything else working here." She glanced at Joseph. "Even if I did, I can't . . . weave . . . calibrate . . . more than one to—sometimes— three data flows at a time. Joseph can do dozens."

Joseph frowned. Sweat beaded his forehead even though a light breeze blew from the lake toward us.

Tom sighed. "Okay. We don't have to do all the work this minute. Chelo, can you stay here while the others go round up some firewood and explore a little?"

"Sure," I said.

Tom looked at Alicia. "Alicia—you're a roamer. Can you lead these three safely? Stay together?"

Alicia's mouth made a surprised little "o." I would have bet a good meal no one had ever asked her to be in charge of anything before. "Just for firewood?" she asked. "Just for a little while?"

"Just for firewood," Tom repeated, smiling at her. "Just for a little while."

Paloma glanced at Alicia. "Do you want me to go?"

Alicia shook her head solemnly. "I can do it. We'll be back soon."

"Be careful," Tom said. "A half an hour at most. Use the earset if you need us."

Alicia put a hand up to her ear, cupping the tiny wireless communications device. They were rare artifacts from *Traveler* that Artistos could not yet manufacture replacements for. She smiled and turned, and the others followed her.

Paloma and I sat quietly and watched their backs as they retreated across the clearing, Alicia in the lead, trailed by Kayleen and Joseph. The bell announced their leaving in three short chirps. After they had passed from our sight, Tom turned to me. "Chelo, do you know how it works?"

"I can't do it. Whatever the genemod is for reading data flows, I don't have it."

Paloma quietly said, "I've watched Kayleen for a long time, trying to figure it out. She calls it 'Blood, bone, and brain,' chants those words when she goes into reading data. She says that's how she feels it; it starts like a heartbeat and then she feels it deeply, everywhere in her body, and only then can she read it and understand it. But I think it's really in her nervous system." She sighed. "I did as much research as I could. The Deerfly databases refer to the skill—they call it 'reading the wind.' But they just say it's a common genemod. Not how it's done, or if it breeds true. I suspect you have to be born with it. I don't think it's a skill you can graft later, like you can change skin color or strength anytime you're willing to accept a mod. But that's about all I know." She pursed her lips. "Our ancestors limited us severely when they chose not to include the science around genemods in our databases. I suppose they didn't want us to be tempted."

I looked at Paloma curiously. Was it a temptation? Did she want to be like us?

Tom stood and paced a bit, and looked in the direction the others had gone. "We know Joseph's fear is stopping him. I don't know how to change that for him, and we have some complex work to do, later on. Kayleen could do this one, but I want Joseph to do it." He paused. "I want to start small with him. This node is still sending good diagnostics; it simply isn't hooking into the others. There's another one nearby that is in the same shape; the monitor picked it up. We can probably get this one back into the main net now, since they replaced the ones lost in the rock fall." He sat down next to Paloma. "I want Joseph to have as few distractions as possible, for me and Chelo to be the only ones with him, and to see what he can do. As soon as he gets back. Before he has time to brood more about failing just now." He looked from me to Paloma. "What do you think?"

Paloma nodded.

"Maybe it would be easier for him if it was just me," I offered.

"No. Remember, we're in the wild."

He was right. I glanced at the stunner on his belt. "Okay." I wanted another answer. "Tom? What happens if Joseph can't do this?"

"Then we'll try again."

"I mean all trip, ever."

"I don't know. The whole colony loses a measure of safety, and you lose a lever for acceptance." He hesitated and swallowed. "None of us wants to need you, particularly Nava and people like Wei-Wei and Ruth that can't forget the war, but it would be foolishness not to use skills that help us survive here."

What he didn't say, but I knew, was that the trip would affect our rights.

So we set it up. Alicia and Kayleen and Joseph returned with an armload of firewood each, and Paloma took Kayleen and Alicia back out to collect herbs and fruit and dig for the long thin roots of licorice-vine, carrying her stunner.

Joseph and I walked close to the edge of the perimeter. We examined the tiny pod on top of the data spike; it looked physically whole. Even though the earthquake had undoubtedly flung the top around, perhaps jerking the data pod into its current silence, the pole had remained firmly lodged in the ground.

As we started back, Joseph walked slowly, looking down. "I shouldn't have let Nava manipulate me so easily. I don't think I can do even this. My body has forgotten the data."

"Paloma told me they called this skill 'reading the wind.'"

"Who is they?"

"I don't know. She found it in the databases. I guess 'they' is the other *altered*. We should ask her for access."

He frowned. Even though we were part of the science guild, we had less access to the university and history portion of the records than children half our ages. His voice was bitter. "Maybe we can read over her shoulder."

"Maybe." Database queries were tracked. We'd learned that the hard way. Joseph had broken past security three years ago, and been severely chastised by Steven for it. I could still hear Steven's voice as he said, "Your abilities are a sacred trust. If you misuse them we will see that you never use them again." It was one of the few times I remember Steven raising his voice at Joseph. As far as I knew, Joseph had never again disobeyed. Although, I reflected, we may need him to in the future. If things went badly this trip. If he still could. I shook my head to clear the thoughts. We needed to prove how honorable we were, not how clever we were. I took Joseph's hand and said, "Maybe we can earn access."

He flashed me a wry grin. "If I can do anything at all anymore."

I took his hand. "I'm proud of you for trying."

Tom had laid out a blanket near the stumps. "The data monitor picks up a strong signal here, so this should be all right, and I want us away from the edge of the forest." Tom sat on a stump near enough to hear what we said, but far enough away so I didn't feel crowded. He looked away from us, toward the lake, as if trying his best to help us pretend he wasn't there.

Joseph stretched out on the blanket, and I sat on a flat stump near enough to touch him. His eyes held a spark of fear. But he dutifully closed them, his long limbs still, so the only movement I saw was his chest rising and falling with his even, slow breaths, his eyelids fluttering. I placed one hand on his shoulder, another on his calf, letting him feel me there with him.

He mouthed the words "Blood, bone, and brain," and suddenly the way he held his body seemed just right, felt right, felt the way it had when he'd done this a thousand times before, like he had slipped just a bit away from me. A soft breeze blew wisps of my hair back. A smile played across Joseph's mouth. He started dictating the diagnostic stream to me, "It sees other nodes, two of them, but barely. Can't connect. No good handshake. Initial failure happened the day of the earthquake." His eyes snapped open, and he shuddered, clenching his fists.

He pushed himself up to a sitting position, eyes wild, mouth in a tight line. "Dammit, Chelo, I couldn't stay. I got there. I did." He looked lost. "The diagnostic was in my head, perfectly, and then it . . . I dropped out."

"You were mentioning the day of the earthquake," I whispered.

He nodded. "I know. It just . . . fled. Suddenly I didn't have it anymore, couldn't hear it anymore."

Tom had turned toward us. "Can you try again?"

Joseph picked at the grass between his legs. His words were bitter. "Well, I have to, don't I? Isn't that what this whole trip is about?" He looked up at Tom, his eyes ablaze with resentment. "Not fixing the network, but fixing Joseph, so he can perform on command."

He was only partly right. "No, Joseph," I said. "Not just about that. It's about Alicia feeling her freedom, about us being away from town for a while, about fixing the network whether or not you help. Why else do you think Kayleen and Paloma are along?"

He didn't reply.

I remembered my conversation with Nava. But how was I supposed to make Joseph able to do this? "So it's not totally about you. But this is your gift. This is what you were designed for."

"I didn't ask to be designed."

That was new. I'd thought it, probably we all had, but I'd never heard Joseph say it out loud. "We are what we are. There's no point in wishing it away."

He lay back down and closed his eyes again, trying again for the diagnostics. Out here in the wild, he looked like prey, like a small quiet animal, trusting me and Tom for protection.

Three more tries, and every time he pulled out within moments. On the fourth try, he couldn't find the thread at all. He stood and started folding the blanket, not looking at me or Tom.

My stomach growled and my shadow had grown long enough to mingle with Tom's. Clouds gathered in the east, bunching up above the mountains on the far side of the lake, darkening the blue of the water. The breeze blew fast and steady.

Joseph walked off, heading for the cabin. Tom and I both watched him go, and Tom said, "It's okay. Let him have some time. I really hoped that would work."

I hated thinking of how Joseph must feel, how his success mattered so much. A brief flash of anger at Nava coursed through me, making my hands shake. She'd made him come out here, made him ride the High Road, forced him to do this thing he couldn't do. But what would I have done? What had I done? At least now Joseph was actively trying.

My thoughts were interrupted by the noisy return of the others, arms laden with herbs and fruit.

The wooden cabin was simple, only three rooms, two bedrooms, and a great room with a fireplace and kitchen and a table and chairs. The kitchen had running water. A metal woodstove that must have been hard to drag up here stood in one corner. There was no power except the small sun-batteries we carried, so after dark fell we lit candles we'd found in the cupboard, and talked, yawning, for about an hour before scattering to sleep.

Tom and Joseph took one bedroom, Paloma and Kayleen the other one, and Alicia and I slept on the floor in the great room. Alicia's breathing slipped into the steady rhythm of sleep only moments after the sounds of people settling in quieted, but I lay awake in my blankets on the hard floor for a long time. The big patterns on Fremont seemed clear to me: our struggle to prove ourselves, the difficulty the original humans had accepting us, Akashi's strengths as a storyteller and band leader balanced against Nava's power. The interdependence of the town and the roamers. The lingering effects of the war. Joseph's struggle was closest to me of all, but ideas about how to help him escaped me completely.

After an hour of lying still and quiet, trying to will my body to sleep, I opened the door and slipped outside. Thunderclouds still hung far to the north. A deep-throated growl of thunder floated across the lake, and jagged lightning forked the sky over the mountains. The air smelled like electricity. Yet, above me, stars scattered across the darkness like tiny spring field flowers, and the moon Dreamcatcher hung low in the south, full and bright, some details of its cratered surface visible. Small animals rustled the brush on the far side of the clearing. I hugged myself against the chill, wishing I'd brought a blanket.

Three meteors, close together, flashed overhead. At least one of them was big, still glowing as it plummeted down below the dark silhouette of the mountains, falling toward the clouds as if it were lightning from deep space. I couldn't tell if the meteor landed in the sea or burned up above it. I sat in the bowl of a crater, and imagined the searing impact of the stone that made it, the scattering of rocks and life and steam.

A few moments later, the perimeter alarms went off, toning for demon dogs. A high yip, and then another one, and then the alarms stopped. Apparently, the pack was not interested enough in us to push past the noise. Still, I shivered. A demon pack had killed two children last year.

Fremont was deadly, and more so without the nets. Fremont surrounded me, naked and dangerous and wild, like a great predator. I shivered and slipped back inside.

11

HUNTING

～

The sharp scent of a fire in the woodstove teased me awake, my belly growling. I opened my eyes to see Paloma padding past in her bare feet, holding a pot of water for morning tea. She grinned down at me. "Late sleeper?"

I scrambled up. Alicia stood in the kitchen, peeling twin-tree fruit and cutting up apples. She raised an eyebrow at me as I folded my blankets and stacked them next to hers. I mumbled a good morning at her and stepped outside, stretching, breathing in the cool air, blinking at thin clouds torched bright pink by sunrise. The morning smelled of the lake, the hebras, the dew-damp grass; entirely different from Artistos's human-filled morning scents of cooking food, of the oily tang of gears at the flour mill and the chuffing metal smelter. I felt free of some familiar oppressiveness, full instead of the exhilaration of adventure, tinged only a little by my fears of the previous night.

I returned to find Tom tilting his head, clearly speaking into his earset. "Nava?"

Only Tom's side of the conversation was audible. Alicia had stopped near him, probably listening as close as I was.

"Yes, we're safe." He frowned, pursing his lips at whatever Nava was telling him.

"No, not yet," and then, "I'll talk to you soon. Let us finish the lake circuit." Whatever she said next, Tom's voice rose. "Just trust me, all right. Give me some time." He walked outside, taking even his half of the conversation away from us.

He came back in a few minutes later, a scowl marring his round face. Whatever the conversation was, it didn't make him happy.

Kayleen pushed awkwardly through the door, breathless, a bunch of thumb-sized round purple pongaberries held triumphantly in her right hand. Her arms bore long thin scratches from the pongaberry tree, and her skin was slicked with a light sheen of sweat. "Good morning! I've been to the lake and there's no wind so it's like a mirror and the sun is making it pink. I saw a huge bird I've never seen before, but I think Liam mentioned; it was fishing." She stopped for a panting breath. "I found the pongaberry tree on the way back. It's going to be a great day."

Joseph appeared in the doorway of the back bedroom, sleepy-eyed, and frowning slightly. "You're awfully cheerful."

Tom looked around the room, like one of the herd dogs we used for the goats, making sure we were all there. His voice sounded clipped and edgy. "First, Kayleen, no going out by yourself. Not even in full daylight and inside our perimeter. Everyone travels in teams of at least two, all the time."

Kayleen nodded, her sunny demeanor falling away, her cheeks flushing with embarrassment. Tom continued. "We should be on the road by midday. I think Kayleen and Paloma should fix this node, and Chelo and Alicia pack us up and water and graze the hebras. All right?" He picked up the gear pack and stowed it back in the saddlebags.

I glanced at Paloma, who nodded. "That's fine with me," I said.

Joseph had sat at the table, and now he stared at his hands, concentrating fiercely on his knuckles, as if trying to shut the whole room of us out of his thoughts. Tom cleared his throat, watching Joseph, perhaps hoping Joseph would look at him. But Joseph just stared at the rough-hewn wooden floor. Tom leaned in toward him, speaking loudly. "And Joseph and I are going hunting."

Joseph looked up, a surprised smile transforming his face. Only people allowed to carry stunners hunted; certainly none of us.

Paloma didn't look at all surprised, but covered a small smile of her own. "Well, eat first." She passed the plate of fruit toward Joseph.

I took a pongaberry, narrowing my eyes at my little brother. "Be careful. I heard a pack of demon dogs last night."

Joseph ignored the fruit, his eyes fastened on Tom, looking ready to jump up and leave that moment.

Tom laughed and took a cup of tea from Paloma's outstretched hand. He stood to sip it, even though there was a chair right in front of him. "An empty stomach won't kill him. We won't be gone long." Tom proceeded to pop two pongaberries in his mouth at once. Juice escaped and ran purple down his chin.

Joseph grimaced and ate a pongaberry himself. "Good job, Kayleen," he mumbled, wiping his mouth and reaching for an apple.

I bit down on the pongaberry I'd been holding in my mouth, savoring the sudden sweetness coating my tongue.

Twenty minutes later Joseph and Tom rode away on Legs and Sugar Wheat, the rumps of the hebras disappearing into thick foliage. Tom was getting Joseph away while Kayleen and Paloma fixed the node. Anything that excited Joseph was good. Besides, fresh djuri tasted better than jerky.

Alicia and I headed for the corral. She leaned in toward me, her voice low. "So what's the story with Nava? I can't tell what she thinks of us."

Water from the stream flowed through an exposed pipe to a hand pump. I worked the lever, starting fresh water running into the hebras' trough. Once the flow was properly started, I locked the pump handle up, and leaned through the fence, feeling the cool water on my fingertips. Alicia's question seemed less straightforward than it would have a few weeks ago. "She . . . she's never liked us much. But now, since she's leading Artistos, she's got to deal with us. She doesn't trust us. She's even told me so." Stripes pushed ahead of the other five hebras, snuffling my fingers on the edge of the corral, and then plunging her nose into the cool water. "But I've been learning that maybe she'll be fair. If we don't give her any excuses to treat us badly."

"Don't she and Tom lead together?"

"Sort of. It's not like when Therese and Steven were alive." The words didn't hurt quite as much as I expected them to. "They worked together, like partners. But Nava tells Tom what to do, and he lets her. Mostly." I shrugged. "She sent him with us. I think he's been charged with getting Joseph to do what Nava wants." I chewed on my lip.

Alicia reached through the bars toward Ink, rubbing her black nose. "I think he agreed to come to get away from Nava. He sure didn't sound happy with her this morning. He doesn't mind being bossed around?"

"They mostly get along. Or at least he mostly does what she asks, but it's responsible stuff like directing half the rebuilding. Besides, she listens to him sometimes. I don't know if she ever listens to anyone else. But I've heard them argue twice since they moved in." I reached into the corral and scratched Stripes below the beard. She lifted her head and curled her upper lip, her warm brown eyes beaming pleasure.

Alicia opened the gate and slipped into the corral. She sounded wary. "I heard Nava was a war hero."

I followed her into the corral, untangling two lead lines from the fence, remembering Nava's story. It seemed a confidence, so I didn't pass it on to Alicia, but I wondered what she would think of it. "I'm pretty sure Tom was, too. Maybe we should ask Paloma."

She frowned at me, stopping momentarily, brushing the hair back over her shoulder. "Doesn't it feel strange to you that our parents' killers are Artistos's heroes?"

"They're all we have." I watched her, but she didn't look directly at me, just focused on the two ropes in her hands, running them through her fingers, adjusting out the kinks. I considered her question. Alicia had little reason to trust anyone; I shouldn't assume she trusted me. "Sky is your friend."

She nodded. "I know. I just wish our parents had won."

I had thought that myself once. Before Steven and Therese and Paloma and Gianna started treating us better. Before

I cared about anyone in Artistos. "Better the war never happened. That our people never came here, or that they and the others learned to live together." That everyone we loved was still alive.

She glanced at the center of the clearing, where Kayleen and Paloma sat next to each other on the ring of stumps, heads together. Paloma was laughing at something Kayleen had said. Alicia sighed. "Kayleen's lucky. Out of all of us, only she and Liam have adults who love them."

"Joseph and I used to." I turned away from her, blinking back tears. Sometimes I could talk about them without pain now, but other times it snuck up, sharp and heavy. "Tom is okay. He seems really good with Joseph, and I guess we get along, too. At first, I hated living with Nava—she's so rude and so always-busy and so bossy. She doesn't talk to us much unless she's telling us what to do. We make her uncomfortable." I turned the water off. "But I don't think she hates us anymore. I guess I'm still not sure. Really, you and Bryan have had it the worst. You worst of all." A stray thought crossed my mind. Alicia had been with us sometimes when we were little, but her mom had stayed back from the fighting. Chiaro hadn't watched her when she watched us. "Do you remember your real parents? At all?"

She stared at Kayleen and Paloma, then seemed to look beyond them, as if seeing the past. "I can't see their faces anymore." Her voice was soft, so soft I could barely hear her. Stripes nudged me, and I pushed her head away, straining to hear Alicia. "But I remember being happy. My memories kept me warm and safe all the first few years I was with the band. It helped me feel okay about myself."

I clipped a lead line to Stripes, and another to one of the pack animals. "Do you feel okay now?"

She shook her head. "I feel better now that I'm away from Ruth and Bella and Michael. I don't care if I ever see them again." She reached for Ink's head harness, clipping the lead on. "But I don't know what will happen to me. To us."

"I don't know either," I said. "Come on, let's go." We walked two hebras each out, including Ink and Stripes.

She stayed silent until we reached the center of the field

and let the hebras graze. Her voice was stronger, as if she had returned to the present, and to our predicament. "Do you trust them? Any of them?"

I didn't, not really. Maybe Akashi, but he had his band to lead. "I guess I trust them to do what they think is right. So that's what I try to understand, to influence."

She narrowed her eyes. "So you do what they want so that they'll think it's right to help you?"

I turned away from her, watching Stripes tear huge hunks of grass with her wide sharp teeth. "I guess . . . I guess we often do what they want. But they never asked us to work on the network; Joseph and Kayleen figured out how to do that by themselves. Paloma and Therese only encouraged them after they saw it worked. But what they want and what we want are often the same thing. In Artistos. We all want to live."

She nodded. "Bella and Michael always told me what to do. I did it, I had to. But every time I got away from them, I ran, or I climbed, or I threw rocks. I practiced being strong and fast as often as I could." She glanced at me, a little sideways glance, as if whatever I said next mattered to her.

"I guess . . . I guess we try not to shock them. When we run at our speed, we do it in our own place, back behind the mills. I mean, some people have seen us. We just don't rub it in."

"Did you ever get in trouble for running?"

"Wei-Wei glares at us."

She laughed. "That's not too bad." She stood and looked out over the lake. "They never locked me up before, but they kept me near them whenever they caught me acting like myself." She leaned down to pick a yellow flower and stood, both leads and the flower in one hand, plucking the long spiked petals with the other. A light wind off the lake blew her hair back, emphasizing the healing bruises on her cheek. "What do you want, Chelo? You're the one who spoke up for us before the Town Council. You're the oldest, the one the others all listen to. Even Liam. What do you want for us?"

"To be safe. To learn as much as we can about who we are and what we can do. To have normal lives." I chewed on my lip, hesitating, looking for the right words. "To help Fremont, or maybe to fly away."

"I like the flying away idea."

Stripes pulled on her lead, and handling two animals became a chore, interrupting the conversation. We grazed the hebras for an hour, rotating them halfway through. What conversations were occurring back in Artistos? Alicia's questions had started a hundred more questions, a river of questions, running inside me. I sang songs to the oblivious hebras, trying to capture some coherent meaning from the tumbling possibilities. All my energy had been spent keeping us safe. Sort of. Except for Alicia's bruises and Joseph's fear.

Kayleen finished fixing the node and Paloma tested it. Alicia and I packed everything except the perimeter bells. The hebras stood placidly, fed and watered, their saddles and face harnesses set out neatly in a row by the corral. The four of us sat in the log circle, Paloma regaling us with tales of seeking herbs for her salves while I twisted my fingers in my hair, worrying.

We jumped to our feet as Tom and Joseph crashed out from under the trees into the clearing, Joseph in the lead, setting off the entrance tones. Joseph sawed on the reins, pulling Legs to an awkward stop just in front of us. The hebra shifted uneasily. A dead djuri, dressed and bled, lay across Legs's saddle bump and two dead jumping prickles hung from the back of his saddle. A wide grin split Joseph's face. "I got them all!" he crowed.

Tom pulled Sugar Wheat up next to Legs. His eyes flashed approval and some other emotion I couldn't quite read—jealousy, concern? Disbelief? "It was incredible to watch."

"You didn't let him use the stunner?" Paloma asked.

He looked at her like she'd grown two heads. "Of course not." He dismounted, and reached up to pull the djuri body down, so it fell onto the grass with a solid whump. It looked sad, all the grace gone from its slender legs. Its long neck had been snapped, so the head twisted backward, resting unnaturally on its curving black horns. Legs sidestepped, as if trying to get as far away from the dead animal as possible.

Joseph almost glowed, his eyes flushed and bright with achievement. "I just . . . I tied Legs up near the edge of a clearing. I got the prickles first." He pointed. The jumping prickles hung from their long spiky tails, tied on with leather straps looped through the saddle rings. They were end-of-summer fat, tan spiky balls twice the size of my fist, their long, strong legs hanging limply, their sharp fur bent and broken. "I jumped ahead of them. That's all. I just . . . I could tell where they were going to be, and I was there before them." He smiled again, holding out his palms, so I could see the shallow scratches the prickles' hair had dug into his skin.

Tom laughed. "It was like you knew how to scare them *just so,* so they'd jump *just so,* and you'd simply be there." He looked at Paloma. "He *caught* them. I've never seen anyone catch a prickle bare-handed before."

Paloma grimaced, holding her hands out in front of her, as if imagining one of the sharp-furred beasts in her own palms.

"And the djuri?" Kayleen asked.

Joseph looked down at the dead animal. "I caught it."

"You caught it? Running?" Paloma asked, skepticism warring with wonder on her face. Djuri were fast, faster than hebras.

Alicia looked at me, as if to say, "See, we should run," a saucy light in her eyes and a quiet grin on her bruised face. I grinned back. We were, after all, with Tom and Paloma. They didn't seem to mind our skills.

This must be how Jenna lived, how she protected us. I looked at Joseph's face. Somehow it seemed different, like the transformation when he first began connecting to the data networks. Maybe this was what he needed: confidence. I smiled at Tom's cleverness, then glanced over at him, catching his eye.

He winked at me. He jumped down from Sugar Wheat and handed his reins to Paloma.

Paloma reached her free hand out to take Legs's reins from Joseph as well. "How about Alicia and Kayleen care for these two and saddle the rest? Joseph and Chelo can take down the perimeter, and you, Tom, can skin this beast. I'll skin the jumping prickles."

"Joseph should help prepare his own kills."

Paloma frowned, her tone serious. "Hmmmmm. Next time. For now, I'd like to talk to you."

Did she want to talk about Joseph's hunting? But she had known; she hadn't seemed surprised this morning. So maybe she wanted to talk about *how* Joseph hunted? I bit my lip. Surely Paloma and Tom weren't testing us? Paloma knew how fast and strong we were, even if Tom was still learning.

Joseph and I started at the closest edge to the cabin and began pulling down the little perimeter data nodes one by one, flipping tiny switches to turn them off and stowing them in a blanket for safekeeping. As we reached the back of the cabin, out of sight of everyone else, I heard a low hiss. I jumped, glancing after the sound.

Jenna stood casually against a near-elm trunk, a slow approving smile on her ravaged face. Dressed in well-worn leather pants, a leather vest over a brown hemp shirt, and low boots, she blended with the background. I was sure my eyes had passed over her at least once before she made a noise. She looked wild, feral, part of the forest.

Joseph regarded her quietly, as if trying to reconcile seeing her here with his expectations. "What do you want?" he asked.

For answer, she threw Joseph a thin pipe as long as his arm. It gleamed in the sunshine, turning lazily over and over, crossing the distance between them. Joseph caught it easily, and held it lightly, turning it one way and then the next. It glowed like the skin of *New Making*.

We manufactured nothing like it in our shops. I glanced from the pipe to Jenna and she tossed a second item, much smaller, to me. My hand came out naturally and plucked a small smooth object from the air. It only filled half my palm, and felt light, like a flower or a seed. It looked like the same material as the pipe. Was *New Making* so light? The smooth flattened sphere bore a single marking: a set of three interlocking diamonds, etched or inlaid so the black diamonds were smooth to the touch, seamless between silver and black. "These are ours," Jenna said.

I looked over at her. "Ours?"

"You are outside Artistos now. If you look closely, look in places only you can go, you will find traces of us. You have not forgotten who you are."

Joseph and I glanced at each other, and I saw my own wonderment and confusion reflected in his eyes. "What are they?" I asked.

She squatted, balancing easily with her back against the tree trunk. "The pipe is from a wrecked vehicle. Just a spare part. It has no value, except to show you that you have not seen everything in Artistos. The data button holds information. You need reading thread to access it."

I closed my fist around the button. "Do you have any? What does it look like?"

Her face was serious, her single eye burning with energy. "Joseph can find you some. If he listens. Keep it. You may share it with our people, but not with Tom or Paloma. Or anyone else from Artistos."

"Why?"

Jenna's one eye twinkled and her mouth pulled into a slightly twisted smile. "They have more in Artistos. But they have never shared them with you. Ask yourself why."

I nodded. Jenna thrilled me, excited me, puzzled me, scared me, but I was tired of knowing nothing. "You, too, are withholding information. Tell us more about this thread."

She looked startled, just for a moment, and a small smile touched her mouth. She leaned in toward me. "I am giving you information as fast as you can use it. Find some reading thread, find out more about us, and earn the next piece of information." She held her hand out for the pipe.

Joseph returned it to her, giving it a wistful glance, and I wished for time to touch it myself, to see if it felt like *New Making*'s skin. But Jenna's hand closed on the pipe. She smiled at Joseph and said, "Good hunting today. But break the djuri's neck faster; it did not have to feel pain."

So she had watched him hunt. I wished I had seen it.

Joseph smiled back, and something, some look, perhaps an energy built on the shared experience of being hunters, passed between them. "I will." He held his hand out for the data button, and I passed it to him reluctantly. As his fist closed across it, he started, his eyes widening. "I am the reader," he said, suddenly, opening his fist again and then sitting, closing his eyes, as if trying to fall into his inner silence and access whatever tales the button had to tell.

So we were right about Jenna's earlier reference to a key.

Joseph stirred, opening his eyes again, looking quizzically at Jenna.

"Not yet," Jenna said. "You don't have the strength or the facility." She laughed. "Nor the machinery. You need a tool to help you."

He pursed his lips, then looked away from us, staring at a set of twintrees twining above the near-elm. He swallowed. "Kayleen?" he asked. "Can Kayleen do this? Am I the only one?"

Jenna nodded. "Kayleen may never have the strength. Your parents built you and one more for this task."

"One more?" I asked.

Jenna spoke slowly, sadly. "One more who is dead now. Dead and gone twelve years. You were not the only children. Just the only ones left alive, left here. You six and I are all of us still here." She straightened, fixing both me and Joseph with her one eye. A feat. "I must go. Remember not to show that to your guardians."

She faded into the forest as if she had never been there.

Tools and keys. But to what end? What did she want?

Joseph pocketed the button, and even though I wanted to ask for it back, I kept my silence. We finished the perimeter and returned to find everyone ready to depart. As we rode away, I looked back, hoping for a glimpse of Jenna.

Our path looped near the lake, and I managed to pull Stripes up next to Joseph in one wide patch that bordered a rocky beach. I leaned in toward him. "What did you feel when you first held the button?"

He glanced ahead, checking that Paloma, who had the front, and Tom, who had the rear, were out of earshot. Alicia and Kayleen struggled between us and Tom, managing one pack hebra each, clearly too occupied to overhear us. "I felt a hum deep inside—like this thing, rather than the data nets we manage, was what I was born to hear. I don't know how to explain it better. I can't read it like I can the nets, but even now I can feel it in my pocket, as if it is alive."

"Does it feel good?"

He licked his lips. "It scares me. Even more than the data nets. But not in the same way. On the nets, I'm afraid of going back to the day Steven and Therese died, or of something else happening. Of knowing things I can't control. This is different. Like it's teasing me." He brushed a biting-fly from Legs's neck. "I'm certain that if I learn how to read it, something will change in me. Something big."

At least his words showed some clarity about why he could no longer fix simple nodes. "Well, it sounds like Jenna thinks that won't happen right away. Do you want me to hold it?"

"Not yet."

After a three-hour ride, we found the next data stake in a clearing that ran downslope to the stony lake bank, the shallows full of grass and weeds that smelled like rotting vegetation and mud. The sun's evening rays slanted through the trees above us in golden beams. There was no convenient cabin or corral, so Tom and Paloma went off together to put up the perimeter alarms in a big half circle arching from lake bank to lake bank, leaving the four of us to water and hobble the hebras and pitch the tents.

We stripped the tack from the animals, clipped on lead lines, and walked them, two for each of us, toward a small clear stream that ran along the far edge of the clearing. Along the way, we passed a jumble of rocks scarred with long black melted lines. Who had sheltered behind the rocks, hunched low while someone else shot at them with a weapon that melted rock? Probably people from Artistos. Weapons that strong surely belonged to the *altered*. To us.

Did Jenna have any? I shivered, uncomfortable and suddenly cold.

We reached the stream and six thirsty hebras plunged their noses into the water as one, the outer two waiting, watching.

Joseph glanced at me, patting his pocket with one hand. I

cleared my throat to get attention, waiting until Alicia's and Kayleen's eyes were on me. "Jenna came to see us while we were taking down the perimeter this afternoon."

Alicia's eyes sparkled with excitement and she said, "Really? Here? What did she want?"

Joseph pulled the data button from his pocket, taking one of the two leads Kayleen held from her hand, and dropping the flattened silvery button in her hand. Kayleen immediately closed her fist around it and said, "Oh." Her eyes widened almost like Joseph's had. So she could sense whatever he felt.

Joseph watched her closely. "What do you feel?"

She closed her eyes. "Like I've felt this before." She looked at me. "Chelo—you're the oldest. Do you remember seeing these?"

I tried to recall the neatly stacked and ordered items in our parents' tent, but what I saw was just Chiaro's round face and almond eyes, her dark hair pulled back into a ponytail, perpetual worry pulling the corners of her eyes and mouth downward. I shook my head, scanning my memories again. "They had a lot of things, and I do remember silver things, which must have been made of this stuff. But I don't remember anything like this."

Alicia plucked the button from Kayleen's hand. "It's . . . light. But it doesn't make me feel strange."

I took it from her, glad to hold it in my hand again. It lay in my palm, light and bright and silent. "That's all right, Alicia. I don't feel anything either. It must be related to Joseph and Kayleen being able to '*read the wind*'—that's a term Paloma taught me about their skill."

Alicia gave me a quick hard look. "Paloma knows about our *alterations*? What we can do?"

Kayleen pursed her lips. "Of course she does. She tries to study them. She stands up for us."

Alicia's brows furrowed. "Are you sure?"

Kayleen watched Alicia warily. "She's my mom."

"Paloma's okay," I echoed. "I think she wishes she could run as fast as we can." I handed the button back to Joseph and watched Stripes raise her head, water dripping from her beard. "She's tried to study us, to study *alterations*. But she says she hasn't learned much. She told me the original humans didn't bring any real information in their databases, just some side references."

"What do we do with that thing?" Kayleen asked. "Did Jenna tell you what it's for?"

"Just that it's called a data button. And that she doesn't want us to talk to Paloma or Tom about it. She said Joseph needed to learn more about the data nets before he can use it, and that he needs to find something."

Joseph put the button back in his pocket. "She told us to look for hidden places where the *altered* lived and fought."

"And died," Alicia muttered under her breath.

"But I want to show it to Paloma," Kayleen said.

I shook my head. "Jenna is everywhere. Apparently she watched the hunt today, too. She would know. Then she might not give us anything else." It was getting cooler and darker. I pulled on Stripes's lead line. "We'd better get the tents set up."

There was no more time for talk that night. Paloma and Tom returned as we finished pitching the three tents; the biggest for Kayleen and Paloma, smaller tents for Tom and Joseph, and for Alicia and me. Kayleen and Paloma made a stew of dried corn and the jumping prickles, and Tom and Joseph roasted djuri steaks. Before I climbed into the tent, full and sleepy, I noticed two more meteors burning across the sky. It was a rare moonless hour, and the flashes of light shone like tiny suns as they burned up above us.

Surely Gianna was cataloguing them back home. I bit back a brief wave of loneliness.

The hebras whickered softly and low wind waves gurgled through the plants and washed rocks softly against each other on the beach below us. As I drifted off to sleep, my last waking thought was to wonder if our parents had ever slept here, listening to the same water, watching the same moons.

Either set.

Perhaps our parents had fought each other on this very same beach.

12

MY OWN KILLING

The next morning I crawled out of an empty tent to a surly sky and the smell of impending rain. Alicia sat on a blanket next to Joseph, combing her hair. I sat beside them. I wished them good morning, then glanced at Joseph a second time. Dark circles spread under his eyes and his hair stuck up in the back, as if he'd slept badly. He held the data button in his hand, shivering slightly in the morning air. I frowned at him. "Are you okay? Did you sleep out here?"

"No." He blinked as the gray dawn slowly grew lighter, tossing the data button from hand to hand. "I'm not sure I slept at all."

Why hadn't Tom come to get him, made him get some sleep? "You were out here alone all night?"

"Yes." He looked out over the lake, avoiding my eyes. "I decided to stay up until I could fix the node."

"Did you?"

A short, ironic laugh escaped his lips. "I'm still awake, right? I can hear it, though. Whenever I want. I listened to the diagnostics all night. I can hear the node Kayleen fixed yesterday. Even now. And a third one, farther away." He pointed past us, in the direction we would go in when we left. "But I can't change anything in them. I don't understand why."

Alicia handed him her comb. "Maybe you're trying too hard."

"Maybe." He swiped the comb through his hair perfunctorily and handed it back. He grunted. "Look, I'm going to take a walk." He stood shakily.

He looked like he might fall back down. At least he was trying to fix the nodes, but staying up all night surely wasn't the best way to go about it. "Maybe you should go get some sleep."

He shook his head. "I think I'll do something useful. I'm going to water the hebras."

Alicia's mouth drew down tightly, and she scrambled up next to him, putting a hand on his forearm. "Let me help you."

He shook her arm away. "I'd rather be alone."

Alicia blinked, surprised, her eyes flashing pain but her face suddenly impassive, as if a mask had covered her delicate features.

I took Alicia's hand and, together, we watched him pocket the data button and walk away. She squeezed my hand in return. "He can't water eight hebras."

"I know. But let him try. He gets downright moody lately, and it's best to leave him alone when he's like this. He's safe enough; we can see him."

Joseph led Legs out behind him, the hebra nipping playfully at his shoulder and Joseph brushing him away. I figured Legs would eventually win, and Joseph would have to smile. The other hebras looked at us as if to say, "Me, too," but I managed to ignore them for the moment by turning my attention back to Alicia.

She jerked the comb through her hair; I heard strands ripping. Her usual expressions were reappearing slowly, anger and loss and excitement becoming visible together, fading up through the mask. Subsuming herself must be how she survived the East Band. And I'd never known; perhaps I'd simply read the mask and not the girl all along? I kept my voice gentle, hoping to coax the true Alicia to the surface. "Are you always up so early?"

She let go of the hank of hair in her left hand and stood, pacing slowly around me. Trust and fear rippled across her eyes and her delicate fingers clenched, and relaxed, and clenched again. "I haven't been able to sleep more than a few hours a night since Varay died. And last night, I dreamed we left here, took the *New Making,* but I'd left something behind and had to come back. Only I could never tell what I left behind." She stopped and looked out over the water. A single raindrop fell on her forearm, glistening. She ignored it. "I didn't want to come back. I can't imagine what I would miss here."

I pointed at the lake. Its surface glowed dark under the clouds, ruffled by a cool wind. It was just possible to make out the crater rim on the far side, mountains rising up beyond it, the far ones improbably touched with sunshine. "Fremont is beautiful. Being alive, being here." I touched her arm. "We have each other."

"And people who think we want to kill them." She sighed. "I'm sorry, I don't mean to be such lousy company. I just . . . I don't fit in. I don't even fit in with you three. You and Joseph are so close you hardly have to talk, and Kayleen talks whole paragraphs to you and barely says a word at a time to me."

A flush of embarrassment heated my face. "Alicia, you belong with us. You'll see." Rain started falling in big fat drops. The hebras whickered. "We always looked you up. Every time the band came."

She cupped her hands, catching raindrops, watching them splash off her palm. "I used to dream I could stay behind with you and Joseph and Bryan, that I could live in a house instead of a wagon and wake up in the same place every day."

The hebras bugled at us. We relented, each taking two beasts to the water, staying ten meters upstream from Joseph, ignoring him like he was ignoring us.

As we got back, fat slow raindrops gave way to a sharp stinging downpour. Joseph remained by the stream with Legs. Paloma helped us put the animals away while Tom and Kayleen prepared hot tea, and cooked up a scramble of the leftover meat from Joseph's hunt and the rest of our fresh supplies from Artistos. By the time breakfast was served in Kayleen and Paloma's big tent, Alicia's long hair stuck to her back in thick wet ropes, and we were both soaked through and shivering. Joseph came in, clutching a dry shirt that he changed into before eating silently. He fell asleep along the south wall of the tent.

"Can we go back to the cabin?" Kayleen asked from her spot near Joseph's feet. "I'm cold."

Tom pulled up a sat-shot on his data reader, overlaid the blue line of our progress and the green line of the path, and pointed out the next node, by a small cabin nestled in an oblong meadow. "This is only a little farther. The road to it looks clear. I don't see any trail damage between here and there." He sighed and looked out at the rain. "Kayleen? Can you fix this node from inside?"

She sighed. "I think so. Except I'm too darned cold and shivery to do anything useful."

Tom grinned and handed Kayleen the blanket he had wrapped about his shoulders. "Here. Use this. I'd rather keep going."

Kayleen took the blanket, huddling deep inside it. "In the rain?"

"It will let off sometime today."

Kayleen sighed. She closed her eyes and lay back, still shivering slightly. Alicia watched her closely. There was little to see: Kayleen lying still with her eyes closed and her arms folded across her stomach. After a while she opened her eyes and said, "All right. I'm done. This was easier than the last one, and it's hooked all the way back to Artistos. Let's go."

Tom glanced at his data reader. "Confirmed." He smiled wryly, watching Joseph sleep. We were fixing the network, but this was not what Nava had sent us out for. Joseph snored softly from his corner. If he could just break through, we could finish a lot faster and get back home.

Paloma peered out the tent door. Water fell fast and hard. Drops plinking in a nearby puddle made concentric rings of water like stones in the river. "I think we should wait for this to slow down."

Kayleen snorted and lay back down.

The rain didn't slow. Tom got up and checked on the animals, returning soaked.

We waited.

Sometime past midday, thunder crackled overhead and jagged forks of lightning filled the sky. Joseph woke and sat peering out the door, watching the storm. Kayleen and Paloma wrote busily on their data readers, recording the details of the journey. I listened to the rain, listened for the boundary bells, and to the hebras' footfalls as they shifted uneasily in their hobbles. Alicia scooted close to Joseph, not touching him, and looked outside, both of them silent. I caught the glimmer of unshed tears in her eyes at one point, and wondered what she was feeling and why, but decided not to ask her in the crowded tent.

Joseph smiled, apparently drinking in the raw electric fury that danced overhead.

I pulled out my flute, playing softly. Liam had never found time to teach me, and the notes came out wobbly and uneven. I wondered what Bryan and Liam were doing, and if the storm touched them, too.

The thunder finally passed us by, falling away so we could hardly hear it, and the sky cleared to cerulean blue, washed bright and shining. A fresh set of thunderheads piled over the mountains beyond the lake, but for now, we emerged from hiding into sparkling rivulets of water touched by sunlight. We packed quickly, drying the tents with dirty clothes, stuffing all of the damp things into one bag to hang out later.

As we pulled ourselves up the knotted mounting ropes, I looked over at Alicia and whispered, "It's a beautiful afternoon. Can you see it—see how pretty the lake is?"

She shook her head.

But Joseph smiled momentarily, looking better for his nap. I leaned over to Tom, who had one of the pack animals. "Can we ride ahead?" I asked. "Just for a bit? Give the animals some exercise?"

He frowned at me, but looked around. Paloma had the other pack hebra; they couldn't move fast. The path in front of us was clear and wide, the clouds far enough away to offer no immediate threat.

A dark hint of resolution in his eyes and the set of his mouth telegraphed that he was about to refuse me.

I smiled as brightly as I could. "We really need a break. I'll be watchful; we all will. We can stay in contact on the earsets." I tapped my ear lightly. Kayleen and I both wore them this morning. "Please?"

He glanced at Paloma, who gave a short little nod before saying, "They have to grow up sometime."

"I guess I'm outnumbered. Be careful. It's only a few kilometers to the cabin anyway. But no running—it's muddy. And check in with us every few minutes."

"Thanks!" I smiled at the others. "Let's go!"

We took off at the hebra's fastest walking gait, shifting into a slow run as soon as we were around a corner and out of Tom's and Paloma's sight. Alicia leaned down over Ink's neck, laughing, and Kayleen and Joseph ran next to each other, barely bothering to pull the hebras' pace back at all. Mud from the animals' split hooves splattered up onto my feet and pants. The beasts seemed to feel as happy in the small freedom as we did, stretching easily into a gentle run, noses forward, ears pricked. The path stayed wide and clear, except for two small storm-water streams. Stripes took the lead in the absence of Sugar Wheat.

Stripes slowed as we ran alongside a small cliff. The trail narrowed and turned away from the water, rising steeply up-hill through a stand of tent trees and yellowing fall ladies that brushed at us with lacy leaves. Boulders lined the path. We passed one that had probably fallen in the quake, shattering the trunk of a small evergreen tree. The top leaves were already brown with death.

I pulled Stripes back to an even slower walk, suddenly cautious, bunching the others behind me. We crested a small hill, keeping the hebras close together. Below us, the long stream-cut valley and small cabin from the sat-shot sparkled as sunshine touched puddles of standing water and glittered on three streams that ran into the valley, joining just before they poured into the lake.

I narrowed my eyes. The valley was too low to make sense for a data spike; signal wouldn't climb up the steep valley walls. I finally spotted the spike a few meters to our left, nearly hidden by a pile of rocks, clearly good line-of-sight all the way across the lake and far up and down both banks. Three pods were strapped together near the top; a major node.

Alicia whispered, "Djuri."

I squinted down at the meadow. Sure enough, three djuri grazed below us, one quite near the cabin. A soft breeze blew the hair from my face, filling my nostrils with the soft musk of djuri, the damp grass, all mixed together. I spotted another one, then another. Surely there was a whole herd. "Tom," I spoke into the earset. "I think we're here. I can see the cabin."

He laughed. "Then you've been moving too fast."

"We're safe," I protested.

Joseph dismounted and handed his reins to Kayleen. I expected him to head for the spike, but he simply stood, very still, looking down.

"Tom, I'll get right back to you, okay?"

"Everything's all right?"

"Sure. We're fine."

"Well, we're at least a half hour behind you. Sugar Wheat has a bad stone bruise, we're going slow."

"All right. We'll check the cabin out."

"Be careful."

As soon as I closed the connection, I dismounted and stood next to Joseph. "What are you doing? We're not as safe on foot."

He handed me Legs's reins, and in a fit of stupidity, I took them. Then he was gone, down-trail, moving silently but fast.

I thrust both sets of reins at Alicia, and spoke to them both. "Stay here! You can see on all sides, and it's safe. Stall Tom if he calls." I followed Joseph, who was already fifty meters ahead of me. I dislodged a pebble, and Joseph stopped and turned, his fingers over his mouth, signaling me to be quiet.

Then I knew.

He intended to hunt a djuri. I glanced down at the animals. They all looked bigger than the one he'd caught the day before. I gestured to him to wait. He stood his ground, still except for his fingers, which drummed against his thighs.

When I reached him I whispered in his ear. "There could be other predators there."

He shook his head. "Remember, I can hear the data nets again."

"Aren't they broken?"

"Two nodes here still talk to each other. Really, it's okay. I'd know if there was anything as big as a paw-cat here. Relax." He grinned at me, eyes dancing, face flushed with excitement. "Come on. You'll see."

The net out here was more porous than the perimeter nets at home, or the ones we set up every night, but he had seen the paw-cat just before the quake, along the High Road.

He continued down the path and I followed, resistant to every step. We shouldn't be doing this. We should be sticking together, like a herd of hebras, watchful. I glanced back up the path. Kayleen and Alicia had both dismounted, and stood watching, each holding two hebras.

Joseph waited for me at the edge of the meadow. Scrub trees protected us from the djuri's sight, and the wind still blew in our favor. He leaned in close, whispering. "The trick is to get close to them, catch them unaware. Then run alongside the one you pick. Keep with it. Yesterday, my djuri wore out before I did. When you can, catch the horns and twist, breaking the neck. You have to pull backward. Only do it fast. That's what Jenna was talking about yesterday."

I scanned the meadow. Two groups of five or six djuri stood bunched together, and three single djuri scattered around them, heads up. Watchers, like hebra herds had watchers? I didn't know; I'd never seen wild djuri so close. Was Jenna watching us even now? "How are we going to get close?"

He grinned back at me. "Belly crawl. Pretend you're a paw-cat. On my signal, run."

I didn't like either part of that idea, but I followed him out. He wasn't exactly on his belly; just moving low on all fours, poised to run. The thigh-high yellow grass slowed us. White tufts of grass seed blew in the wind, sticking in his hair, my hair. Surely the djuri would see us move the grass. Other predators, too. I glanced behind us. Nothing followed us. But

I could still see Alicia and Kayleen and the four hebras. Didn't the djuri see them? What was Joseph thinking? I could stop this. Jump up and scream, scare the djuri. But Joseph? How would he feel, then?

A sharp rock stabbed my palm.

I slowed, bringing my focus to the task at hand, discarding worries. I no longer looked back and up, but just followed Joseph's feet, sliding as silently as possible through the grass. Every once in a while, his head rose up slowly, then down, and we changed direction. The djuri smell, dusty coat and grass and dung and forest, grew more distinct from the scent of the grasses.

Joseph whispered, "Go right, then forward."

I obeyed. Were Tom and Paloma listening? My breath sounded loud in my ears. Every strand of grass my body displaced slid noisily along my clothes, every footstep made a crunching sound. Was I really going to do this? Was I crazy?

Joseph's whisper again, high and excited. "Now!" He leaped up, running fast.

I, too, leaped up and found a startled djuri five meters from me, veering away even as I saw the fear in its eyes, its tiny flared nostrils, pink inside. The horns were small, just longer than my fingers. Young.

It bounded.

I followed.

It gained distance, flying away from me, rump bouncing, hooves flashing. I pushed, keeping pace again, but now behind. Ten steps, twenty, then thirty. More. Too many to count. As it neared the stream, it slowed, turning away from the water.

I gasped little ragged breaths, remembered Bryan had taught me to breathe through my nose, shifted, felt air feed my lungs, my belly, my legs. I gained a meter on the djuri. Grass pulled at my pant legs, threatening to catch my feet and throw me headlong. A sharp pain ran up my leg from the paw-cat scratch.

Joseph yelled triumph and Tom yelled anger into my earset and Kayleen screamed encouragement from the top of the trail, all in a tunnel far behind my focus, which had drilled down onto the heaving sides of the beast, the dun color of its hide, now soaked with sweat, the dark stripe that started in a vee at the horns and flowed along its backbone to its tail. It strained for air. Its head bobbed almost as high as mine, but its legs were shorter, thinner. Less powerful. We ran, now almost side by side.

My eyes met its eyes. Its fear smelled.

I breathed in sharply and lunged. My left hand caught its neck, halfway up, grasped the sparse little mane. It stumbled. I clasped a horn with my right hand and jerked backward. The djuri tumbled sideways, screaming in a high shrill voice, a sound like Jinks's scream just before the paw-cats got her. I tripped, catapulting past the fallen djuri before stopping myself on all fours, knees and palms, head down, heaving, pulling air in great gulps.

As soon as I could, I stood. My legs wobbled as I walked the ten long steps back to the animal. It lay on its side, still breathing. No fear filled its eyes now, only pain. I leaned down and patted its head briefly. I no longer wanted its death, but one leg splayed awkwardly, a shard of white bone breaking the skin.

Someone groaned and whimpered and I realized it was my own voice. I clamped my mouth shut, stopping the noise. All movement seemed unnaturally slow. I placed one hand on each horn, gripped firmly, and twisted, hard.

Bone splintered. A horrible sound.

The pain leaked from the djuri's eyes, replaced by a still dark pool that reflected my own sweat-stained face back at me, the way a sphere reflects: oddly. My hair was wild about my shoulders, my mouth open, my eyes wide. I stood, looking away from its eyes, looking for Joseph.

The din in my ears resolved into voices; Kayleen and Tom on the earset and Joseph near me. All of them at once. I screamed, "Quiet!" and everyone obeyed, instantly. I had no idea what to say into that silence. "I just killed something and its eyes mirror mine," didn't seem quite right. My breath was still fast, and surely loud enough to deafen them all. "I . . . I'd like to report . . . a successful . . . dinner catch."

Joseph laughed, a hard, nearly maniacal laugh, and I

joined him, releasing the fear and adrenaline and shock of the hunt. Suddenly my muscles hurt, my leg hurt, my palm where I'd slapped the rock hurt. My heart pounded. But beneath the pain, elation. I beat the animal. I had become a hunter. It felt completely strange, like a skin that fit perfectly but had never existed before, even in my imagination.

Joseph came and stood by me, his sides heaving, his face covered in sweat and dirt, blood on his hands. His eyes shone. I hugged him, tightly, and we stood for a long moment together, brother and sister in something new. I made sure the communications link was closed and whispered in his ear, "Thank you."

He looked down at my kill, nodding. "You're welcome."

I looked around for Jenna, but saw no sign of her. If she had watched our hunt, she didn't bother to reveal herself to us.

Joseph's djuri was bigger than mine, and a clean kill. The blood came from Joseph's hand, which had been scored by one long, graceful horn. His animal was too big to move, so we pulled mine to his, and stood over them. Mine looked small in death, and eyeing it, I became unsure what to do next. Our large knives were in our pack, back with Tom and Paloma. Joseph had the small one he used to whittle his animals. He took it out, staring at it. It looked entirely inadequate for the job.

We looked up at the sound of a hebra's fast footfalls, and Tom's voice. "Chelo! Joseph!" He was galloping Paloma's hebra, Sand, looking around wildly. I glanced up the trail. There was no sign of Paloma, or of Kayleen or Alicia either, although Stripes and Legs stood at the top of the path where we'd left them, apparently hobbled. Tom jerked his head toward them. His voice had a new angry edge I'd never heard in him. "Get your animals and get back down here, now."

"Where's Alicia and Kayleen?" I asked.

"I sent them back after Paloma." He glared down at me, a look that left me feeling flayed and childish. "I had to leave her alone to come watch over you." He panted. "Alone. Out there." He turned his glare on Joseph. "Never, never hunt without a stunner." He gestured at the carcasses. "Dead animals attract paw-cats. I'll watch the carcasses while you bring your hebras down here where they're safe."

"It's safe," Joseph said, evenly, but despite his measured words, the anger in his voice matched Tom's anger. "I can hear the nets. Two nodes work here." He pointed toward the high node by the hebras. "And so does the big one, partly. It's enough net to identify anything the size of a paw-cat coming into this valley."

Tom pursed his lips, still looking around. "Not demon dogs or wild orries. Get your animals."

We turned as one, heading back across the meadow slowly, the grass harder to walk through than it had been to run through, the effort burning my thighs. I glanced at Joseph, who walked with his head down. "He's angry."

"I know," Joseph mumbled, and we kept going, sharing a shocked tired silence. As we neared the top, Joseph stopped for a moment, a puzzled look on his face. His hand slipped into his pocket and he brought out the data button. "I feel something. There's more here. More of these. Somewhere nearby." He flipped the button over and over in his bloodstained palm, a thoughtful look on his face. "We have to find whatever it is."

I sighed, wondering how much we'd regret the hunt. "Well, I suspect they won't let us go anywhere alone for a little while."

He smiled. "It was worth it."

"Maybe."

Stripes snorted at me, shaking her head. The look in her eyes seemed changed, as if she saw me as a predator, as if my hunting had changed something between us. Maybe that was my imagination, but she stood still, looking away from me as I pulled into the saddle.

We rode down, and shortly thereafter, Paloma, Kayleen, Alicia, and all five hebras started down the path. Paloma had dismounted and led Sugar Wheat, who favored her right fore-leg slightly as she slowly picked her way down the hill. Even back on level ground, Paloma continued to walk, and Kayleen and Alicia rode slowly alongside her, each leading one pack animal. As they neared us they looked away. I supposed they must have been getting quite a lecture on the way here.

Paloma reached Tom, a tired smile crossing her face, but not touching her eyes. She gestured toward Sugar Wheat. "We may be here a day or two while her foot heals."

Tom nodded curtly. Joseph and I looked at each other, and he fingered his pocket meaningfully. Perhaps we would have time to look for whatever he sensed.

One look into Tom's hard eyes drove us to work. He made us bleed and skin and dress the dead djuri, all the time watching our every move, speaking only to give direction. We took it, silent unless we had a question. It was hard, rough work. Once, Paloma came out and started to help, but Tom looked at her, frowning. "Go on," he said. "Go back and let them do this."

By the time we had stacks of meat and bones and hide separated into piles, my back and legs and hands felt sore and raw. The sun used the thunderheads for a palette, and the sky became a nearly black canvas behind the bright clouds. The rising wind blew cold against my sweaty face.

But we weren't done.

With no corral here and the storm coming, we strung a high-line between two low trees at the edge of the clearing, fifty meters from the cabin. We tied the animals to the high-line, hoping to provide them some shelter and still keep them from being targets for lightning. Then, Tom made us find our own firewood and light a large fire, burning the bones and hide. The fire stank so badly for the first hour that we huddled upwind, tending it, and the others stayed inside.

Afterward, we cooked djuri steaks on sticks stuck over the fire, our faces dancing light and shadow from the flames, our arms so tired we could barely hold the sticks. Tom watched us speculatively, a strange look in his eyes.

If I had to describe it, I would say curiosity, respect, and an emotion I'd never seen him direct to us before. Fear. It made me cringe.

13

STORMS AND TESTS

Thunder boomed directly over the cabin. My eyes flew open, meeting blackness. Even the coals in the woodstove had stopped glowing through the crack in the door. Blankets rustled. A lighter clicked and then dancing candlelight illuminated the single room we slept huddled together in. Next to me, Kayleen sat upright, looking around. "Wow, that was a big one." She rubbed at her eyes. Water sluiced down on the roof, sounding more like a river than mere rain. Somewhere near the back wall, water dripped onto the floor.

One of the hebras bugled outside, a high frightened noise.

Tom stumbled past me, stopped briefly at the door to pull on his boots, and called out, "Some help here. Something's out there." Then he was gone, the door ajar behind him, his stunner tucked into his belt.

Kayleen and I glanced at each other. I listened for alarms, but the wind and pounding rain would have obscured them anyway. I stood and pulled on my pants, then my boots. Kayleen scrambled up, too. Paloma mumbled, "What's happening?"

Kayleen looked up from retrieving one long boot from under her blankets. "Something's wrong, Mom. Tom just went out."

"I can see that," Paloma said, pointing toward the open door, the candlelight flickering on her face and hand. "What is it?"

I stood in the doorway, ready to go, bouncing with worry. "I don't know. Tom said something's out there."

Paloma pushed her blankets off. "He went out by himself?"

"We're going, too." Kayleen shoved her bare foot into her found boot.

Paloma stood up. "Okay. I'll rouse the others, we'll follow."

Alicia's eyes were wide open. Joseph still slept, his blanket pulled over his head. Kayleen and I rushed out the door, pushing it closed behind us.

A flash of lightning illuminated Tom's figure standing by a melee of frightened hebras. Thunder rolled overhead even before the lightning flash faded. Ink's right foot was tangled in her lead. Sugar Wheat, on the end, stood still, but Sand, next to her, pulled back, her eyes wide, trying to break free. Then the lightning passed, the moonless dark blinding me to all except dark on dark shifting forms. Kayleen and I ran toward the thrashing animals, following the sound of their hooves, their rushed and frightened breath, their nervous calls.

Another flash of light, and I saw Tom point toward the far end of the line. His words were hard to make out over the storm. "Separate the animals. Carefully. One each."

Kayleen bent over one of the pack hebras' tangled lead lines, trying to work it free. It seemed to take forever. I stepped up and pulled the high-line taut to help her. She flashed me a brief grin, finished, and handed me the lead. I stepped back, pulling the hebra with me, dodging its stamping feet, bracing against its bulk as it sidled nervously sideways into me.

Something screamed to my right. A hunter. Paw-cat? Not demon dog. No time to think. It must be a paw-cat. My heart pounded. Kayleen freed the second pack animal just as Joseph, Paloma, and Alicia ran up to us. I thrust the end of the line in my hand to Paloma, felt her fingers close around it, and plunged back toward the animals. Another bolt of lightning seared my vision. Tom yelled, "Joseph— here. To me."

Joseph ran, and Tom stepped back, pulling his stunner out, holding it pointed at the ground, looking around. He yelled at Joseph, "Grab Sand!" Joseph turned and obeyed, pulling the frightened animal from the line. Sand reared up, her head back, her mouth open in a scream. Joseph dodged her feet, tugged hard on her lead, and she came down, standing and trembling, nostrils blowing.

"Let the pack hebras loose," Tom yelled. Paloma, close to me, reached in to unclip the lead from the animal she held. It head-butted her, and she went down, sideways, her foot at the wrong angle. A small shriek of pain escaped her lips. She pulled herself back up, using the lead.

My hands were still free. I ran to the beast and reached for the bottom of its face harness. It reared, almost jerking me from my feet, but I yanked down, unclipped the lead, and fell. I rolled, dodging the hebra's frantic hooves, dark dangerous hammers against a dark sky. As soon as it was free it stopped and stood looking down at me, feet planted, eyes wild. Paloma used the lead as a whip, and it turned and ran.

"Why?" I yelled at her as we turned back toward the line.

"So it can protect itself," she spat through clenched teeth, and then fell again, holding her ankle.

I reached down to help her. She waved me away, her face twisted with pain. "Loose the other animals."

Tom appeared by her side, his hair and face wild and wet. "Go!" he urged me. "Let the other pack animal go. Try to keep the riding beasts, get them near the cabin."

I turned back to the others. Alicia held both Ink and Sand with difficulty, Ink staying near her while Sand did her best to pull away. Sugar Wheat was loose, but she stood her ground, watching.

Sugar Wheat was the key; the closest thing to a herd leader they had. "Joseph!" I held out my hand for Legs's lead. "Get Sugar Wheat. Lead her toward the cabin."

He tossed me the lead, then ran toward Sugar Wheat, grabbing her head harness, while I struggled, like Alicia, to hold on to two unhappy hebras. A wild hunter's scream came from between us and the cabin. Sugar Wheat pulled free, bounding from sight in an instant. Lightning flashed.

Tom stood straddling Paloma. He turned, braced, and fired his stunner. A paw-cat yelped, then faded into the grass, running away.

Legs jerked me around, and I turned, looking for Joseph in the darkness. I couldn't see him or Sugar Wheat. My heart raced. There would be more paw-cats. I struggled with the soaked and frightened hebras, trying to pull them toward the cabin. They resisted. Mud and wet grass pulled at my feet.

Rain and dark folded Tom away from my sight, but he must have continued shooting. Another paw-cat screamed in pain.

Stripes jerked free and ran, trailing the lead line dangerously. She disappeared in the darkness and driving rain. I whispered a small prayer for her safety, all I had time for since Legs showed every sign of wanting to follow Stripes.

Sugar Wheat pounded toward us, Joseph astride, struggling to use the lead line for control. It would never have worked on Legs or Stripes, but Sugar Wheat obeyed.

How did he get up on her without a saddle or mounting rope? No time to ask.

Joseph succeeded in pulling the tall beast to a stop. She twisted her neck around and bugled, a high long noise that raised the hair on the back of my neck. Legs stopped fighting me and looked toward Sugar Wheat, trembling but still. Sugar Wheat repeated the strange call, and all of the frightened animals stilled and looked at her.

A voice spoke from the darkness. Jenna. "Now, lead them back to the cabin. I'll make sure everything is all right out here."

Tom blinked, looking from Joseph astride the blowing hebra to the spot of darkness that had spoken to him. Jenna was completely invisible, at least to me.

Tom looked from his stunner to Paloma, then shoved the stunner in the back of his pants and bent down and gathered Paloma into his arms, cradling her close to him. He headed for the cabin. Sugar Wheat and Joseph followed, the hebra limping slightly. Behind them, the rest of us strung out in a line, threading through damp grass and puddles up to our ankles. I talked to Legs to calm him, to keep him on track. A flash of forked lightning seemed to rise from the meadow itself, and as thunder crashed about us I almost lost Legs as he jerked back, but Sugar Wheat repeated her call. Legs let me gather him back into line, dancing and snorting.

When we reached the cabin, Tom carried Paloma inside. The rest of us stayed out shivering in the rain and lightning, holding the animals, speaking soothing words.

I kept looking out into the darkness, hoping to spot Stripes or Jenna, but there was no sign of either, not even when lightning turned the whole clearing to daylight for seconds at a time. I listened for more paw-cats, but the only sounds I could distinguish except for the storm were ours.

After a long time, the thunder and lightning spun over the ridge of the crater rim, and the rain slowed from a sluicing torrent to a steady soaking dampness. Tom came out and built a makeshift high-line close to the cabin.

"What about the pack hebras?" Kayleen asked. "And Stripes?"

Tom sighed, his voice edged with worry and exhaustion. "We'll look for them in the morning. In the meantime, your mom sprained her ankle pretty badly. It's not broken, but it hurts. She could use your company." He watched us all as we trooped toward the door. "Good job. Thank you."

Inside, Kayleen nestled next to Paloma, holding her hand. Paloma's foot was propped up on two blankets rolled together. Her ankle looked twice its normal size. She stayed very still, head near Kayleen, her face white with pain.

I settled in a dry corner, still shivering. Every muscle hurt. I turned toward the wall and stripped off my soaked shirt, trading it for my last clean dry shirt. The hunt, the skinning and the fire, and then the crazy rain-sodden fight with the hebras had altogether become too much. My eyes hung half-open as Tom lit a fire and started water. He brought the first cup of tea to Paloma, helping her sit up a little, stopping to gently brush his fingertips over her swollen ankle. A tender look passed between them, and then Paloma dipped her head, drinking her tea.

Tom squatted near me, looking in my eyes. "How are you doing, Chelo?"

I reached for the tea, sipping it, feeling its incredible warmth in my cold belly. "Not so good. Stripes is gone."

"I know." He shook his head. "We'll find her tomorrow."

I swallowed another sip of tea, struggling to hold Tom's eyes with my own. "Did . . . did that happen because we hunted yesterday?"

Tom remained still, balanced in a squat, one hand on the floor, gazing at me. His eyes were warm, devoid of the fear I'd spotted earlier by the fire. He stayed silent for so long I grew sure he blamed us, but he said, "No. It was no one's fault. I taught Joseph to hunt." He paused. "More accurately, I gave him permission to teach himself, and he taught you. We took good care of the carcasses. It's more likely the paw-cats were drawn to the hebras." He smiled. "Dinner on a string. We set it right up for them. We'll post watches tomorrow night, two people each." He pushed himself up, looking slightly wobbly himself, and went to pour another cup of tea.

I never found out who got the third cup of tea. I fell fast asleep sitting up, in spite of Stripes, of Jenna, in spite of myself.

When I next opened my eyes, it was because the smell of frying djuri steak had worked its way into my dreams. Someone had stretched me out and covered me with two blankets. I pushed them off and sat up. Tom lay next to me, snoring softly, his round face slack. I watched him a moment, recalling his kind words from just before I passed out. His dark graying hair was mussed and he had one arm flung up over his head, one splayed out to the side. There were tiny lines I'd never really noticed around his eyes.

Kayleen stood over the stove, turning thin strips of back-strap meat carefully, her focus completely on the task at hand. She too looked wrung out; her hair was tangled and she moved slowly and deliberately. Paloma lay where I'd last seen her, her ankle propped up. Someone had bandaged it in the night. Her eyes were closed but her body looked too tense to be asleep. Alicia and Joseph were nowhere to be seen. I listened, and finally heard voices outside near where we'd tied up the hebras.

I stumbled to the outhouse. Afterward, I glanced toward Joseph and Alicia. They stood close, heads bent together. Joseph said something that made Alicia laugh softly. I decided not to interrupt, and instead bent down to the stream and splashed cold running water on my face, then scrubbed my hands and feet in the bracing water.

I looked toward the hebras, counting five. So Stripes hadn't come home in the night. At least it would be a good day to look for her.

Small silver fish darted under my splashing feet. The weather had changed again; sunshine warmed my shoulders. The sun had fully risen, the jarring light of full day filled the now-peaceful meadow. Destiny hung pale in the sky, near the sun. Cloudless bright blue sky hung over the dark blue lake.

I went in to help Kayleen with breakfast. Joseph and Alicia had come back inside, and Joseph was shaking Tom gently. "Do you want to get up for breakfast?"

Tom grunted and shook his head and Joseph stopped, looking down at him quizzically. Paloma spoke up from her nest of blankets. "Leave him be. He was up all night, checking on the hebras and listening for . . . for anything."

We ate in near silence, too tired for conversation. As we were finishing breakfast, Alicia asked, "Where does Jenna stay?" She looked thoughtfully at her nearly empty plate. "She could have come in and had breakfast. I've never seen her, not up close."

I finished the last bite of my meat. "I've never seen her inside anywhere."

The door swung open. Jenna might as well have heard us talking. She stood in the doorway, wearing the same forest-colored clothing we'd seen her in two days ago, dry and clean. A small smile touched her twisted face.

Alicia babbled. "Would . . . thanks for helping us last night . . . would you like breakfast?"

Jenna smiled. "My pleasure." She ducked just inside the doorway, running her gaze across the room. She seemed happy enough with what she saw. She stayed.

"You can come in," Kayleen suggested.

"I like it here." Jenna's strangely folded face wrinkled even more as she looked at Paloma. "How is your ankle?"

Paloma gazed back at her, apparently nonplussed to see her there. "I bet I can ride, but I can't walk."

"Your lead hebra is lamer than yesterday. Better if neither of you walk or ride for a few days."

Paloma grimaced, but didn't argue. "Thank you for helping us last night. What can we do for you?"

"I came to take Chelo and Joseph to search for your missing beasts."

Joseph looked hopeful. Tom stirred, pushing himself up to a sitting position, blinking at Jenna in amazement. "I thought you were a dream."

She looked down at him, a small smile touching her lips. "No. But we should not waste more time. We'll go find the hebras."

Tom stretched and yawned. He moved slowly. Now that they were open, his eyes looked bloodshot with exhaustion. "Mmmmm. I'll go," he mumbled. "Give me a moment."

Jenna met his gaze steadily. She gestured toward Paloma. "There should be a capable adult here. I will take Chelo and Joseph and we will find the animals. It only needs three of us."

Tom drew his brows together, as if the thought of us going off together just wasn't all right. He yawned again, apparently so exhausted that even Jenna's surprising presence wasn't enough to shock him fully awake.

Alicia's eyes shone up at Jenna, curious and intense. "I want to go, too."

Jenna kept her eye on Tom, forcing a decision with the intensity of her gaze. It felt like having a wild predator in the room, a force of nature bending all of us to her will.

Paloma broke the tension, her voice husky and laced with pain. "Let them go. Jenna will not let any harm come to them, and you are in no shape for that job. Besides, I'd like you here."

Tom smiled at her. "I'm outnumbered." He glanced at Jenna. "Take Alicia, too. She's a roamer, she'll know the trails." He glanced from me to Jenna and back. "Come back at least an hour before dark? Whether you find them or not. Will you take hebras?"

Jenna shook her head. "We do not need riding beasts. Besides, it would make it harder to bring the others back." She smiled. "And yes, I am hungry."

While we packed water and a light lunch, I watched Jenna sit cross-legged on the floor, as if she were a normal person, a family member, eating fried djuri I had caught with my bare hands and exclaiming politely about the quality of the cooking. I bit down on my tongue, checking to be sure I felt pain, to be sure I was awake. Sure enough, it hurt.

"Take two earsets," Tom suggested, rummaging in his coat pocket and handing me two of the small devices.

I stuck one over my ear, handed the other to Joseph.

Kayleen looked worried. She hadn't asked to go with us. Perhaps she didn't want to leave Paloma. "Check in, okay? I'll wear an earset, too, so I can be your contact."

I liked that idea. It would be nice if our main contact was one of us. Kayleen understood things Tom and Paloma didn't. Couldn't.

While I was rummaging through my pack, I noticed my paper and pens. I hadn't had time for them, but maybe Paloma would like to use them—she often drew plants and flowers and herbs she found. I handed them to her, stopping only long enough to acknowledge her startled smile.

Jenna stood in the doorway, frowning, as we gathered our final goods, said our good-byes. At last, we stood by her in the doorway, ready. She frowned down at us, then reached for our bags. She stripped out everything but the water and the earsets, leaving a small pile of goat jerky, apples, and even a shirt by the door. I looked at Joseph and giggled nervously. "I guess we travel light."

Jenna glared at me, and saying nothing more, she went out the door and took off, loping quickly across the meadow. We tumbled outside, finding our feet, running bunched together, trailing far behind her. We never set off the exit bells. Did the storm or the plunging animals destroy them, or did Jenna just know how to magically avoid our nets?

By the time we reached the end of the meadow she had

become invisible again. We stopped and stood in a knot, staring at each other, blowing, our breath coming in gasps. Alicia caught her breath first, and called out, "Jenna?"

There was no answer.

Alicia's cheeks were red from exertion, and she flexed her fingers and danced a little, ready to keep moving. I suspected this was just the beginning of a long day, and laughed. "We'll have to find her. She doesn't teach with words, not often."

Alicia blinked, absorbing the information. Then she adjusted. "So what do we look for? Tracks?" She gazed at the muddy ground. "Should be easy enough, here."

Our tracks showed clearly in the mud. I was sure this was where Jenna had left the meadow. I'd marked it by the redberry bushes that stuck out farther into the meadow here than anywhere else nearby. But Jenna's tracks were invisible, as if she ran on air.

I leaned down to look at the grass, trying to spot broken stems.

Joseph said, "You won't see anything. Think your way through this. I saw her leave through here. And you agree, right? That's why you stopped?"

I nodded.

"So, we're tracking hebras. Looking for signs of them. So she wants to find high ground. She'd go up." He pointed to a gravelly wash with a thin stream through it. "That goes up, and it's easier than pushing through underbrush. There's no regular trail here."

We followed him up. Around the first bend, Jenna sat idly on a rock, a patient look on her face. She smiled. "Good. That did not take too long. But don't bother looking for the hebras."

Were they dead? Or had they run home? I pictured Nava's face if three riderless hebras showed up in Artistos. "Why not?"

"Because there is something else I need to show you."

I didn't need her to add that this was a unique opportunity. We were away from all the adults in Artistos, on our own. Outside the data nets. I remembered Jinks, though. "Can we try and find Stripes, too?"

"Later." She turned and bounded easily up the damp streambed, her steps sure and silent. We followed, almost as sure but not nearly as silent. She lost us again quickly, but we kept going. She wouldn't let us stray far. Whatever she wanted us to see was important to her. I thought of Joseph's words yesterday, and turned to him. "Do you feel . . . what you felt yesterday? From the data button?"

He nodded. "Stronger."

Perhaps she wasn't making us find the thread ourselves. After last night, maybe she thought we'd never make it.

I shook my head to clear it, trying to focus on the wild rush up the hill the way I had focused on the djuri. Right hand reaching for a jagged gray rock, pulling up, left foot swinging wide to find purchase on a little dark shelf of volcanic rock, slipping, grabbing, finding a big flat stable rock, squatting and jumping, almost sliding off the next target, my hand splashing in cool shallow water, birds twittering overhead, the scent of wild mountain-fern . . . How did Jenna make it up here so fast with one arm?

By the time we found her again my palms were raw, I'd bumped one knee, and the long muscles in my thighs quivered.

She laughed at us as we clawed our way up a short sharp cliff to her. Our perch was near the top of the crater rim. We could see all the way across Little Lace Lake and farther, past the mountains on the other side. Alicia pointed out the rising dark clouds that marked the volcano, Rage, on the far southern tip of the continent, belching steam and fire.

Alicia and Joseph looked as ragged as I felt. Jenna didn't sport a single scratch.

She didn't say a thing, just watched us gulp water. She pointed, and we followed her finger to a tall pongaberry tree.

But Kayleen wasn't with us.

We must have looked confused. Jenna sighed and took off her shirt, handing it to me. I wondered what Joseph thought about her tanned breasts. The one by her missing arm drooped slightly. We didn't get a long look. She jumped up and ran for the tree, hopping easily from one boulder to another, down to the ground, and making another jump. Her balance was perfect. The muscles in her back stood out, the ones on her right side, the one with the arm, at least twice as thick and ropy as the others. She appeared to have no fat on her long body at all.

She *walked* up the pongaberry tree, almost in line with its slender trunk. Her feet seemed to find easy purchase on the rough bark, and her arm shimmied up the tree with easy, if jerky, motion. I held my breath, afraid she'd fall and yet sure she wouldn't. The first half of the tall tree had no branches, no leaves, and once past that point, Jenna moved even easier, using the thin swirling branches as footholds and a hand-hold. A fat bunch of berries nestled near the trunk a meter above her head, well over thirty meters above the ground. She stood on two branches on tiptoe, and reached for the stem where the berries attached to a branch, the stem fully as thick as the branch they attached to. She jerked and freed the plump berries. Two purple berries fell down through the leaves and then the open air, into the brush below. Jenna clamped the berry stem between her teeth and descended as easily as she'd climbed up.

She returned, handing around the berries, and simply said, "It would be good for you to practice your physical strengths." She only had one scratch. Every time Kayleen harvested pongaberries she looked like the spiky leaves had used her for target practice.

Alicia glanced at me and grinned. We did practice, but clearly not nearly enough.

Jenna pulled her shirt back on with no further comment. She must have dressed again for us, for our Artistan up-bringing. Certainly, I'd never gone shirtless.

The berries were sweet and warm from the sun. As I ate my share, energy filled my body. The others looked better as well. The rest helped us as well as the berries; all of us had stopped gasping for air and the red flush had fallen away from Alicia's and Joseph's faces.

The next part of our journey took us along a faint trail over the top of the rim, away from the lake. We stopped briefly at the crest. Blue sea lined the horizon. Far to our right, the edge of the Grass Plains showed yellow-green. Everything else fell away in forested hills, marching north and north and north. The sun was almost directly overhead. Wherever we were going, we wouldn't have much time there before we had to turn back.

We wound down a faint path, Jenna periodically pointing out markers: a rare single twintree trunk, a rock shaped like a bird, a deadfall near-elm with three tall live trees growing in it, including a round baby tent tree.

Jenna stopped on a long, flat rock with a great clear view on nearly all sides. She stood still for a long time, looking outward, apparently lost in thought. She turned back around and swept her gaze over us all, letting it linger for the longest on Alicia. Then she touched my earset. "Call home. Tell them we haven't found the hebras yet. And don't say how far we've come."

I tapped the set to activate it. "Kayleen?"

Her voice was excited. "Did you find them? Did you keep up with Jenna? Did she tell you anything interesting? Are you on your way back?"

"Not yet." Then I added inventively, "But we're following tracks. How's Paloma?"

"She still can't walk. She has a fever, but Tom says it will pass, that it's just because of the swelling. Paloma had some of her salve in her bag, and Tom rubbed it on her ankle to kill her pain."

Silence for a moment. Then Kayleen's voice again. "Tom says to be sure you get back before dark. Well before dark."

"Okay, we'll try." I hung up quickly, suddenly guilty.

Jenna nodded at me and then told Joseph, "Tell me what you feel. Tell me which direction we should go."

Joseph sat and closed his eyes. "I . . . I can feel it. It's all around, though."

"What direction?"

He shrugged. "I can't tell."

Jenna frowned. "Chelo, sit next to him. Support his back."

I obeyed. Joseph leaned into me, smelling of sweat and mountain-fern and pongaberries. I braced one hand on the warm solid rock under me and put the other on Joseph's shoulder. He sat still for a long moment, the space of ten heartbeats, and then he opened his eyes, a surprised look on his face. "Down," he said. "Under me."

Jenna nodded approvingly and walked to the end of the long warm stone, turned, and hanging from her one arm, dropped from view. I crawled to the end of the rock and looked down. Jenna stood on another flat rock below her, a rock so flat it looked metal. I frowned and looked at the rock we sat on. It was rough, natural. But the one below was not. Joseph and Alicia both bent over next to me. Alicia made a soft amazed sound, and twisted around, dropping easily to stand next to Jenna. Whatever she saw there, her eyes grew wide and her mouth dropped open.

Joseph and I scrambled after them.

THE CAVE

We dropped from the rough exposed rock to land, bent-kneed and noisy, on the smooth surface beside Jenna and Alicia. We straightened to look into the dark mouth of a cave at least as big as the science guild hall. The floor was cut flat, the walls a mix of smooth surfaces and natural rock. The ceiling was smooth as the floor, and dry. Doors faded in the darkness, set into the smooth walls. At least two wide corridors branched away. The air smelled clear, vaguely dusty, but not damp or chemical or mossy like the caves I'd been in before. This smelled . . . controlled.

Jenna turned and pointed outward. Trees and jumbled rocks

would hide this opening from even direct sunshine within an hour or two. Thirty meters downslope, it would be nearly invisible. Jenna's voice was firm and careful as she swept her hand in front of her, encompassing the land on all sides of the entrance. "Even if you can find this place from out there, do not come in this way. Only use the way I showed you." She pointed up to the rock we'd dropped from. I looked up. How do we get out, then? It was too far to jump.

"Climb." She showed us clever footholds in the rock near the edge of the cave mouth. She demonstrated. It required one awkward jump and much strength; Jenna's arm quivered at how she had to torque to hold her weight nearly upside down at one point. She landed back beside us and said, "See? Normal humans cannot do that."

No, it would take our strength. Kayleen's nearly prehensile feet would come in handy. It could be done with a backpack, but not with very much weight. But two people could haul stuff out; one on top, where we jumped from, and one below. And of course, Tom or anyone could get in and out with rope.

"Why not come from the other way?" Joseph looked dubious about the exit technique Jenna had just shown us. "It looks easier."

Jenna spoke matter-of-factly. "You would die. There are traps."

I drew in a sharp breath. The trees and rocks outside looked completely natural, safe. Thick redberry bushes and tall thorn sage bunched together, blocking easy access. Behind them, near-elm. No tent trees. Perhaps they'd been cleared? Tent trees were great to hide in, and with the cave here, they could hide enemies. "What kind of traps? Where are they?"

This time she looked at me. "You can earn that knowledge. Just don't come up from there, don't betray my trust bringing you here."

So she trusted us enough to show us this place, but not enough to share all of its secrets.

Joseph squinted into the cleared sunny area between us

and the brush, probably also scanning for the elusive traps. "Jenna, why did you tell us to look for the cave if it's booby-trapped?"

"I turned the systems off after we talked. Then I changed my mind."

"Did something happen?" Alicia asked. "Or is it because we weren't finding it on our own?"

Jenna frowned, as if Alicia's questions interrupted her train of thought. "Circumstances gave me this unexpected chance." She shrugged, but excitement flashed from her one eye. "I do not have time to wait forever for you to learn all you need to know, or for Joseph to fix the data nets." Then she smiled. "Besides, you were busy absorbing other lessons."

So she had seen our hunt. She gazed far out into the distance, apparently lost in thought. A trick of light highlighted spiderwebs of weathered wrinkles around her one good eye and the corners of her mouth. The place where her other eye had been was a sunken scar, red and angry around the edges. Her gray hair hung in a long twist down her back, the ends uneven and straggly. She lived a harder life than the rest of us, and after Nava's story, I was curious about Jenna's as well. What pain drove her?

She licked her lips. "There is much in this cave which it would be best if no one sees."

So show *us*, I urged her silently. But she remained in the cave's mouth, still looking out. Alicia asked, "Are there other places we shouldn't go? Other traps?"

She turned to face us. "Not nearby."

I fidgeted, wanting to be inside the cave, to see what was so carefully hidden. "Can we come back here?"

She grinned at me. "Answer that yourself."

I pursed my lips, thinking, then grinned back. "Sure. You wouldn't have been so careful to show us how to get in and out if it we couldn't come back."

Her smile faded. "Best if I am with you. There is much in here you would not understand, and some you could do harm with." She licked her lips. "Harm to yourselves or others." Her eyes flicked toward the sun, already past midday. "Today, you will only see a very little bit of the parts of your heritage that are here."

"Is this where you got the pipe and the data button?"

"I've gathered nearly everything of ours, and put it in here. There is another, smaller cache that Akashi knows about. But even Akashi has not seen this." Jenna turned around and walked into the cave, the three of us following like baby chicks, until we were surrounded by stone and weak light.

The cave felt full of new knowledge, knowledge of ourselves. Our parents. Surely they, or at least the *altered,* had lived here, based from here, fought from here. I wished Bryan and Liam could see this. Kayleen. I wished we were all together.

Jenna prompted, "Okay, Joseph, now where?"

He blinked and scanned the cave. At least three tunnels led in different directions. Small alcoves hid in shadows. "I don't know."

Jenna sighed exaggeratedly. "What did you just learn?"

I stepped over to him, folding him in my arms. He leaned into me, smelling of sweat and pongaberries, letting me take his weight. His eyes closed. I braced myself to balance him. He was so heavy my leg shook and I wished we'd thought to sit down, like on the rock above the cave.

It seemed like a long time before he straightened and walked toward a wide shadowed doorway in the left back corner. The rest of us followed.

Alicia whispered to me, "What do you do to help him?"

I shook my head. "I don't know. I guess I've always helped him."

"Could I help him?"

Jenna answered, "Not as much as Chelo. She and he are one blood; brother and sister. Even though Chelo is deaf to the nets, her physical closeness soothes Joseph. It has to do with Chelo's own genemods."

My breath caught in my throat. "And what are they? What am I?"

Would she avoid the question, change the topic like she did with me so often? But she licked her lips and answered,

"A caretaker, a planner. An influencer. That is your special gift."

"Will I be as strong as you?"

"If you develop your body. But it's more important to develop your instincts. Separate your goals from the goals others have given you. Almost anything you want, you will be able to make happen. By suggesting, by making choices about how and when to offer what information, and to whom. Joseph can thread data, but you can thread life, thread politics. But you must learn who you are first, decide what you want. Because, you see, you will often get what you want." It was a very long speech for her, and after that she fell silent.

Joseph had stopped by the doorway, listening. "I always do better when Chelo is around."

Alicia looked long-faced. "Does that mean I can't help him the same way?"

"You, Alicia, are a risk-taker. Perhaps there will be a time when that is exactly what he needs most." Jenna turned to Joseph. "Here, you'll need light." She handed him a shiny silver canister, wide as my wrist, half as long as my forearm. I had not seen her carrying it, or seen her pick it up.

Joseph turned the cylinder over and over in his hands.

Jenna laughed. "Figure it out."

Joseph ran his fingers along the smooth surface. It reminded me of both the skin and the mystery of the *New Making*. He drew his brows together and twisted his mouth up. He carefully placed both palms, one on either side, flat against the lower portion of the cylinder. Light bloomed from the top, startling Joseph so much he nearly dropped the cylinder.

"How did you know to try that?" I asked.

He shook his head. "It felt . . . warmer there. But I don't know if that was physical, or something else. This new—energy field—feels different from the Artistos data."

And suddenly I started giggling, picturing us so serious, so intent, so . . . like children with new toys. "It's . . . it's just a flashlight . . . a flashlight."

He clutched it to himself, looking at me strangely. He

clearly didn't quite get my change of perspective. Neither did Alicia. Their solemn confused faces only made me laugh harder. Artistos had flashlights. They turned on differently. They weren't as bright. But they were small enough to fit in pockets or slip on belts. Perhaps we were not so high-and-mighty-different as I'd wanted to believe, not in some ways.

Jenna watched me, her eye flashing approval of my laughter. She did not laugh herself, though.

As my giggles died down I reached for the flashlight, wanting to try it myself, see if this was yet another thing only Joseph could do.

Joseph shook his head and kept it. I might have argued, but the cave was far more interesting than the flashlight.

Joseph shone the light in the doorway, and then followed the bright circle inside, turning to light our steps as well. A short hallway, maybe three meters long. The light played across smooth walls, all clearly tool-cut. The hallway widened into a square chamber. The flashlight's beam bobbed around the room. Rows of stone shelves lined one wall. The other three walls were flat and featureless. Joseph flicked the light back at the shelves, running it slowly along each shelf. The light stopped and hovered, illuminating five data buttons in a pile on the bottom shelf. The symbols on the surface of each button looked different. Next to them stretched a leather strap, nearly a meter long. Colorful threads wove a diamond pattern into the leather.

There was nothing else of interest in the room. Clearly, Jenna had set us up to find only these things. I watched her. She watched Joseph closely, almost hungrily, like a new mother watching a baby take its first steps.

Joseph's hand was immediately drawn to the strap. He picked it up, holding it. "Reading threads."

Jenna smiled, a bright twisted smile of approval. "Good."

He ran his hands along the length of the leather. It wasn't new, but it was still supple. "But how do I use it?"

"Tie it . . . tie it around your head."

He handed the light to Alicia and complied. The ends of

the straps hung down, light against his dark hair, falling nearly to his shoulders.

Alicia watched the whole process closely, leaning in, careful how she handled the light. She reached a slender white hand to touch the headband. "How does it work?"

"The threads woven into the leather read wireless data from the buttons, and connecting with his temples and scalp, they build a direct bridge to Joseph's circulatory system, and to the nanocytes in his blood. His body was enhanced, using genetics, to accept the nanocytes as part of him."

"Nanocytes?"

"Tiny machines. Even if you spill his blood and look at it with a common microscope, you will not see them. But they will allow Joseph to read and relate to many threads of data at once. More than he has ever managed. But first, he'll need to learn how."

"So Kayleen has the same things in her blood, only fewer of them?" I asked.

Jenna shrugged. "She probably has as many. But she seems less naturally attuned to them. Back home, we could fix that with a single session. Here, she will have to learn herself. You might try working with Kayleen the same way you work with Joseph and see if it helps."

"But I don't have these nanocytes? And Alicia doesn't have them?"

"Neither do I," Jenna replied. She turned her attention back to Joseph. "You can actually wear that anywhere—but on your head it will look like a decoration, and draw less comment. If you choose, you may wear it somewhere else, like under clothing. It must touch skin." She reached over and adjusted the position of the band on his head, so slightly I couldn't tell the difference. Perhaps she just wanted to touch it. "Our wind readers sewed the threads into clothing. Pants legs, shirtsleeves, helmets, even socks."

I glanced at the workmanship. Jenna hadn't made it, not with one hand. "Where did this come from?"

Jenna looked at Joseph rather than me. "It was your father's. David Lee's."

I had remembered the David, but not the Lee. I repeated it in my head. David Lee. David Lee.

Joseph closed his eyes and put his fingertips on the band. We had nothing of theirs. I had regretted that a thousand times, wished for even a small memento. Jenna's words had clearly affected Joseph as deeply as they had me; I thought for a moment he would cry. But instead, he straightened and gazed evenly at Jenna. "How do I make it work?"

Jenna looked away. "I cannot use one. This is the most sophisticated remote communication we had here, the closest thing to being truly net connected, as if we were in civilized space. Whatever physical technique allows you to read the Fremont data nets, you will want to do something similar to read the buttons. David was the best of us, and he once described it for me as 'slipping sideways to the data wind.' Perhaps that will help you."

Joseph blinked. "I . . . I don't feel anything."

Jenna picked up a data button and handed it to him. As his hand closed around it, his eyes widened. Fear flicked across them.

"Relax," Jenna said.

I stepped to his side. "Here, sit with me."

He and I curled on the hard stone floor, Joseph's head against my shoulder, my arm flung over his chest. His heart beat fast against my palm.

He was silent a long time. When he spoke, his voice was full of wonder. "How do I show the others what I see?"

Jenna frowned and cocked her head. "Do you understand any of it?"

He shook his head. "It's a jumble of images. I can see those. Some of them. Things I've never seen before. And words I can't understand. But maybe if I can show it to Chelo and Alicia and Kayleen, they can help me figure it out."

"There are tools for that. But they are not so . . . easy to conceal." Jenna pursed her lips, as if trying to make a decision.

"Are they here?" Alicia asked. "Can we see? What's on the data buttons, anyway?"

Jenna stood and mumbled, low, as if to herself, "I set this

up here in case you needed it. I guess you do." She reached up to the top shelf and pulled a small silver square from the back.

She kept the square in her hands, held close, as if it were an eggshell. It was about twice the size of a data button, still small enough for Jenna to conceal by closing her fist. "This is a sacred trust. I've only found two more that work on Fremont. Artistos's leaders will recognize this if they see it, and take it from you." She fixed her eyes on me. "Do you understand?"

I nodded.

She was not done. "You cannot use this near any of the self-styled original humans. Not even Tom and Paloma." She glanced at Alicia. "Not your friends, not any of them. Not in town. Only away." Then she seemed to come to an answer. "I will take it back from you before you return to Artistos. That is best. But you can conceal it around Tom and Paloma, and I do not know when you will have such freedom again."

So she understood the gist of the discussions going on back in Fremont. Perhaps that was what drove her to finally reveal so much to us openly.

Jenna handed the square to me. It was surprisingly light, and decorated like the data buttons with smooth symbols I didn't recognize.

Jenna placed her palm over the top of the box in my hand, twisted, and it opened. She dropped a data button into it and closed the lid. A rectangle of light blossomed a meter from me.

I frowned. "It's a data projector. We have those in Artistos."

"You do not have any like these. The ones the crippled humans use in Fremont do not read our data."

Of course.

Jenna watched me closely, then said, "Be careful about assuming you understand our technology because you understand what Artistos has. Some of it is very different."

Jenna showed us how to start and stop the stream of data and pictures, using specific pressure points. When I turned on the projector, images of spaceships like *New Making,* and bigger than *New Making,* moved across the face of a planet. "Where is that?" I asked.

"That's Silver's Home. We came from there."

My eyes were glued to the pictures. The planet had much more land than Fremont. Large seas, or maybe large lakes, dotted it. Both poles were almost all ice, and a wide river, almost a sea, fractured the two continents directly centered in the moving picture. Jenna was the only person on Fremont born somewhere else. I had never thought of it before. "Were you born there?"

She reached over and stopped the playback. "There's no time for much more talk today." She glanced at Joseph. "The headband transmits all of the data on a button, or even multiple buttons, directly into you. You will be able to cross-reference and search and use this up to the limit of your capabilities. It is the same tool you use for the Fremont data nets, but on our frequency. By definition, none of Artistos's people have any ability to use data thread, and I doubt they even know what they are. As far as I know, you can keep it, wear it. It can be a gift from me. Tom and Paloma, at least, will accept that."

Joseph fingered the headband, then took it off. "I . . . can't wear it now. It's too confusing. I'll work with it."

Jenna smiled at him. "Your ability to work the nets should return as you learn to use that. In fact, it may grow stronger, as if you are exercising muscles you've seldom used." She reached her hand down to help Joseph stand, and looked directly at him, her single eye boring into his rapt, focused gaze. "Fear will stop you. The knowledge you stand to gain, or for that matter, the help you can give Artistos, is something to value, to learn from."

He nodded, silent for a moment. "But . . . but how do I stop the fear?"

"Trust yourself. Trust who you will become."

His gaze slid uncertainly away from hers, and he mumbled, "I'll try."

"Don't try," she said. "Simply do it. Use Chelo to help you . . . she makes you stronger."

Alicia moved the light stick toward the short hallway, and we stepped out into the larger cave, blinking at the light.

Jenna glanced at the box in my hand. "That can only play a single thread at a time; it is not even as powerful as Joseph is now. It will make some information accessible to you directly, but in a very linear fashion. It was designed for young children. You should have had it when you were six or seven. If it falls into the wrong hands, that same data—much of which has been concealed from the people here—will be available to them. They will never be able to use Joseph's data thread, they are not made for it. It is conceivable they could figure out the button box."

I swallowed. "I will protect it."

"Only you. Do not leave it, ever. Even with your brethren."

Alicia crossed her arms over her chest. "So I can't use it alone? Chelo has to be with me?"

"Yes. Chelo is the keeper."

I was briefly taken aback by the charge, and felt the responsibility she laid on me like a geas. Was it because we were the same, had the same genemods? Or because I was the oldest? This wouldn't help my relationship with Alicia. I looked Jenna in the eye. "All right. Tell me when you want it back."

"What data have you given us?" Alicia asked.

Jenna stood and started for the door of the alcove. "Children's data, on the first button I gave Joseph. History and culture on another. I know a few are training programs for the colonists. Navigation and maintenance and health and how to land on a planet and live there. That's all I could find. Consider it the education you were denied. Now, we should go."

Alicia narrowed her eyes. "Why go back?" She looked from me to Joseph. "You two can hunt. I'm sure I can, too. We have data now, we can learn." Her gaze slid to Jenna's. "Why can't we live with you, free?"

Jenna threw back her head and laughed, and didn't answer Alicia except to cock her eyebrow at me.

There were many reasons not to live alone. The most important ones were all people. "Kayleen. Bryan is back in Artistos. Liam is with Akashi. I couldn't abandon them."

"Well, me, then." She sounded wistful. "I could live free. I don't want to go back. I don't even know where I'm staying, who I'm staying with." Her gaze was still on Jenna, her eyes full of longing. "Please? Can I live with you?"

Jenna met Alicia's eyes, offering a hard look in exchange for Alicia's longing. "There is little freedom in my life, Alicia." She gazed out of the cave, seeming to see something different than the brush and trees and rocks that were actually there. "I am trying to gain more freedom than you can imagine. Perhaps I will be able to share it." She shook herself, as if leaving some painful memory behind. "In the meantime, you all have at least some measure of safety down there." She gestured toward Artistos. "In my life, there are many dawns I am surprised to see at all. It is no life for you."

Alicia frowned. "But my life is no good, either. They laugh at me, they hate me. They locked me up."

I stepped close to Alicia, putting one hand on her shoulder. "It will be better for you now. I promise." I had no idea how I would keep the promise, but I meant it.

She looked away, her eyes full of tears. I didn't know her well enough to tell if they were tears of anger or tears of sadness. I let her turn away to stand at the edge of the cave, her shoulders heaving.

Jenna remained silent while Alicia gathered herself. Joseph stepped near Alicia, as if offering himself, but she didn't turn or acknowledge him. Then Jenna handed me the flashlight, which was still on, even though sun touched us here in the cave's mouth. The flashlight was surprisingly light, like the box I had in my pocket, like holding a twig. "Turn it off," she said.

It worked almost exactly like the box. A palm touch, a twist. "Jenna? Would this work for . . . for someone who isn't *altered*?"

"Yes. It works on sunshine. You must always stow it where it can feed on the sun's power." She set it on a little shelf near the cave mouth. "Now, watch me again."

She did the jump and twist and pulled herself up, then dropped again from the cave roof, standing ready to help us.

As she showed Joseph, I took a last long look around the cave. I wanted to stay longer, to learn more. Fantastic stories we could tell about being stuck outside all night played through my head. But there was Paloma, injured. And Kayleen and Tom. And the hebras. "Stripes? Will we find the hebras on the way back?"

Jenna glanced over her shoulder. "What do you think?"

"Yes."

She made us twist out of the cave twice each, being sure we knew how to do it. By the time we stood on the roof-rock, ready to start back, the sun was three-quarters of the way gone.

Shortly after we crested the rim, Jenna veered off, down a different path than the gravel wash we had taken up the crater face. We followed after her, running easily downslope on a clear trail that switchbacked neatly downward, one small slope after another. This would have been much easier to go up than the boulder wash. If not as fast. Trees and underbrush clung precariously to the steep sides of the crater. I smelled redberry bushes and the meadow and the fire from the cabin.

I smelled the hebras just before Jenna turned down a faint twist of path that veered from the main one. Telltale cloven hoofprints showed in the muddy path. She motioned for us to stop, and then ducked into the trees. She emerged with all three beasts. Stripes came up to me and butted my chest with her head, and I breathed a huge sigh of relief and happiness. I scratched Stripes under the chin, laughing and giggling and calling her a silly beast for running away.

She made soft contented noises in her throat, apparently just as happy to see me.

"I missed you," I crooned into her ears.

Jenna watched me with a wry smile. "You know," she said, "hebras are good, smart animals, but there are places you could design exactly what you wanted for a pet, have it grown just for you. Even have it bonded to you."

I simply hugged Stripes closer.

"Yes, well, and you have to go," Jenna said.

"How did you keep them safe?" I asked.

She shook her head. "I can only teach you so much in one day." She held my eyes for a moment. "Take care. Take care of the button box. Don't get caught."

I nodded, my nose still buried in Stripes's shoulder. "Aren't you coming with us?"

But she was already gone. As before, I couldn't see her footprints.

WAR STORIES AND SUCCESS

By the time we found an old stump to use for a mounting block, the light had shaded to the soft gold that heralded dusk. The pack hebras refused to be ridden, standing stock still and ignoring all forms of encouragement either Alicia or Joseph could think of to offer. Stripes let me ride her bareback, although she swiveled her head around and looked at me balefully, as if telling me off for forgetting to drag tack up here. She took over the lead in Sugar Wheat's absence, herding the other two. I pretty much hung on and let her trot up and down our tiny line. Between bouncing on Stripes's backbone and running our conversations with Jenna over and over in my head, I felt dazed and bruised by the time we reached the edge of the meadow. There were so many questions I hadn't had time to ask. About our parents. About us.

Tom waited for us by the new, closer high-line. The hebras called greetings as soon as they were in sight of each other, dancing and perking their ears forward. A sigh of relief escaped as I finally slid from Stripes's back to stand on wobbly legs next to Tom. He looked around, as if expecting Jenna.

I answered his unspoken question. "She's gone again. But we wouldn't have found the hebras without her."

"Where were they?" Tom asked.

I waved toward the wall of forest marching toward the crater rim. "Up there. It took a while."

Tom and I helped Joseph and Alicia tie up the pack animals, and then we all dragged into the cabin to find Kayleen standing over a stew pot that smelled of djuri and pol-roots and herbs. Sweat beaded her forehead as she lifted a spoon for a taste, smiling at us. My stomach rolled with hunger. We'd run after Jenna, scrambled up the wash, been in and out of the cave, and herded the hebras home with nothing more than water and pongaberries since breakfast.

Kayleen spooned up bowls of her stew, a proud grin on her face. "I made it all myself. It kept me from wishing I was with you."

"Mmmmm." I took a steaming bowl from her hands and set it on the floor in front of me. "I wish you *had* been there. We're exhausted."

"You look like it. Your hands are all scratched up."

Alicia grimaced tiredly. "We had to scramble up a lot of rocks and gravel."

I shot her a warning glance. We didn't want to give away the location of the cave. Her eyes flicked away from mine, but her grimace told me she understood. "They were hiding in a bunch of trees halfway to the rim," she added. "It took a long time to find them."

Tom frowned, looking confused. "Everything is so muddy it should have been easy to track them."

I choked down my bite of the spicy stew, swallowing a pol-root almost whole. "Hard to see where they'd gone through the grassy parts and the water." The little lies adding up made me squirm. "Anyway, we caught them."

Paloma nestled in a pile of saddlebags and blankets, her foot up on a full pack stuffed soft with dirty clothes. I turned to her, asking, "How's the ankle? And Sugar Wheat?"

Paloma shook her head slowly. "We'll both be okay with a

little rest. But nothing got done. We didn't work on the net nodes at all today." She yawned. "I think we were all too tired. So we'll do that tomorrow. I don't know how you three had the energy to keep going all day. Maybe if both me and the silly beast out there rest, we can keep going in a day or two. But we probably shouldn't ride Sugar Wheat for a few days." She set down her own empty bowl. "How was being with Jenna all day? I've never seen her as friendly as she was this morning."

Unanswered questions aside, I was still reeling from how much information Jenna *had* shared with us. "You know, she's always quiet. But she's a good tracker."

Joseph must have decided to follow Jenna's advice to hide the headband in the open. He pulled it out of his pocket. "She gave me this. To hold my hair out of my eyes when I hunt. Isn't it neat?"

Tom handed his bowl to Kayleen and turned to look at both of us, his face stern. "I want you two to promise not to hunt without permission. It's dangerous."

Joseph and I glanced at each other, and he gave a tiny nod. Accepting that as acquiescence, I said, "Sure, we'll ask first. I'm sorry." I shrugged, trying to make it look unimportant, remembering the fear in Tom's eyes after we killed the two djuri. "I just wanted to try it. I didn't really like it *that* much." It was only partly a lie. I didn't like the killing part, but the chasing had been wonderful.

Tom's gaze stayed on us. "I want a promise that you won't hunt, or do anything else . . . anything else I wouldn't like . . . without asking first."

A vision of the inside of the cave filled my head. "I'll try. But it's dangerous out here, and sometimes we'll have to act." There, that would leave a little room for freedom.

Tom nodded. His voice sounded stiff as he said, "Thank you." He turned to Joseph. "You, too. I want your promise as well. I am responsible for you both."

Joseph mumbled assent, his focus on the leather strap he ran gently, almost reverently, through his hands.

Paloma and Kayleen both reached out for it at the same time. Joseph set it in Paloma's hands. "Look at the embroidery.

There's silver and copper threads in there, so it looks different any way you turn it, and it shines in the sun." Joseph's face was a study in innocent enthusiasm.

Paloma, too, ran the leather strap through her fingers, almost an echo of Joseph's actions, her face noncommittal. She passed it to Tom, who sat between her and the woodstove. He held the reader up to the firelight. The flickering light danced on his face, and caught the metallic threads woven into the leather. He looked at it for a long time, fingering it.

Joseph watched him carefully, a guarded look on his face.

Tom kept the headband, looking at Joseph, appearing unsure what to say next. "You may not be able to keep it. Hunter is leery of any *altered* artifacts, and he is still responsible for security. He made us scrub the whole area around Artistos clean, and there's still a standing order to bring back anything we find and give it to him."

My hands balled into fists all on their own, and I took a deep breath, commanding them to release. Joseph needed the headband. It was the only thing we had of our parents'. I could not imagine handing it meekly to Hunter.

Joseph apparently agreed. His mouth was a tight hard line and his eyes bored into Tom's, pressuring him.

Tom gazed back, evenly, fingering the reader.

They stared at each other that way so long I thought no one would give, would look away. After the tenth breath I counted, neither had changed position. I silently willed Joseph to relax, to give Tom an opening to relent. Joseph didn't relax; Tom turned his eyes away. He looked down at the headband and shrugged. "I suppose a piece of decorated leather can't be too harmful. You can keep it for now, but you must show it to Hunter when you get back." He handed the reader back to Joseph, who passed it to Kayleen. "Did Jenna give anybody else anything?"

I resisted an urge to feel for the box in my pocket. Alicia and I shook our heads, each of us paying close attention to our food.

Paloma spoke up from her corner. "I remember when we were all scared of her. Some people still are, but I'd like the opportunity to visit with her more, learn more about her and her people. We are, I hope, ready to all live together rather than fight." She fixed us momentarily with her bright green eyes, as if to make sure we caught her message. A caution to us. "If you see her again, will you tell her I'd love to talk with her someday?"

I wondered how much Kayleen told Paloma about our periodic short meetings with Jenna.

Alicia asked, "Do you know how she lost her arm?"

Paloma and Tom glanced at each other. Paloma smiled softly at Tom. "No reason not to tell war stories. They're growing up."

Tom looked uncomfortably at the scuffed wood floor of the cabin. I felt him caught between Paloma and Nava, between someone who trusted us and someone who didn't, between a woman he liked and a woman he loved.

He would have to make up his own mind, but I spoke into his silence. "Nava told me some of her war stories the night before we left."

Joseph narrowed his eyes at me. I hadn't told Joseph Nava's story. I'd planned to, but it had seemed too personal, and I wasn't through digesting the implications. Besides, he'd had his own worries. I added, "I'd like to hear your stories, hear anything you know about Jenna."

Tom looked up at me, then at Paloma. "Well, I'm already in for it when Nava figures out these two can hunt, and I started it." Tom's gaze slid to Joseph. "I just . . . didn't expect . . . I thought you would flush djuri and I'd shoot them."

He cracked his knuckles and drank from his glass of water. "I'll tell her after Joseph finishes figuring things out, goes back to his work on the nets. Then I can tie his new self-confidence to the hunting."

"But you will tell her?" Paloma asked.

"I never lie to Nava. How can she lead if we hide things from her?"

So we weren't the only ones keeping small secrets. Tom wasn't lying, but he wasn't telling either. Yet. It was hard to picture Nava or Wei-Wei or even Hunter being thrilled that we could bring down food with our bare hands. I bet we'd have to hunt in secret like we had to run in secret. They hated displays of our skills, even though Jenna's skills helped keep them safe. Because Jenna's skills helped keep them safe?

I set my already empty bowl in front of me and scooted back against the wall. Kayleen moved a little closer to me, to a better spot to watch Paloma. Alicia and Joseph already sat close together, not touching. Still, even from a meter away, I felt a new closeness between them.

Paloma cleared her throat and her face went momentarily slack, as if she were sneaking into the past. "I first saw Jenna just after the *altered* landed. I don't remember being afraid then. I remember being curious. We were only a few years older than you. Me and Tom and Nava and Karin and Pam and . . ." Her voice trailed off, and she swallowed hard. "It doesn't matter. Most of them died. Hunter and his wife, Sarah, ran the colony then. But none of us had any power yet. So we watched, fascinated, as the delegation from the ship walked past us, heading to meet with Hunter and Sarah and Wei-Wei and the guild leaders. We didn't have a culture guild yet. That was created after the war by a group of older people, too old to fight, who made group dinners and kept Commons and River Walk Parks clean . . . and later, it became the natural home for the wounded." She shook her head, as if to clear it of memories. "I'm sorry, I'm digressing.

"Jenna was with the first delegation. They *all* towered over us, at least a head taller, some more. Like you, now. Otherwise, none of them looked very different from us. Healthy, almost glowing with health and strength. Perhaps they chose the least *altered* in appearance to keep from frightening us. Jenna had short hair then, and of course she wasn't hurt yet. She walked with more grace than I had ever seen in anyone, as if she glided. I thought her beautiful and exotic. She took notes about Artistos, and I saw her deep in conversation with Sarah sometimes, and even laughing." Paloma stopped for a moment, the faraway look relaxing her face.

Joseph shifted position nervously, his eyes fixed on Paloma.

I tried to picture Jenna laughing. Jenna beautiful. Jenna whole. She had smiled more than usual yesterday. No matter how hard I tried, the only Jenna I could see gazed at me from one eye.

Paloma continued. "But Jenna's laughter died away. As we and the *altered* grew more wary of each other, her face became more like stone. She always seemed to notice everything. She began to seem more haughty than beautiful to me, like an ice-woman sent to watch us. But even though I overheard arguments between the *altered* and our own leaders, I don't recall hearing her voice in the fights. Those of us who still lived with our parents weren't allowed to attend any meetings with them, so we got information secondhand, or from listening outside of locked doors." A little ghostly smile flew across her face and disappeared. "Therese and Steven were older than us, and sometimes included. They told us the *altered* leaders treated Jenna as important, that they asked her advice on some things, and brought her to almost every meeting."

Paloma shifted, moving her leg a little. Tom handed her a cup of water. She sipped some and set the cup near her hand.

"And then the war started. The *altered* camped outside of Artistos, in the field past the hebra barns where we grow hemp now. Some of our young men and theirs clashed. People died, and the *altered* who weren't still with their ships on the Grass Plains moved up the High Road and settled around here, near the lakes. We found three camps after the war, and burned them. Hunter made us burn them." She looked down at her hands, which twisted in her lap. "I'm wandering again. It is so easy to get lost in those years." She fell silent, chewing on her lip. Heart pain hovered in her eyes and settled into the tiny lines on her face.

"How did she lose her arm?" Alicia prompted. "And her eye?"

Tom looked at Paloma and nodded. "I was there." He picked up the thread of the story. "It was near the last fight. I hadn't seen Jenna fighting, not directly. Some *altered* who came here had only subtle changes, like you. The fighters were the strangest of the *altered*. They had physical advantages over us. More legs or arms or reflexes or . . . one had four eyes, two in the back of her head. God, there were a lot of them, and they killed us so easily." He opened the door on the woodstove and piled in two more small logs. "But there were more of us, and so in the last fight, we knew we would either win or die. But you know the basics of that fight?"

Everyone in Artistos knew the stories and songs. Desperate, the original humans had committed all of their resources to a single fight at a newly discovered camp. Half the remaining *altered* were there, either counting on secrecy or needing to meet for some other reason. We never knew why the opportunity existed. But Hunter exploited it. For the first time, they died and we didn't. Or vice versa. It made my head hurt to belong to both sides. I responded to Tom. "Yes, we know the story."

"I was in the last fight. So were Steven and Therese, and almost everyone else. Nava ran messages back and forth between the fighters and Artistos. Paloma worked in our field hospital. The fight was . . . terrible." He closed his eyes briefly and Paloma took his hand, squeezing it, and then releasing it again before he continued. "There's no value to you in the details. We thought we had killed all of them when Geordie spotted Jenna and a man and a child running away from us up a draw. We hardly had any weapons left—just homemade rocket launchers and some stunners we'd modified to carry enough punch to kill. The child was too young to run; Jenna held it to her breast. We could see the child, but we'd been fired on by the *altered* for years, lost our own children, our parents, our brothers and sisters. We burned with anger. In retrospect, that's no excuse for firing on an enemy who was running away." He swallowed, and cleared his throat. "For firing at a child."

Tom ran his hands over the light stubble of gray beard sprouting from his chin and stood and stretched. He walked to the door and opened it, looking out at the hebras, letting the cool scents of evening and damp grass and running water compete with the spicy stew.

I glanced around. Kayleen's dark eyes watered and she looked up in a corner, away from all of us, her skin a pale white. Joseph fidgeted, rearranging his weight, apparently unable to be still. Tears streamed silently down Alicia's face.

We waited for Tom to start again, watching as he carefully levered himself back down next to Paloma. "Geordie sent a rocket after the three of them. The rocket launchers made noise when they were fired, and so the man with Jenna had time to turn and fire on Geordie. They were like that—so fast they could react as if they knew our intent before we did. Maybe he heard Geordie take aim. I don't know." Tom paused and licked his lips. "Geordie's aim was good. The rocket exploded square in the middle of the little group. The rockets were full of shrapnel, of hard metal that burst in a wide pattern with every explosion. So anything near the explosion should have died.

"I ran up the hill to Geordie, only to find he had been shot through the head. He died as I was carrying him back down the hill. I didn't stop to check on the group up there. If I had, I would have found Jenna alive, and I would have killed her then." He reached for Paloma's water glass and took a sip, licking his lips. I thought perhaps he was done, but he went on. "I thought about that a lot over the years. How it might have been kinder to her to have killed her."

The subtext was the same, whether it came from Tom or Nava. *If we'd just killed everyone, killed Jenna, killed you kids, then life would be easy.*

Perhaps Joseph heard the same unspoken words. His hands were clenched so tightly in his lap the knuckles whitened, but his voice came out even and reasonable. "But if you had killed her, Jenna wouldn't protect Artistos like she does."

Tom frowned. "Things are never as simple as they seem."

Paloma picked the story up. "I climbed that hill with a clean-up detail two days later. Hunter had us searching the whole area, bringing all the *altered* weapons and bodies and artifacts and food . . . everything . . . down to a big pile to be burned. So three or four of us went up the hill to find anything left after Geordie's rocket. We found pieces of the child and of the man, and a hand that must have been Jenna's. Two of us followed a bloody trail for an hour before we lost it. After we reported what we'd found, Hunter himself tried. He, too, lost Jenna's trail. And then Hunter was pulled back to town, into the debate about you six." She raised her eyes and gazed at us contemplatively.

Tom broke the quiet moment, his voice soft. "In the last fight we killed so many of them, so ruthlessly. We had to. But we hated ourselves for it." He looked at me thoughtfully. "Chelo? How did you feel when you killed the djuri?"

I hesitated. "In the end, after it was too late, I didn't want to kill it anymore."

Tom nodded and waited a moment before saying, "I think you lived only because we were so tired of killing by then."

I swallowed, and took Kayleen's hand. She scooted a little closer to me.

Paloma whispered, watching Kayleen closely, "I'm glad that we didn't . . . that you're here."

"Me, too," I said.

Paloma held up a hand, clearly asking for silence. "We were all so busy recovering and rebuilding that we didn't make it back to Jenna's cold trail. The ship was gone, our enemies gone with it.

"We had, at most, one damaged enemy left. At first, Hunter was convinced Jenna lived, and posted special watches. After a month passed with no sign of her, we assumed she had died after all.

"No one saw her until the following winter, which was particularly cold. She haunted the edges of town. She had somehow managed to slip inside the boundaries. People chased her. Some to kill her, some to catch her. She was elusive, amazingly fast, and she did no harm. Some people spoke of missing ears of corn, or once a small goat, but no one could produce real evidence. There must have been many opportunities for her to kill us, but she didn't take any of them. After a while, she started killing predators and bringing them to town under the cover of darkness, so we'd find dead paw-cats or full clutches of demon dogs."

"I remember," I said carefully, "I remember how people used to chase her."

Paloma shifted again, her eyes still pained. "I'm sure she

must be lonely. I imagine she very much liked spending the day with you today."

I nodded.

Paloma's voice held a note of longing as she said, "I would like to know if she ever tells you any interesting stories."

I pushed myself up. "She doesn't seem used to talking."

"No," Paloma said, "I imagine not."

Joseph stared at his hands, at the leather band in them. "Do you know if our parents left with *Journey* or if they died here?"

Paloma shook her head. "We don't know who they were."

I expected that answer; Therese and Steven had answered the same way.

We were all unusually quiet preparing for bed. Tom looked over at us. "You three look tired. I'll take the first watch over the hebras tonight. Kayleen can keep me company. We'll wake up Joseph and Chelo later on."

Joseph answered, his voice heavy with exhaustion. "Okay. Tom—let *me* work on the nodes tomorrow? I think I can do it now."

Tom nodded, smiled at Joseph, and he and Kayleen slipped quietly through the door.

I crawled into my bedroll, grateful to be both still and horizontal, to have avoided first watch. My body relaxed long before my mind. Had Jenna chosen to live to protect us? What did she want from us and for us? Now that we were nearly grown, what could we offer her back?

Always, I thought of helping the colony in terms of keeping ourselves safe, avoiding their prejudices, becoming useful in exchange for being allowed to live with a semblance of freedom. Sometimes in terms of sheer survival. Neither seemed like enough tonight. Safety was not a worthy goal all by itself and survival was simply instinct. We had no dreams, no direction.

Jenna was right; we needed to know what we wanted.

Where was Jenna anyway? Was she staying in the cave tonight, or perched nearby, watching the cabin, watching us?

It seemed like I had only truly slept for moments when

Kayleen shook my shoulder and whispered, "Wake up. Your watch."

"Hmmmm . . . did anything happen?"

"Yeah. We got cold. Take blankets."

She was right. The chill air outside smelled like decaying fall leaves, like the night after a storm when all the water has not yet sunk into the ground or risen to the air. We settled on some wide low stones with a good view of the high-line and the cabin. At first, I sat sleepily next to my brother, welcoming the cold against my cheeks, watching Wishstone, Faith, Hope, and Summer hang above us. Four-moon nights were said to encourage contemplation, a fit to my mood. The hebras dozed standing, heads down, clearly too uneasy to lie down as they sometimes did back home. Night birds called calmly back and forth to each other. I imagined any of them might be Jenna, patiently watching, blending in.

Joseph broke the silence first. "Come closer, Chelo. It's too risky to use the projector here, so close, but I want to try the headband. I can tell you what I see."

I scooted over next to him, so we shared a single blanket between us and the wet grass, and I draped the blanket Kayleen had urged me to bring so it covered both of our shoulders. "Do you have one of the buttons with you?" I whispered.

He nodded. "But first, I'm going to fix the node. The one on the ridge. I've heard the whole local net all day, and I can feel its imbalance inside me. It's driving me nuts." He held my hand, leaning into me, his head against my shoulder. I slipped my arm across his back. It had been one of his favorite positions to rest in when he was ten.

"Go on, little brother, read the wind."

He nodded, mumbling, "Blood, bone, and brain." I watched his eyes drift closed and then returned to scanning the sounds and shadows of the clearing and nearby forest, making sure we were safe. Joseph became steadily limper in my arms, heavier. His eyes fluttered and he thrashed softly, restless. It took longer than usual, even longer than the easy past, before he said, "Okay, Chelo, I have it. Node 89A sees two other nodes here, 90A and 91B, both up near the top. It should be able to talk to 102A across the lake. 89A is healthy enough. It's reaching the far side, but all it gets is static. I can't quite—twist it—no. We'll need to replace the far side."

He sounded confident. Himself. As if the headband erased his fear.

"Now . . . linking backward, into Kayleen's work. Easy slide, follow . . . follow . . . data returning to Artistos: seismic, weather, temperature . . ." His voice trailed to nothing. His skin warmed slightly beneath my fingertips. The reddish moon, Summer, slid behind the crater rim, near the cave. I imagined it filling the cave with soft light, landing on Jenna's face, softening her rough features, turning Jenna in her sleep to the beautiful woman that first came here.

Joseph drifted, his eyes fluttering, his lips moving, but silent, as if he had no need to tell me exactly what he did, where he went. He felt far away and I curled myself closer around him, tucking the blanket in, watching carefully.

A small shower of meteors spun through the sky, brilliant points of fire and light. The hebras shifted and stamped their feet. Joseph stayed a quiet heavy lump in my arms for so long I lost the feeling in my legs. I shifted a little to become more comfortable and hummed quietly to keep myself awake, wishing I'd brought the flute out here.

Joseph's far arm rose, stretching, and my hand slid down to his waist. He pushed himself up partway, and I shifted again, finding a comfortable spot. He tilted his head toward me. "It worked." His dark eyes were bright and happy, as if the data of Fremont fed him. He whispered, "I want to go back to Artistos and sit in the middle of the web and see what I can do."

"We have work to do out here first."

He grinned, eyes alight as if a secret wanted to burst from them. "Only a little. Two nodes on the far side need physical replacement, and one is missing entirely. I know where they all are. Everything else is done."

I blinked at him. "The whole lake ring? Just like that?"

Jenna had said the data threads would help him, but she hadn't seemed to expect this much this soon. But then, she was like me. Deaf to whatever data flowed here. She might be guessing what to do for Joseph.

He sat the rest of the way up, still grinning. "There's more. I can sense the cave, and nodes way up by the Fish Mountains. From here. It's as if I can feel everything on this part of the web, all the way back to Artistos. I can feel it now, while I'm talking to you. I can hold the threads." His words tumbled out one on the other, loud in the quiet night.

I put a hand over his mouth, shushing him gently. "Tom will be able to tell this is fixed as soon as he turns on his data reader. Artistos will see the new data. Do we want that?"

"Isn't that what we came here for?"

"But so fast? I want time for you to learn to use the headband, for the rest of us to try the projector, maybe time to spend with Jenna." I looked out over the clearing, watching the moonlight touch the grass tips and the streams. "I'm not ready to go back yet."

His eyes looked dreamy even in the wan moonlight, as if he were half in conversation with me while the rest of him rode the winds of data. His energy felt light and confident. "I . . . no, it's okay. They can know these are fixed. We still have the physical work to do. That will take a few days. Then I want to go find Liam."

"Is that in Tom's plans? I thought we were just going to fix the lake nodes and maybe a few more."

"We'll make up a reason." He stood, bouncing up and down on his feet, holding a hand out to me. He radiated confidence, and more. The boy from before the earthquake was back, clothed in an extra coat of success. I took his hand, letting him pull me up, his ebullient energy infecting me even through the soft haze of my exhaustion.

"So, this is really easier now than before?"

"It's like jumping in the sea for the first time, when all you've ever known are streams."

I followed him to the hebra string, where he woke Legs from a drowsy sleep with a gentle slap on his neck. Legs snorted and turned a scathing look on Joseph, and I thought if the hebra could speak he would say, *Why are you waking me, why now? Go to sleep, silly human. It's just past the middle of the night.*

Joseph laughed and patted Legs, stroking his neck and the long nearly healed scar on his haunch. Legs whickered contentedly.

"Is it because of the headband? Is that why you can see our data, the Artistos data, so clearly again?"

He slipped it off and handed it to me. It felt warm from his head, and the fine metal strands woven through the pattern were smooth and slick. I tied it around my own head. Wearing something my father had worn seemed to weave a connection to him through the years, a physical link I could no longer remember directly.

Joseph came and circled me in his arms, a hard hug full of energy and excitement. "It's not just the threads . . . I can still feel the network. Remember, even yesterday, I felt the nodes." He released me and stood close, but not touching. "And now, I don't need your touch to keep feeling them, although I think I did to get started. I feel like I'm being tuned."

"Tuned?"

"Becoming more like myself." He frowned, looking deeply, earnestly into my eyes. "I didn't know before that this was something Dad could do—I don't really remember him at all. Not like you do."

"I can't see his face anymore. I remember Chiaro more, and the day she brought us to town. It must have been the same day everyone left." I thought about Tom and Paloma's story. "The day we were almost murdered. She had all six of us, and everyone was old enough to walk, but Liam and Alicia could barely manage. Chiaro's face and her side were bloody. She kept telling us to hurry. She took us to Commons Park, and we all had to hold hands the whole way. You could barely walk, and Liam and I pulled you between us."

The memory made me shiver. "A group of people came and Chiaro talked to them. There were a lot of them. She fell. Her blood stained the grass. She was asking the people to take care of us, and then Therese and Steven led us all away."

Joseph was quiet for a few moments before he spoke again. "I wish we remembered more about Dad. I'm glad I'm like him, that we have the same mods."

My sleepy thoughts about goals came back to me. "What do you want? For us? We *will* be adults. I want us to be free adults." I pointed out a meteor flashing briefly above the dark silhouette of the crater rim. "What can Nava do? They won't kill us, not now. They need us.

"But do we want to just be part of the colony? Do we want to help lead it? We could become our own band of roamers."

He held his hand out, and I took the reader off my head and placed it in his palm. He closed his fist around the band, and held it up to his eye level, watching it closely, as if it were a bird or a flower. "It depends, Chelo. It depends on what we learn. Right now, I want to use this to learn what Jenna knows. We've learned more this week than in all of the years before. I want to understand who we are, and then maybe I can answer your question."

It would take time for me and Kayleen and Alicia to watch the projector, for any of us to communicate with Liam and Bryan, for Joseph to understand how to use the headband. It seemed important to come to a shared goal, to include all of us. Maybe even including Jenna. "Think about it, little brother. This trip won't take forever, and we need a direction before we return to Artistos. We will need to know what we want to be when we grow up before we can bargain to get it."

He nodded, tying the headband back over his dark hair. It was surely a trick of the moonlight, but he looked older, as if even his shape had changed overnight and become nearly a man's shape. Faith, the largest moon, hung over Joseph's head and the smaller Hope reflected in his eyes as he looked up to meet mine. "And what do you want?"

"I want to be happy. I want to prove to all of them that we are true humans, I want the freedom to make our own decisions. I want full access to their databases, and to ours. Now we know we have our own." I chewed on my lip. "I want our own culture, side by side with theirs."

He laughed. "You may have to fight to get all that."

"I don't want any wars." I yawned. "I want to sleep."

Joseph bounced on the balls of his feet. He stretched, tall, as if he were reaching for the sky. "I'm not sleepy. Will you go in and wake Alicia up, then? She can help me watch until dawn."

"All right. But remember to be watchful. We're not out here just to talk." I gave him another hug. "Glad to have you back. I've missed my happy brother."

He kissed me on the cheek, his lips warm and dry. "Thanks for being there. You've always been there for me."

I returned his kiss. "Good night."

As I walked quietly back to the cabin I wondered again about Jenna. Was she nearby? What did she want?

Three more meteors streaked the sky. Simultaneously, our small boundary bells rang the lowest possible earthquake tones and the ground shivered under my feet, once, and again.

I didn't go back and check on Joseph. A quake would not spook him tonight.

16

MONSTERS?

The next morning I rubbed at crusted gritty eyes as the even light of midmorning poured in through the one window. It felt like I'd slept minutes, even though the light promised hours had passed. It hurt to sit up.

The only movement in the room was Paloma's right arm, where she sat propped in the single stream of sunlight. Her fingers spun over the paper, drawing a field of blue flowers over green grass, dipping rhythmically in and out of the jar of blue ink; a contrast to the stillness of the rest of her body. She smiled at me, then flicked her eyes toward Joseph and Alicia, her smile twisting to puzzled question.

They slept close together, under a single green blanket. Alicia's long hair covered her face. His face slack with sleep, Joseph looked both content and young. His right hand clutched the headband, and the other held the blanket up over both of them. It looked like Alicia had an arm thrown over his waist, although I couldn't be sure because the blanket covered them.

Yesterday, I had promised myself I'd think about this today, and I shut my eyes briefly, sighing. I looked at Paloma and opened my hands in a gesture of futility.

She grimaced, a sign she wasn't much happier than I was about the situation, and whispered, "Good morning. They just came in at dawn. Would you help me to the outhouse?"

I nodded and pushed myself up. My legs protested at the idea of movement and my hands still stung from yesterday's adventures. Offering Paloma an arm, I helped her up. Joseph and Alicia didn't even stir as we walked carefully past them and through the door, shutting it quietly. A warm fall day greeted us, the sky a cloudless soft blue, the hills dotted with little scraps of yellow and red signaling the near-elm and fall ladies turning with the season.

Paloma leaned on me, letting me take much of her weight every other step. Her head came just past my shoulder, and this close, little gray wisps showed against her blond hair. Dry leaves crunched under our feet, even though small mud puddles still filled low spots.

"Where are Kayleen and Tom?" I asked.

"They went to the node." She must have misinterpreted my startled look, because she said, "Yes, Tom remembered Joseph asking to work on it. He's just having Kayleen tell him what she thinks is wrong."

I suspected they'd be back soon, but didn't say it out loud. "Do you have any idea what I should do about Joseph and Alicia?"

Paloma grimaced at a slight wrong step, but kept her balance. "Has Joseph talked to you about Alicia?"

I shook my head. "I think Alicia started it."

"Well, she must feel very lost out here. Are you sure you want advice?"

I grinned. "Can't hurt."

"If you tell teenagers not to do something, they often think it's a great idea. You may be his sister, but you're older than both of them by a couple of years." She smiled up at me. "Almost an adult yourself. If I were you, I'd encourage Joseph to talk, but I'd only offer advice if he asks. Tom and I can keep them from being alone together too much by making sure they are on different watches."

"He asked me to wake her up last night. I was so tired I didn't even think about it, but they were alone for hours."

"Well, Tom's caught up some on sleep. We could make sure either me or Tom is awake all the time."

That wouldn't help us try out the projector. "Maybe I'll just take a watch with Alicia tonight. You need to rest enough for your ankle to heal."

She laughed. "I don't need that much babying. We'll work it out." She stopped for a moment to catch her breath. "It might be best to stay out of it until one of them approaches you, which they will if they don't see you as an enemy." She sighed. "Don't, by the way, be sure that you can or should stop them. Regardless of what people in Artistos think, you all will pair up sometime."

I remembered Liam's farewell kiss on the top of my head, and the feel of Bryan's arms around me the last day before we left. "I know. It just seems we should wait until the discussion in Artistos is over. Until we have our freedom as adults."

Paloma laughed, a friendly laugh tinged with irony. "You're delusional. Being an adult does not make you free, and emotions seldom honor reason."

I frowned and helped her step carefully down a steep spot. We arrived at our destination, took turns, and started our return trip. Tom and Kayleen met us on the way back, just outside the cabin. "All of them?" Tom's tone told me he was talking into his earset, probably to Nava. "I'll call you back." He tapped the set to close the connection, and when he looked at me his jaw was still tight and the little muscles near his ears trembled. He looked angry, both with us and with Nava. "What did you do last night? Why didn't you tell me?"

He didn't need to be mad at Joseph for doing what he'd asked him to do. I smiled up at him, trying to counter his anger. "Well, I haven't seen you since I woke up. I'd be happy to tell you now."

His expression settled some, relaxing. "I'm sorry. We're all tired." He swiped at his eyes, as if underscoring the point. "Kayleen and I went to fix this node, and it had been done. Then Nava called and said the whole lake ring is working this morning. Did Joseph do all that?"

I nodded. "Last night, while we were on watch. He was happy he figured out how to get back into it. You should have seen him—he was almost dancing. Remember, he's been able to read the nodes since before we went hunting. He just couldn't change them until last night. I don't know what he figured out."

Kayleen clapped her hands together. "I knew it was Joseph."

Tom looked puzzled, and gestured at the Fremont data reader he held in his right hand. "Well, he fixed more in one night than he would have been able to in three days before all this." He narrowed his eyes. "Did Jenna teach him anything? Does it have something to do with that thing she gave him?"

I shook my head. "I asked him the same question. He said no. Besides, remember? He *was* reading the nodes before we went with Jenna. She didn't tell him anything about how to fix them except to suggest he stop being afraid—the same advice you've been giving him. She told me she can't do it, that she's as deaf to them as I am."

Tom frowned. "Yeah, we used to worry about her. Jenna seems to be able to slide through the perimeters as if they aren't there—the *altered* all seemed to do that." He paused. "Except you six. But we never found any evidence that she changed anything."

"We didn't set off the alarms yesterday when we were with her." Was Jenna honest with us about not reading data like Joseph and Kayleen? Or did she know some other trick?

Tom just shook his head quietly. "I wish I knew how she did that. I better wake Joseph up and ask him about the nodes. Nava's wanting some answers."

Kayleen stepped over near me and Paloma, and smiled up at Tom. "Isn't this what she wanted? For him to fix things? Just tell her he did what she wanted and let him sleep. He's exhausted."

Tom sighed and touched Kayleen's shoulder lightly. "Maybe you're right. It's been a tough few days. Nava and Gianna are compiling a list of what's fixed and what's not. They'll send it to me. I'll call Nava back and confirm that Joseph did the fixing, and let her know he's sleeping." He started to turn away, then he glanced back at Paloma. "Here, I'll help you back. Kayleen and Chelo can tend the hebras."

So I lost my chance to ask Paloma more questions, but gained a long-overdue opportunity to fill Kayleen in on our trip with Jenna. I took it, telling the story in order as we led the hebras out for food and water one at a time. Predictably, she asked a hundred questions I had no answer for. After we tied the last hebras back onto the line, she grinned at me, her eyes bright with excitement. "So, let me see the projector."

I glanced at the cabin. No movement. We stood behind the hebras, out of direct line-of-sight, and I slid the small box out of my pocket and handed it to her. She fingered it, and held it up. It appeared seamless. She immediately drew the same conclusion I had. "So, however this works, maybe the *New Making* works the same?"

"It looks like it's made out of the same stuff." I showed her how to open it, how the data button nestled inside the box, fitting perfectly.

She closed her eyes, holding the box in both hands close in to her belly, swaying gently. "I feel it. Like—but not like—our data. I felt it more when the box was open, as if the box itself hides some of the buttons' . . . I don't know what word to use. Attention? Signal?"

"I still don't feel anything from either."

She opened her eyes, an excited smile on her face. "Turn it on."

"Not here." We *would* have to take some risks to use it at all. I'd been afraid to use it last night, even though the watch with Joseph would have been safe enough, in retrospect. "We need to come up with a reason to be away from Tom and Paloma."

"Well, let's go pick berries." She grinned, still excited, reminding me of Joseph the night before. "I'm hungry anyway. But we better ask. I'll go." She handed me back the projector and bounded toward the cabin. The uncomfortable feeling of widening deception felt only slightly weaker than the burning feeling of knowledge I'd wanted—no, needed—all my life, sitting in my pocket.

Kayleen returned with two earsets and a backpack to carry the berries back in. "Tom sent these just in case we get into trouble." She led. "Tom and I found three pongaberry trees yesterday. You can practice."

I groaned.

She gave me a sly grin. "But you don't have to take your shirt off."

"Good." I followed her for almost ten minutes. We passed through the boundary, setting the exit bells ringing. It *would* be handy to have a way to pass barriers unheralded. Something else to ask Jenna about. We wound up a path lined with spiky green and gold trip-vine, stepping carefully to avoid being caught or scratched.

Kayleen stopped at the base of the biggest of three pongaberry trees and kicked her shoes off. She had a silly grin on her face. "Race you?"

I shook my head ruefully, kicking off my own shoes. Watching Jenna was one thing, but getting up the tree myself was sure to be another. The dun and dark brown bark ridges ran vertically, making for bad toeholds, and the trunk of the smallest tree rose a full twelve meters before there was a branch to grab. Sighing, I stood at the bottom of the tree, feeling the rough deadfall leaves and small branches through the soles of my bare feet. I set one hand on the tree, trying to remember how Jenna had started up.

Kayleen called to me, and I glanced over to find her halfway up, her long feet acting almost like extra hands.

I tried a little leap up the tree trunk. One foot found barely acceptable purchase and the other slid off, pulling me down to my knees. I tried again, with nearly the same result, then stood still, eyeing the tree. It had to be about strength and balance. Jenna had been almost vertical. I started over, my belly near the rough bark, using both of my hands to grab halfway around the bole. That way, I managed a full two meters before I lost it and fell down, stinging the soles of my feet.

Kayleen waved at me from the bottom of the branches of her tree, her face framed in the wide green and yellow leaves, laughing.

I made it ten meters, and stopped, stuck, afraid to go back down, unsure how to go up. My arms twitched and shivered at the strength required to hold on. Kayleen called down, "Relax."

I closed my eyes. Surely this wasn't as hard as it looked, as it felt. Jenna did it with one arm. I could do it with two. I started back up, slowly, carefully, one step, another, another, keeping my belly close to the tree. I didn't look up or down, just at the bark in front of me, picking out the imperfections in color and the places wood-ants or summer moths nested.

I counted breaths and slow unsure steps.

My head bumped something hard. A branch. I reached up, found a firm grip, and climbing became easier, stepping in the cracks where the branches met the trunk, pulling up, finally enclosed in so many wide green leaves and broad branches they got in my way. The end of each leaf sported a nasty thorn, and one raked across my shoulder, drawing a thin bead of blood. I looked around. No pongaberries.

Kayleen now stood at the bottom of my tree. "Up and to your left."

I followed her directions, finally locating a big bunch of berries. Looking past them, I saw the meadow, then picked out the hebras and the line of smoke from the cabin's fire. The midday sun danced on the lake and reflected points of light all along the streams that cut through the valley. I glanced down, and wished I hadn't. Kayleen looked very small.

I reached for the stem, pulling, tugging harder than I expected to have to. The stem separated from the branch with a snap and I nearly lost my balance, nearly dropped the berries. I stuck the stem in my teeth, like Jenna had, and headed down-trunk. Down was easier, but even so, I earned two new scratches on my right forearm and slipped the last few meters. Kayleen had to catch me to keep me from landing on my butt. Lucky for her, she had the good grace to hold her face neutral, and say, "Good job."

I breathed a sigh of relief to see her holding two bunches of fat purple berries. We had enough.

We sat near each other on the ground, the berries next to us, and I slipped the box out of my pocket and showed Kayleen how to turn it on. It still held the button Jenna had placed in it in the cave, and the first image to shimmer into being was of Silver's Home. "That's the place we saw in the cave, Kayleen, the planet Jenna called Silver's Home."

Kayleen—eyes round with amazement—watched tiny silver ships like *New Making* fly through the air three feet in front of us, above the image of the strange planet; constructs of light with no substance. The projection drew my attention from Kayleen, from the world around me, so that, like Kayleen, I watched closely, entranced.

We saw a planet full of energy and people and ships, a planet that was owned by our people, like Fremont was owned by its predators and its wildness.

There was no sound until Kayleen found a way to stroke the box to produce a narrator's voice that spoke softly into the mountain-fern and redberry that surrounded us. It took me a moment to be sure it was our language. The accent was a little off, the vowels more rounded, the words spoken faster than we spoke. Enough words were entirely unfamiliar that I couldn't pull meaning from the monologue.

At first, it appeared to be an encyclopedia description, like we had seen in school about some of the original human worlds: Deerfly, Green Sands, and historical Earth. The voice described population (two and a half billion—a number higher than anything we had counted except stars), and then it talked about trade, like between us and the roamers. Silver's Home apparently sold information and education relating to genetically modified people like us, including training and databases. They manufactured ships and weapons in low orbit and on one of their two moons; hence the vast multitude of ships moving around the planet like moths congregating to a candle flame.

What they bought was less clear, but seemed to be related to information and visitors to the world who came to study there.

I was keenly aware of time passing. How long before Tom and Paloma decided we'd been gone too long? I reached for the box to turn it off, but Kayleen blocked my hand and shook her head furiously. "No. Wait. You worry too much. We'll say you were learning to climb pongaberry trees. Look—it's showing individual people."

A series of images marched briefly across the air; the narrator talked about each one for only a few sentences each. I didn't understand most of the words. "No. It's not individuals. It's types." I pointed at an image of a tall woman with four arms. "Watch." The next image was equally tall, with only two arms, and something that looked like the wings of a bird. A third image was shorter, with bunched powerful muscles in the shoulders and thighs. It could have been Bryan, only drawn with every difference between him and the original humans exaggerated.

I stopped for a moment to look around, half hoping Jenna would show, afraid I'd see Tom's round face peering out from behind a tree, watching us. I hadn't even been listening for predators, and we were beyond the boundary.

"I think you're right," Kayleen mused. "It's a display of available genemods. Some of those pictures could match the *altered* we've heard about from the war."

When we saw a hairless woman with two eyes in the back of her head, I felt sure we were on the right track. They were all ugly, except maybe the woman with four arms, who had her own gentle grace. I looked down at my hands. We were not nearly so alien as the images in front of us. These were the monsters who had fought for Artistos. Or our brethren who had fought for Artistos. I remembered when we camped on the beach and I saw traces of a fight, and wanted both sides to have been safe. But we had not been made as different as these people. I was glad of that, but why? So we'd fit in here?

Kayleen leaned forward, watching the play of light closely as image after image paraded in front of her eyes. I passed my hand between her eyes and a figure with elongated arms and legs. "We have to go."

She nodded, still focused on the projected image.

I reached around and turned the reader off. "We'll find some more time soon."

"This is going to be hard," she said. "We don't have time to just watch random images." She stood up, brushing dirt from her pants, and bent to slip her shoes back on. "We'll never get what we need moving this slowly. Not even if we have all day to watch."

"I know." I slid my own shoes on and slipped the box back into the relative safety of my pocket. Maybe Joseph had made progress. "Do you think you could navigate the way you follow the data from the nodes?"

"It didn't work. I'm seeing this, not feeling it inside me. I didn't see an interface, or a list of contents, or search boxes." She picked up two bunches of berries. "But there has to be something else if Jenna can use the projectors. We'll just have to figure it out."

We stuffed the berries in the pack and raced back, jumping over logs, chasing each other, tossing the pack back and forth as if it were a ball. Playing.

As we walked into the cabin, we held up our pongaberry haul triumphantly, only to find Joseph and Alicia still sound asleep. Tom and Paloma sat quietly, talking. We passed around berries, saving some for the sleepers. The sweet berry smell permeated the cabin. After eating our fill, I jumped back up. "We're going to brush the hebras. Come get us when they wake up."

Tom nodded, and Kayleen and I went outside. "Search terms . . ." she mused.

Warmed by sunshine and slightly sleepy from night watches, we brushed mud from the hebras' coats, boosting each other up on their backs to get at their long necks. I started with Legs, working in silence. Then I leaned against Ink's side. "I want to know why the *altered* even came here in the first place. What did they want, except to live here?"

Kayleen picked up my thoughts. "Fremont's not prime real estate. The databases talk about hundreds of better planets, or at least planets that are easier to live on than this one. The original humans came here because they wanted someplace no one else wanted. But why did the *altered* come? And why were they willing to get in a war, to die, to stay here?"

I hesitated a moment. "Maybe they wanted something they could only get here?" I turned back to Ink, quietly brushing her belly and down her legs, picking at matted mud.

"The most useful thing to know," Kayleen proclaimed while she sat backward on Sand, brushing her rump awkwardly, "would be how to get into the *New Making*. There must be tons of information there, maybe whole databases."

"I'd like to do more than get in it. I'd like to fly it."

Kayleen snorted. "And where would we go? Do you want to go to Silver's Home? We're not weird enough. To Deerfly? We're too weird."

"I don't know."

Kayleen boosted me up onto Stripes's back. Stripes swiveled her head to watch me, bending close enough that her hot breath warmed my stomach. I scratched her ears with the bristles and used my fingers to comb out her beard.

We knew Bryan's parents were dead, but we knew nothing about the rest of them. Surely there were records. Surely Jenna knew, at least some of it. It wasn't lost on me that she could answer most of our questions directly, but was making us hunt the answers on our own.

We finished the hebras, hurrying back in to find Joseph and Alicia still asleep. My sleepy brother had slept long enough. I busied myself repacking and folding and finding small ways to make noise. Paloma laughed at me, catching on, then joined in, singing and stacking the wood next to her noisily. Even Tom seemed to be hiding a smile, though he was intent on his data reading device, taking notes.

Alicia woke up first, sitting up and pushing her tangled dark hair into some sense of order behind her shoulders. "I'm starved," she mumbled, glancing out the window. "How did it get so late?"

"You were up until dawn," Paloma said.

"Oh, that's right." Alicia flopped back down, only to bounce up for a handful of pongaberries Kayleen offered her. Then she did the rest of my work for me, luring Joseph up with two berries she waved under his nose. He swiped at her with one hand, but took one of the berries with the other and joined her in pushing back the blankets.

Tom watched Joseph speculatively as he and Alicia headed outside. As soon as they came back in, Tom asked, "So . . . what did you do last night?"

Joseph peered at Tom through half-open sleepy eyes. "You sound as if I've done something bad," he mumbled.

Tom's eyes narrowed. "No. But everything seems to be working around here. Rather suddenly."

"Well?" Joseph cocked an eyebrow. "That's what you wanted, right?"

Tom stood up, poured himself a cup of tea, and palmed two more berries out of the pile we'd been saving for Alicia and Joseph. His voice didn't have the anger he'd shown me on the path this morning, but he didn't seem particularly pleased either. "I just don't know how you did so much. I checked the local nodes yesterday while you were out rounding up hebras, and you were right—three of them did work, barely, but they weren't talking to the Artistos net at all. This morning, Nava called me and said every single node that they don't think is physically broken works better than it ever has before. She's not getting any dropped data. None. I'm just . . . surprised, I guess."

Alicia clapped her hands together softly, drawing everyone's attention. "Isn't that what you wanted?" She looked exasperated, her dark hair a tangled mess, her lips a thin line in her narrow face. "It's like hunting. You wanted Joseph to hunt if he could flush beasts for you, but when Chelo and Joseph, and surely the rest of us, can kill for ourselves, you don't like it." Her voice rose, almost scolding. "You don't like it at all. You wanted Joseph to learn to fix nodes again, and you tried really hard to help him. I know, I saw you."

She paused, rubbing her hands together, holding Tom's eyes with her own. Tom sat up straighter than a moment before, his arms crossed over his torso as if warding off Alicia's words. His eyes looked like he wanted to laugh, while his crossed arms and stern expression told me he was frustrated with her.

She continued, her voice now almost defiant, but shaky. "And now he can, and I can tell by how you're sitting, how your voice is, everything, that you don't like this either." Her bottom lip trembled. "And you're the two people Chelo tells me are the most sympathetic to us. If this is what I can expect in Artistos, I'd be better off by myself somewhere, where I can be as strong as I want to be, as fast as I can, as capable . . ." She put her hands up over her face and turned toward the wall, away from Joseph, away from the rest of us.

I dragged my gaze from her, from her third cry in as many days, to watch Tom's face, and Paloma's.

Tom chewed at his lower lip, and looked like he was working hard to swallow words that begged to come out of him. I caught a glance between Paloma and Kayleen. Kayleen seemed to know how to interpret Paloma's look, because she slid over close to Alicia and set an arm on Alicia's shaking back.

Tom leaned over to Joseph, ignoring Alicia and her outburst. "Yes, we came here to fix the net. Good job."

Joseph took one of Alicia's hands, but answered Tom evenly. "Well, I see you've been working on the maps. Can we start this afternoon? I want to finish the ones that are broken, and then I think we'll have time to pick up even more of the net than we planned. I'd like to see Akashi and Liam before we go home."

Tom glanced at Paloma, who said, "I can ride. Can Sugar Wheat go yet?"

Tom hesitated briefly before answering. "Yes, but I don't

think we should ride her. Or run her. Maybe Chelo and Joseph can double up."

Alicia turned back toward us and removed her hands from her face, exposing red cheeks wet from tears, and said, "We don't all need to ride. We can keep up. Go ahead and ride Ink, and I'll run. If I get tired, I'll trade with one of the others."

Once more, I saw Tom swallow his first reaction. He nodded curtly. "Well, then, pack up. There's a rough spot on the trail about two kilometers ahead. We should be able to get past it tonight if we get packed in the next half hour."

Packing took us forty-five minutes, but at least four hours of daylight remained when we rode on, passing through the narrow end of the valley to ride along the lake. We followed a beach trail, winding between forested cliffs and the water, dotted here and there with trickling waterfalls.

Sure enough, Alicia ran just ahead of us. The hebras moved just faster than our natural walk, and so Alicia loped along with plenty of time to make small side trips to pick up stones and throw them in the water or just run ahead and stand, watching and waiting for us, her hands on her hips.

After a while, Joseph dismounted and handed me Legs's lead line, running alongside her. They ran easily, laughing and pointing out waterfalls to each other, looking like young healthy gods. I scratched Stripes's ears. "Hey, girl, I'd love to run, too, but someone has to ride and manage you and the pack animals." Stripes turned her head back toward me and lifted her lower lip in what I fancied was the hebra version of a smile.

We rounded a corner in the path to find a quake-slumped cliff. Gray and brown gravel and boulders, broken bushes, and shattered trees spilled across the path and into the lake. Tom rode along it, inland and down to the water, and back again, looking for a passable trail.

Joseph and Alicia clambered up on the fall. Finally, Alicia stood on the top of the unsteady berm, calling out, "There's djuri tracks here. I bet if we lead the hebras they'll make it."

Joseph carried Paloma. Tom led two pack animals while I managed Stripes and Legs, Alicia took Sugar Wheat and

Ink, and Kayleen led Sand and her own hebra, Longface. Even without our weight, the hebras sometimes sank almost to their knees in the loose material. Joseph's idea to take them across without extra weight had been right. We sank in sand to our ankles, and once I fell in a soft sinkhole up to my waist and Kayleen had to pull me out with a rope. It took nearly an hour to get all of us across the berm.

We rode another hour, tired. I kept wondering when we'd stop, but Tom appeared to have a destination in mind. Finally, we came up over a little hill. There, in the middle of a valley that had been purposely cleared, stood the biggest tent tree I had ever seen. A guild hall would fit under its canopy.

We camped inside, near the huge spreading trunk, tying the hebras on the other side of our camp but still under the canopy. We strung the barrier right at the edge of the tree and left two people at a time to tend a small fire all night. No animals bothered us, but it was no place for the projector.

Tom assigned Alicia and me the last watch that night, and we sat sleepily feeding small sticks into the fire, making sure it neither winked out, nor grew big enough to flood the canopy with smoke or threaten the tent tree.

"Have you ever seen a tent tree this big?" I asked Alicia.

"Yes . . . two others. One is even bigger. Sky said it must be over a thousand years old."

I looked up at the thick canopy above us, the bottom leaves yellow from lack of direct sunlight. The tree creaked and groaned and made tiny snapping noises, and its leaves rubbed together almost like crickets. "It sounds like it's singing to us, Alicia. Like it has its own song."

She laughed, softly, almost a whisper. "Sky told me Akashi said everything has its own song." She stared at the small fire, and fed it a dried brown tent tree leaf, which curled in on the edges and then burst into a small yellow flame as it lost its form. "Maybe we need our own song."

I smiled and got up to get my flute. When I returned, Alicia put her fingers to her lips and stood, rummaging quietly in her own pack. She returned with a flute that was nearly a twin of mine, except that the wood had been worn shiny with use. Shells hung from it for decoration instead of feathers.

"Did Liam make that?" I asked.

She glanced down at the flute in her hands almost reverently. "It was Varay's. I took it the day after I brought his body back. No one noticed. He would have wanted me to have it." She turned it over and over in her hands, caressing it. "I just haven't had the heart to play it." Then she raised it to her lips, blowing softly, and a sweet sad song seemed to fill all of the empty space in the tent tree.

A few minutes later Joseph joined us, gently tapping his drum and smiling at Alicia. The three of us played for twenty minutes, watching as the first light began to steal into the tree, greening the leaves and dimming the firelight.

17

NEWS OF BRYAN

We led the hebras out from under the canopy of the big tent tree just as full daylight painted the dew-spangled grass bright. Alicia and Joseph stopped at the edge of the path, holding the pack hebras' lines, waiting for the rest of us to mount up.

Tom laughed softly at them, his eyes sparkling with amusement. "I think it's a great morning for Kayleen to run with Alicia." He mounted Ink, gazing down at Alicia. "And stay in sight, okay? I lost track of you and Joseph a few times yesterday."

Alicia blushed, but her eyes darkened and narrowed. Joseph shrugged, his look more distant than disturbed. Kayleen and Alicia stood to the side while Joseph pulled himself up on Legs and took Sugar Wheat's lead line.

The wide path threaded through rolling grassy foothills dotted with small stands of trees, the hills rising to the mountains behind us, almost opposite the fork where we began our trip around the lake. Joseph rode by himself, keeping Legs at least three meters from all of us, even riding off-trail to maintain his distance. Kayleen and Alicia ran ahead of us, staying in sight, but barely. Tom called them back twice, cautioning them to stay near.

After observing Joseph's silent treatment for fifteen minutes, I rode up next to him and said, "You know, you can't afford to make Tom angry. We need his support."

Joseph nodded, but didn't move any closer to the others. His eyes stared straight ahead under the headband. After about ten minutes, my logic must have sunk in, because he pulled Legs over close to Ink, and began a conversation with Tom. I rode next to Paloma, her face pinched white with pain, and tried to distract her with chatter about the various trees and late-blooming flowers by the trail.

We stopped briefly at the next spike. We all led the hebras to the lake bank to drink. Afterward, Tom dug out his data reader to confirm that the pod worked. As soon as Tom closed the reader with a satisfied grunt and put it back in his pack, we traded runners, boosting Kayleen onto Legs, and Alicia onto Stripes.

Joseph and I ran near each other. The midmorning sun and the exertion of running combined to draw a light sweat on my forearms and scalp almost immediately. We slowed to clamber over a small mud and gravel slide, more likely caused by the recent rains than the quake. He glanced sideways at me. "Thanks, sis. I'm sorry I'm so distracted. I'm having trouble understanding what's on this darn thing."

"And I thought you were pouting about not running with your sweetheart."

"At least mine's here." He blushed and looked away.

"I don't have a sweetheart." Damn him.

He laughed. "Nope—you have two. You and Kayleen are going to have to work that out." He gave me a smug glance. "I'll stick to Alicia. She needs me."

Alicia needed a lot more than Joseph. But he didn't offer

anything else about how he felt, and Paloma's suggestion to wait until he wanted advice held my tongue. "What's going on with the headband?"

We'd crossed the slide, but kept to a walk, waiting for the others to maneuver the hebras across the muddy patch. "I'm seeing a lot, but I don't understand what I see, yet. The data button I chose seems to be about a fight—not a war, more like an argument—that happened back where the *altered* came from."

"Was it about genemods?"

He shook his head. "No. I think it was about artificial intelligences and about money."

I understood both terms. Vaguely. They were in our history books. We bartered instead of using money, and we had computers. All of our computers and communications gear, even the earsets and the pods, came from dwindling stores on *Traveler*. But as far as I could tell they weren't intelligent. At least, they didn't talk or make their own decisions except within parameters we gave them. We told them what to do; they didn't tell us what to do. "Can you direct it—I mean, can you navigate the data?"

"Not yet." The others were gaining on us, so we opened into a slow run. Joseph waited until we'd widened the gap before continuing. "I was trying to figure that out when you interrupted me. Part of the problem is I can't seem to turn off the Fremont nets and listen just to the data button—I get it all." He turned his face toward me briefly, grinning. "Thanks for stopping me from falling into myself."

I leaped over a particularly wide fallen log, stopped, and dragged it off the path, out of the way of the others. "Kayleen and I watched the projector yesterday morning while you slept. We couldn't find a way to control it. Let us know if you figure out how to navigate the data."

"What did you see?" Joseph asked.

I struggled for words to describe what we'd seen. "People . . . like us, only more. Really different. And what you saw in the cave—more of Silver's Home. It's big, and there are a lot of people there. Billions. There was a narrator, but we couldn't tell what he said much either. I don't know how to use anything we learned. We're running out of time to figure all this out. As soon as we get back to Artistos I have to give Jenna the projector and Hunter might take your headband."

"No one's taking the headband."

"Are we going to fight over it?" I asked.

"I'm not letting anyone have it. I'll try to buy us some time, set it up with Tom to fix nodes near the roamers." He grinned at me, his eyes flashing. "Get you some time with Liam."

I blushed. "That's not the most important thing on my mind."

He sped up a little, running ahead of me. I followed on his heels, relaxing into the easy rhythm of the run. After a while all that occupied my attention was the swell and fall of the path, the periodic slowing to allow the hebras to catch up, and the easy pleasant movement of my body.

By the time Tom called to us to slow down because we were where the next spike was supposed to be—one we needed to replace—my breath came harder and my whole body felt flushed with exertion. A wide valley spilled out between two mountains, the valley itself dotted with smaller hills. The lake lapped at brown mud beaches lined with spiky grass, browning with fall.

We couldn't see the spike. Tom dug a spare pod out of its safe nest inside one of the packs, and headed up a little hill to the location he found on his data reader. Paloma and Kayleen promised to set out a light lunch of the last of the djuri meat and some of our dried food while Alicia and Joseph and I took the hebras to water.

We took off our shoes, rolled up our pants legs, and splashed out a few meters so the hebras could drink clear water. The cool lake swirled around my ankles, sending tingles up my legs after the long, hot run-and-scramble to get here.

Alicia smiled at Joseph, standing as close to him as possible while managing two hebras at a time, but none of us had a free hand and the two of them didn't touch. Even so, I felt energy between them that I was no part of.

We brought the last animals back and started taking lunch, as finger food, from a tray Kayleen and Paloma had arranged artfully. Tom glanced at Joseph. "I replaced the node. Had to dig the spike out of the ground—it had been stuck up in some rocks and must have fallen in the earthquake. The old one was smashed. You can help calibrate the new one after lunch if you'd like to."

Joseph took a bite of djuri and said, "It's done."

Tom cocked an eyebrow at him. "Already?"

Joseph grinned proudly. "I sensed it as soon as it came up, about five minutes after you put it in. I tweaked it. It's operating fine."

Tom's expression said he didn't want to believe Joseph. He bit into a dried tomato, chewing thoughtfully. "Do you mean it's on, or it's talking to all the other nodes, or what?"

Before Joseph had time to answer, Tom tapped his ear to indicate a call on his earset. "Hello?" He listened for a moment, then said, "Yes, Joseph fixed it." He paused. "Good to hear." He glanced at Joseph and gave him a thumbs-up. "Yes, we're fine."

I waved to get his attention. "Tom?"

He said, "Hold on," looking at me.

"Can I talk to Bryan?"

Tom's eyes flashed alarm as if my request disturbed him. He spoke carefully into the earset. "Chelo would like to talk to Bryan. Is that possible?"

He listened for a moment, and then hung up. He didn't look at me as he said, "He's not available."

It would be a workday in Artistos. Surely that was what they meant, although I didn't like what I'd seen cross Tom's eyes, however briefly. "Maybe later?" I asked.

He was silent for a moment, looking out over the lake. "I'll see what I can do." He switched subjects. "Nava says you did a great job on the node; it's clearer than it was before the quake. Apparently they all are. Nava said our equipment can't calibrate so finely. What changed?"

It was Joseph's turn to look away. "I feel stronger than before. That's all. I can do more, faster." He glanced briefly at Alicia, blushing a little. "Maybe I just grew up some."

Tom chewed on his lower lip, still looking unhappy. "Maybe you did," he mumbled.

Alicia sighed exaggeratedly. "Isn't fixing stuff what he got sent out here to do? I don't understand you at all."

Paloma put a hand on Alicia's arm. "Yes, it is. Tom's just tired."

Tom took a piece of djuri and held it up. "You caught this. You or your sister. And you're doing more for us than you ever have, better. I . . . wanted you to succeed. You kids have done well in a difficult situation. But . . . heck . . ." He lowered his hand and his eyes, looking at the blanket in front of him. "Maybe I'm jealous. Maybe I'm not sure what the people in Artistos will think if you do too well." He glanced at Alicia. "This is hard for us, too." He returned his gaze to Joseph, who looked right back at him. "It will help to have the nodes working right, make this winter easier. Just be sure that whatever you do is for the colony. That's all I ask."

Paloma took her hand away from Alicia's arm, twisting to gaze directly into her eyes. They contrasted neatly; a tall blond woman with straight hair and soft eyes and an even taller dark-haired girl with flyaway hair and hard eyes. As thin as Paloma was, she looked rounded compared to Alicia. When she spoke, her voice was soft, pitched barely loud enough for the rest of us to hear. "Alicia . . . this is hard for you. It's not fair for us, either. It's just how it is, and we all have to figure out how to manage." She glanced over at Kayleen. "Kayleen has brought me more joy than any other human being, been a daughter to me. And yet she's always been in danger, and now, now you are all so old we can no longer protect you. And you may be in more danger than ever before."

Paloma's comment went with the fear I'd seen in Tom's eyes. "What's going on back in Artistos?" I asked.

Tom and Paloma both avoided my eyes.

"Tell me," I insisted.

Paloma said, "Bryan got in a fight."

My stomach felt instantly weak, and I saw Bryan's face when I told him good-bye, remembered the anger that was always in him. But he wouldn't have started anything. He'd promised me. "Is he safe?"

"He's all right," Tom said.

Why didn't they tell us before? I stiffened. "When, and how? With who?"

"Just after we left. We didn't want to stop Joseph's healing, didn't want you to want to go back home. There's nothing you could do anyway." Tom shifted uncomfortably, looking at his hands. "He's locked up."

We were two days away from home if we kept a hard pace. Paloma's ankle wouldn't take that. Anger and fear crept into my voice even though I tried not to feel them. "Someone must have started it. Not Bryan. He would never start a fight."

Paloma whispered softly. "I told Nava that he wouldn't have started it." She surely knew about our periodic arguments with some of the other young people from Kayleen.

Tom added, "I don't have many details. Nava told me that Bryan broke Garmin's arm."

This was bad. I could see Garmin's face, taunting us, hear his harsh tones. I snapped, "Garmin baits us all the time. I'm sure he started it. I can't tell you how often Bryan has ignored him—I know he never started any of the arguments we had. We all learned to ignore Garmin."

Tom looked surprised, as if the idea that we had our own troubles with people our age hadn't occurred to him.

Alicia started gathering the lunch things, even though most of the food was still uneaten. "We're going back," she said.

"It's three-day-old news," Tom said. "We're finishing lunch, and we're going on to the next node, and then we'll decide if we go back or go on. Nava asked us to stay out here."

"So Nava told you to keep this from us?" I demanded.

Tom shook his head. "We all talked about it together."

Alicia stopped, still holding the tray, and glared at him, her violet eyes snapping with anger, her long dark hair loosely back from her face, exposing her slender neck. "I'm sick to death of people not telling me things. I'm tired of being told what to do. Of other people making decisions for me." Every muscle in her body looked tense.

Her anger felt dangerous, its heat thawing my own anger and betrayal.

"Alicia." I took the food tray from her hands and set it down. "We aren't done with our lunch. Do you expect to just barge into Artistos and break him out? We have to think." I stood looking down at her, realizing I couldn't have the conversation I needed around Tom and Paloma. "Come on, Alicia, Joseph, Kayleen—let's go talk." I looked at Paloma, and said, "You just told us that you can't solve our problems for us. You're right. You helped us get out here, helped keep Alicia safe, but this time we make our own decisions."

Paloma gulped and looked at Kayleen. A tear streaked down Paloma's cheek. Tom frowned, but he bobbed his head in a short nod. "Don't go far."

Just out of earshot would be fine. No one else had moved. "Well?"

Alicia rocked back on her heels. "Did you hear me? I'm tired of being told what to do. No one made you my keeper either, Chelo."

Kayleen answered by standing up and stepping next to me, taking my hand.

Alicia didn't move, just stayed in her squat on the blanket, a coiled spring ready to fly. Her face was set, her jaw tight. Only her eyes showed anything but anger. In them, uncertainty flashed.

Joseph went over next to her, putting his hand on her back, looking at me with a terrible ripped expression on his face, as if he were caught in two conflicting moon tides. I held his eyes, willing him to walk to my side, our gazes both unwavering for at least five breaths. It seemed like the entire lunch party had frozen in place, waiting for movement.

Joseph dropped his eyes.

Instead of walking over to me, he squatted down to Alicia, looking her in the eyes, holding his hand out. His hand hung there in the air for a long time before she took it, standing and following him to join Kayleen and me. I gestured ahead of us, and Joseph and Alicia, hand in hand, led us down toward the lake bank. None of us looked back to where Tom and Paloma sat silently, but I felt them watching us, felt a small gulf opening between us and their support.

We sat near where we'd taken the hebras out, the lake spreading in front of us, the mountains that held the cave—held relics of our past and future—to our left, barely visible beyond the curve of Little Lace Lake. A light wind blew off the lake, smelling of water and moss and soaked logs. Alicia sat nestled in Joseph's arm on my left, Kayleen on my right. "All right," I said. "This is bad. We don't know how bad. We know Bryan's in trouble, and that he can't get himself out of it. And I suspect whatever happened hasn't helped us."

"Mom will support us," Kayleen said. "And Tom."

Alicia sat up straighter, looking past me to Kayleen, her eyes cool. "Really? They didn't tell us about Bryan."

"And what would have happened if they had?" I asked. "Would we have spent the day with Jenna, learned the things we learned? No one wants to go get Bryan as much as I do. But what if we go back and they lock us up? What if we go back and we can't change anything? We need a plan."

"Bryan and Liam broke me out," Alicia said. "I can't bear to leave him there, not after he helped me."

"And you couldn't bear to be locked up again, either," I snapped. "We're doing what they want, and we're learning things they don't know about, things we need to know. It's impossible to talk to Jenna for long in Artistos, even when we aren't being watched carefully. She stops it herself. She knows better than to draw attention."

"I wonder if she knows what's going on in Artistos?" Kayleen asked. "Is that why she showed us the cave?"

"Maybe she's there now," Joseph said, "looking after Bryan."

Alicia stood up, standing with her back to the lake, watching the three of us. "So no matter what, you're dependent on someone else? On Tom and Paloma, or on Jenna?"

I watched her carefully as I said, "Don't underestimate the people in Artistos just because we are stronger than any one of them. You heard Tom and Paloma's story the other day. Three hundred people stronger than us—adults who understood what and who they are—lost a war with Artistos. We couldn't win."

She gazed back at me, her face as angry as when she crouched on the blanket.

I continued, trying to soften my voice, to draw her in. "But you're right. We must decide what we want. Not what anyone else wants for us. But even then, we may need help."

Alicia sat back down, still close to Joseph, but this time not touching him. "I know what I want. I want to live by ourselves, just us. There's six of us. Seven if you count Jenna. That's enough to start our own town, or to be our own band. Liam and I know how to travel, and you four know how to farm and grow things."

"Six." I swallowed. "Or seven. It's not an adequate breeding pool. I know that from how carefully we keep records, and how the Town Council has to approve marriages. Six won't do unless we learn more about genetics ourselves, and can design out defects. I don't even know if we have that information here." I glanced at Joseph. "Or the tools."

He shook his head. "We might have the data. I have almost no idea what Jenna gave us yet, for the most part. Even if I could, it's not like learning to pick corn. It would take training."

"Paloma understands as much genetics as anyone here," Kayleen said.

Alicia grimaced.

I held up my hands for silence. "Okay, so Alicia wants us to live by ourselves. There are some problems there, but let's each have a chance to talk. Kayleen?"

She tucked her knees in close to her, wrapping her arms around them, and glanced over her shoulder toward Tom and Paloma before speaking. "I want to live by ourselves, in one big house, but in Artistos. I would feel safer there, and I don't want to leave Mom."

"Joseph?" I asked.

"I'm with Alicia. We can hunt, I bet we can kill predators, and we wouldn't have to hide anything. I want to be free to go to the cave, to see Jenna, to travel." He scooted closer to Alicia and squeezed her around the waist, then leaned in to kiss the top of her head. "I'm tired of being told what to do." He frowned. "But I know what you want, Chelo. Like Kayleen, you want to live in Artistos."

I chewed on my lip. He was right, and that meant we were split. "You and Alicia could join the West Band." I glanced at Kayleen. "Or maybe we all could. We don't have the skills, today, to live completely apart, not even as a group. But there's something else I've been thinking about." I made sure to look each of them in the eye, to make them nod before I looked away. "We've always helped out. Maybe we did it for the wrong reasons. But the best outcome for us and everyone in Artistos is for them to let us live there, and to value our skills. We have something to offer them."

"I don't care if they all die," Alicia said, sliding a little away from Joseph. "It would be a lot easier on us."

Kayleen stiffened, her eyes flashing. "But I do," she snapped. "I don't like them all, and they don't all like me, but I love Paloma and Akashi and Liam and Bryan and even Tom. Gianna. We have friends there."

"I have no friends in Artistos," Alicia said, her voice even and flat, unemotional. "And only one good friend in the band. Just Sky."

Joseph pulled her into him. I could have planted my own kiss on his cheek when he said, "Chelo's right. We can help. If we can't figure out how to make them let us help, we leave until they will let us. They'll need us someday. For more than fixing data networks. Jenna's probably saved twenty lives so far with her predator kills. They'll see."

Alicia shook her head. "I don't want to live in Artistos or to help them. But I want to stick with you three for now. That will have to be enough."

It wasn't. We needed to be united, and even Joseph didn't yet see that living on our own, away from Artistos, wasn't all right. I drummed my fingers and fidgeted. "Okay," I said. "We know we don't want to be told what to do and we're tired of living with the adults. So we know what we don't want. We know two of us want to live in town and two don't."

They all nodded. Alicia said, "Now that the preliminary chat is out of the way, what do we *do*? We can't ignore Bryan."

I shook my head. "I don't know. We better talk to Liam. Maybe I can get Tom to let us do that."

"I don't want to let Tom off the hook for not telling us," Alicia said.

"And so we . . . do what?" Kayleen asked. "Ignore him?"

Alicia shook her head. "I feel like a prisoner."

I had no counter . . . I felt the same way. But I didn't want to agree and feed her anger. "All right. Joseph, there's one more node here to fix. Can we get to it tonight?"

He nodded. "It's only a few hours away. After that, there's nothing left to do but make our way around the lake."

I looked at the far shore, calculating in my head. "We'll still have to camp one more night. It's too far to get back to the fork before dark. Let's talk to Liam, and then decide what to do next. I want to get Bryan out of Artistos, but I don't know how to do that yet."

"We could break him out if Jenna helped," Alicia said. "She can get through the boundaries."

The idea made me squirm uncomfortably. "We need to find out what's happening first." I glanced at the sun, which had started its afternoon transit. "Let's talk again as soon as we camp—maybe all four of us taking the first watch. Whatever we have to do." I stood. "But first, we should move. Sitting and talking all day won't help Bryan."

I took Kayleen's hand, reaching my free hand for Joseph's. He took mine and then took Alicia's. I wanted us to walk back looking united, even though we had agreed on very little. The gesture was pretty much wasted on Tom and Paloma, who were so deep in conversation they didn't notice us until we were almost back in camp. They had packed up, and sat ready to go.

"Kayleen and Alicia—it's your turn to run," I said. Alicia favored me with a brief glare, but they obeyed, standing while Joseph and Tom helped Paloma mount up. Tom and

Paloma did not ask us any questions, nor did they seem surprised that we were ready to just keep going. I glanced over at Tom. "I'd like to set a fast pace."

He nodded. "Well, then. Take the lead."

I drew in a breath and made my voice sound calm. "I want to talk to Liam when we stop."

He looked long and hard at me. "I'll talk to Akashi."

So the balance of power between us was shifting, but not entirely. If it was this hard to get Tom and Paloma to let us choose our own path, how much harder would it be to convince Nava, Hunter, and Wei-Wei?

This time, I let Joseph ride by himself. They'd just assume he was lost in thought about Bryan, and perhaps he could figure out something about Bryan. I asked Tom and Paloma what else was happening in Artistos, but they offered no more information. I couldn't tell if they had none, or just weren't willing to share.

We settled into a quiet and uncomfortable ride. Alicia pointed out fresh paw-cat tracks once, a reminder to keep good watch.

After an hour, we traded runners out. Joseph and I stayed close to the others, nervous of paw-cats and both quiet.

The next data spike had simply lost its power, probably not even related to the quake. Tom and Joseph worked quietly together. Paloma made no protest when Tom agreed with us that we could keep going for another hour to take advantage of the light.

We camped in the open, on a little muddy beach in the last set of hills before the path intersected the fuller and deeper Little Lace Forest. Tom and Kayleen laid the perimeter bells, building a U-shape with the lake at the opening of the U. When they finished, Tom said, "Okay, now we need some firewood. Why don't you four go out together? You'll be safer that way. I'll pitch the tents while you're gone. Gather a lot of wood—we're so in the open here that I'd like a big fire to ward off any predators."

In other words, he and Paloma wanted to be alone. I met his eyes. "I want to be here when you talk to Akashi."

He nodded. "I know you do."

I held out my hand. "Can we have an earset in case we need it?"

Tom shook his head. "Not until we all talk, later. Just stay close enough to yell if you need us."

Who was he trying to keep us from communicating with? I frowned, but turned anyway and started off. The other three followed me. We set off the perimeter bells as we passed outside the safe zone.

I led us to a downed tree I had spotted on our way in, in a small grove just a little ways back along the path.

Joseph and Alicia walked together a little bit ahead of Kayleen and me, holding hands. Kayleen turned toward me, giggling. "Will you look at them?"

I remembered Trading Day, when it had seemed like Joseph had a crush on Kayleen. "Do you mind?" I asked her.

She shook her head. "I didn't want to be Joseph's girlfriend. And he needed something to drag him out of his shell—better he hunts a girl than the local wildlife. They're kind of cute together."

"So you don't like hunting?"

She shrugged. "Someone's got to do it. I don't want to. But I do worry for her, and for him because of her. She cried on our last run. Earlier, she stayed angry the whole time."

"Did you try to talk to her? Alicia told me a few days ago that she feels like you don't like her."

Kayleen scowled. "She's not making it easy to like her."

Joseph and Alicia reached the downed tree ahead of us and started ripping off branches, Joseph filling Alicia's arms. As I held out my arms for a pile of wood, he asked me, "So, what are we going to do? Go back tomorrow?"

"I want to. But maybe we need to stay out until you understand more."

He laid two heavy branches across my outstretched arms and started adding smaller pieces. "I made some progress this afternoon. I can separate the two strands of data now, but I still can't control the new one."

Alicia asked, "Can you read the Artistos data? Can you find out what's happening in town? I hate waiting for them to tell us."

Joseph silently finished giving me a full load of branches. The rough edges scratched my bare hands. He turned and ripped off another branch, as wide as his biceps, the cracking sound satisfying. When he turned back to hand the branch to Kayleen, he said, "I probably could. But I don't think I can do it without leaving traces. Yet. I was probing the net a few hours ago. I think we better wait until we're closer; they'll just shut down the nets if they think I'm poking around. Remember how Tom said Hunter had them watching for signs that Jenna might be in there? I got in a lot of trouble when I got caught at that years ago, and that means they'll remember I can do it."

I glanced at Alicia. "I think it's best not to probe. Not now." I sighed and shifted the load of wood a little, speaking softly to Joseph. "But you should be ready."

He kept adding branches to Kayleen's pile. "I know. I don't like it, but I can certainly do it. But I can only do it for sure once." He picked up two branches for himself. "I'll travel light. Someone should have their hands basically free."

So we walked back, slowly, burdened with piles of wood. My legs were tired from the run, and I felt like sitting down around a fire and not moving would be the best thing in the whole world. The sun had fallen far enough that we walked in twilight, even though it still shone on the tops of the hills above us.

I felt like an outsider to Artistos, like I was planning, or at least preparing for, an assault on my home.

18

THE FORK IN THE PATH

$\backsim$

Tom smiled and joked as he helped us stack the wood by a fire pit he had dug and surrounded with gray river stones. His voice trembled a little, as if the friendliness was being dragged over some other feeling I couldn't identify; maybe worry about what we would do next, or better, remorse over hiding information about Bryan from us.

As soon as we finished, Tom motioned us to gather near Paloma. She lay nestled in a pile of saddlebags, her foot propped up, looking small and tired in the near-dark. Kayleen squeezed next to Paloma and rubbed her shoulders, and the rest of us gathered in close.

Tom held a hand up for attention. "Time to call the West Band." He gestured toward the data reader next to him, like Paloma, propped in saddlebags. It surprised me that he had set it up to route the other side of the conversation from his earset through its speakers. He took his earset off and twisted it, changing channels to match the roamers' frequency. He fit the set back over his ear, the small dark knob visible like a black stone beneath his earlobe. "Akashi?"

"Here. Tom?" Akashi's voice was barely recognizable through the tinny high-pitched speakers. We all leaned in closer to hear him.

"We can all hear you; we patched you through some speakers. How are you? How is the band?" Tom asked.

Akashi sounded too happy, stage-cheerful. "Hello, everyone. We're wintering at the edge of High Canyon Falls, near

Hunter's Stream. We're almost settled, and Liam just returned from setting the dragonbirds free. No one's been hurt. Are you still out fixing data nets? How is that going?"

A small ironic laugh escaped Tom's lips. "Oddly. We're making good enough progress we'll have time to come up your way."

There was no answer for so long that Tom asked, "Are you there?"

"Yes. Perhaps that is better than going back to Artistos right now." Akashi's next words were measured. "Fixing the nets up here would be good; we'd like to get our communications with Artistos clear."

Tom raised his eyebrows as us, asking us wordlessly.

Alicia grimaced and shook her head, her eyes dark and angry. *Don't agree.* Joseph's dark eyes met mine, unreadable, but he held Alicia's hand. Torn again, I suspected; wanting to follow Alicia anywhere, but not yet shorn of *all* good sense. Beside me, Kayleen smiled encouragement, her expression eager. She would want to see Liam. I did, too. As much as I wanted to free Bryan, riding back to Artistos didn't feel right. I looked back at Tom, nodding. I'd take responsibility for getting Alicia there.

Alicia pursed her lips and looked away, her body rigid. She said nothing.

"All right," Tom said. "We're almost all the way around the lake. We'll be back where we separated from Liam, at the fork in the High Road, by midafternoon tomorrow. Which way do we go from there?"

"Don't. Stay put. I'll send a guide. That will be faster."

"We have a map," Tom protested. "And Alicia. Surely she knows how to find a roamer band."

"Yes, but you don't know all the dangers." Akashi seemed to be picking his words carefully.

Tom pursed his lips, glancing from me to Alicia to Joseph. "When will someone meet us there?" he asked Akashi.

"Sometime in the morning, the day after tomorrow. If you camp by the river, back up to the cliff. It's safer."

"All right," Tom said. "Paloma twisted her ankle a few days ago. We ride slowly."

"I'm sorry to hear that. Tell her good traveling. We'll talk when you get here." The crackle in the speakers deadened to stillness.

Tom turned off the data reader. "Shall we eat?"

Hours later, Tom and Kayleen woke Alicia and me for the second watch over the hebras. Destiny hung directly overhead, lighting our way as we walked Ink and Sand down for water. The grass was already so wet with dew that I slipped twice as we made our way to the bank, careful to stay inside the perimeter. Far off, behind us in the hills, I heard a pack of demon dogs, and the call of two wild hebras, probably herd lookouts giving direction. Ink danced and threw her head, perhaps reacting to the dogs and the wild band of hebras. Sand pricked one ear forward and one back, but otherwise she simply pulled me down toward the lake. Two clear silver paths of moonlight, from Destiny and Summer, reflected on the dark water, intersecting in a V near the shore. We stood in the moonlight while Ink and Sand drank in quick slurps, one at a time, the other always standing and listening, ears swiveling.

"Why did you let Tom decide what we would do?" Alicia asked.

"Because he chose the right thing for us. I don't like making Bryan wait, but we need more information, more time. We need to find Jenna." I sighed. "Or let her find us." Stripes lifted her head and butted me gently, asking for a scratch. Her beard dripped water. I scratched her anyway. "We can't risk Hunter taking the headband, not yet. Not until"—I swallowed—"not until we have a good way to keep it. I bet things at home are worse than Tom is saying. Akashi was too quiet. He didn't sound like he wanted to say anything specific. I bet he knows about Bryan. Besides, Akashi's advice is almost always good."

"Waiting for someone else to tell you what to do again?"

What? Who wouldn't want to listen to Akashi? "Should I just do the opposite, by reflex? We're going to have to pick our battles."

She nodded, her profile nearly a silhouette. Her voice was almost belligerent as she said, "I hate agreeing with you about that. I hate waiting. I've waited all my life to be free of the band. Only . . . only I'm not really free. There's always something to keep me from doing what I want." She reached into the shallow water and picked up a stone, skipping it across the lake surface. Ink warbled at her and splashed water on her torso with her head. Alicia glared at her hebra, then splashed Ink back softly, laughing. She looked at me. "I'm sorry. I'm fighting everything. That's not fair."

I reached toward her, but she pulled away, leading Ink toward the bank. We rotated through the rest of the beasts in awkward silence, and went to sit by the fire.

Kayleen and Joseph were there, sharing a log for a seat. Flames crackled and snapped in a good-sized fire, releasing sparks to drift briefly over our heads, red stars winking out one by one.

Kayleen said, "We had to wait for Tom to go to sleep. Joseph wiggled out of the tent right past him, and he kept right on snoring. Joseph wanted to talk to us, and this is a good time. Isn't the fire pretty?"

I laughed and gave her a little hug. "Shhhhh . . . you'll wake your mom. Yes, it's pretty." I looked over at Joseph. The fire's reflection danced in his dark eyes. His fingers drummed on his knees and his right foot tapped impatiently against his left calf.

"What did you find?" I asked.

He kept his voice low. "I changed data buttons, and the one I'm reading now is about the *New Making*."

"Can you fly it?" Alicia asked.

He laughed. "Hardly. I don't even know yet if this data button will tell me how to. But I know some of what it looks like inside, how they expected the crew to live. I know how to make food and use the toilet and take a shower, and what the sleeping rooms look like. It's not that same silver inside. It's got lots of color, mostly soft blues and greens. It's pretty simple outside the living areas; pipes and storage—lots of storage." He threw a small log on the fire, watching as yellow flames embraced it. "I want to get in there and see what they left. There may be ships. The button shows ships. Smaller than the ones we use to go back and forth to *Traveler*. But I don't remember any stories about them—us—using ships like that. Do you?"

I shook my head. "No. The *New Making* doesn't look big enough to hold ships inside it."

"These were only about six times as big as a wagon." He looked at Kayleen. "It has a big garden. Paloma would love it."

"I bet the garden is dead after all this time," Kayleen mused.

"Well"—Joseph shrugged—"there's that. I wish I could show you the pictures I've been seeing in my head. Maybe after a while I can figure it out."

"Can you pipe what you see through the projector?" Kayleen asked.

I shook my head. "Jenna said not to risk it near anyone."

Kayleen looked pained. "Paloma and Tom wouldn't turn us in. I know they wouldn't." She picked up a stone and threw it out across the water, so Ink and Sand both raised their heads. "But you're right. Did you see anything else?"

He shook his head. "No. And . . . I don't think the projector would show you the data the way I see it . . . it's layered and twisty, and I have to follow idea-threads, which work like a bad knot. Data lays on data and points to data, image on image." He stared at the fire for a few moments, then yawned. "I don't exactly know how to direct questions yet . . . I just sometimes know how to go down a path of questions that relate, one to another. If I make up my own new question in my head, I don't know how to start answering it." He yawned again. "I thought you'd want to know about the ship."

He glanced at Alicia and gave me a hopeful look, but I said, "Go to sleep." I told him the same thing I'd told Alicia earlier. "We'll save our energy for the important fights."

He nodded, gave Alicia a slightly too long hug, and slipped back into the darkness. *New Making*. I had yearned to see inside it for so long, had been entranced and puzzled by its mysteries. Alicia had dreamed of it. Joseph had obsessed about it when he was about ten, drawing pictures of it every evening. And now we were learning something about it. At last. At least Joseph was. The projector nearly burned in my pocket, but I resisted, feeding small sticks into the fire and humming.

Tom and Joseph together relieved us for the next watch, pretty much ruining any chance to find out if Joseph had learned more about the ship. But maybe, I thought as I yawned sleepily, maybe he and Tom would repair some of the damage they'd been inflicting on each other.

Long before I had enough sleep, I woke to the smell of fish cooking over the fire. The windless air was surprisingly cool. I pulled on my shoes and coat and took a seat by the fire. "You guys were fishing?"

Tom laughed. "I taught him to hunt. I figured I'd teach him to lake fish."

Joseph was already good at fishing the Lace River. I glanced over at him, and he grinned and stretched his arms in front of him. "We thought we'd better make breakfast before we woke you sleepyheads." He gestured toward the tents. "So how about if you wake everyone and we eat and go?"

"How about she has a cup of tea first?" Tom asked. He nodded at Joseph. "You can go wake the others. Give me a few minutes to talk to Chelo."

I curled my hands around the cup Tom handed me, enjoying the warmth, watching a flock of small brown birds dart over the trees we'd taken the wood from.

Tom pitched his voice low, leaning in toward me. "Paloma and I are a little worried about you and Joseph and Kayleen, about the choices you might make. We are more worried about Alicia. She doesn't listen. At best, she's a distraction for Joseph. At worst . . . well, she might lead you into trouble." I was sure he meant to say something worse about Alicia, but instead he just scraped the fish over with his knife, concentrating on the pan and the fire. When he finished, he looked at me. "Can you control her?"

Not really. No. Joseph would never forgive me if I said the wrong thing, and got Alicia locked up with Bryan. Tom was asking about control, but how would I control her? How had I so far? "Alicia trusts us more than she trusts anyone. And she wants family. So, yes, I think I can." A log disintegrated into glowing coals. "She can only earn your trust, or not, if she's free to make decisions." I sipped at my tea again, thinking about goals. "And you need to earn hers. In fact, remind Nava the trust she wants isn't a one-way effort. Tell her that I need her to take good care of Bryan, and that we'll do our best to take care of Alicia."

He blinked, looking startled at my audacity.

I heard Kayleen chattering at Paloma and took our last moment of quiet to add, "Thank you for all you've done. You did help Joseph."

He nodded, watching the fire and not me, and said, "It's getting hard to know what helps him, or you, and what hurts."

I stood up and went to help organize camp.

By early afternoon, we finally finished circumnavigating Little Lace Lake, coming back to the point where we'd first seen the lake, at the top of the crater wall. It had taken six nights to return to this spot; it seemed as if a year had passed. I felt different than I had cresting the crater on the way over, but the same problems we had left, and worse, waited below in Artistos.

From the crater wall, it was only half an hour back to the three-way fork. Following Akashi's suggestion, we nestled our tents against the gray-black cliff, so the stream ran between us and the road. A thin line of forest filled the gap, and thankfully, someone had built a corral we could use for the hebras, shaded by near-elm and river whites. We laid the perimeter to include the corral.

When I went to fill my canteen at the stream, I looked back, and could hardly see our camp. If I hadn't known where we were, my eyes would have slid across the tents. I stopped and looked down the path, toward Artistos, and my feet wanted to start down: to return to this past spring, to collecting herbs for soap with Therese; to run stealthily and fast to the center of town by the hospital and liberate Bryan from the dark jail; to gallop down the cliff and stop near the *New Making,* safely, alone except for my brother, to open the ship and peel its secrets.

I could do none of those things, not now.

On the way back, I petted each of the hebras in turn. "Well, Stripes," I whispered. "At least we'll see Liam and Akashi."

After a cold dinner, and just as full dark cloaked us all, I followed Alicia into our tent, leaving Tom and Kayleen the job of tending fire and taking first watch. I meant to stay up and chat with Alicia, but I was out cold as soon as I closed the door behind me.

I woke, groggy, realizing I had dreamed the entrance bells chimed friendly entry. Or did they? I listened carefully. Nothing. Then a step outside the tent.

Cold air assaulted my cheek. Someone opening the tent door from outside.

Did Alicia hear it, too? I couldn't hear her breathing. I extended my arm, expecting to touch her arm or shoulder. Her bedroll was merely a jumble of empty blankets. And it wasn't Alicia coming in, whoever it was smelled wrong. Joseph? No . . . not his smells. I blinked, staying still. Traces of the hot fiery scents of the smelter, of Artistos. Adrenaline surged through me, so it took an act of will to stay still. What to do? Play as if I were asleep? Who was here?

"Come out, Chelo."

Nava.

I pushed blankets away, the cool air bracing me further. Holding my voice to a casual tone was hard. "I'm coming." I pushed through the door into a blast of even cooler air, looking around.

Nava stood a few feet away from me, her hands at rest. Her own voice sounded like mine; a strained attempt at casual conversation. "It's time for you to come home."

Stars spotted the dark, moonless sky. "It's the middle of the night," I said, looking around. The fire was ten meters from the tent, splashing light on Tom, who stood at one side of it, and Kayleen and Paloma, close together, on the other. Two men stood so far out of the firelight I couldn't make out their identities for sure. Sweeping my gaze across the broad circle of darkness, I picked out two figures leaning against trees and another standing in the corral, scratching Sand's forehead gently, looking in our direction. I squinted, recognizing Stile by the way he moved, one arm a little jerky. He'd brought us the little urns full of Steven's and Therese's ashes. He had always been kind enough to us. He clipped a lead to Sand's face harness and then reached for Ink.

"Where is your brother?" Nava asked. "And Alicia?" The way she said Alicia's name worried me.

I looked around. Alicia and Joseph both appeared to be missing. Had Alicia talked Joseph into going after Bryan by themselves? Was that why Nava was here? Was she trying to tell if I sent them? I shivered and stepped toward the fire. It was too bad I was apparently the last one to wake—any surprise on Tom's and Paloma's faces would have registered and fled by now. I looked anyway, and saw only resignation. Had they known about this?

"I don't know where they are." I turned to face Nava. "Do you?" I asked her, forcing a calm I didn't feel. "Do you know where they went?"

She seemed startled that I would ask her. "No."

I calculated my chances of bolting, including the chance of getting Kayleen to come away from Paloma's side and run with me, find my brother and Alicia. Not good. Paloma and Kayleen stood close, holding hands, Kayleen supporting some of Paloma's weight. Any escape for Kayleen meant abandoning Paloma. She'd never do that, even though Paloma, surely, was safe from Nava.

Nava stepped inside the flickering light of the small fire, so there was a circle of five of us. She held a stunner in one hand, pointed toward the ground.

"Why are you here?" I asked her, watching Tom's face

rather than hers. Tom squinted and a tight clench of his jaw muscles narrowed his round face.

She must have seen me look at Tom because she stepped nearer to him even though she spoke to me. "I thought I should explain about Bryan, thought you needed to know from me what happened. You asked to be included in the discussions at home."

Right. She brought at least five men to invite us back casually. I stalled. "I would love to know what you have been talking about. And about Bryan." My voice shook, and I fought to sound firm. "Why don't you sit here by the fire and tell me?"

"I'll tell you everything when we get back."

Tom put a hand on her shoulder and leaned down to look into her eyes. I'm sure he thought we would not hear, but I was close enough to understand his hissing whisper. "What's this about? You didn't tell me you were coming up here."

She flicked her eyes at me. "Later."

"No. Now." He looked around. "But not here. Come with me." He pulled at her arm, pulling away.

Her own reply was as low and hard as his. "When we get back."

He stopped pulling on her, looking back and forth between Nava and me.

"Stile?" Nava called. "Are you ready?"

"Almost," he called back, his voice coming from near the hebras.

I looked around carefully again, counting six of them, including Nava. No, more. They must have ridden here, so at least one person watched their hebras. And two of us, if I thought of Tom and Paloma as neutral and Joseph and Alicia as escaped. Were they in Artistos, or had they just gone off somewhere to kiss and talk? I swallowed, alone and outnumbered. "Nava? We did what you wanted. We fixed things. Joseph learned to go back into the data nets. Why are you forcing us home?"

She licked her lips. Her eyes looked like Joseph's when Alicia and I asked him for different things. So she was torn.

Her words, however, belied the indecision in her eyes. "I'm offering you the voice you wanted, encouraging you to come back. We want you all to come back for now."

"So it's an invitation that we can refuse?"

She swallowed hard and licked her lips yet again, the conflict in her eyes even brighter, her neck and cheeks flushed red. "Town Council is recalling you. It can't be refused. They chose me to come. Of all of us, I know you best." She paused, looking down and then back at me. "I thought you would prefer me."

"And they are recalling us for?"

"I told you. To include you in the talks we're having."

Sure, just so we could have our equal say. I didn't believe her. "And I am to come back to my own room and live with you?"

She hesitated. Like Tom, she couldn't flat-out lie. Or wouldn't. So foolish or not, I would try to escape. I shrugged, doing my best to look resigned. "It doesn't appear like you're leaving me any choices. It will take time to pack and put the fire out. And don't you want to find Joseph and Alicia first?"

She looked at the two men behind me. "Search the camp." They faded into the darkness.

Kayleen's eyes were fixed on Nava's, her brow furrowed, her face pale. We shared a glance, and I could tell from the fear in her eyes that she knew what I did—we could not go with Nava.

Paloma spoke up, her usual soft voice full of anger. "I won't go back until I know what you plan for my daughter. And why. Bryan breaking Garmin's arm does not begin to justify you stealing in here in the middle of the night."

Paloma was right. They had sent a force to capture us, when we would have come home on our own in a few days or weeks, riding happily into town.

Nava paced, scowling, her shoulders rigid. She took a steadying breath, and then another. She seemed to calm a little. "You have to obey the Council, Paloma."

"Not this time." Paloma stood her ground, feet planted. "Don't test me when the order is about my child."

Paloma was very popular. Forcing her might be a test for Nava, back home. Instead of taking her on directly, Nava simply said, "We will bring Chelo and Kayleen home."

I stepped next to Kayleen and Paloma. Nava didn't like it—she gestured me away. I stood my ground, taking Paloma's other hand. It trembled in mine, or perhaps our hands trembled together.

"Look," Nava said, "you're overreacting. It's going to be fine. Council just wants to talk to you. If they wanted to hurt you, they would have sent us to do that. We're simply here to escort you back to Artistos."

I didn't think for a minute that she believed her own words, or her own reasonable tone. Escort us to jail? Not home. I'd already established that. "We're not going."

Nava brought the barrel of the stunner up.

Tom stepped between Nava and us, between his wife and us.

Nava's face crumpled, as if the strength had gone out of her. She dropped the stunner barrel back down, her eyes glittering with tears that didn't quite spill down her cheeks. She opened her mouth as if to speak, then looked away.

Tom spoke firmly. "I am Town Council. I did not agree. I suggest you tell me what's driving this, and let me make a decision."

"We had a quorum." Nava's lower lip trembled and she bit it hard, as if trying to control it with her teeth.

Anger laced Tom's voice, making it lower and fuller. "Nava. My vote does matter, my opinion matters. At least to me. And unless you remove me from the Council, it matters to Artistos. Whatever drove you up here, you chose not to include me, even though we talked every day." His jaw trembled and he stopped for breath, staring at her, trying to force an answer.

She searched his eyes, tears now flowing down her cheeks in small streams that reflected the firelight.

A voice from behind us and to the right, behind the two shadowy figures I hadn't been able to identify. "I believe I mentioned that little problem to you, Nava." Akashi. Akashi himself. My heart raced.

She swore softly, and anger replaced the vulnerability in her face. Her whole body trembled. Her knuckles on the gun were white. "Tom was in the physical company of the people we were talking about. We couldn't risk alerting them. And we don't know how much Joseph can read the nets."

"I think the problem is that you do know he can read it, all of it, and you are afraid he'll exercise his ability. Hiding things from this particular set of young adults won't serve us well, Nava." I followed Akashi's voice to see him between two trees, mounted on a hebra. He held his own stunner in his hand, casually pointed just a bit away from Nava, and clearly not at us. "Put your gun in your pocket," he said, evenly, as if he were asking her to have a cup of tea.

She looked down at the gun in her hand, then at Tom, then stood still, gazing at Akashi, her neck red, her eyes blazing with frustration. She slowly, exaggeratedly, slid the stunner into her right front pocket, making a production of the movement.

Akashi didn't drop his gun. "Now, why don't you ask Stile to go ahead and get the tack on the hebras, including the pack beasts, and one for Alicia and one for Joseph, and lead them out to the road. I'm positive you won't stun anyone. We'll just head on down and camp by the spaceport. You can see us coming, we can see you coming. After you cool off a bit, we can all meet and talk."

"I don't think that's a good idea," Nava said, glaring not at Akashi but at Tom.

Akashi's voice was still evening-tea reasonable as he said, "Like you, I brought company. We don't want anything except friendship between roamers and Artistos."

Nava, defeated, hung her head and mumbled, "You can saddle your own damn hebras." She looked at Tom, a huge question in her eyes.

She didn't let the question cross her lips, but Tom crossed to her, standing by her side. He looked in Akashi's direction, and said, "I will go back to Artistos for now. I think I'm needed there."

Paloma looked from Tom to Nava. Her voice was firm, and louder than usual as she proclaimed, "I'm staying with my daughter." Nava jerked her head quickly, a tiny unsurprised nod, and Tom mouthed the word "good" over Nava's head, so that we could see.

Akashi turned his hebra around, riding toward the road. He stood there, apparently alone, a dark silhouette standing silently in a dark night, watching. I smiled when I saw Tom saddle Sugar Wheat. His choice would slow the group down and leave us the best hebras.

Nava and Tom led the others away, down the hill toward Artistos. Although it was hard to tell for sure in the darkness, I didn't see either of them look back.

There were eight of them. Eight, to bring back four. I wondered if Nava knew it would not have been enough to make us come quietly. Was it Akashi's presence that convinced her to leave, or Joseph's and Alicia's absence?

19

THE FIRST ROAD

After Nava and her force of would-be captors clattered around the bend, down toward Artistos, Akashi whistled softly into the silence they left behind. A few moments later, Liam rode up next to Akashi, emerging into the edge of the firelight. He grinned at his father. "Nice job!" Liam's light hair looked dark in the low firelight, his eyes like dark pebbles in the dark lake of his face.

"There's only you two?" Kayleen asked, her eyes wide above her smile of welcome and relief. I felt the same.

A small smile crossed Akashi's face. "Apparently, that was

enough." He gazed out over the camp. "There are also only two of you here," he pointed out. "And Paloma, of course." He smiled at her. "Thank you for staying. Joseph and Alicia are with Jenna."

I released a breath I hadn't realized I was holding, knowing they were safe. Or at least not captured, or hurt.

"Tom and I were taking the watch together, and we didn't see them leave." Paloma drew her brows together in a puzzled look. "We didn't hear them leave, either. How did they get through the perimeter?"

"Mom," Kayleen said, "I'm sure Joseph just turned the perimeters off." She giggled, releasing stress and adrenaline. "At least he turned them back on. Otherwise we wouldn't have known when Nava showed up."

I hadn't known. We were all exhausted; too exhausted. I'd slept four hours at most, and more sleep didn't seem likely. How did Joseph and Alicia end up with Jenna, anyway? They hadn't even left a note. Why didn't Jenna take me? The silence of the bells meant she must have come all the way into camp.

Liam interrupted my unspoken questions. "We better get ready to move. We need to be at the spaceport before they send a welcoming committee. That grass will hide a host of people."

I shivered. It hid paw-cats rather well, too.

"What happened in Artistos to make them come after us?" Kayleen asked.

Akashi answered. "Some idiots beat Bryan up, pretty badly. He'll recover, if they let him. Artistos has become more"—he spread his hands out in front of him—"divided since you left."

I should never have left Bryan. Never. Fear for him swept through me in a dizzying wave. "When? When did he get beat up?"

"Last night. Jenna tried to stop them, but they ran her off. Shot at her again." Akashi sounded disgusted.

No wonder she came here. But what for? Why didn't she wake us all? Maybe Nava and the others were close on her heels.

Akashi said, "You scare them enough they want you where they can see you. Now they'll have to fill Tom in, and Tom can drag that out, buying us some time. I hope." He paused, looking toward Artistos. "But don't count on it."

"Who beat him?" Paloma asked.

"Kids. Garmin's friends, apparently."

"Do you know how the fight with Garmin started?" I asked. "How he broke Garmin's arm? It's not like him."

"The same thing," Liam said. "A bunch of kids hating someone different." He sounded disgusted and his jaw looked tight with anger. "I heard two of Bryan's *brothers* even helped." He, too, looked down toward Artistos. "Bryan's alive, and not likely to get any worse. I hear he's in the hospital. We should pack up."

Akashi said, "Liam's right. We need to move. We'll take the First Road, so best, perhaps, to pack goods on riding hebras and loose the pack hebras. They'll go home."

"But what if we need them later?"

Liam rode over next to me, looking down, concerned. "You've never been down the First Road. It will be hard enough to manage extra hebras for Joseph and Alicia. With luck, they'll find us before we get to the trail."

I reached a hand up to him and he took it, squeezing quickly, and the warmth from his touch went all the way up my arm to my chest.

Then he swung down, and shifted his gaze away from me. "Paloma—you're still hurt. We'll take care of packing. You can be our watcher." He led her to a spot by the stream where she would have a good view of both directions of the High Road and be able to call out any trouble to us.

Akashi marshaled us through the process of gathering camp, shoving saddlebags to bulging with unfolded clothes and blankets, and saddling the hebras.

Liam returned from helping Paloma. He climbed up Ink's mounting strap, balancing with each foot in a separate mounting rung, trying to help me tie a pack meant to sling over a bare back to the top of Ink's saddle. He whispered at me. "I'm happy to see you."

"Me too," I replied. "Did you know they were coming?"

"No." He threaded an extra lead line from the back saddle ring over to the rings on either side of the saddle hump. "Here—hold this."

I took the line while he leaned on the pack, flattening it in the middle, pulling the line tighter. He continued. "We were about to ride into camp when we saw Joseph and Jenna and Alicia. They were heading up toward the lake. Jenna told us not to expect them until sometime tomorrow afternoon."

Going to the cave. For what? I couldn't ask.

"Akashi had me wait outside camp when we first spotted Nava. Dad's been included in some of the talk, via earset, since he is part of Town Council." He grimaced. "No one told him they were coming here. They betrayed him. He thinks they heard our conversation with you yesterday and wanted to beat our 'guide.'" He reached a hand for the line, his fingers brushing my arm lightly, leaving a trail of warmth. "We were just lucky no one saw us." He tied the line expertly, using a slipknot he could manage with one hand and his teeth.

"I'm glad you came," I said, my voice husky.

"Me too."

After he climbed down, I leaned into him, not thinking, and kissed him on the lips. Briefly.

He raised his eyebrows in surprise, but grinned and went off to loose the extra hebras while I blushed, thankful for the darkness.

Liam and Kayleen bundled Paloma on Sand, and then Akashi and Liam each took one spare beast.

"Have either of you been up or down the First Road?" Liam asked, looking from me to Kayleen.

We both shook our heads.

"All right. Do what we say when we get there." Liam patted his hebra, a tall animal with a dark hide spotted with light streaks—not quite stripes like my own animal, but like the sun falling through a glade in strips of light. "This is Star."

I put a hand out to stroke Star's soft cheek. "What about the others?" I fretted. "Will they know how to find us?"

Akashi laughed. "Quit worrying about Joseph. He's nearly grown, and Jenna is with them anyway."

The rest of us mounted, and followed Akashi to the right fork, which rose up the middle of a low hill. Deepening shades of dark implied a sharp drop twenty feet to our right, and a low rise made a dark slash to the left. The path was wide enough for us to ride five abreast. Ink and Legs, unhappy to be temporary pack beasts, pranced at the flanks of the outside mounts. Even going uphill, Akashi and Liam kept the hebras breathing hard up, their long necks extended. The beasts seemed to sense our worries as they responded to our urges for speed.

Stars, but no moons, filled the sky overhead, offering little light. Every once in a while, a meteor streaked overhead, a bright snake arcing across the sky. One briefly lit the path in front of us with a flickering yellow-white light.

Our passage sounded noisy against the quiet of the sleeping forest. I was sure that if we yelled, they would hear us all the way down in Artistos. Akashi and Liam rode on the two sides, Paloma next to Akashi, then Kayleen, and me next to Liam. Kayleen chattered softly. "Where is the First Road? Paloma told me about it, but she didn't say where it started or ended. Why don't you use it to get to Artistos?"

Akashi answered her. "The High Road is faster, and besides, the First Road is too steep for wagons."

"Is it safe at night?" Paloma asked.

"No." Akashi's voice was matter-of-fact. "But Destiny will rise by the time we get there. It will help." He changed his tone into a comic query. "Unless you prefer to ride through town?"

Twenty minutes later, Akashi pulled up by a wide spot in the road. Sure enough, Destiny's light now touched our side of the mountains. The path we were leaving turned, rising upward, toward the mountain passes, wide and clear and well used. A dark and narrow path branched west, heading down into thick forest.

"Liam," Akashi called. "You lead. Then the girls, then the two extra hebras, then Paloma. I'll take the last spot. Go slowly."

Liam handed Ink's reins to Paloma, and started down the narrow path, watching over his shoulder, his face lit by moonlight: a beacon. Kayleen and I rode up together, and I wanted to ride ahead of her to be closer to Liam, but I pulled back on Stripes and let her go.

Akashi said, "Chelo, take Ink, but unclip her lead line as soon as you know we're all on the path, put her between you and Kayleen."

After only a hundred meters or so the path dropped suddenly downward, and Stripes leaned back, haunches into the hill, her forelegs trembling. "Shouldn't we walk?" I called ahead.

"Not yet," Liam called back. "But we should make noise; sing or something. Be sure any predators know there are too many of us."

I encouraged Stripes gently with my heels. She turned her head back to glare at me, but then grunted and started gingerly down. Kayleen hummed the first bars of a traveling song, and we all sang it together, Akashi's voice so loud and sweet it carried all the way to me. Here, with trees to absorb the sound, I was sure Artistos would not hear it. Too bad. It would be good for them to hear us singing.

The path straightened again, still narrow, surrounded by the darkness of thick trees. I shivered, looking for paw-cat on the bigger branches. But whether it was our singing or the time of night or just luck, nothing leaped at us. Ink and Legs stayed in formation with no one leading them; the trail was too narrow for them to turn or pass. Down, and flat, and down, and only once a little up, and down, and down; walking twice, leading hebras down slopes so steep we all slid; crossing a stream twice, and down. In three hours, we didn't quite run out of songs, and we didn't stop, even once. My throat hurt from singing when Akashi called, "Chelo. We have Legs. Get Ink."

I dismounted, unsteady on my feet after so long in the saddle. I slipped up behind Ink, caught her head harness, and clipped the lead I'd carried on my own saddle back onto her. Ink tossed her head, but let me do it. I was so tired that climbing back up the mounting rope to Stripes's back was nearly impossible, and I lay straddle across her for a moment before swinging up and urging her to follow Longface. Sure enough, the trail widened and the trees opened in front of us onto the Grass Plains.

New Making gleamed with Destiny's light.

The hebras' heads rose, their ears pricked forward, and they swung their heads back and forth, as if drawing energy from being back on the Grass Plains.

Akashi stopped us fifty meters before the spaceport, in a wide rocky spot on the path. "Stay here. I'm going to ride out and make sure the spaceport is empty."

"Be careful," Liam said.

"It hasn't gotten so bad that anyone will shoot *me*," Akashi said. "But keep good watch, and stay mounted." He turned and rode toward the spaceport, disappearing from sight long before we lost track of the sound of his saddle creaking and his hebras' footsteps.

Moonlight illuminated tiny pain lines creasing Paloma's forehead. She held up one hand. "Liam. What else has happened? We know about the fight, the first one, but either Nava told Tom very little"—she paused and frowned—"or he told me almost nothing of what she said."

Liam cleared his throat and took a drink of water from the bottle strapped to his saddle. "Ruth. Ruth went back to Artistos, waiting only until we were past the fork and gone."

I groaned, picturing her and Nava laughing in the kitchen the same day she accused Alicia, the same day we'd been almost thrown out of town.

Liam continued. "Ruth took a few of the people in her band that sided with her the most, leaving everyone else to set up winter camp. Once she got to Artistos, she started arguing with everyone she could, I guess, and demanding that a decision to keep you all under some kind of house arrest be made before you got back. Wei-Wei backed her. Lyssa disagreed, but she's not nearly as loud. Hunter and Nava didn't say either way, I guess. Nava's the one who talked to Akashi, and he said she's divided."

"She is," I said. "You saw her up there. If she'd really wanted to take us into custody, she'd have tried harder."

"She's not exactly fighting for us," Liam said. "Akashi's mad at her. I think he's mad at all of them. For treating you so badly."

"Anything else?" Paloma asked.

Liam shook his head. "Not that I know of. Remember, we weren't there either."

For a few moments we were all silent. The first bit of daylight began to fill the sky. A cool morning wind blew across my face and ruffled Stripes's thick dense fur, the beginning of her winter coat.

"When will Joseph and Alicia and Jenna join us?" Kayleen asked.

"I don't know." He turned to Paloma. "What happened to your foot?"

We filled him in on our trip around the lake, leaving out only the cave and the headband and data buttons. When we talked about hunting, he laughed. "I've been hunting for years. Akashi encourages my strengths." He looked sideways at me. "Did you like it?"

I laughed, touched that he thought I might not, touched that he cared what I felt. "Not as much as Joseph did."

Leaving out the parts we weren't ready to tell Paloma made the trip sound less interesting, and Kayleen and I shared a miserable look when we pretended we had found the hebras. But I wasn't ready to trust Paloma with things Jenna wanted secret, even though I wanted to, since she had chosen to stick with us.

After we finished, Liam looked over his shoulder, probably watching for Akashi. Daylight began to frost the tips of the grasses with sunshine. Liam frowned.

Kayleen smiled tiredly at him. "Tell us about the dragonbirds."

Liam smiled at her. "Well, they started squawking when we were about two kilometers from Dragon Lake. Loudly, like they were screaming. They did that when we took them, too. And then we saw a whole family of the birds, looking like flying redberry bushes, tracking the wagon. I bet ten of them followed us. The two in the cage screamed even louder as the other birds got closer. I thought the loose birds might attack, so I let the caged ones out." His eyes sparkled, as if the memory was a good one. "They all joined up and flew back to the lake, squawking and telling stories, and then they all . . . disappeared . . . into the redberry bushes." He smiled softly. "It makes me wonder what else lives so camouflaged here. With all the predators we have, it's a good strategy. I bet we miss a lot."

Akashi rode back up, coming from the other direction. I noticed the lines around his eyes looked deep, and that his cheeks were dark and puffy. We had had four hours of sleep at the fork, but they had surely ridden all night. His smile was as warm as ever, though. "It's all clear."

The perimeter bells chimed friendly entry as we finally clattered into the spaceport, heading straight for the water trough.

As Stripes began drinking, I started to strip her saddle but Akashi said, "Not yet. There's more to do."

"What?" Kayleen asked. "Aren't we staying here?"

He nodded. "We've got to make it safe, first. And before they send anyone down the hill." He glanced up at the sun, now just fully risen. "We have to do it now."

"What are we going to do?" Kayleen asked.

"You're going to take the hebras inside the hangar, and blindfold them," Akashi said.

I blinked, understanding dawning slowly. "You're going to burn the grass."

"Yes. I was hoping for a storm, so they might think it was lightning-sparked. But we're going to do it anyway. The grass is ready; it happens about this time every year."

"But what about the animals?" I asked. "We saw a herd of wild hebras last time we were here, and"—I shivered—"paw-cats. And there's rabbits and jumping prickles and . . ."

Akashi held up a hand to quiet me. "All of the bigger animals will outrun the fire, especially today, with no wind. Smaller ones will hole up and the fire will burn over them. Some will die. Many of the animals here live only that year between fires, and their young shelter in eggs laid belowground, safe until next spring. It's the way of these plains, Chelo."

We would still cost them at least days of their lives. "Well, what about Joseph and Alicia and Jenna?"

Akashi spoke patiently. "Jenna will know as soon as she smells smoke. She'll keep everyone safe."

I swallowed again, my eyes watering. "At least there's no wind," I said. "We can get it going every direction at once."

"Good girl."

I frowned. "Why inside the hangar?"

"Artistos has satellites. No point in giving away how few of us there are."

Oh.

He nodded at me, and I swallowed hard, and led Stripes toward the hangar.

We piled the tack, all except the head harnesses and lead lines, just outside the hangar door and set Paloma by it to watch, with a damp shirt and a bucket of water to keep it damp next to her. If the smoke got too bad, she'd come inside or breathe through the shirt.

Fire itself was no issue; the spaceport had survived two hundred years of natural grass fires.

We blindfolded the hebras, and Kayleen and I each took two, giving Liam three for the moment. Kayleen had Longface and Sand, I had Stripes and Legs, and Liam had Ink, Star, and Akashi's whitish hebra, Lightning. Standing in the quiet barn with the animals, dead tired, it seemed to take a long time before anything happened.

The huge shuttles the colonists used to carry goods down from *Traveler* were dark hulks above us, heavy and almost spooky in the thin light that crept through the tiny windows and in around the door.

Lightning and Legs shifted uneasily, then Stripes lifted her blindfolded head and bugled, sounding like Sugar Wheat had the night of the lightning storm.

Only then did I begin to smell the smoke. I'd smelled it before—every time the plains burned we hunkered down in Artistos, staying inside for the day it took the cleansing fire to burn the plains to smoldering stubble. It was stronger here, stinging my eyes, and first Stripes and then Legs tried to pull away. It grew darker, and I pictured smoke filling the air, obscuring the morning sun.

Akashi darted in the door. "Talk to them." He grabbed Lightning and Ink, and Liam took Sand from Kayleen. "Get some distance between us. Don't let them bunch or run."

My arms quickly tired from hanging on to the leads.

The perimeter rang entrance. "What's that?" I whispered.

"Animals," Liam whispered back. "Maybe hebras or paw-cats on their way to the forest. They'll pass through."

The bells rang exit.

"See?" he whispered.

We talked and soothed and whispered and sang, our eyes stinging. I lost track of time in the dim gloom of the smoky hangar, as if I had been there forever and would be there for-ever. Bells rang and rang again and fell silent.

Finally, Stripes leaned down and nuzzled me, content ap-parently that the fire would not chase her down.

"Okay," Akashi said, "slowly now, take one blindfold at a time off."

We stayed in the hangar with the hebras for another fif-teen minutes, ensuring that they were all right. Then we walked, blinking from the smoke, outside the door to join Paloma by the pile of saddles.

We stood in the middle of death.

All around us, blackened grass attested to the killing power of the fire. Beyond the large concrete pad, beyond the blackened expanse of grass, red tongues of fire still burned, all moving away from us. A light breeze blew in off the sea, carrying most of the smoke toward Artistos. What would Bryan think as he smelled the fire? Would he know we set it? Were people in Artistos telling him anything? I swallowed, my throat raw from singing, from talking to the beasts, from smoke. Maybe Tom. Surely Tom would check on him.

Kayleen looked out at the devastation, and said, "I wish we hadn't done this."

Akashi said, "We had to. This place is too big to defend by ourselves if people can sneak up on us."

Paloma looked out over the burning plains, her eyes red

and watery, her hair hanging in strings, dark with smoke. Her voice cracked as she asked, "Will it come to that, Akashi?"

He stood, watching the fire, a faraway look in his eyes, his mouth a hard slash in his face. "I hope not, Paloma. I truly hope not. I feel as if the war never ended."

But this time you're on our side. I went and stood by him, then gave him a fierce hug.

He leaned into my hug, returning it, smelling like smoke and fire and sweat.

20

A DECLARATION OF WAR

The fire spent all day spreading out from the spaceport, a ten-and-twenty-foot flame wall flaring, racing to its natural barriers: sea, river, cliff, and steep, wet mountainside. Following, a red-gold carpet of low fire slowly finished the first flame's work; behind that, smoke and black.

I took the first watch, staring at the fire, feeling the hot wind of change and danger it represented. Afterward, when my eyes stung from smoke, I slept, snuggled in blankets outside the hangar, secure in the knowledge that nothing could approach us for now. The fire would be a barrier to the return of Joseph, Jenna, and Alicia, but it would also be a beacon to them, telling them where to find us.

I dreamed of running animals, racing in front of the fire, of red-and-yellow winged birds flying into the fire, becoming the fire, melting into single red eggs shaped like *New Making,* of the eggs rocking in sunshine, cracks widening in their sides. I watched to see what came out of the eggs. But something shook the ground, an earthquake . . .

. . . Kayleen's hand on my shoulder. "Wake up. We're all meeting for dinner."

Watches lasted two hours. I had slept, fire or not, for eight glorious hours.

I pushed off my blanket, and the dream, looking around. No one but Kayleen and me were in sight; everyone else must be awake and elsewhere. Figures moved in the keeper's cabin windows. The scent of smoke and ash filled—everything. I stood. The first night stars glimmered over Artistos, shining weakly through gray smoke-stained sky. In the west, the sun shone bloodred just above the water, torching the smoky air with shades of red: blood, brick, and russet.

Kayleen stood beside me, transfixed by the sunset. "That's beautiful," she whispered.

I put an arm over her shoulder and drew her close. "Yes." Joseph and I used to love watching fire sunsets. "Is anyone coming yet?"

Kayleen shook her head. "Akashi expects Jenna and the others soon. He said not to expect anyone from Artistos until tomorrow. I just washed my hair in the trough—it felt wonderful. You should, too—gets the smoke smell away. Come on, let's eat!"

Surely the keeper's cabin had a shower? Shrugging, I dutifully followed Kayleen to the cold, bracing trough water and cleaned up, changing into clothes that had been too dirty to wear two days ago. At least they didn't smell like they'd been roasted in grass-fire all night. Walking to the cabin, I felt better than I'd felt in days.

Akashi and Paloma had cooked up a thick vegetable and root stew and a crumbly golden corn bread I recognized as Paloma's. Full serving plates filled the tiny table in the keeper's kitchen. Akashi nodded at us. "Grab a plate. We're eating outside, by the far corner."

The corn bread steamed as I split it, smelling like home. I sniffed, breaking off a corner and letting it melt under my tongue before smothering the rest with spicy stew. I wanted to stand like a rude two-year-old and just eat right there, to feed the growling beast in my stomach.

I did lick my fingers, then dip them in stew at the edge of my plate, and lick them again, as Kayleen and I followed Paloma and Akashi across concrete tinted gray with tiny flecks of ash, a test of self-control as my stew cooled beneath my nose. Paloma sat on the concrete corner of the spaceport closest to Artistos. She looked up at us, grinning.

Kayleen stopped, eyes wide with protest. "Mom? How did you get way out here?"

"I walked." Paloma sounded distracted, her focus on the fire. "Some sleep and some time without being on a big lurching beast helped. So did Akashi; he resplinted my ankle." She laughed softly. "But I'm still really slow."

Kayleen sat next to her mom, frowning in consternation. "Just don't reinjure it, okay?"

I sat, plate on my lap, finally able to fork enough food into my mouth at once to feel warmth radiate through my belly. The fire was easily visible east, toward Artistos, and north, at the edge of the mountains. There, lacking rain, it would slowly consume green underbrush, making more smoke than flame until it ran out of easy fuel. Redberries and mountain-fern were notoriously fire-resistant. To the west and south, small puffs of low smoke announced the fire had already run into sea and river.

The cloudless night sky was sure evidence of our guilt as fire-setters.

"So, Akashi," Paloma said, "what do we do next?"

"It's up to *us*," I said. It was time for us to make choices, for the *altered* to stand up for themselves. Paloma and Steven and Therese had taught us to be quiet and invisible. I knew, now, that was the wrong choice. I glanced at Akashi, noticing a spark of approval in his eyes. "We need to make these decisions."

Paloma narrowed her eyes, gazing at her daughter, frowning. "Whatever you decide affects me." She looked at Akashi. "The West Band, too. I'm not willing to give up my voice."

I understood. It was like being forced out of Artistos just as the conversation about our own future started. Akashi and Paloma had helped us. But our freedom was at stake; not theirs. I was the oldest. Joseph, at least, was my direct responsibility. And what he needed, what I needed . . . we all needed. Freedom and knowledge.

"I'm sorry, Paloma, we do want to hear from you. You, and Akashi, and Tom, too, if he returns. I trust you. But I'm not sure this is a vote." I groped for the right words. "We have the biggest stake; we can die."

"The chance of losing a child is a bigger stake than you can know, Chelo," she replied. As if to emphasize her point, a small quake shivered beneath us, rattling the plates against the concrete.

"I do want to hear from you," I repeated, closing my eyes for a brief moment, searching for wisdom. I opened my eyes to find Akashi watching me closely, waiting. "Akashi. You're Town Council. Everyone but you is in Artistos, now. Will they make a decision without consulting you?"

"I hold my Council position as West Band leader. They may try to negotiate with Mayah instead of me, but that won't hurt our cause." He glanced toward Liam, who was sitting next to Paloma. "Mayah loves Liam like I do, and she loves me."

His matter-of-fact trust in Mayah warmed me. Therese and Steven had been like them; Tom and Nava were cool together, and almost never tender with each other. Far better to be like Mayah and Akashi. "Okay," I said. "But what if they cut Mayah off, too? Can they, or do the town rules prohibit that?"

"A majority can vote a Council position closed," Paloma said. "But if they vote Akashi off, they vote out the West Band. I don't think they will. The band, by law, gets to choose its representative on Town Council. It's traditionally the leader, but the band could choose someone else."

Kayleen scowled down at the ground, scuffing her feet through the ash. "I don't want to talk about politics, I want to talk about how we get Bryan back. I want to know he is all right."

"Me, too." I sighed. Even Kayleen did not see. "It is not so simple. We have to win this with politics—with discussion. Not by fighting."

She frowned at me. "So how do you plan to use politics to find out how Bryan is?"

I shook my head. I had questions, but no answers; my struggles to find a future vision we all shared hadn't quite borne fruit. Time. I needed time.

A low sound grabbed my attention, deep and throaty, like the machinery in the mill that kept the heavy rollers spinning. It seemed to come from the sea. A memory stirred, fuzzy, of being little, still with Chiaro, and frightened of *this* sound.

I leaped up, looking toward the noise. No light, just noise; not loud, but getting louder, coming toward us. Lights bloomed, growing bigger, fast. Three round white lights, and two tiny red ones. We were all on our feet, looking. Akashi's voice, awed and angry. "Skimmer. I thought they were all destroyed."

Kayleen started to dart away, out into the dark grass, but Paloma yelled, "Kayleen, it's okay. It has to be Jenna."

Akashi ran toward the hangar, and we followed, the three of us outdistancing him easily, Liam ahead, and then me and Kayleen next to each other. Liam stopped by the small door, the piles of tack, fumbling for the lead lines. "Get the animals. They'll want to put it in here."

The hebras stood in a dark, quivering knot behind one of the shuttles, the big animals dwarfed by the flying machine. We walked through the near-dark, calling to them. Liam flicked on the big overhead lights, startling the hebras. They flattened farther against the wall as the noise grew, the pitch changing, surely signaling that whatever approached was slowing. Ink and Star made low frightened sounds deep in their throats.

We held two beasts each, and Liam was reaching for Legs's head harness, when the wide door the shuttles used creaked and rolled up, and the lights in the building clicked on, stopping all of us momentarily, human and hebra. Legs darted around Liam and started running for the door. I struggled with Stripes and Star as they nearly pulled me from my feet, trying to follow. Akashi stepped toward Legs, his arms windmilling, trying to slow the big beast, but Legs darted left and around, and fled out the big hangar door just before the skimmer's lights shone directly on us, coming inside. The noise shook the floor and the walls, and I was too busy with Stripes and Star to look, pulling them out of the path, as far away from the skimmer as I could, trying like hell not to share my fear with them, to stay calm, to calm them.

Then, silence. The big door closed. The hebras quieted.

The skimmer shimmered: the same bright silver of *New Making*. A flattened cylinder with two raked-back stubby wings, sitting on five wheels, only a quarter the size of the shuttles, and new and sleek in contrast to the bigger, older shuttles.

Someone flicked its lights off.

What if it wasn't Jenna and Joseph and Alicia? What if Hunter had kept it hidden with the other *altered* artifacts he'd confiscated?

A door on the top popped open in two parts, rising like tiny square wings, and Joseph stood up, screaming. "We did it! We flew!"

I unclipped the leads, left them lying there, and ran toward Joseph, reaching him just as he finished climbing down, clutching him to me. "Wow!" With such a machine, we could . . . we could travel anywhere, we could explore, maybe even get to Islandia.

Joseph pulled free, grabbed my arms, and grinned into my face. "Jenna had it hidden. She couldn't fly it." He laughed. "But I could. I flew it, Chelo. She told me Dad loved skimmers—I love this one, I loved flying. You could see everything. Even the *New Making* looked tiny."

Alicia jumped down and stood next to Joseph. Kayleen ran up, Liam and Akashi on her heels. "You flew it?" Kayleen asked.

Joseph glowed, like he'd glowed after hunting, full of excitement and adrenaline. "You've got to try this. It's so . . . so fast. I saw places we've never been, places someone walking could never go."

Jenna jumped down next, standing behind Alicia and Joseph, her eye shining with excitement. She looked around. "Odd choice for a barn."

Legs! "Did you see which way Legs went?" I asked.

Akashi grunted. "He'll come back after he quits being scared. His herd is here." He looked at Jenna. "Where the hell were you hiding that thing? And why bring it out now?"

She shrugged, but from the look Joseph gave me, I knew it was the cave. I squinted at the skimmer, trying to picture it rolling out of the cave, suddenly understanding why the cave floor had been so smooth. It was a landing pad. Did they clear the brush or just fly through it? Only then did I think of Artistos at all. "You know, you probably just scared the hell out of Artistos."

Jenna's eye sparkled as she waved off my concerns. "We went around and came in from the sea. Joseph needed to practice flying on something small."

The skimmer didn't look small to me. She'd had the skimmer and couldn't fly it. Lack of ability to read data, or being short one arm, or both? I chewed on my lip, thinking. *Altered* in possession of *altered* technology. Joseph able to fly. Nava and Hunter would hate it. Worse, it would scare them. And I'd been worried about their reaction to *hunting*.

What was Jenna doing?

I shivered, feeling pushed, manipulated. I glared at the skimmer, wishing it away, but of course, it stayed exactly where it was, alluring and beautiful and powerful and polished.

Stripes came up and sniffed at the nose of the skimmer, whickering softly, which started Kayleen laughing, then me, then the rest.

But it wasn't funny. Nothing was funny. Not now. "Come on," I said. "Let's go outside and catch up." I wanted to be away from the skimmer, to be outside in familiar surroundings. To draw the others' attention from the sleek machine.

Liam hesitated, walking up to the skimmer, touching it. His touch reminding me of Tom's loving inspection of the bigger and squatter shuttles the day we sent Therese's and Steven's ashes to the sea, the day Jinks died. Tom's eyes had held that same look of awe and hunger.

Liam's face was transfixed, bright, as he walked under the skimmer, his head almost brushing the bottom, circling around to the back where the engines cooled with light crackling and popping sounds. "Can I climb inside?" he asked, directing the question to Jenna.

Jenna smiled, apparently pleased with his interest. "You can help unload her soon. This is the *Burning Void*. Her range is anywhere on Jini."

"How many people will she hold?" Liam asked.

"All of us," Alicia said. "There's room for eight. More if you're willing to be uncomfortable."

If Tom had worried about the headband, what would he think now? I interrupted Liam's entranced tour of the skimmer by saying, "You know, you three might as well have outright declared war on Artistos."

Alicia's eyes flashed at me, happy and defiant. She knew. Jenna frowned. "If they saw us, they can choose to see it that way. They chose to shoot at me."

That stopped me cold. She was right. "I'm sorry, Jenna. I'm sorry for all the wrong things done to you, by anyone. Maybe they declared war when they beat up Bryan or when they shot at you, or years ago, before I was born. I'm sick and tired of it, too."

She nodded and looked away, watching the hebras who were watching her as if entranced.

I couldn't let it stop there. "Jenna—you've helped us and taught us and led us here. But I will not be led blindly into a fight. I . . . I still want to resolve this without anyone dying."

She turned toward me, a small smile on her lips. "I will let you try. But you must be willing to discuss at least defense. I am tired of being hunted, and I will not stand for more of it."

I swallowed and nodded, then looked at the others, who had watched the two of us, rapt. "Come on," I insisted, desperate now to get away from the skimmer, to think through the implications. The people of Artistos had killed our parents; they would kill us if we scared them enough. "We can't just stand here. We need to decide what to do next."

Jenna glanced at Stripes, who was still nuzzling up to the

ship, curious and unafraid. "We should get the hebras into the corral."

Akashi spoke up from behind me, his voice shaking, as if he were attempting a wry sarcasm he didn't feel. "It *is* an odd barn. We were trying to hide our strength from the satellites."

"I turned them off," Joseph said. We all stopped, silent.

He what?

Did he think we were more powerful than they were? The six of us here? They still had Bryan, dammit, and we *needed* the colony. Or we would be hunted. Seven Jennas. We didn't know as much as she did. They'd pick us off one by one.

Paloma hobbled in the doorway, then stood stock-still, her mouth wide open. She shook her head, as if she, too, wanted the skimmer to disappear.

"Look," I said, "Kayleen and Alicia—you two get the hebras to the corral by the keeper's cabin. And take the tack over, too. We may be making a little trip." I glanced at the rest of them. "You four, come on. We need to talk. The others can join us as soon as they finish."

Silence fell. Everyone watched me. No one moved.

I turned and started walking toward Paloma, toward the door, praying they would follow. My footsteps were the only ones I heard until I was halfway across the hangar. Three steps, seven, ten.

Twenty.

No one followed, no one made a sound.

Thirty.

Kayleen's voice, shaky, calling to Stripes.

Footsteps behind me. I wanted to turn around, to be sure I knew who followed me, but I was afraid that if I stopped they would stop, and time was not our friend. Satellites or not, what were our chances that no one saw, or heard, the skimmer?

I kept going, passing Paloma, through the door. I didn't stop until I could see Artistos, see if any lights came down the hill, see if they reacted to the skimmer.

No unusual light came from town. Whether they saw the skimmer or not, they were not rushing down to overwhelm us. The others stopped near me. Enough light fell from the high windows of the hangar for me to see their faces.

I looked to Akashi first, starting with small things I should have thought of earlier. "Do you have any earsets?"

"Liam and I each have one."

I glanced at Paloma. "How about you?"

She pursed her lips. "Tom had them, and he took them with him."

"So they don't know that we can communicate with them?" I asked.

"I'm required to carry one all the time," Akashi said.

"And Nava and the crowd she brought with her saw you. Have they tried to contact you?"

He shook his head. "Not yet."

Why? Why was Artistos silent? I glared at Joseph, who looked sheepish, as if it was just dawning on him that turning off the satellites was a poor idea. "What else did you turn off? Can they use the earsets?"

He looked down at the ground between his feet. "They can talk inside their immediate perimeter. That's all." He raised his head and stared at me. His face showed no sign of the exhilaration he'd shone with climbing up out of the *Burning Void*. Instead, his eyes smoldered with resentment. He used to give me looks like that when he was seven or eight and I encouraged him to set aside toys and work. He mumbled, "I left them their perimeter, so they'd be safe." Then his head came up and he looked around at the group of us. "Where's Tom?"

So he hadn't been paying attention to all the details. I found the sign of weakness oddly encouraging. I pointed to Artistos. "After you and Alicia snuck off with Jenna, Nava brought a group to invite us home. We refused. Tom went with Nava. Paloma didn't."

Joseph blinked. "Oh." Then he said, "Oh. They're mad at us already."

Good. About time he felt the consequences of his choices. I chewed at my lip. "Yes. Akashi stopped them, and then he and Liam led us down here. I'm sure they suspect us of any problems on the net, especially after you turned out to be so good at fixing communications."

He mumbled again, "I'm sorry."

I watched Akashi and Paloma while I spoke to Joseph. "I think we should open communications. And restore all of Artistos's abilities. If we're really, really lucky, they didn't see the skimmer. It will be invisible to them in the hangar, even with the satellites."

Akashi nodded encouragingly. Paloma smiled. Jenna glared at me but held her tongue. I swallowed and continued. "Okay, Joseph, be sure you can turn them back on, but hold off for a moment." I stared at him until he nodded.

Alicia and Kayleen jogged up. They must have made short work of corraling the hebras. Was Alicia talking Joseph into going so deep into the nets, daring so much?

Jenna. No matter that Joseph had turned off the nets, and flown the skimmer, Jenna was the architect of his choices. "Jenna, why did you bring the skimmer?"

She raised the eyebrow over her one eye, looking surprised that I was questioning her. Well, maybe we should question her. We'd asked her questions, but never questioned her actions before. She had been a . . . a goddess or something. A mythic figure. What did she want?

She took a step back, then another, distancing herself a little from all of us. She looked like she wanted to run, but she held her ground, watching me. I was still missing something. I knew it. I looked back at Jenna. "You did not need to bring the skimmer here just to let Joseph practice flying. You've been hiding it for years, a treasure. What else did you bring with you?"

Alicia answered the question for Jenna. "We brought weapons. Personal weapons, enough for all of us."

Jenna frowned and gave a quick hard nod. I got two quick impressions: Jenna wasn't happy Alicia told us about the weapons, and she didn't trust Alicia any more than I did. "Jenna?" I said.

She nodded. "In case we need to defend ourselves."

Alicia added, "In case we need to save Bryan."

I swallowed. The bad choices were adding up fast. Saving Bryan was great, killing people in Artistos to do it wasn't. Maybe Alicia had killed Varay. I no longer discounted the possibility. She was not like us. What had Jenna called her back in the cave? A risk-taker? Maybe a pointless risk-taker would have been a better description.

And my brother loved her.

I knew what to do next, anyway. And everyone was here to hear it.

But who should contact whom?

"Akashi? Can I use an earset?"

He nodded, his face serious. "Liam?"

Liam fished in his pocket, extending his palm, an earset lying loose in it. It struck me how close in size it was to a data button, and I laughed a little, thinking of my laughter over the flashlights in the cave.

Akashi and Liam looked puzzled, so I stuffed the laughter, took the earset, and nodded at Joseph. "Turn their access back on."

He hesitated. "Are you sure, sis?"

I hesitated for a moment. "Silence seems to have confused them so far, but it won't confuse them for long. If we can at least talk to them, we might be able to figure out what they're doing."

Joseph spoke up. "As far as I can tell, they're talking. There's not much activity in Artistos."

So he could see. "Do you know what they're saying?"

He gave me an exasperated look. "I haven't had time to listen. I could. But I've been taking skimmer lessons." He shifted uncomfortably, a slightly guilty look on his face. "Do you want to wait until morning to turn on the data?" he asked.

"No. You gave them something. Then you took it away. Give it back."

Liam spoke up. "Maybe Joseph should turn on their data now, but we could wait and contact them in a few hours, so they don't connect the two actions quite so tightly?"

I licked my lips, glancing from the hangar to the charred plains, to the last bit of flame I could still see, a thin line of red-orange between us and Artistos. I shook my head. "That's attractive, but I think it's more important that we call them. I don't want to call them in the middle of the night;

that would seem too desperate. If Nava gives me her word, she'll keep it."

Joseph stepped over near me, leaning on me a little. Physical closeness still helped him. I still helped him. I blinked back sudden tears. It was a small glimmer of hope. He'd gone beyond me in just a week, gone from introverted and broken to become more capable than I had ever dreamed he could be.

To reaching too far?

His head rested against my shoulder. His skin was still soft and childlike, his long lashes lying dark against his cheek. A surge of tenderness overwhelmed me. Perhaps Liam also saw Joseph's vulnerability, and mine, because he stepped over and stood on the other side of me, providing stability. He smelled of smoke and hebra and, faintly, of corn bread. I inhaled deeply.

It seemed that we stood there a long time, me centered between Joseph and Liam; Akashi watching the three of us; Kayleen standing beside Paloma, taking some of Paloma's weight; Jenna and Alicia both standing alone.

Stars filled the night sky. Destiny had not yet risen, and small, pale Hope was about to fall into the sea for the night. A cool breeze blew my hair back from my face, blew in the smell of the sea as well as the smoky char from the grasslands.

I wanted Joseph to hurry, so I could talk before I lost my nerve.

His head rose, and he blinked. "Okay, they have everything, and they know they have it all. It works better than it ever has before." He swayed on his feet, his face pasty white. Liam stepped past me and helped him to the ground, sitting so Joseph's head rested on his thigh.

Joseph looked up at me, whispering, "Good luck, sis," and then he closed his eyes. Out cold.

I glared at Jenna. Had she let him sleep since she took him from our camp? "Someone get him a blanket."

Alicia jogged over to our sleeping pile by the hangar and brought two, one for a pillow. She looked tender as she covered Joseph, running a hand along his cheek.

I shivered and set the earset to Artistos's frequency. The

call would go to the science guild, which had doubled as Town Council headquarters under Therese and Steven. It had not been changed by the time we left. "Artistos, this is Chelo calling for Nava."

Silence.

I called again.

Gianna's voice, high and . . . relieved. "Chelo? Are you okay?"

"Yeah, we're okay. For now. How about you?"

"Communications are back on. They said you turned them off. That Joseph turned them off. I said he wouldn't do that. He wouldn't?"

Bless her support. I said nothing, unable to explain.

She continued. "I heard he's working well on the nets again. Can you ask him to check on the asteroid shower trajectories? I'm seeing two that might be problems."

I looked down at my sleeping brother. "Yeah, Gianna, as soon as he wakes up. I'll ask him." I looked up at the sky; no meteors now.

"Please don't wait until morning," she said.

"Why?"

"I just—I need better data. Joseph has been better than me at interpreting multiple data sources since he was seven."

I smiled at that, looking down at Joseph, who slumbered on at my feet, mouth open, snoring softly. "What do you want me to tell him, specifically?"

"Ask him to cross-correlate the trajectories using multiple data points. I think some may come close to town, and I want someone else to verify my findings, and Joseph's the only one who can do better than me."

"I'll ask him. You can call us, you know. It's good to hear your voice. How's Bryan?"

She hesitated. "I don't know."

"Really, Gianna? No one will tell me anything. I'm so worried . . ."

"I know, honey. But all I know is that they took him to the hospital. I've been busy watching sky rocks."

"All right, let me talk to Nava, or Tom if you can't find Nava."

"Hold on. I'll get her."

I filled the others in on the conversation while I waited, glancing periodically at the rockless sky.

Nava's voice crackled in my ear, frosty and distant. "Hello, Chelo. I trust the fire was your signal that you arrived safely."

"Nava." I hesitated, reaching for the right words. "Nava, this has gone very wrong, and we need to talk."

"Come here, and we'll talk."

"How is Bryan?"

"Bryan is . . . recovering." The line was silent. I left it that way, waiting for her to elaborate. It was a long time before she spoke. "He is . . . nothing permanent. But he's hurt. It wasn't my choice, and I didn't order it. He was . . . in custody. For something he did do, and for which he must answer."

Her voice told me it would be pointless to ask if he could travel. She knew she had a hostage. "I want a meeting. We mean you no harm, but after your trip up to the fork, I'm not sure Artistos means us no harm. Not after Bryan." I stopped there, picturing Bryan's face. Gentle, angry Bryan. In pain. I wanted to see him.

"Come here, and I will guarantee your safety."

I shook my head, knowing she couldn't see it. "We should meet somewhere more neutral than Artistos."

More silence. "We are not willing to go to the spaceport."

"Then meet us halfway. The road here will be passable by tomorrow; the fire will have burned out. Meet us . . . after breakfast. After full light."

Her response was quick. "What guarantee will *we* have of safety?"

"My word." I needed no hesitation for that answer. "My word, your word, and a neutral location will have to do. This is a pattern, the same pattern that started the Ten Years War. Only no one has died yet. No one needs to. Trust, Nava. We have never harmed you."

She didn't sound convinced as she said, "I will talk to the other Councilors."

"Akashi is here. He will come to the meeting." I glanced at him; he nodded. I tried to pitch my voice as friendly as I could, to reach across the void between me and Nava, to touch her. "Do you remember when we took that walk the day before we left? I asked what you needed, and you said for us to fix the data networks. We did that."

"And to see how dangerous Alicia is. You are all dangerous. Bryan snapped Garmin's arm as if it were a twig."

"People our age beat him up. People who could, should, be his friends. His *brothers* helped."

"Point," she said. She sighed heavily. Her voice had lost its frost, but it had not gained warmth; just exhaustion. "I will talk to the Council."

"Thank you. Please call me back tonight so we can be prepared."

"I will let you know by morning."

I turned to the group, meeting their eyes one by one. "Nava will let us know if they'll meet with us."

At first, no one commented. Alicia spoke from her position on the ground next to Joseph. "I think we should go get Bryan tonight. Use the skimmer, land across the river, and get Bryan. They won't expect us. The fire will stop them, and they will expect us to be stopped, as well."

I wanted to agree with her. I wanted Bryan. But it was wrong. "We don't know if they saw the skimmer. If they didn't, we don't want them to. Besides, we don't know what kind of defenses they have."

Akashi nodded. "Best to let the talks happen. Artistos is well defended." He looked pointedly at Paloma.

Paloma nodded, chewing her lip. "We shot down skimmers." She swallowed. "I shot one down, myself. There are mortars stored in the armory. My guess is that they still work."

Alicia said nothing else, but her violet eyes blazed with frustration. I'd have to watch her, talk to Joseph when he woke. But for now, I let it lie.

There was no point in setting firm watches. Most of us had slept nearly all day. Except Alicia and Joseph and Jenna. I walked over and retrieved a few blankets, tossing them to Alicia. "Alicia, why don't you stay with Joseph? Sleep some if you can. The rest of us can unload the skimmer and take turns on watch for a while."

Akashi held up his hand. "Chelo?" He waited for everyone else to notice, to pay attention. Even Jenna, who still stood a few feet back from us, stopped. "Chelo. I don't know if there is a solution here, but I thought someone should acknowledge you. I acknowledge you. Thank you for trying for peace."

Alicia pointedly looked away.

Jenna watched me carefully, her face unreadable. I wanted her approval, but clearly I would have to settle for acceptance. If I even had that much. She was a force I had no idea how to truly manage, or even understand. She knew so much, so very much. She alone, of all of us *altered,* understood being shot at.

I amended that thought. Perhaps Alicia did, too, in a way. Bryan was learning. Akashi and Paloma had been in the war; they wanted peace. But Jenna? I had to figure out what she wanted. I nodded at Akashi. "Thank you. We will all have to work together. Perhaps there is a good choice here."

Kayleen gave me a soft, encouraging smile, and all of us except for Alicia turned and started walking toward the hangar. After a few steps, I stopped. "No. At least one must watch. That way Alicia can sleep. Kayleen?"

She nodded, and turned back toward Alicia and Joseph. I felt immediately better.

As we neared the hangar, Liam came up beside me and put an arm around my shoulders. It warmed me. It reminded me of walking back from the tent tree to Artistos the day the roamers came back, when Bryan helped me walk because my leg was stiff. I curled my arm around Liam's waist, feeling his strides, the slip and movement of his thigh muscles. I liked the feel of him next to me.

21

WEAPONS AND HISTORY

∽

As soon as we stepped inside the hangar, Liam separated from me, jogging toward the skimmer. I felt his absence immediately, a cold place near my side where he had been.

He glanced back at Jenna. She nodded, and he clambered up the ladder into the still-open door. She followed him, the two of them ducking down, disappearing. Moments later, a wide rectangle of silver skin rose up from the back of the skimmer. I did not realize how silent the mechanism was, we all were, until a short sharp bang shook the floor lightly under my feet as the ramp touched the concrete. The opening revealed a cargo bay filled with boxes. Liam and Jenna appeared inside the bay.

Akashi jogged quickly up the ramp and stopped dead at the top, staring unhappily down at the boxes. "You know, Jenna," he said sadly, "we once promised to leave the past buried."

She spoke slowly. "I remember *my* promise precisely. *To keep the peace.* I did not break it."

He shook his head but did not pursue the conversation.

She strode over to the smallest of the boxes, hiked it up under her one arm, and brought it down to a corner in the hangar. Akashi and Liam and I helped, until seven boxes were stacked; three together in one pile, and four in another. The three were *New Making* metal, the four all of Fremont forest wood.

Jenna started with one of the metal boxes. She pulled out

a blanket, doubling it over so it made a cushion against the concrete floor. She reached into the box, and took out a wrapped round silver ball, carefully removing a silver cloth that swaddled it, and putting it down gently on the blanket, as if it were a baby.

"What is that?" I asked.

Akashi answered, his voice trembling. "If you throw that ball into a group of people, it will kill everyone close to it." I tore my gaze from the ball, looking at him. His eyes were— sad. A simple word, but his face looked as if all the hope had gone from it.

Liam asked, "What is in it?"

Jenna reached back into the box, pulling out a second ball. "These have some explosive and bits of metal in them." She pulled out a third and looked up at Akashi, finally acknowledging the disgust in his voice. "I hope that we don't need to use them. But if we have to defend this place"—her gaze swung to me—"they will be useful. They throw . . . shrapnel, in a large area."

I swallowed. I'd promised to talk about defense, but this was not talk. Jenna reached back into the box, and I watched, fascinated and repelled. No wonder Hunter kept every *altered* artifact he found. He was keeping Artistos safe, not hiding our heritage from us. Or both. The headband and projector were neutral, and we could use them for good. The skimmer. The ball's only purpose seemed to be to kill.

Everything Jenna pulled out was unfamiliar. Twice she wedged boxes between her powerful thighs to gain the leverage to open them with one hand. A long box produced a long stick that Jenna described as a rifle, meant to kill at a distance. Jenna handled everything herself, setting each item or group of items a little apart from the others. She used her mouth when she needed to, when just one arm wasn't enough; an extra appendage to help unwrap objects encased in soft material.

We stood around her in a loose half circle.

No one spoke or offered to help.

Akashi and Paloma looked miserable; Akashi glaring as if he wanted the box and all of its contents to sink into some deep hole somewhere, Paloma as if she might get sick to her stomach at a feather's touch. Liam looked curious, but kept his distance and his tongue. I counted fifteen things. Fifteen weapons, I was sure. Five were the same: small cylinders as long as my palm, thin on the ends but fatter in the middle, shaped for a hand to hold; all of *New Making* metal.

When Jenna finished with the one box, she seemed tired. She sighed, glanced at the other boxes, but didn't reach for them. She lay a second blanket atop everything but the five small cylinders, and said, "The covered items are for me only. Do not touch them. Do you understand?"

"What do we do if anyone else comes?" Liam asked.

"Do not go near these things." She pointed to the others, and looked up at Akashi and Paloma. "You know what these are?"

"Microwave guns," Akashi said.

"The simplest and least lethal choices I had available." Jenna watched Liam and me this time. "They're small enough to hide easily. To use one, just apply pressure. Grip it with your fingers to fire it." She placed the cylinder between her big toe and the one next to it, held it, and twisted with her hand. "There, now it's activated. It will have power for up to a week, then it can be recharged. You will, of course, draw down its power if you use it." Then she pointed it at the wall and squeezed. There was almost no noise; just a tiny click that I suspected normal human ears would miss with any background noise at all.

"See," she said, "nothing happened. There has to be a target in range . . . something for it to hit. A living target, animal or human." She held the cylinder out to me. "Then after the click, it will hum softly while it's being fired, and a light will show what you're hitting. The noise and light have nothing to do with the microwave beam; they're for you, so you can tell what the gun is doing. Whatever you hit will immediately feel intense pain. The damage will only be permanent if you fire on the same spot for more than a few seconds. It is a very smart simple weapon."

I didn't want to take it. We had always been refused even hunting stunners; I had never even held one. The small cylinder felt heavy for its size, a good fit to my hand. Holding it seemed to split me—Chelo after holding a gun felt as changed as Chelo after hunting. Simply taking the gun felt like the moment I knew I had to kill the djuri I'd downed, that I'd gone too far to save its life. A shiver ran deep inside me, along my spine and up and down the back of my legs, my neck.

Jenna watched me carefully. "Keep the nose pointed at the ground, even when it's off."

I adjusted the angle of my wrist.

"If you fire this at a person, or an animal, they will feel like they are burning. You cannot hold it on long enough to kill easily; but it can kill. It disables even from a distance. Effectively, although temporarily. We will practice with it later."

I swallowed, sure of myself, and spoke clearly and evenly so there was no mistaking my words. "I won't need this."

Akashi spoke from beside me. "I hope not. But tomorrow, tomorrow when you meet whoever comes from Artistos, you should assume they will have weapons capable of killing you. No matter how much strength and speed you have, you aren't combat-trained."

"Hand it to Liam," Jenna said, her voice as even as mine.

I felt lighter as soon as it went from my hand to his. I looked back at Jenna, who held another microwave gun out to me. She said, "Carry it. Put it in your pocket. Get used to it. I'll show you how to fire it later."

And so Liam and I both ended up with weapons, small ones, but in my pocket, the gun seemed heavy and huge, so big that I felt for it a few times, expecting it to fill my pocket to bulging, to mess up my balance, even though it was, in truth, much smaller than a flashlight. The projector was bulkier, and I hadn't worried much about being caught with it.

At first, neither Akashi nor Paloma would take a weapon. Paloma looked miserable when Jenna held one out to her, saying, "No one will shoot at me."

Jenna shook her head lightly. "They may shoot at your daughter and you may want to protect her."

Paloma nodded, her eyes wet but her face resolved. "I hate this." She took the gun and pocketed it instantly.

Akashi also armed himself, with no argument. Now there was one cylinder left. And three people. "Jenna—will you take the last one?" I asked.

She waved her hand over the blanket. "Do not worry about me."

All those times she showed up with dead paw-cats across her back. Did she use weapons, or kill them with her brute force? I had always thought she used her physical skills . . .

"The last one is for Joseph," she said.

I did not like that. But Kayleen was too impetuous, Alicia too likely to use a weapon. I nodded. "Let him sleep for a few hours."

She shrugged. "Not for long. I need him. Chelo? You know not to show that unless you plan to use it?"

"I don't intend to ever show it to anyone."

Jenna stood up and gestured toward the *Burning Void*. "You wanted to see inside?"

We climbed, briefly, one by one, into the skimmer; a row of soft seats clearly designed for multiple body types, with straps. There were two screens in front and one on each side; dead now, but surely for navigation. I was positive that when the skimmer flew, data flowed throughout the cabin. Data Joseph or Kayleen could immerse themselves in, but which would forever be invisible and silent for me. There were two pilot seats in back, similar to ours, but with buttons on the armrests. The walls were all smooth and rounded inside; utilitarian.

We were gawking when we should be getting ready, planning, doing *something*. There was much I still needed to know. "Jenna? Will you take a walk with me?"

She nodded, and we all climbed back out of the skimmer. The ramp folded in again, becoming smooth skin. Jenna looked at Liam, who was watching the sleek ship, a thoughtful look on his face. "Can you unpack the wooden boxes?" she asked. "They are . . . gear. Clothing and supplies. Nothing in them will hurt you."

Liam nodded, eager. Akashi asked, "Okay if Paloma and I stay to help?"

Jenna hesitated a moment, and said, "All right."

She and I walked out of the hangar and under the stars. On her way out, Jenna stopped by the skimmer and picked up the paw-cat cloak she'd worn the day they investigated Alicia's claims. Draped in cat fur, walking with feline grace, she looked like a predator all over again. I swallowed hard, suddenly a little afraid of her. I took a breath. "Jenna? What do you want?"

She walked in silence for a while, her strides longer than mine; I had to jog to keep up with her. The cooling night forced me to wrap my arms around myself for warmth, wishing for a coat. Jenna must have noticed, because she veered toward the keeper's cabin. Finally she said, "I want to go home."

Fremont was home; I'd dreamed of leaving. A daydream; a thing to want but never a thing to have. Never a possible thing. To find a home where we fit! Confused, I listened to the crunch of my feet on the ash-covered concrete for a while. I remembered the questions Kayleen and I had mapped while grooming the hebras. "Why did you come here? Why did the *altered* come at all?"

Her response was quick. "Why did the first colonists come?"

"To . . . to find a place they could live like they wanted. A place no one else wanted enough to fight for."

"That is why we came. Fremont has raw materials. We brought tools and knowledge to transform it into a paradise; we were more prepared than the original colonists. We planned and scrimped and saved and traded and sacrificed to obtain this world. In the end, we were able to purchase it straight out."

"You what?"

"We bought rights to Fremont. For a hundred thousand years. Artistos's ancestors filed a claim for it, with the Planetary Registry. The surety they gave collapsed in the markets, invalidating the claim. We bought rights to Fremont. We knew about the old claim—that's how we found it, since it's not near any commercial systems. We didn't imagine the claimants were still here, or that they'd even ever gotten here. No record existed, and why would settlers choose to close off all contact with the greater world? They never even confirmed their claim." She hesitated. "We followed the laws. Our affinity grouping is not rich enough to write off such a loss. We pooled all of our resources to come here, to build our new home."

I didn't know what to make of her words. They sounded like the narrator's voice, on the projector, the day Kayleen and I were trying to pull meanings from strange words under the pongaberry trees. Besides, what difference could it possibly make? The *Traveler* brought the colonists here, but it was a one-way journey. The ship had no fuel to return, no pilots. Fremont's residents were not going anywhere, no matter who had what claim. "What is an affinity grouping?"

She stopped. "I shouldn't have expected you to understand all that. An affinity group is a set of beings that chooses similar lifestyles and shares an economic future—that owns the same things. Like the original humans that started Artistos. It is like . . . like an extended family, only more diverse. An affinity group will stand up for its members when no one else will."

"So me and Joseph and Kayleen and Liam and Bryan and Alicia are an affinity group?"

She paused. "You are part of ours." After a few moments, she said, "You *could* make a separate group." She waved her hand up at the sky. "Out there. If you had any resources. But you don't, not yet."

I changed the subject a little. "But now you want to go home. Silver's Home?"

We had arrived at the keeper's cabin, and I rummaged through my pack for my coat, shrugging it on quickly. We went back outside and continued walking.

I had just about decided she wasn't going to answer me when she stopped near the edge of the concrete pad, folding down cross-legged twenty meters from the *New Making,* close enough that it loomed above us. The ground around the pad the ship rested on had burned black, but *New Making*'s outer skin showed no scars from the fire, no sign it had been affected in any way. "We came from Silver's Home, and the others most likely returned there."

My heart leaped into my throat. "Were my parents there? Did they get away?"

She shook her head, and I swallowed, unbidden tears stinging my eyes. My breath caught, hard, sobs struggling to break free of my throat.

Her one eye never left me. The scars across her face shifted. Softened? "I said that wrong," she said, "I'm sorry. The bodies were all burned. They buried the ashes. I was . . . incapacitated for a long time, after. Surely they all thought me dead with everyone else. So I don't know who escaped. Enough to fly away, and at least one pilot. Your father was a pilot."

The tears that had come to my eyes fell anyway, even with this uncertain news. It was nearly as bad—maybe it was worse—than knowing them dead. I knew Chiaro was dead. I still missed her, in a small place inside. Therese and Steven were dead; I helped burn their bodies and scatter their ashes. I knew there was no hope of seeing any of them again. Not knowing, still, about my first parents was harder. "How many other pilots were there?" I asked.

"There were three left last time I counted. Joseph was born to be a pilot."

Joseph was born to be a pilot. I stuttered her words back at her. "Jo . . . Joseph—was born to be a pilot?"

"Joseph can fly the *New Making*."

I blinked, stunned. Joseph? Fly the *New Making*? "Now?" I asked.

She nodded. "He'll need to learn, and we have to check the ship's systems out. It will take a day or two."

A day or two.

While I struggled to keep peace here, Jenna had worked to get us all away safely. I could see the pattern, the way she and I had been working together, loosely bound more by her goals than mine. Jenna could help us figure out where to go. There was something more than family out there for us, maybe. If they survived. I hated the war all over again, and loved Jenna all over again, even though some inner part of me screamed caution.

"Is Joseph the only one that can fly the ship?" I asked.

Jenna nodded.

"Not Kayleen?"

"Kayleen might learn, in time. Not nearly so quickly as Joseph."

I shook my head in frustration. "If Joseph was born to be a pilot, what was I born for?"

She smiled. "You were born to help me—a politician, a strategist, and Kayleen to work the data nets. Bryan to be a fighter, a strong man. Liam, like you, to lead. Alicia to experiment. And others to be other things . . . but they are all dead."

The child that was killed, that Jenna held when the rocket tore her arm away. I'd forgotten about it in the rush of skimmers and fires and tactics and needing to negotiate some kind of peace. "Jenna? I heard that the day of the last fight you had a child with you. It was one of us, wasn't it? What was that child born to be?"

Jenna's words came out packed with longing, but sharp and short, so that her very voice carried pain and loss such as I had never heard in a single human voice except, perhaps, in the wailing of funeral rites, the songs around the pyres. "She was . . . she had . . . she was going to be our geneticist, our surgeon. All but one were killed. She . . . could have helped us all. Helped you. You see . . . it takes maintenance to keep us alive for hundreds of years. Care. Care I can't give you."

Care she couldn't give herself. I let silence fall again after that. I had no answer for the pain I heard in her, which seemed as deep as Little Lace Lake. I had lost the heart to ask if the child was hers. I didn't want to know. Silence itself became oppressive, the echo of Jenna's tone filling the emptiness between us.

I headed for more comfortable territory. "You asked us to keep the projector and the headband secret. It can't matter anymore. We should tell Tom and Paloma how we're learning, and Liam. They know you had that skimmer somewhere."

She nodded. "You're right. But not yet where the cave is."

We sat. I breathed in the silence, the nearly still spaceport, the lack of action, the choices that hung in front of me, so heavy as to be nearly visible. The cool breeze blowing in from the sea carried salt as much as smoke, and stars glittered above us. I thought about what Jenna had said, about the things we were born to be, and whether or not we could be them. Joseph had been miserable and unhappy when he tried to be a pipe fitter, and excited since Jenna showed him the cave, and gave him the headband. Since he started learning to be what he was born for.

Could I choose not to be a leader? We had skills designed for a colony of *altered,* but useful here, now, as well. Were all of our choices foreordained?

A meteor streaked near the horizon, a red flare disappearing over the tops of the mountains that rose a distance behind the *New Making*. A small thing. A reminder of my conversation with Gianna.

I had never been alone with Jenna for so long. There were so many questions, but it seemed like such an odd time to ask them. Like they should wait for . . . some change to happen. To be past this crisis. Surely we would have time for long talks in the ship (in the ship!). But that was soft thinking, and I needed to make sure we could get away, make sure that whatever happened was right for us. All I knew of this affinity group was Jenna, and it was up to me to save us six. Not her. I had to remember that. It would be so easy to forget, to let someone else decide for us. "What is back on Silver's Home? What will happen to us if we go there?"

She cocked her head and shifted her gaze from the ship to me. "It depends on who made it back. If our people made it back and did well, then maybe they are still there and maybe we have some resources." She shrugged. "My sister stayed. I'd like to know if she lives. If our people are coming back here." She looked away again, watching the silent silver ship. "They might be on their way here now. It takes six to ten years for a round trip. We could pass each other in the space between places."

Somehow I had never thought of Jenna with family. Jenna was always crazy and alone and distant, and now she sat here next to me, close actually, and she had spoken of a girl who might have been her child and of a sister far away.

I remembered trying to touch Nava, how I hadn't touched her, how when I'd tried she'd pulled away.

Jenna's palm rested on the concrete, holding some of her weight. Close enough to touch. "Did I tell you I climbed a pongaberry tree?" I touched her hand with mine, briefly, my hand withdrawing of its own accord, and I forced it back and over her palm, laid it down on top of her rough hand even though I had to stretch and reach to do so.

"That's good," she said, and shifted her weight, turning her hand under mine to grasp it with her strong fingers. Her palm felt warm and dry. "You need to learn your capabilities."

We sat that way for three or four minutes. I wished I knew what was in her head, her heart. Her fingers clutching mine did not tell me.

Then her hand withdrew quickly and she pushed herself up. "I—need to check on the others." And she was gone, a silhouette in the dark, running so lightly back toward the hangar that I couldn't hear her footsteps.

I stared at the *New Making*. Joseph was made to fly that ship. My father flew that ship. Soon, I might finally be inside her, see inside her.

If only Bryan were here.

What if I left, and my parents still lived, and came here looking for me? If we all left, would Artistos get along, or did they really need our skills, and would they ever let us use them? Was there any life available here for Joseph? And if I didn't let Joseph, and thus Jenna, go, was I dooming her to die, broken and maybe soon, when she could be healed? What would life be like without Paloma and Gianna, or even Tom? Leaving was simple, and yet it wasn't.

The night was half gone, and I needed to be ready for the coming . . . confrontation. I walked back, following Jenna's footsteps, slowly, alone under the stars. I passed the keeper's cabin and the hangar, and went to Joseph.

He and Alicia curled like one being under the same blanket. In sleep, the lines of pain and anger that often creased Alicia's forehead and lined her mouth had gone, and she looked . . . vulnerable. Joseph looked like a boy who wanted to be a starship captain, not a young man who might become one soon. Surely the right answers were here, surely home was here. Surely we could wait before making these decisions.

I knelt beside them, hearing Gianna's exhortation in my head. Maybe I could wake just Joseph. I reached out and shook his shoulder gently. He curled his arm tighter, pulling Alicia closer against him, grunting. I tried again. He opened one eye. "Mmmmmm . . ."

"Wake up," I whispered. "I need you."

He moved Alicia's arm from his waist and pushed himself up, shivering as the cold air hit him. I stood and started walking toward the unruly pile of goods by the hangar, gesturing for him to follow me.

He crawled completely free of Alicia, turned and covered her, and padded silently after me. He took a blanket from my outstretched hand and wrapped himself in it, then stood leaning against the hangar wall. "I . . . I'm sorry I couldn't stay awake. What happened? Did you hear anything about Bryan?"

"I'm meeting Nava tomorrow morning." I glanced at my chrono. "Or more accurately, in about eight hours. If she calls to confirm. But she will. She's keeping Bryan hostage in Artistos. She didn't give me much detail about how he is, but I think they beat him up pretty bad. Garmin's friends."

His jaw tightened and he stood straighter. "We're in trouble."

"And you need to be careful not to scare them; not to do anything else to show off. I'm pretty sure they . . . some of them . . . would welcome any excuse to be rid of us. Maybe even if they had to kill us. Not everyone. I talked to Gianna, and that's why I woke you up."

"How is Gianna? Is she mad at me? What did she say?"

"She's nervous about meteors. She wants your read on the data nets, something about cross-correlating multiple data points. You better talk to her to get the details."

"So Nava maybe wants to kill us and Gianna maybe wants us to save them all?" Joseph raised an eyebrow and shook his head. "I think that's a clear sign it's time to go. Jenna wants me to help her check out the *New Making*." He looked toward the ship, as if hungry to be back inside it.

I had known that was what he wanted, but only now could I really feel the sharp knife of his desire to leave. "Joseph." I used my best big-sister voice. "I know. We may have to use the ship. I don't know what to do about that. But don't forget Bryan, and that Kayleen and Akashi and Liam may not want to go. Don't forget the good Therese and Steven did for us.

"Please look into the meteors, and get back to Gianna. I know you can figure out how to message her."

His gaze was still pinned to the *New Making*. I wondered if he was even then reading data. Finally he said, "Well, I don't exactly want a meteor to fall on the *New Making*. But I'm not very good with space-based data streams. Gianna only let me use them once before." He paused, stilled completely, and then his face brightened. "I'm pretty sure I can get to them."

Jenna materialized, as if out of thin air, next to him. Damn. How did she move so quietly?

She cleared her throat. "I think I can help. Come, Joseph, let's open *New Making*. There's better access to data there."

He smiled at her, his face lighting up. He turned toward me. "Coming, Chelo?"

My body suddenly felt cold inside. "I'll be there soon. I need to find Paloma and Liam and Akashi and tell them about the headband and the data reader and the cave."

"I've told them," Jenna said. "All of that is small compared to the *New Making*. Let's go."

"Someone has to stay on watch." Why didn't I want to go? The coming meeting was important; getting ready. I missed Bryan. The hebras needed water. I didn't want to do this thing I had wanted all my life. And then I caught Joseph looking at me from the corner of his eye, as if I had perhaps gone a bit insane, and I suddenly knew why I detested the ship in that moment. The *New Making* had already stolen Joseph. I could see it in his face, his eyes, in the set of his body. Nothing tied him here, not even me. If I wanted to be with my little brother, to watch over him, I needed to go with him. I hugged him, holding him tight, not caring that Jenna was there to watch. He smelled like the skimmer and smoke and hebra.

"All right. Maybe Akashi and Paloma can hold watch. I still have the earset; they can reach us if they need anything."

Joseph smiled. "Good. I'm going to wake Alicia up. We should all see this together."

So all of the *altered* on Fremont, except Bryan, all of us gathered around the ship that had brought our families here twenty-two years ago. My fear and anger at the ship had melted away, replaced by dread, directed at the future, but not at the simple metal of this ship I had wanted to see inside my whole life. Besides, I had to know if it was safe, if we *could* use it. If it could carry my brother away from me, or both of us away from everything we'd ever known.

The cool soft night wind blew my hair against my face. Stars spread above us, and far off, I could hear the low rumble of the sea.

Jenna stopped outside the ship, turning around, facing us. "A few days before the last battle," she said, "we had a conversation. Your parents were there—at least Alicia's father, Kayleen's mother, and Chelo and Joseph's mother and father. The rest were already dead."

Kayleen drew in a little tight breath next to me and clutched my hand. Liam stepped closer, but hardly reacted otherwise, his focus on the ship.

Jenna continued, not missing a beat. "We took only the *Journey*; there weren't enough of us left to fill even one ship. Leaving *New Making* behind would both draw us back, and be a story for Fremont's children. We didn't know that those would be our children." She stopped, struggling for words. Her voice lost volume, catching in her throat, and I had to strain to hear her. "So this ship is meant to be your tool as much as mine."

I took a step closer to her, and Liam and Kayleen matched me, the three of us staying close, Kayleen still clutching my hand. Liam slipped an arm over my shoulder, and I felt his hip against mine, a return of the closeness I'd felt on the walk to the hangar earlier. Joseph and Alicia, also holding hands, marched past Jenna up to the ship's sleek gleaming side. They looked small next to it. Alicia held a hand out, stroking the outside metal as if it were a lover. I had only stood this close to it a few times, and never had I felt so . . . awed. We were about to step inside the *New Making*.

Jenna cleared her throat, gathering our attention back to her. "We will go inside, all of us together, but you must stay with me. Do you understand?"

We all nodded.

Movement. Just behind Jenna and to the left, a ramp folded down in the same way as the skimmer ramp. Out here, with wind and insects and the sound of our feet shuffling, I could barely hear the movement of the door. It appeared to fold out from the ship with magic. "Jenna?" Kayleen asked. "How is it so quiet? How come I didn't know the door was there?"

"Materials. Our materials are nearly perfect. Nanotechnology. The ship is nanosteel and carbon and diamond, all of the materials manufactured, and coated with active protectant."

"So why doesn't Artistos use such perfect materials?" I could imagine windows and doors and signs and pots and a million things made of such smooth, clean metal.

She shook her head. "They probably didn't have the resources to bring such technology with them." She turned, gesturing to us to follow, and started walking to the ramp. Her mutter barely reached me. "They may have chosen not to."

That sounded right to me. They were such stubborn people, so afraid of change. And it seemed they liked to do everything the hard way . . .

And then I was following Jenna up the ramp, and I didn't care about Artistos or Fremont, or why we had no such metal.

New Making demanded all of my attention.

22

THE *NEW MAKING*

We walked up the ramp toward the *New Making*. Jenna first, then Joseph and Alicia, and then me in the middle and Kayleen and Liam following. Liam didn't run up to the *New Making* the way he'd run up to the skimmer. I looked behind me once. Starlight illuminated beads of sweat on Kayleen's face, and Liam smiled encouragingly at me, his eyes wide as he looked past me toward the entrance. I followed his gaze.

The tall, narrow doorway displayed only darkness. Air spilled out, smelling of oil, clean metal, water, and even, faintly, of plants. I had expected stale air or decay; it had been still for twenty years, and closed up, certainly, since the end of the war twelve years ago—since its sister ship, the *Journey,* fled.

Jenna touched something inside the opening and light bloomed, illuminating a corridor beyond. The walls glowed a soft blue, the floor a soft silver, and four red lines ran through the round corridor: top, bottom, right, and left. Bumps of various sizes rose from all of the walls except the floor. "What are these?" I asked.

Joseph, just ahead of me, already had an answer. "Handholds for free fall." Despite my earlier fear, a curious thrill filled me. Joseph and I had dreamed of this moment all of our growing years, and now I would see inside our biggest mystery.

The door slid shut behind us. We walked twenty or so steps and then Jenna stopped and pointed up. "Follow me."

Colorfully painted pipes, and more hand bumps, lined the vertical corridor. She used the bumps as footsteps and hand-holds, moving up. Her progress was fast, strong, but lurching, her missing arm clearly a problem, giving her a gait similar to her pongaberry tree climb. I watched her, waiting my turn. If she went home, she could almost certainly fix her arm. A world that could make four-armed people and perfect metal could replace a missing arm.

Joseph and then Alicia went next, and I followed, then Kayleen, Liam trailing. I reassessed my opinion of Jenna's progress. We were slower; finding the right rhythm to reach and pull and reach again took time.

"Jenna," Liam called up. "Is this the only way around the ship?"

Her laughter echoed down the shaft. "No. But until I've checked them out, it's safer than the elevators."

We went up, and up, and up before we passed a horizontal corridor. Kayleen and I, next to each other, stared into the dark tunnel.

Something moved.

I sucked in my breath. Kayleen screamed.

"What?" Jenna called down.

"Something's alive in here."

She laughed. "A maintenance bot."

Kayleen blushed. I felt sheepish for being scared. Of course starships had automated systems to take care of things. I'd read about robots. We had machines on Fremont to help unload raw materials, handle ores, mill flour, and make pipes. But they did not move without specific direction from a human.

Two more levels up, my arms and calves burned from the climb. Jenna finally took a horizontal corridor lined with square doors outlined in different colors: black, deep blue, and maroon. The air still smelled fresh, and now the plant smell I'd sensed at the very bottom of the ship was stronger, mixed with winter forest scents of decay and rot and wet plants. Jenna opened a door about halfway down, and stood in the frame for a moment, frowning. The smell of flowers and herbs and dead plants was so strong I held my nose.

Light spilled into the corridor, bright, like sunlight, streaming around Jenna's spare form. Then she stepped through and motioned us in.

The room was a chaos of green and brown. Dry, dead plants thrust naked stems and curled brown leaves between healthy green shoots. Two bots scuttled away from us, and two more lay on the floor, unmoving. Jenna walked up to one of the inert bots and kicked it. It slid along the floor without changing the position of its limbs, and she stood and frowned down at it, shaking her head. She prowled around, poking at planters. Half were empty, neatly empty, no dirt and nothing but dead leaves fallen from the remaining planters. They had been put away the way we put away the fields each year. Of the rest, straggly green, healthy green, brown, and black competed about evenly.

There was barely more room than necessary to walk between the stacked planters. I didn't see any dirt, didn't smell dirt. I walked up and stuck my fingertips into a planter. Starship soil was clear and wet and squishy. I wiped my hand on my pants.

I would never have guessed anything lived inside the ship. It had always been a dead thing, a statue, like the little statue of the first Town Council in the park. And yet it was alive. Camouflage. Like the dragonbirds; something happening under our noses that we didn't know how to see.

Kayleen followed Jenna, her eyes wide. "Did the light stay on the whole time we were growing up? Do robots make the plants grow? Do you need to eat in cold sleep? Is any of this good to eat?"

Jenna kept walking, ignoring Kayleen, who fell silent and stared after her. Jenna appeared to be looking for something. She stopped at a long narrow box. Feathery green tops I recognized from our greenhouses stuck out of it, only bigger. I smiled when she proved me right and plucked six carrots. Then she held the carrots under one of the first things I recognized easily. A water spigot. When Jenna touched a button with her elbow, clear water flowed.

We had a water treatment plant in town. It was finicky, affected by quakes and cold and heat and too little or too much rain. Yet clear water flowed out of a system no human had touched for twelve years. Jenna waved her handful of wet carrots, a gesture that took in the whole room. "The air systems will adjust for humidity because I picked carrots and rinsed them for you." She handed each of us a carrot. Mine was heavy and fat and off-color; yellower than carrots from home, nearly white at the tip. When I bit into it, it crunched perfectly in my mouth, but it barely had any flavor at all.

Jenna made one more trip around the garden. Kayleen trailed her. The garden, the ship, fascinated me. But time passed in the real world. Town Council was surely planning their next moves, and Akashi and Paloma were probably worried about us. As Jenna and Kayleen neared us, I said, "I thought we were looking for meteor data."

Jenna looked distracted. "We are. The garden was on the way, and I needed to check it. There are other food stores, but the garden will be our fresh food. It was a good place to stop to see how well the maintenance bots have kept the ship. I thought you'd like to see it."

I picked at a dry dead leaf. "It doesn't look very healthy."

Jenna waved her hand at the greenery. "This is not the highest priority for the bots. There are other ways to get nutrients. But if the garden is this healthy, the rest of the ship is probably ready, although I'll run complete diagnostics before we leave."

Liam stepped toward me, looking at Jenna, his eyes narrow. "Before who leaves?"

"Joseph can fly her," Jenna said softly. Joseph and Alicia nodded, standing close together. So she had already sold them.

I stood stock-still, crumpling the dead leaf in my hand, watching Liam's face.

"How?" Liam demanded.

I suddenly sensed the huge jump between data nets and starships. The danger.

Jenna spoke patiently. "I have to show him. Give him the right gear. That's where we're going next. The ship mostly flies on automated systems. He'll need to understand basic interfaces and monitor streams of data. The same thing he already does." She sounded slightly exasperated, as if she were talking to young children. "There is a pilot computer to help him; he will be able to speak to it after he has some training." Jenna turned toward the door and started walking.

Liam grabbed my shoulder, his voice rough. "Chelo—you can't agree with this." The others turned to look at us, bunching up by the door. Jenna turned, too, holding still, her gaze on me.

I glanced at Jenna, at Joseph. "We can't go without Bryan. But . . . what if we do need it? Someday?" I was babbling, betraying my uncertainty. What did I *know*? "Liam—we can't leave now. We can't do anything until I meet with Nava, until we get Bryan. I don't know how Town Council is going to treat us, not since Therese and Steven died. And Akashi and Nava drew weapons on each other. I'm carrying a microwave gun."

Joseph and Alicia looked startled. They'd been asleep when Jenna unpacked the weapons.

I kept going, not letting their look stop me. "They threw Bryan in jail and let him get beaten up. They withheld information from Tom. It makes sense to see if the ship can fly." I looked at Jenna. "You're not planning to leave soon, right? Not before we have Bryan and not if we can stay here?"

Jenna said, "Not before we have Bryan."

"I don't want to go anywhere." Liam's face was set, his eyes hard and accusing. "You talk about other parents; maybe you have other parents, but mine are here. You heard Jenna. My *altered* parents are dead for sure. I want to stay with Akashi and Mayah, and my band."

Kayleen stepped up next to him, her eyes darting between me and Jenna and Joseph. "Me, too. I want to stay here."

"Look, all of you." I swept my eyes across the whole bunch of them, including Jenna. The decision had to be ours, not Jenna's. Not entirely Jenna's. And she'd given me the perfect opening, outside, before we came in. "This is *our* starship. Didn't you hear Jenna outside? Ours." I paused, letting my words sink in.

Joseph gave me a bright smile, Alicia looked positively triumphant, and Kayleen and Liam thoughtful. I drew a deep breath. "Maybe we will fly it away, someday. First, we have to get out of the mess here, and not by flying into some great unknown that could be worse. Not by running, unless they make us run." I paused again, and again they stayed quiet, watching me. "Look, I've wanted to be inside this ship as long as I can remember, wanted to fly it to space or even just to Islandia. We need to see this. We have to learn."

Liam's scowl relaxed. Kayleen offered me a tiny smile, still not happy, but clearly she and Liam now believed we would not leave this minute and abandon Artistos for the stars. Jenna, standing behind Joseph and Alicia, nodded at me, seeming to agree. But the agreement didn't reach her eyes. She wanted to go. And she wanted to make the call, not me. But outside, before we came in, Jenna told us this was our ship. I would use those words again if I needed to.

Joseph looked as torn as he'd looked for the past few days. Alicia radiated anger, standing stiff, chin up. She spoke into the silence I'd left without looking at me. "We should get Bryan now. So we can leave. Take the skimmer and fly in and get him."

Liam said, "We should get Bryan right away, for Bryan's sake. But it's not that easy."

I nodded. "Liam's right, but not tonight. Let's see what Jenna wants to show us, see if it can help Joseph and Gianna figure out about the meteors. That is the only thing, except tomorrow's meeting, with a time limit."

Jenna took advantage of my comment to pass through the door and head up the corridor. We all followed her. As far as I could tell, none of us wanted exactly the same thing. Joseph wanted to fly; Alicia to flee. Liam wanted to stay and lead in his father's footsteps, Kayleen to follow, to help. And I wanted . . . I wanted to do it all. Jenna, Jenna just wanted to go home. That sounded so simple.

Damn leading. It was harder than it looked.

Ten more minutes of following Jenna through corridors, and we were in a big square room filled with a single table and eighteen chairs, all of them bolted to the floor. One wall held a sink and a small set of cabinets. Two of the walls had screens, the third was a surface for drawing on: there were colored marks, green circles and blue arrows and black symbols I didn't understand. Perhaps they'd been here twenty years. Perhaps my parents had made those marks.

Jenna stood in the doorway, gesturing for us to sit. Then she said, "Stay here. I'll be right back." She disappeared through the door. For a moment, we all sat and blinked, looking around. The air smelled good; no tang of the sickly garden. The colors and textures were all new, all wrong, and they drove me to restless fidgeting.

Kayleen broke the awkward silence first. "So what do we do if meteors are heading at us? How worried did Gianna sound? What can we do about it, anyway?"

Liam cleared his throat. "There are crater lakes everywhere. And just plain craters. Most of them are pretty small . . . Little Lace Lake is the biggest I've seen."

The lake took five days to ride around, maybe three without stopping except to sleep. We'd stopped a lot. I pictured it in my head, something big enough to make that crater, carve those tall, steep walls. Something big enough to make a hole that took days to ride around. I shivered.

Liam leaned forward, sweeping our attention to him with the intensity in his dark eyes. "Lorrie and her husband, Jacob, are our best biologists. They think the ecosystem here is as sparse as it is"—he held up a hand to forestall the question that immediately jumped to Kayleen's face—"compared to Deerfly and Earth, because there are so many geologic events. Meteors, volcanoes, earthquakes. We roamers see signs of old impacts all over the place." He tugged at his braid, running it through his fingers. His eyes shone with energy and his hand nervously stroked the fine smooth surface of the table. "I could count a hundred places that they've hit if I tried." He paused. "But there are a lot more places that they haven't."

Alicia said, "I've seen a lot of craters, too, and Liam's right. We'd have to just stay out of the way. Lots of meteorites aren't big enough to make craters of any size—they just . . . land. Cause small problems. We found a burned-out section of forest a few years ago. Klauss said a meteor started the fire. He spent two days looking for it, although he never found it. So if there was a crater, it was so small we didn't see it. It would be just terrible luck to be right where something like that hit."

No point in getting too worried about something we couldn't control. I sighed. "So we don't really know anything until we know if, and where, one might hit." I glanced at Joseph. "Gianna did sound worried, but not . . . not too scared."

Jenna came in, carrying two bundles awkwardly. She handed the first to Joseph; a rich blue coat shot through with the same type of embroidery as the headband he still wore. White piping lined the collar and the ends of the sleeves and ran up by the buttons at the opening. The coat shimmered, softly enough to draw the eye rather than repel it. I would watch anyone wearing something so beautiful.

Joseph's eyes shone as he ran his hands along the fabric, holding it up and looking at the finely crafted pockets and turned-up collar. He stood and slid his arms into it, shrugging it on. The coat was about two sizes too big; his fingers barely poked through the arms and the bottom of the coat fell almost to his knees. He grinned, fingering the fine worked edges, and sat back down, closing his eyes. His hand reached for the headband and he pushed it toward me across the table. "Keep this for me?"

I took it, placing it carefully in my coat pocket.

Jenna turned to Kayleen. "Here. This is an assortment of possibilities for you to try." She handed Kayleen a pristine folded emerald-green vest with black piping, a battered cap, and a pair of loose-legged pants that tied at the ankle; filmy and totally unsuitable to wear in the cold outdoors. "These are like Joseph's headband—they will work with the data buttons. They are not tuned to the ship, but you need to start somewhere."

Kayleen's eyes widened as she picked up the hat.

Jenna turned back to Joseph, still sitting straight up, eyes closed, his body relaxed. "Joseph!" she said. He opened his eyes, coming back from wherever he'd drifted when he donned the coat. "You're wearing a pilot's uniform, or at least, half of one. It should be plenty, as strong as you are. With that, you can access the ship's systems, and control the screens in here. Or at least, with some practice. It won't help you access data from *Traveler,* but we're better off with our own data. A cross-reference. We dropped two satellites in orbit when we came, we'll pull data on the meteor shower from those. It may take a while for you to learn, but I'll stay and help you." She looked around the room, sweeping her gaze across us all, her face thoughtful. "I think . . . that the rest of you should go back. There are more useful tasks for you outside, and you should get some sleep." She looked at me. "Chelo, I'd leave you here to help Joseph, but Kayleen will have to fill that role since I want to work with her, too." Her face softened, looking genuinely concerned. "You should sleep, or try to sleep. It's always easiest to negotiate on a belly full of sleep."

Alicia said, "Can I stay? I want to learn more about the ship."

Jenna frowned at her. "We need to concentrate."

Alicia gave Joseph a beseeching look. He didn't even notice, his eyes riveted on the bright silver buttons on the front of the coat, exactly the size of data buttons. I squinted at them. Maybe they *were* data buttons. Practical.

Alicia shook her head, watching Joseph ignore her, her mouth a tight angry line in the center of her face.

The crumpled brown hat now sat on Kayleen's head and she was already slipping on the vest. Jenna laughed. "One at a time. You'll confuse yourself. Joseph—will you hand her the data button with the information on the ship?"

He blinked, and fished in his pocket. Kayleen took the hat off, then reached for the button Joseph held out for her.

Jenna fixed them both with a stare. "You two, stay here," she commanded. They both nodded, Kayleen looking puzzled and Joseph with a silly grin on his face and his eyes closed again. A stab of jealousy ran through me. Why couldn't I see what he saw?

Then she turned to us. "Liam—you lead us out."

Liam gave her a startled glance, but she held her arm out in a go-on gesture. He grimaced and went through the door, the rest of us following. We took three wrong turns, every one grating on my sense of urgency. Typical Jenna, making us learn the hard way. As we wound down, the scent of charred grass from outside began to mix with the more sterile scents of the ship's corridors.

At the bottom of the ramp, Jenna said, "I'll meet you in two hours, at the hangar. It will be getting light then."

"But what if we need you before that?" I asked.

"You'll manage." She gave me a small quirky half smile, and disappeared back up the silver walkway toward the ship. We stayed, watching, until the ramp folded back up and it was impossible to tell where it had been.

I realized I had no idea how to open the door from outside.

ALICIA'S BETRAYAL

Liam and Alicia and I jogged back toward the hangar, keeping close to each other. No one talked, as if being inside the belly of *New Making* had stunned us all. Alicia looked like she might bite anyone who spoke, and Liam seemed to have fallen inside himself.

What if Jenna took off with Joseph and Kayleen? What if something went wrong in the ship—if Joseph or Kayleen got hurt? What if Nava didn't come to talk, or if she brought an invasion force? Where would we go? The sea and the river and the cliffs made effective barriers—we'd have to go back up the First Road. Surely people in Artistos knew where the First Road intersected the High Road? What if we had to flee and Liam wouldn't come, or we didn't have Bryan?

I was not going to sleep. But Jenna's advice was good; rest, at least, would surely help.

We found Akashi and Paloma standing near the corner where we had eaten earlier, watching the last fading bits of flame lick at the cliff bottom below Artistos. "Did anything happen?" I asked.

"Nava called and said they'd meet us halfway two hours after dawn. Otherwise, it's been quiet. Where are Kayleen and Joseph?"

Liam said, "With Jenna in the *New Making*. They're trying to figure out what condition the ship is in, and looking for meteors."

Paloma blew out a long breath, a worried look on her face. "In the *New Making*? Does it work?"

Liam shrugged. "There's a half-alive garden growing in it. Jenna says it can fly."

Paloma's eyes widened. "A garden? After all this time?" Her gaze turned out the window, toward the silver ship, and she smiled.

Liam walked up and touched her on the shoulder. "It's not a good idea. It's running away. Jenna isn't a trained pilot. She says so herself. Neither is Joseph, but Jenna thinks he can fly it."

Paloma turned to look at me, her eyes searching mine, digging for my answers. "Chelo?"

I swallowed, picturing Joseph's face after he fixed the lake ring, after he flew the skimmer. I looked at each of them in turn, stopping last on Alicia's hard, violet gaze. "I think he can do it." I glanced at Liam. "But I'm not sure it's the right thing to do. Not yet."

Akashi hadn't stopped staring at the far-off line of flames. "Right for who? For you, and Liam, maybe not." He glanced at Paloma. "Or for Kayleen. Hard for me to say." He turned to Alicia. She watched him closely, her eyes wide, as he said, "It could be a good idea for someone with no happiness here to see if there is happiness somewhere else."

She smiled up at him, wide-eyed.

He continued. "But sometimes you find you love what you threw away."

Alicia didn't flinch. "And sometimes you find your destiny." She turned away, watching out the window like Paloma had, but instead of looking speculatively at the ship, she looked starved.

Akashi shrugged, looking at me and Liam. "Your skills are useful here. It will be sad for Fremont if you all leave." He swallowed, his eyes shining and damp. "But the choice is yours to make."

I smiled wryly, sure he wanted Liam and me to stay, sure he wouldn't interfere with whatever we chose. His eyes reminded me of how I felt about Joseph's choice, which I couldn't make for him. If Joseph stayed, no one went, so he could choose for us all, but I couldn't choose for him.

But Alicia? I remembered our second night around the lake. "Do you recall your dream, Alicia? About how you left, but you found you had left something behind?"

She stared at me, then nodded. Her voice was soft and firm as she said, "I also remember telling you that I couldn't imagine what I might have left behind that mattered. Now I can. I couldn't bear to leave Joseph behind, or Bryan jailed." Her face brightened. "But Joseph will go. He has to. So now, it's just Bryan."

I wondered if that mattered so much to her. She knew Bryan as a rescuer, as the friend who had helped Liam free her when she herself was locked up, but she didn't know him well, didn't know how he looked after us, how he loved dogs and loved to climb . . . I shook my head. Maybe I was underestimating her. "I'll work on that tomorrow."

Alicia looked down at the ground, then back at me, her gaze measuring. "I want us all to go. Everyone here, and maybe Sky. Sky would love it. But I'd go with just Joseph and Jenna."

"I don't know what to do," I replied, struggling not to show how much part of me wanted to go, had always wanted to go. "I'll try and get Bryan free. Then we can make any choice we want."

"By talking?" Alicia asked. "You're going to free him by talking?"

I looked around at the others. I suddenly felt exhausted, drained. I didn't want to defend my choices to anyone, wanted instead to just be alone, to think, to think about Joseph in his shimmering pilot's coat, to think about Nava and how to make her see us instead of her fears about us. . . . Every one of the things I needed to think through exhausted me, all by themselves. "I . . . need to prepare for tomorrow. I'm going to take a walk. Maybe out there." I gestured toward the dark stubble. "I want to be alone."

Akashi looked at the charred ground outside the concrete he stood on. "Not alone. Take Liam, at least, with you. Paloma and I will keep watching." He paused, examining the blackened plains in the pale starlight. "Should be okay in boots. Watch for hot spots—they'll be white ash. The black should be fine to walk on by now. And don't go so far we can't see you."

"Thanks." What about Alicia? I didn't want her to go with us, not really. I didn't even want Liam, not then. Alicia's restless energy would be a distraction. But she needed something to do. "Alicia, can you check on the hebras? Make sure they can be saddled easily, and fill some packs with enough food and water for a few days, so we're ready to ride out of here and meet Nava?"

Her eyes narrowed, and I braced for an argument. Instead, she simply nodded and faded away toward the corral.

Liam looked at me tenderly, his gaze full of concern. For me.

I swallowed, unable to tear my eyes away from him.

He said, "Come on, I want to get something first. I owe you a flute lesson."

"Flutes?" I frowned, unable to quite think about flutes; there was peace on Artistos to think about, and losing my little brother, Alicia and Jenna and the spaceship . . .

He laughed, probably at the look on my face. "I owe you a lesson. Remember when I gave you the flute? Give yourself a break, a rest. Even Jenna said you needed to rest."

Akashi clapped his son on the back. "Good idea, Liam— give her something unrelated to think about." He gazed at me, his eyes as worried as Liam's. "Sometimes, Chelo, giving the confused part of your brain a chance to work on something else lets your real wisdom bubble up."

Liam led me back to the packs, and I pulled out the flute he had given me. He dug into his own pack and produced a long thin bundle, wrapped in maroon cloth and tied with a light yellow rope. He undid the rope with one hand and unwrapped a flute made of darkwood and inlaid with small stones. "I didn't quite know why I packed this, but it . . . felt right." He held the flute out to me, turning it a little so the stones reflected light. "See how some of the stones change color in the light? A few are crystals. Akashi and I made this together when I was ten. I found all the stones myself, mostly in streambeds." He pointed at a milky stone with flashing azure and gold flecks in it. "This one was at the bottom of a waterfall."

I took the flute and ran my fingers over the little round stones. "It's pretty." The wood had been carved so the stones looked like a river or a snake, a sinuous line of color spiraling around the wood, avoiding only the top, where the little line of finger holes marched. I carefully handed him back the flute. "Let's go."

He bowed exaggeratedly, his braid nearly touching the cement slab. A gesture meant for the stage on Story Night. He gave a little flourish of his hand. "After you."

I don't know why it seemed funny, but it did. I laughed, a genuine belly laugh, and took off at a fast walk, shaking my head. Apparently Liam had learned his father's sense of theater well. Suddenly I wanted the longest flute lesson I could get; the biggest possible break from worry about the meeting. As we passed from the concrete onto the plains, the ground crunched under our feet and tiny clouds of ash puffed up.

We sat on top of a pile of rocks nearly as tall as we were, with a view in every direction. In front of us, the last of the flame wall toward Artistos was no longer even a complete line, whole sections had guttered out for lack of fuel. Darkness cloaked every other direction. The plains were unusually silent, surely a result of the fire. Only two moons were visible. Summer hung over the sea behind us, a reddish crescent providing only faint light, and Plowman looked like an oversized star above Artistos. The moonlight was wan enough that the Milky Way spun over our heads, a visible link between us and other inhabited planets, between us and Deerfly and Earth. The spaceport huddled behind us, a dark line punctuated with the big dark box of the hangar and the tall spire of the *New Making,* which showed no sign of the people I knew were inside.

Liam sat close enough to me for me to feel his warmth, not quite touching. I brought my flute up to my mouth and blew softly, playing "Season's End," a children's song about harvest that I'd managed to pick out most of the notes for. My hands shook, maybe because Liam was so close, maybe because I'd just been inside the *New Making,* maybe because I might leave my home soon, or be sundered from my brother, my only blood family. I struggled to focus on the notes, to put as much of myself as I had available into the tune.

Liam knew the song, joining me, filling in the few notes I hadn't quite managed. I watched his fingers carefully, following him as best I could. Near the end of the song, I missed a note entirely, shattering the melody with a small cacophony. We shared a nervous, companionable laugh. "Here," he said, "follow this one. Listen first, though. Close your eyes."

Haunting soft notes filled the empty space around us, the pitch and transitions perfect. Liam's playing transported me, lifted me. I had never heard the song, but it sounded like a journey, and water, and fire, and love. It sounded like the trip we had just taken only without the tension or the hunt or the altercation with Nava. I listened until he finished, and then sat in silence for a moment afterward.

He whispered, as if not wanting to break the song's spell. "It's called 'Two Souls' Water.' Are you ready to try?"

We played together, working on the same song for twenty minutes. Liam stopped from time to time to show me a complicated fingering. As we came to the end after the third time through, I set my flute down. Enough self-indulgence. I stared at Artistos, at the sky beginning to lighten just a bit above the town. Only a few hours left.

Liam took my hand in his. "Are you scared?"

I nodded. "Scared I won't succeed, scared I'll want to use the weapon, scared they'll scare me. I don't know. Maybe I'm most afraid I won't be able to pull this off and something will happen to Bryan, or Joseph, or to . . . any of you."

"Do you love Bryan?" he asked, letting go of my hand and placing his palm on my cheek. His eyes searched mine. My face felt warm.

"Of course I do." I swallowed. "I love him . . . he's like Joseph, like my brother. Like . . . Kayleen. He's family."

"But you haven't promised him anything else, anything more?"

I shook my head. "I haven't . . ." I clamped down on my words. It was too soon for this discussion, our world too perilous. But it mattered, mattered in my final choices. Liam did not want to go, and I did.

He waited for me to respond. I wanted to lean into him and let him hold me. I wanted him to kiss me, and more, but this was not the time. I felt caught, unable to move toward him or away.

His arm fell around my shoulder and I closed my eyes and leaned into him, my head down on his shoulder. His arm tightened around me, gathering me in. "I'm . . . I'm not ready yet," I murmured into his shoulder. "I have to finish this."

He pulled me even closer. "Then just let me hold you a moment. Do you want that?"

I nodded, and let myself drink in his warmth, his smells, his open offer of more. A little part of myself longed to break into that possible future now, to do more than hold him, to at least promise him more. I breathed deeply, in and out, and he matched me breath for breath, and for just a moment it seemed like we were the same: the same heartbeat, the same breath, the same heat.

I opened my eyes and watched light spread farther above Artistos, washing out the stars on the sunward side of the sky. I pushed away, gently, hating the end of this peaceful moment. I wanted to stay here and kiss Liam and play the flute and let him hold me. But there was no time, and today,

I had to try to make more time for us. For all of us *altered*. "Thank you," I said, softly.

He nodded, smiling, and did the best little half bow possible from a sitting position. "Your wish is my command."

"Well, I can't have what I wish right now. We've got to go saddle the hebras."

He cocked his head, still grinning. "Well, that's a wish."

We started walking back, our flutes cradled in our outside arms, holding hands. We stopped just before stepping onto the concrete pad, turning to look back across the burned plain now that the sun spilled light generously onto the black and ash-gray plains.

Liam pointed. "What's that?"

I followed his finger, and saw movement behind the spaceport. A black hebra and black-haired rider. Dark enough to barely pick out against the dark, burned plains. Heading toward the First Road. So far away they were already tiny. My heart fell. "Ink." I knew what she'd chosen. "Alicia's gone after Bryan. She's too smart to try to go up the cliff road, so she's going around." We had to stop her.

Liam's startled tone rang with disbelief. "By herself?"

I squinted. "Apparently. Besides, who would she take? Joseph's not likely to leave the *New Making,* or Jenna, right now. Akashi and Paloma wouldn't condone this." Rising anger at her erased my sense of peace. "She could ruin everything."

"I know," he said. He squeezed me briefly, and we ran back to the spaceport. There was no way to stop her now, she had too much of a lead. Maybe, just maybe, Akashi and Paloma had sent her on an errand. Maybe she hadn't gone on her own.

Akashi and Paloma were in the keeper's cabin, making a breakfast of corn bread and applesauce. Akashi turned as we came in, and his face changed as he saw ours. "What's wrong?"

"Alicia," I said. "Alicia took Ink and she's gone up the First Road. I think she's taking the back way into Artistos."

Akashi's expression hardened. He glanced at Paloma. "Can you watch this?"

She pursed her lips and a quick deep sigh escaped. "Sure."

Akashi passed Liam and me and headed straight for the hangar. Liam and I followed. We caught up to him staring at the blanket-covered pile of weapons. The microwave gun had been lying out, uncovered. It was gone. "Wasn't the gun there?" I asked.

He nodded quickly. "It looks like she took it." He flicked back the blanket Jenna had covered her weapons with and counted. There were nine. One of the silver killing balls was missing. Akashi looked up at us, his face grim, his eyes full of anger and fear. "I'm sure she's going after Bryan. She wasn't here when Jenna unpacked this—she was out with Joseph. Does she even know what the hell she has?"

I glanced down at my chrono. "They should be along in a few minutes. They're already late." Why? What kept them?

"What about your stunner?" Liam asked Akashi.

Akashi shook his head. "It's in the cabin. I still have that. All she has are *altered* weapons." He stared down at the pile of weapons for a few moments, and it seemed like he grew both angrier and older as he stood there, his eyes sad and his mouth drawn into a grimace. His voice caught as he said, "She made her own choice. There is nothing for us to do now, but wait and see what that choice brings her."

I ground my teeth. I couldn't leave to chase her; I had to meet Nava. There was nothing to do until Jenna and Joseph and Kayleen returned. It galled to stay here, talking, but she was beyond catching now. "Will you tell Nava?" I asked him.

He looked me straight in the eye. "Will you?"

I shook my head. "No . . . well, I don't think so. I have to think of Bryan first, I just have to." What if I had to choose between them? I'd choose Bryan, but Alicia, no matter how wrong she was, Alicia was one of us, one of my kind. Ruth had made her what she was, but surely Ruth's damage could be undone. "She could ruin everything." I looked up at Akashi, hoping he'd understand my next words. "But telling on her . . . telling on her ruins something else. We've never betrayed each other. We six are all we have."

His response was quick. "You have us. Me and Paloma

and Mayah and Gianna and dozens more I can name." His eyes were hard as river stones.

I swallowed. "I'm sorry, Akashi. You're right." I stammered. I had hurt him. How to help him understand? "That's why I don't want to just jump in *New Making* and fly away. You are here. People we love are here. It's just, just that we are the only ones like ourselves. And if I can save Alicia from her own stupidity, I will."

"Good luck." He sounded like he saw no chance to save Alicia, or save ourselves from her. Or maybe that was just how I felt, so that became what I saw in his eyes and heard in his voice.

Akashi started walking back toward the keeper's cabin. His next question clearly wasn't looking for an answer. Yet. "So, Chelo, has Alicia betrayed herself, or you, or no one?"

I must have looked puzzled, because Liam leaned down and whispered in my ear, "He does that a lot. To make you think. But don't get caught in his mind knots—some can't be untied." He grinned at me, and for a moment, the situation felt just a little lighter, a little more bearable. I grinned back.

He reached toward me, offering a hand, but I didn't take it. "Not now," I whispered. I couldn't. If only I hadn't been so selfish, hadn't taken time for myself and been happy to have Liam along and alone. If I had taken Alicia with me, too, this wouldn't have happened.

24

REACTIONS AND CHOICES

By the time we got back to the keeper's cabin, the sun had painted the whole plain with light, illuminating the fire-black rocks and ash, warming me enough to open my coat. Paloma looked up with a wan smile as we came in, her face rigid with ill-concealed tension. "Did she take any weapons with her?"

Akashi nodded.

Paloma blew out a hard breath and blinked, then sighed. "Come on, eat. You'll need your strength."

"Have you seen the others?" I asked.

She shook her head, handing me a plate of steaming corn bread piled with applesauce.

Akashi smiled at Paloma as he took his own plate. "I could smell the applesauce from outside the door."

She smiled tiredly. "Well, and it's corn bread again. If we stay here another few days we'll have to figure out how to re-provision. Eat."

I heard footsteps outside. Joseph, Kayleen, and Jenna rushed in. "We've got a problem," Kayleen said. "Joseph did what Gianna asked. There's a swarm of little meteors that are going to hit near here, here and Artistos, but it's really worse than that; a big one is headed for the ocean near Islandia." She slowed down to catch her breath. "It might make a wave big enough to swamp us, but he doesn't know how to calculate that."

Islandia was almost half the world away.

Paloma reached for her daughter, pulling Kayleen close. "Are they going to hit today?"

Joseph shook his head.

Paloma released Kayleen with a sigh and handed out plates to the rest of us. "So, everybody eat. We can decide what to do over breakfast." I'd never heard her quite so forceful.

Joseph's and Kayleen's news, on top of Alicia's desertion, had withered my appetite to ash, but I took my plate to the table anyway. I moved next to Joseph and whispered, "Did you talk to Gianna?"

"No, Jenna said I should talk to you first." Only then did he blink and look around more closely. "Where's Alicia?"

I sighed heavily. "Gone. Fill your plate. Sit down. I'll tell you."

He obeyed, quickly, sitting and looking at me expectantly, anger darkening his eyes and pulling his face taut. Within two minutes, all seven of us had wedged around the table meant for six. "Where's Alicia?" Joseph demanded.

Akashi glanced at me questioningly. I nodded at him, and a tiny strained smile crossed his face. My news. I cleared my throat. "Alicia took Ink, and a microwave gun, and"—I glanced at Jenna—"and a round silver ball from Jenna's pile—and she left, heading toward the First Road." Jenna's face paled. Anger quickly chased the surprise from her face, and her mouth went tight and hard. So she hadn't suggested it, or given Alicia permission.

I stabbed at my corn bread, smashing it on the plate. "She left a half hour ago. Liam and I saw her leave, but by then she was too far away to catch on foot. My guess is she's taking the First Road to Artistos to try to rescue Bryan."

"You should have watched her," Jenna snapped.

My face grew hot. "I know." I glanced at Joseph, who looked confused. He probably didn't even know he'd contributed by ignoring her in the ship.

Akashi's voice dripped disgust. "I could have watched, too. Liam and Chelo were out, and I knew it. Paloma and I were here, near her. We didn't even know she'd gone until they told us."

Joseph asked, "Did she leave me a note?"

"Not that we've found," Paloma said. "Tell us about the meteors."

"A half hour?" Joseph said. "Can't we catch her?"

"I need *you* here," Jenna snapped.

Joseph glared at her, then glowered at the table, looking at no one.

Liam looked at Jenna. "What was in that ball she took?"

Jenna frowned, hesitating. She licked her lips and looked almost sheepish—a look I'd never seen her wear before. It looked ridiculous on her twisted face. "She could kill everything within twenty meters of where she throws it, and do serious harm within fifty. It's meant to damage a crowd."

Paloma spoke up, her voice flat. "And every one of us old enough to have been in the war will recognize it."

"Whether she knows how to use it or not, she can scare people with it."

"They'll shoot her," Joseph said, his face pale. "We have to go after her."

Liam stood up, his plate untouched. His face was set. "I'll go. Chelo can't—and you shouldn't, Joseph. We can't lose you."

Joseph glared at Liam, and I was sure he was going to tell Liam no. Instead, he said, "I'm closing down the nets then, so they can't see either of you coming."

"No," I cried. "Wait. Think about it. We're meeting them soon. With luck, they know nothing about Alicia or the skimmer, and with even more luck"—I looked pointedly at Joseph—"they think losing the nets yesterday was an anomaly. We need to talk, or we start a full-scale war. We'll lose, all of us. They'll kill us all, or we'll have to all fly off, without Alicia, without Bryan, without Liam. We can't do that. Besides, she can't get to Artistos the long way before the meeting."

Liam tugged at his braid. "I should go now if I have any chance of catching her."

Akashi looked at his son, his face a mask of concern. "Liam—she may be committing suicide. You don't have to do this. Stay with us, stay safe." His eyes pleaded with Liam, although his hands and voice were steady. "They must have Bryan in a safe place, must be guarding him. They've probably set the perimeter bells to identify any of you coming in."

Jenna spoke, her voice slow and reluctant. "I can get you through the nets undetected. I'll give you a frizzer."

Akashi instantly diverted his attention to her. "A what?"

"I carry one. It makes me invisible to your data nets. Changes my signature. It's small—you can keep it in your pocket. I brought one for each of us; they're in the *Burning Void*."

I glared at her. Jenna gave up her secrets slowly, but she was offering them. Sooner would have been nice.

Liam looked at Akashi. "I have to go. There's still a chance to stop her, or if I can't do that, to help her. I know Artistos better than she does; she never had the run of town like me. Bryan has to be in the hospital if he's doing as badly as it sounds. It's the only place they have good medical equipment."

I frowned. "But what if he needs care? We don't know how badly they hurt him. Who says we *can* rescue him?"

Jenna spoke up. "There are medical supplies and bots in the ship. I used them after . . . after I lost my arm. I lived in *New Making* for almost a year."

So that was how she survived. I pictured her sneaking alone down to the ship, which I knew was guarded then, stealing aboard, injured, hiding, and finally healing.

I didn't want Liam to go. But Alicia, wild and uncontained, was a clear danger to us as well as herself. "Okay— everyone. Here's what I think we should do."

Liam continued to stand, watching his father's face. Joseph glared at me, his eyes pleading. For what? To shut down the nets? To send him after Alicia, or Liam?

Paloma and Kayleen, next to each other, held hands on the table. Akashi gazed at Liam. No one had taken even a bite of food.

I swallowed, hard, wishing for time. "Liam, go now. Let Jenna take you to saddle Star, get the frizzer. Take an earset, so we can talk to you." I dug in my pocket for the earset I'd used to call Artistos. "That means we'll only have one, but it can't be helped. Try to catch her, to stop her." I glanced at Akashi. He looked back, neither agreeing with nor fighting me. "If she's already done something stupid, don't help her—stay safe. Your goal is to stop her. If you can do that, call us, then come back."

Joseph looked like he burned to say something, but he held his tongue.

I continued. "We'll know the outcome of the talks by the time you find her. We may need to help you two get Bryan if it all goes bad." I caught Liam's attention, pinned his eyes with mine. "Don't get killed. Think of yourself as a scout, not a warrior. Find out what's happening in Artistos for us."

Akashi's face relaxed a little. He broke in. "Liam—do what you need to. But don't save Alicia from herself if it puts you in danger. Do you understand?"

Liam nodded, and stepped next to Akashi, putting his hand on his father's shoulder. "I'll be careful."

Paloma stood, wincing, and started wrapping a piece of corn bread and some dried fruit.

I held the earset out to Liam. "Be careful. If you can all three come home, if you can get Bryan safely, do it. I don't think he's in any danger—apparently he's too hurt to threaten Artistos, and they have every reason to keep him alive. Do you understand? Stopping Alicia is more important than getting Bryan out. They'll kill her if she threatens them; they won't kill him if he stays put." I paused. "I hope."

He stood across the table, looking down at me. His eyes flashed warmth, a hint of a secret smile just for me. "I understand."

Kayleen looked up at Liam. "Maybe . . . maybe you should find Tom. He might be able to help."

Liam nodded and started toward the door, but I realized what I'd forgotten. "Wait." He stopped. "We meet with Nava and whoever she brings in a little over an hour." I swung my gaze to Joseph. "Joseph—I don't want you to mess with Artistos's data nets for now. But you keep the other earset, stay in touch with Liam. If Liam needs the nets down, he can ask for it. But unless he or I ask for it, I want the nets up. In fact, I want you and Gianna to have a civil conversation about the meteors right after we eat. Be helpful. Let them know we're being cooperative."

Joseph frowned, but he nodded slightly, his gaze on Liam. "Can Liam go now?"

I swallowed. "I guess he'd better. But everyone else, stay here. Jenna can help him go." I glanced at her, wondering briefly if she would do what I told her. Take my orders. She had held her silence since hearing about the ball.

Her voice sounded torn and ragged, tired and worried. "I'd go, Liam, but I need to stay here and work on the *New Making*. It might be our only escape route, especially now." She jerked her head toward the door and stood, her shoulders as straight as ever.

I stepped toward her and reached out a hand, not quite touching her. "Jenna, can you give Liam enough frizzers for Bryan and Alicia?"

"Yes." She looked at Liam, not me. "Let's go."

Liam leaned down and hugged Akashi, briefly, then smiled at Paloma and took the package of food she held out to him. He stepped over near me, leaned in, and kissed my cheek. His lips were warm. "Good luck," he whispered.

"Good luck to you, too," I whispered back.

And then Jenna and Liam were gone.

I took my first bite of breakfast. The applesauce had already cooled, and the food tasted like sawdust. How could I have let her go? It was so stupid. I should be the one to go after her, but I had set up my own trap. At least people were listening to me. But was I being just as stupid all over again? How *was* talking going to help anyway?

I swallowed a lump of cold bread and applesauce and looked around the table. It wasn't wrong for me to make the choices. Paloma and Akashi were original colonists; they were not us, no matter that they loved us. I was older than Kayleen and Joseph, and I knew I thought things through better. Jenna—Jenna would fly us all away. She was . . . not us either. Not quite. Fremont wasn't her home. I sighed heavily, and met Akashi's eyes as he looked at me. "I'm sorry, so sorry for letting Alicia go."

He shook his head. "You can't take responsibility for everyone's choices. Only for your own."

I took a drink to wet my dry, scared mouth. "Joseph, tell me about the meteors."

"There are a bunch of small ones coming. Some big enough they'll survive entry into the atmosphere, and fall around Jini, but it's too soon to say where. Maybe here, maybe Artistos, maybe on the far side by Blaze." He looked up at the ceiling, his eyes fixed on a cobweb, as if touching the data again. Only then did I notice he had left the coat in the ship. I reached into my pocket and took out my father's headband, holding it out toward Joseph. He glanced at me, at the headband. "I don't need it anymore. Jenna said I'm stronger than Dad was, stronger than anyone she's met."

I shivered. I wanted my little brother, and he was well beyond me. I fingered the headband, toying with the idea of putting it on. But I couldn't read the wind. I pocketed it.

Paloma prompted Joseph, her face white. "So, what about the big meteor?"

He screwed up his face, as if recalling a list of facts. "It's . . . it's less than a quarter the size of the one that made Little Lace Lake. It won't come down anywhere near us. It could hit Islandia, but the trajectory suggests it will miss it, barely, and land in the ocean." He shrugged. "I don't know what happens after that. Does it make a tsunami? Does it just miss us, and we're okay?" He drummed his fingers on his thigh. "It will make weather—storms or something. Surely it will do at least that."

"Gianna can help you figure that out," Paloma said gently.

Joseph nodded. "I already asked her."

"When will this happen?" Akashi asked.

"We'll go through the shower of smaller ones tonight. It should be over by dawn. The big one is just behind, maybe noon."

After my talk with Nava.

Akashi held his earset out to Joseph. "Go on. Take Kayleen with you, set it up so she can hear, too."

Joseph shook his head. "I'll just go in straight through the nets. I can show Gianna more that way, and Chelo can have the earset. Besides, aren't you required to keep it?"

Akashi left his hand open. "Take it, Joseph. Start your conversation with it. That will scare them less. Then maybe Gianna will let you show her more via the nets, and maybe she'll hide what you're doing. Go ahead and keep it—it's the only way Liam can communicate with you."

I nodded. A good plan; Gianna had always been a friend, had been Therese's friend, too. Her understudy in the science guild, which she now ran. I remembered many nights she'd joined us for dinner. She sounded glad to talk to me last night. It was possible she would keep secrets.

Joseph reached a hand out for the earset, his eyes showing resentment, as if using something so mundane was a chore.

25

ON THE GRASS PLAINS

Paloma, Akashi, and I sat, mounted, looking across the flat plains to Artistos perched on the cliff above us. Joseph, Jenna, and Kayleen stood with us, Joseph next to Kayleen, watching Artistos thoughtfully, his face lined with worry and exhaustion. He had slept the least of all of us, except for Jenna.

Jenna had been the first to spot movement down the cliff road ten minutes ago. A line of hebras snaked slowly down the switchbacked path.

Joseph squinted into the morning sun and said, "I count five."

Five? Who? Nava, for sure. I'd be willing to bet on Tom and Hunter. There was only one way to find out.

Joseph and Gianna had been talking, but they didn't yet know what kind of damage the big asteroid would do. A day remained.

There had been no word from Liam. But he wouldn't call and risk alerting Artistos to Alicia's intent before he knew anything.

The headband shimmered in the sun against Kayleen's dark unruly hair. I had passed it to her for safekeeping. She, after all, could use it.

Jenna patted Stripes with her one hand and looked up at me, her slate-gray eye approving. "You are good, Chelo. Strong. You can do this. Buy us time, time to get the ship ready. Buy me a day. Your brother needs to rest, and there are still things I must teach him."

"I'll do what I can."

"Don't trust them," she said.

I led off, Paloma and Akashi following me, close in. The charred day-after-fire scent filled my nostrils, and made the hebras nervous. They picked their feet up high, and kept their ears forward.

I had planned to bring Liam. I felt his absence, felt how I alone represented us all.

Paloma spoke so softly I could barely make out her words. "It took so little time to come to such a pass. Before the earthquake, everything was fine, even getting better. For you, for Kayleen, for the whole colony. As if we were finally recovering from the damned war."

I leaned forward to pat Stripes's long neck. "Maybe it will be all right."

"I hope so," she said. "What will you do if it isn't?" Her words seemed caught in her throat, as if they didn't want to emerge and be heard. "Will you all fly away in the *New Making* if you can't go back to Artistos? Will you take my daughter?"

I turned in my saddle. Paloma rode straight and comfortably, as if she and Sand belonged together, as if she belonged exploring. She had chosen simple hemp pants and a hemp shirt, flowing and loose, and a thick hemp coat with small hand-carved djuri-horn buttons. Her clothes were rumpled from the saddlebags, but she looked clean and alert. She straightened her reins, over and over, but her face gave away no emotion. Akashi, next to her, wore leather, and he looked very much like Paloma; contained and calm. He, too, dressed simply, his only ornamentation the fringe of his leather coat, decorated with the tiny horn beads Mayah made for trade each year. He had chosen to ride with his stunner visible, the hand grip showing in the waistband of his pants. He could have covered it easily by closing the coat, so it was a conscious decision. He and Paloma both carried the little microwave guns, like me. Neither of them was visible. I took mine out of my pocket and pushed it into a hole in the saddle where I could reach it easily. Then I thought better of it, and pushed it back into my pocket.

I couldn't answer Paloma's question. I asked her a different one. "Would you go with us if we went?"

She looked startled, and then she smiled. She spoke slowly, her voice catching in her throat. "Only if Kayleen must. Artistos needs you, all of you."

"Thank you." I turned back around, facing the coming conversation.

When we were about halfway between the spaceport and the cliff, I pulled Stripes to a stop. A little patch of grass the fire had missed hung on, barely wilted, behind a large pile of stones. Paloma and Akashi stopped next to me, silent. The string of five hebras approached us from the Artistos side, close enough now for me to see the deep red of Nava's hair. I squinted, looking for Tom. Hunter followed Nava, then three more behind her. Stile, Ken, and Ruth. No Tom. Ruth's presence added to my unease.

As they came closer, Stile and Ken stopped, holding back. Bodyguards.

The other three continued. Paloma looked at me questioningly, and I shook my head. Let them come to us.

When Nava was about five meters away, I called out, "Good morning."

She stopped. Looking at Akashi, she said, "Where are the others?"

I spoke. "Which others? I came to talk, and that is what I promised."

Hunter rode up next to Nava, sitting straight in his saddle, his gnarled hands holding the reins loosely. He gazed at me evenly. "I came for Joseph."

I bet he did. "I'm the only one of us here."

Regardless of how age had curled his hands and bent his back, Hunter's eyes peered out of his wrinkled face with a deep distrust. He spoke slowly and clearly, as if I were a recalcitrant subordinate. "Do you remember, on your way out, you promised me that you would take care of your people?"

I nodded.

"Here is what I believe. I believe your brother regained his skills, and more, and that he has made our networks unstable for the past two days. I believe he and Alicia are not even with you anymore. I believe you failed to keep your promise."

The combined gazes of Hunter and Nava made me want to squirm. I drew in a trembling breath and let my own anger at them help me steady my voice. "I took care of them all, and we never disobeyed Paloma or Tom." That was all I had promised him. I had never promised him we would not learn.

Ruth rode up on Nava's other side, gazing at Akashi. Her eyes were dark and flinty, her hair pulled back tightly behind her head. Like Akashi, she wore a stunner in plain view. "Akashi, what are you doing? Why aren't you with *us*?"

Akashi's eyes looked concerned, compassionate, but his voice was cool and distant. "Because you are wrong."

"Where is Joseph?" Hunter asked.

Paloma and Akashi were silent, waiting for me to respond.

Was the power here Hunter or Nava? Nava still led Artistos. I nodded to Hunter, acknowledging that I had heard him, but I spoke to Nava. "We have done nothing wrong. You asked us to fix the networks. We did. We were not with Bryan, and I can't say why he chose as he did, but I know we have all been taunted by Garmin and his friends more than once, and

I know they beat Bryan afterward, that you did not keep Bryan safe."

I let a beat of silence fall, and then followed up. "We have often stayed together to keep each other safe." I made sure Nava watched me. "You sundered us, and then you failed to protect Bryan."

A flash of guilt touched Nava's eyes. She shivered a little, but didn't reply.

I didn't give her a break. "We have simply been ourselves. You and I, Nava, we talked once about how we might grow into ourselves."

A light wind blew Nava's hair from her face, blew up fine ash so it swirled around the hebra's feet. Nava's eyes roamed across us three, drinking in details silently. No one spoke.

I wasn't sure what to say next. I knew what we wanted, and that it started with acknowledgment that we had done nothing wrong. Had I made my point? Not if I looked at Hunter, who regarded me calmly, with the same exact condescending look on his face. Ruth simply watched us, her eyes narrow, her mouth a hard line in her thin face.

Nava's voice grew more formal, her eyes harder. "You must all come back. Chelo, Joseph, Kayleen, and Alicia." She looked at Paloma, a brief smile crossing her face. "Kayleen may continue to stay with Paloma, Joseph and Chelo with me." She addressed me next. "But you must stay in town, and you must not gather together. You must not protest any decisions that we make. We expect you to continue your work in the science guild, Chelo, and Joseph to continue strengthening the nets, but only at our command. He is to stop taking unilateral actions."

"And Alicia, and Liam, and Bryan?" I asked.

Nava hesitated a moment, then continued. "Alicia may choose between living with me in Artistos, or returning to her band." Nava glanced at Ruth. "She has not earned more freedom than that."

Alicia and Nava would be oil and water, and she would not go meekly back to the East Band. Besides, she was off making her own consequences at the moment. "And Bryan?" I asked.

Nava wiped a stray hair out of her face, and looked at Akashi warily. I remembered them standing at the fork, each holding a stunner drawn and ready to fire. She swallowed. "Liam can stay with Akashi."

Akashi eyed her back, the same wariness on his face that hers held. "And Bryan?"

Nava swallowed. "We will decide what to do with Bryan when he recovers. We may base our decision on the behavior of the others."

So she liked having a hostage.

Ruth had worked her way to the side. I glanced at Stile and Ken. They, too, had fanned out. So it wasn't just a game of talk, even if I was the only prey here. "Call Ruth and Ken and Stile back, keep them where I can see them."

Nava looked startled, but made no move. I glanced at Hunter. "We are three to your five, and at least three of you are armed. Smart that none of you has drawn your weapons. I suggest that you don't." I regretted placing the microwave gun in my pocket, where I couldn't reach it easily. Except that sight of it could drive them to violence I still hoped to avoid. I opened my hands. It was hard to keep my voice from shaking. "I am not carrying a stunner. There is no reason for you not to hear me out."

Hunter gave a hand signal and Ruth rode back toward him and Nava.

"The others," Akashi said.

I glanced at Paloma. Sand pranced lightly under her. Paloma's face had gone white and her knuckles, where she clenched her reins, were white also, but her eyes flashed determination and anger. She said nothing.

Hunter called, "Stop where you are for a moment," loud enough for Stile and Ken to hear. They stopped, still too far apart for me to watch.

"Where I can see them both at once." I smiled at Hunter, hoping my smile made up for my trembling hands. "You remember the war better than I do, but I don't want to repeat it, either."

He sighed and nodded at me, his look no longer condescending. "Come closer, you two—stand behind us."

Stile and Ken brought their hebras in closer to the path, not quite as close as I wanted, but it would do. I cleared my throat. "Here is *our* proposal. Joseph and I and Kayleen will come back, and Joseph and I will live by ourselves, in town. We will do you no harm; we will help you, like we always have. We are part of you now, we have fought Fremont like you have, helped rebuild it after the earthquake like you did. Joseph will continue to work on the nets, and to do more. He can build them better and stronger, weave in a better warning system. He will show Gianna everything he does. Bryan will stay with us when he recovers, or by himself if he prefers. Liam and Alicia will go with the West Band for the rest of this season, and be under Akashi's care."

I glanced at Akashi. I had only just thought of this solution for Alicia. He didn't react, and I took it as a sign that he would support it. I turned back to Nava. "Akashi is Town Council. There are four of you here this moment. You can decide. We will promise to work for the good of Artistos, and not to harm anyone unless they harm us first. That is the best promise I can make."

Ruth snapped out, "Alicia cannot simply run free."

Hunter put a hand up, asking Ruth for silence. He spoke slowly. "You are not adults to dictate terms to us. Our terms stand."

"I will be an adult in a year," I said. "Artistos's children have married at my age, and younger, and they are treated as adults when they marry." I watched Nava's face closely. She gave nothing away, just watched me as closely as I watched her. "Akashi will agree, and Tom will." I took a risk. "Lyssa, too." I looked from Nava to Hunter. "You need us. We have skills the colony can use."

Nava looked uncertain. I could see it in her eyes. But it was Hunter who spoke, and his eyes were flint and determination. "We do not negotiate with children. I expect you to come back with us now, and then you can explain your *demands* to the whole Council."

And become another hostage? If I went back, I could be there, where Alicia and Liam were. Maybe. If Liam didn't stop Alicia. If he had to follow her all the way into Artistos.

If she didn't do anything stupid. But I'd be out of touch with everyone else. Jenna had told me not to trust them. "I can't go with you. Please talk to me now."

Hunter shook his head. "You're making a mistake, Chelo. If you speak to the Council they are more likely to believe you."

Nava looked past me, at Akashi and Paloma. "Tell her. Tell her to come back with us."

Paloma said, "It is her choice."

Nava pursed her lips, her eyes flashing anger. "Akashi?" she said.

Akashi gathered himself, as if he were on stage. He sat very straight in his saddle, gazing evenly at them, his stunner clearly visible. "I believe these young people have demonstrated they are adults. No matter what we call them. I will abide by Chelo's wishes, as long as she and the others don't harm the colony. Tell Town Council I support her suggestion, and that we'll take Alicia in the West Band for now."

The three of us held our ground, watching the five of them. A standstill.

Ruth addressed Akashi. "You will regret taking Alicia in if it comes to that."

Akashi ignored her. Time stretched, long moments of quiet, filled by the scent of burned grass carried on a freshening breeze. Hunter nodded at me, his face impassive, his eyes cold and untrusting. "You will be welcome in town if you change your mind."

I returned his nod, hopefully returning to him the same look he gave me. "Thank you."

Ruth and Hunter and Nava turned and rode through Stile and Ken, who let them get a few meters down the path while they watched us.

I glanced at Paloma. "Come on, let's go."

She turned Sand around and she and I started back, Akashi continuing to watch the others, guarding us. After Paloma and I had been riding back for about ten minutes, Akashi rejoined us. "They are all going back," he said.

So that was twice they came for me and returned empty-handed. Would a third time come out the same? "Should I have gone with them?" I asked.

As usual, Akashi didn't exactly answer. "The choice was yours."

"I know. Did it make a difference? Did it even help to talk to them?"

Paloma spoke up. "They would have made you go back if you had Joseph with you. They're afraid of him."

Akashi said, "I agree. If Joseph had been with you, they would have used force. We'd better post careful watches tonight."

I frowned. "At least Jenna has her extra day."

Akashi looked at me, a wry smile on his face. "I hope that turns out to be a good thing."

"Me, too." I pushed Stripes into a gallop. Maybe Joseph had heard from Liam by now. Maybe I *would* go to Artistos tonight. I was dead tired of talking and no one listening. I had counted on this meeting, put all of my attention on the solution that scared me the least. I should have had backup plans. Jenna had backup plans. If we made no progress, the only choice for all of us here would be to leave. I was beginning to warm up to the idea.

26

A RIDE INTO TOWN

As we rode back into the spaceport, no one came to greet us. The light wind that started during our talk with Nava now whipped ash steadily around the hebras' feet, rising in little eddies that made us blink. Legs and Longface, still tied in the corral, called out to Stripes and Sand and Lightning as we rode up. There was no sign of people. Ash blew across the concrete pad like dour smoke, in keeping with my mood.

Surely Jenna would have left someone on watch? A long look in every direction produced no sign of movement. I glanced at Akashi. His brow was creased and his eyes searched the concrete pad. I sighed. "You two stay here, don't dismount. I'll go on foot—I'm faster."

He glanced at Paloma. She'd stripped the brace from her foot for the ride, but she still couldn't walk fast or far. He would stay.

I swung down from Stripes, tying her near the other hebras but outside the corral, and headed toward the keeper's cabin. Ash collected in a long line along the windward wall and dusted the windows. The cabin was empty. I darted over to the hangar, calling out as I pushed open the door. No answer. Circling around the building, I spotted Kayleen huddled out of the wind, sitting with her head down on an arm thrown over drawn-up knees. She still wore the headband, and although this spot was sheltered, she'd clearly been in the wind; her dark curly hair was tangled and gray from the ash.

She didn't move as I walked up to her and bent down. "Kayleen?" I whispered, looking to see if she breathed. Her back rose and fell. At least she was alive. But she didn't respond to my whisper. . . .

I shook her and she opened her eyes, blinking against the bright late-morning light. "Wha . . . oh. You're back."

Relief washed over me. "Are you all right? Are you supposed to be keeping the watch?"

She nodded, sitting up straighter. "Sssorrry. I—I stopped over here to get away from the ash, and I started getting good readings on the perimeter data. I figured I could tell when you came back in; I can hear it all." A dazed look decorated her face. "I've never been able to do that before, hear the whole network."

"But you didn't notice when we came in," I pointed out gently.

"Ohhh . . . yeah, I guess I didn't. I filtered out friendly entry. I've been trying to figure out how to get the alarms to be more sensitive to animal entry. It's an exercise Jenna gave me." She shook her head, as if to clear it. "I can't get it working yet."

The headband was clearly tuning something in Kayleen like it had Joseph. A good thing, except that Kayleen seemed dazed. Jenna and Joseph were undoubtedly in the ship. How was I going to get their attention from out here? Throw stones at the ship and hope they made it ring?

I glanced back at Kayleen, who was beginning to look more alert. "How are you supposed to let them know if you need help?" I asked her.

She frowned. "They trained cameras on the spaceport and they can hear the perimeter. Besides, Joseph can talk to me over the nets."

"Oh?" That implied a connection between our nets and Artistan nets. "Can you call him?"

She drew her brows together and swiped at her unruly hair. "Not yet. He has to open a channel. But he calls every fifteen minutes."

"Has he heard from Liam?"

She shook her head. "What happened?"

"They don't care about you or me or Liam. Joseph scares them—if he'd gone, they would have taken him back. Or killed him. I think the only reason they didn't just ride past me like a fly was because Jenna scares them, and they don't know who's here. I don't think they know if Akashi brought a small army or not. They act—respectful—of him. They don't seem to know about the skimmer, but they weren't exactly a river of information."

"How's Bryan? Any word?"

"No." I reached a hand down to help her up. "They won't say anything about Bryan. Wanted the rest of us to come back and do their bidding, except Alicia—they want to send her back to Ruth—and Liam, who's supposed to stay with Akashi. But I think *that* was meant to soothe Akashi."

Kayleen stood, dropping my hand.

I stepped toward the corral. "Come on, Paloma and Akashi are waiting. It felt weird to ride in and find no one watching for us."

"I'm sorry. I can hold on to a lot of the net now, more than ever, but it pushes the physical world away from me. It's like a flood." She shook her head again, not moving with me, but standing and blinking as if some great light shone in her eyes. "Joseph says I'll get used to it."

"I hope so," I said, worried for her, for us. We were all overtired. Kayleen looked almost drugged. I took another step, and this time she followed. We left the lee of the hangar, stepping into the cool wind, the blowing ash. We'd taken no more than ten steps when Kayleen stumbled, falling all the way to her hands and knees. She turned to look up at me, her eyes rolled so far back in her head I could see mostly whites. "Kayleen! Are you okay?"

She sat down on the concrete and put her hand on her head. "Yes. Joseph says he'll be right down—says Liam called. He wanted to know if you were back." She sneezed.

They'd had a conversation and I couldn't hear either side of it. Spooky. "Did Liam find Alicia?"

She pushed to her feet. "Joseph didn't say. He'll be here soon, though." Between her wind-tangled hair, the circles under her eyes, and the odd, skewed look on her face, Kayleen seemed like a caricature of her usual self. The next thing I knew, she was going to start talking in simple sentences, one at a time.

"Come on." I held my hand out for hers, offering support. She took it, and we walked close together. I watched her steps carefully the whole way. She made it to the corral without any further stumbles.

Paloma and Akashi dismounted as soon as they saw us, and Paloma started loosening Sand's girth rope. I eyed the saddled hebras. "Leave them saddled. Joseph is on his way with news from Liam." I squinted at the *New Making,* trying to see if the ramp was up or down. Just closing—so they were coming. Was anyone in Artistos watching?

Joseph pelted up to us, running all out, followed by Jenna who moved at an easy lope. He stopped near me, struggling for breath. His eyes were wild. "Alicia got in, but she set off the alarms. They'd programmed her as unfriendly entry— loud bells. Everyone in Artistos is looking for her. I turned off their perimeters, so she won't telegraph her location if she leaves, but I'm worried about her." His face showed mixed defiance and desperation. "I . . . I found her once—she was in the park—but now, with the nets off, I can't find her anymore."

Jenna caught up, and stood watching us, her face a mask.

"What about Liam?" I prompted.

Joseph answered. "He's in, too, used his frizzer. It worked. He's looking for Tom. But if anyone sees him, with the hunt on for Alicia . . . I don't know. I don't feel good about this."

Damn. We were too split—too many people in too many places. And the only choices I saw now made it worse. Wait here. Safer. But it left them alone, left Liam alone, and Joseph might not be able to stand it. We did have an open invitation to go to Artistos. "What condition is the ship in?" I asked.

Jenna shook her head. "We need more time. Joseph needs to drill more, and I'm tuning the environmental systems. We *could* leave now, but it's risky. I don't want to leave until tomorrow."

"When?" I asked.

Jenna frowned, and drew her brows together. It took her a moment to answer. "We could leave in the morning. After first light. If Joseph and Kayleen both stay to help."

Paloma's face went white. "Can I help you?" she asked Jenna.

"You're not . . . you don't have the training. You can keep watch."

"But we have to go to Artistos!" Joseph said. "We have to leave now." He started toward the hebras.

I grabbed him and turned him toward me. He nearly pulled away, then gave in, his eyes demanding that I let him go.

"Can you talk to Liam?" I asked him. "Tell him to lay low. Tell him to find Alicia if he can and just stay out of the way. Tell him . . . tell him to tell Alicia we're coming."

"When?" Joseph asked.

"Not you. You heard Jenna. You and Kayleen are staying here." I wracked my brain for the best of the choices running through my head. "Me and Akashi. We'll say we're follow-ing up on the conversation this afternoon. Negotiating terms. That will get us up there."

Joseph glared at me. "But I—"

"No. Tell Liam—now—and I'll get us packed." I looked at Akashi. "Mind being part of a rescue party?"

He gazed at me evenly. "My son is there."

Joseph still stood, watching us. I snapped, "Joseph—go!"

He glared at me, but he stepped a few feet away and I waited until I saw his lips moving before turning back.

I addressed Jenna. "Is the skimmer ready to go?"

She nodded. "You can't fly it."

"I know that. I'm crippled, remember, just like you. We need Joseph for everything."

Jenna took a step back from me, looking as if I had thrown something at her. I sighed, wishing I could bite back my words. "Sorry. I didn't mean that. I'm just—worried about him."

Jenna nodded quietly. "I will watch over him."

"Kayleen, too?"

"Yes."

I leaned in and gave her a little hug. She didn't resist, didn't lean into the hug, but she—softened. I backed off and whispered to her. "Thank you. I will try and buy you enough time to do all this, but I can't promise anything. We'll at least be a diversion."

She nodded, and then *she* reached for me, enfolding me in her one arm. I returned her hug, wrapping my arms tightly around her thin, strong middle, feeling the whipcord strength of the muscles in her back and torso. Solid. She felt solid.

Kayleen tugged on my sleeve. "I might be able to fly the skimmer."

She *was* talking one sentence at a time. "Right now you can't walk and handle that much data. Stay here, learn. Help Jenna and Joseph. Try to be sure he doesn't exhaust himself with worry." If Kayleen was out of her depth, how much was Joseph struggling? He was stronger, but in three days he'd gone from blinded to the nets to reading them all, to control-ling them. To training to fly a starship. Flying the skimmer in between. I glanced at the hangar, at the pile of our stuff, the saddled hebras, the silent ship full of bustling robots and green plants; all to reassure myself this was real.

Akashi was already walking Lightning and Stripes over to water. I needed Jenna, too, but she couldn't be in two places at once any more than Joseph. I shook my head, overwhelmed again by how few of us there were. I had to get Liam and Bryan and Alicia back safely. Somehow.

Joseph stepped back near me, looking earnest. "Liam has the message. I . . . thank you, Chelo. I wish I could go."

"Well, me too." I realized I was tired. My eight hours of sleep had been the previous day, not last night. I sighed. "I should go. The sooner we get there, the better. You can communicate with us okay?"

Joseph reached into his pocket and handed me an earset. "I don't need one of these. I can talk to you anywhere you can get signal."

I looked at him, startled again. Of course. Hadn't he just contacted Liam that way? I was getting used to miracles. In another month, a year, would I still know him? If he left . . . if he had access to a world built for us . . . "Just . . . just take care of yourself. I'll call if we need help, or need you to come get us in the skimmer."

He smiled. "I'll be watching you."

"Not every minute. You have work here. I'll call if we need you. How do I do that?"

"Just say my name. I'll plant a program in the nets to listen for it."

"Did you turn off Artistos's access to the satellites again?"

He nodded. "Except Gianna. I gave her a password entry. I need her . . . to interpret."

"Good." How long would Gianna protect him, though? How much information would she hide from Council? No way to tell. I could hope. "Can you . . ." I hated to ask him for something else. "Can you find out where Bryan is and how he is, and let me know?"

He nodded. "I'll try. The hospital net has been protected. I can crack it, but I think they're hiding something and they're afraid I'll find it."

"Let me be sure I understand. The nets are off for them, but on for you?"

He swallowed. "Their perimeters are down. But not all of their communications. They can use earsets between each other, and query individual nodes with readers. I had to leave some communications up so they'll chatter on it. It's the only way I can get information."

"Can you leave their perimeters up, but turn off the bells? So you can see what's happening? That way you can warn them if you see anything dangerous coming in."

"Great idea." He pursed his lips, momentarily lost in thought. "I'll have to work a few minutes on that, but I think I can. That will give me better information about you, anyway."

I looked away, once more overwhelmed with what he was becoming. "God, little brother. You're growing. Be careful—don't get too sure of yourself. You could make bigger mistakes now."

He laughed softly and I turned my gaze back to him as he said, "You're not doing so bad yourself."

My voice shook. "So are you as scared as me?"

He nodded. "Probably."

I leaned in, gave him a hug, and Kayleen stepped forward and joined us. Paloma's arm slid over my shoulder, and she called out, "Come on, Akashi." Soon, all six of us, including Jenna, were in a single large hug, a warm and hopeful and supporting hug.

We stood that way, a huddle of *altered* and not, old and young, friends. A brief image of Steven and Therese, watching us, pleased, crossed my mind, and I laughed, and soon we were all laughing, edgy tired laughter, but its core was warmth and support.

We drew apart. I stopped at the keeper's cabin before heading for Stripes, procuring two pieces of kitchen twine and a scrap of leather from a utility drawer. I wrapped the gun in the leather, being sure it could be drawn out easily, and used the twine to tie the bundle, including the microwave gun, to the inside of my calf where I could reach it mounted or standing. It felt cold against my skin and the twine chafed.

We loped slowly along the wide road, heading for the closest entrance; up the cliff switchbacks. The wind blew harder and cooler and clouds had begun forming over the ocean. In the two hours it took us to get near the top of the switchbacks, the clouds thickened and darkened, and the air crackled with electricity. Perhaps the plains would have ignited today if we hadn't already done the lightning's job.

We crested the cliff road with a few hours remaining before darkness fell. I entertained myself with hopeful daydreams. Town Council would talk to me and Akashi; I'd be around if anything happened, and maybe, just maybe, I could push Nava to our side. Council wanted Joseph, and not me. Yes, they could use me as a hostage, but they had one already. They would be happy with a go-between.

Joseph was supposed to call me if anything happened, so it was safe enough to presume that Liam and Alicia were still safe, and hopefully together. So we walked Stripes and Lightning placidly through the boundary with no comment at all from the bells. Joseph would know we were here.

The great winch stood just a few meters inside the boundary. The hebra barns spread out just down the road, the deep brown and yellow stubble of harvested cornfield waiting to be turned just ahead of them. Lights shone from the center of town, and farther away, from the smelter across the river. The scent of rich earth and a whiff of the goat pens and someone baking bread rode to me on an eddy of back breeze, and then blew away in the prevailing smoke-scented wind from the plains.

Was this the last time I would ride into Artistos?

I needed information. I pulled Stripes to a stop under the big winch, looking out over the charred plains. The clouds obscured the sea, a wall of grayness to the west, sea and sky and plains confused on the horizon line. Akashi stopped next to me, watching the road. "Joseph?" I spoke softly.

His reply was fast. "You made it."

"So far. What do you know? Did you find out anything about Bryan? Did Alicia get caught yet?"

"Shhhh . . . slow down. You sound like Kayleen. Yes, and no."

"Sorry," I hissed. "Yes what?"

"Bryan's in the hospital. I finally got through their security a few minutes ago. He was beat-up pretty bad. His records show four broken ribs and seven of the bones in one of his feet."

"His foot?"

"Yeah. I guess from kicking something. The records don't tell me how it happened, just what's wrong. Anyway, he didn't do too well on some of the pain medication they gave him. There's a doctor's note that he seems to be allergic to something. They suspect his genetic modifications, of course. His heart stopped once."

"What!"

"Shhhh . . . he's doing better now. In pain, but not medicated, except for normal headache pills. We've had those before with no side effects, so that's what they were willing to give him. But that's got to be like giving a parched person a teaspoon of water."

I winced, agreeing with Joseph's assessment. "Can he walk?"

"With most of the bones in his foot broken?"

"Is it set, in a cast or something?"

"Hang on, I'll check."

In the ensuing moments of silence I looked around. The road was empty. I expected a lookout at the top of the path into Artistos. Was Hunter slipping or was something else going on? Or had there been a lookout who ran off to deliver news of our coming already?

"It's in a cast. That doesn't mean he can walk. I don't understand medical terminology well enough to tell what they've done."

"Okay. What about Alicia and Liam?"

"Liam's still to ground, and he still hasn't seen her. I'm worried."

"Me too. But you'd know if they'd caught her, wouldn't you?"

Dry lightning forked across the sky, brilliant even in the afternoon light. "Did you see that?" I asked.

"What?" he asked in return.

"Lightning. Are you in the ship? At least watch a camera—you love storms."

"Yeah. In my spare time."

"Where is everyone? It's too deserted here."

"Council told women and kids to stay home because of the meteors. A stupid idea, but I think they're really afraid of Alicia. Everyone else is at the amphitheater, or looking for Alicia. They're running the search for Alicia from the amphitheater." He giggled. "But there aren't very many of them—they couldn't use the gather bell."

I struggled to suppress my anger, to keep my voice low. He was laughing at the wrong thing. "Look—since you turned off the data, you're responsible for everyone's safety here. Don't laugh at the lack of bells."

"All right, Miss High-and-Mighty, would you have preferred to have the perimeter on? Or to have seventy people looking for Alicia?"

"No. Sorry. I'm edgy."

Joseph sighed, a soft hissing in my ear. "We all are."

I glanced at Akashi, who gazed up and down the path, his eyes never stopping. I could tell he wanted to move on. He was right—we stood exposed here. I told Joseph, "We're going to keep going."

"Where?"

"To the amphitheater." We had to go where Council was.

"Be careful. Tell Liam where you're going."

"Won't they overhear?"

"I won't let them."

He was playing with his new powers. I needed him to think strategically. "Look—I don't want to draw their attention yet. You tell Liam. Tell him he can call me when he needs to, but we've got to keep going."

A full beat of silence passed. I imagined his face set, his eyes smoldering because I was telling him what to do. He would obey me, though. Sure enough, his next words were laced with careful control. "Okay, I can do that. Call back when you need me."

"Thanks, I will."

A few moments later, riding slowly and deliberately toward

town, we passed three men walking out of the hebra barns. I'd seen them all, and knew two from watching their children. I waved. "Hello, Gary, Louis, how are you?" I called.

They raised their heads and two of them stopped, whispering between themselves. Gary kept walking toward us. His eyes were wary as I drew Stripes to a halt. He nodded a greeting. "Chelo, Akashi. I heard . . . I heard you were against us. But I didn't believe it." He jerked his head toward the other two. "But they do. They said we were going to kill you all, and here you are riding into town." He brightened. "But I knew it was okay." He put a hand on Stripes's front shoulder, stroking her. His eyes were full of concern and confusion, but I read no fear or animosity in them.

I wasn't sure what to say. Akashi beat me to it. "No, it's not okay. But we hope that it will be. Chelo and her friends mean no harm, but some people seem to be afraid of them. We came up to stop the rumors, to assure people that there is no reason for fighting."

Gary shook his head. "Fighting. None of us want that." He looked at me. "Chelo, you were always good with my little ones. They like you. I hope it turns out all right for you."

I smiled at him, grateful for the support. Perhaps it was a good sign that the first person we met was friendly. "I hope so, too. You can tell people we don't want to fight either."

"Is your little brother doing better? I heard he'd gone crazy."

I raised my eyebrows. What was Town Council saying about us? "Joseph's fine. Never better. Who told you he was crazy?"

"My wife, Lucy, she told me they said that at a Town Council meeting. I wasn't there. I was watching Julie and Kim." Gary looked puzzled, then he said, "I told her it was probably just grief, just 'cause you lost your parents that way." He shuffled his feet. "I'm sorry about that."

"Me too, Gary. Will you tell Julie and Kim and Lucy hello for me?"

He blushed. "Sure. Good luck, Chelo."

"Thank you." I nodded and directed Stripes to keep going. As soon as we were out of earshot I said, "Well, at least the whole town isn't up in arms."

Akashi smiled back. "Maybe not. But that was a two-one split. Not as good a sign as I'd like. You handled that well. You sounded calm."

I blushed. Praise from Akashi had once seemed so rare. We passed the fields—empty except for two people who appeared to be searching for someone, but paid *us* no attention—and started into Artistos proper. The next group we saw included May and a few other girls I knew vaguely. Neither Klia nor Garmin was with them. They stayed on the other side of the road, watching covertly, with no greeting. When I looked back a few moments later, they were running up a side road. So much for secrecy. I glanced at Akashi. "Get ready."

"I know. We have a saying in the West Band—when we scatter into small groups for summer research, we say, 'May you find only small deaths.' That means change—death of ideas, and learning, death of ignorance."

He was talking philosophy *now*? I smiled. "Last spring, when you came back and one of your people had died in a fall, but only after he'd found some new herb that you were raving about at the time, you talked about treating death as a friend, as your companion in risks. Might that be more appropriate?"

Akashi looked both surprised and pleased. "If you can learn that from talk. Truly understanding death and change takes years. But death can be your friend through the small deaths as well."

I'd certainly changed in the last few weeks. "You too, Akashi. May you have only small deaths today."

His smile was warm and approving. We continued riding, slowly, as if we had no worries. Just a fall ride. Perhaps that was why some people walked by as if we were not there, as if they didn't see us at all.

No one stopped us. We rode straight through the neat outer streets. A few faces looked out of windows at us, and a child I knew, Fern, waved at me once.

Even the town dogs seemed to be inside.

Activity picked up near the park. People milled about singly or in small groups, most heading to and from the amphitheater.

A figure ran from the park, away from us, intent on a goal. Tom.

Eric the shoemaker passed us and waved a greeting, furtively, but turned quickly away, continuing on whatever errand he was intent on.

Akashi leaned in close to me. "Be careful, Chelo."

I swallowed, imagining death riding behind me, but wanting me to live. A weird image, not exactly cheerful.

Should we run after Tom? Or talk to Council? "Come on, Akashi, we can't ride the hebras in there."

He nodded, but stayed up on Lightning until I got down from Stripes and tied her to the twintree that spread its branches over the top of the amphitheater. As long as no one took her, she'd be close, and maybe I could retrieve her. After I had my hands free, Akashi dismounted and quickly tied Lightning next to Stripes. He frowned at my knot and redid it. It seemed surreal that we were allowed so much time, so much freedom.

Akashi and I walked side by side, stopping at the top, looking down.

Everyone was looking up, the whole amphitheater of people, Nava and Ruth and Hunter and Wei-Wei on the dais, Gianna halfway up the steps, one-handed Chayla with a tray of sandwiches and fruit stopped in the act of climbing the stairs, Ken, Hilario, five or ten other people. Their faces were wrong, Wei-Wei's twisted in fright, Ruth's in anger, everyone standing still as if some huge thing were about to descend on them. Ruth's stunner was in her hand, frozen in position. They looked up, past us, higher than us.

I followed their gaze, up, to where the twintree the hebras were tied to overhung the amphitheater. It was about three meters to the left of the entrance, and nearly that far from the ground. Its long pointed leaves danced in the wind. Partially hidden by the leaves, a slender figure hugged the trunk, legs braced, a head full of wild dark hair exposed and facing toward the assembled Town Council.

Alicia.

In her raised hand, she held a featureless silver ball.

27

THREATS

∽

At the sight of Alicia in the tree—threatening everyone in the amphitheater—I stopped, staring at her as if she must be an apparition. My breath came fast and deep, accompanied by an urge to rip her from the tree and send her running so far away I would never see her again. I hissed at her, "No, Alicia! You can't do this."

"I'm already doing it." Alicia spoke without looking down, her eyes nervously scanning the people spread below her, her words clipped and angry. "Go away. Go stay safe and warm down by the spaceport."

Akashi drew in a whistling breath. "What are you bargaining for, Alicia?" he whispered.

A hint of triumph laced her voice. "Tom is bringing Bryan to me."

I tore my eyes from the tree and looked down. Nava's and Wei-Wei's gazes had swung to me and Akashi. "Traitor," Nava hissed to no one in particular, loud enough for me to hear in the near-silence of the amphitheater. It wasn't clear who she meant—Alicia, or me, or Akashi. But Akashi stiffened.

Alicia's presence above me was heavy, like being under a paw-cat in a tree. I had nothing to say to her. She was wrong.

Joseph? Joseph hadn't warned me! He must not know. I hissed softly, for his sake and not hers, to draw his attention. "Alicia . . ." I hesitated. What to tell him?

Alicia called down from the tree, loud enough for her

voice to carry, "I waited. I stayed hidden until they rode back. I heard them trying to figure out how to capture us all, and I knew that talking did you no good. They're too scared of us to let us go, to let us be. Ever. I heard it in their voices."

"Joseph?" I queried.

There was no immediate answer.

My feet felt rooted; my mind spun. If we walked down, talked to Council, it would negate Alicia's threat. She would not throw the weapon where we were. I had to believe *that*—and Council would anyway. Akashi and I could back up, follow Tom, get Bryan, abandon Alicia to whatever fate she created for herself in the next few moments, abandon Artistos's leaders to whatever fate Alicia created for them in the next few moments. Then it wasn't me, it was her choices.

I couldn't.

I wanted to scream in frustration.

Joseph's voice in my ear. "Sis? Sorry . . . I was . . . doing something. I've been offline . . . I traced back, I can see where you are, where Alicia is. I can't talk to her." I couldn't tell whether his voice shook with fear or anger.

"Neither can I," I retorted.

Nava called up, "Chelo, Akashi. Stop her!"

I wanted to. It was too late. She'd started us down this road, and now we had to negotiate it. If I simply stopped her, if I even could, we would all lose. I called down to Nava. "I'm sorry. I did not choose this."

"How do I know you and Alicia didn't plan this together?" Ruth yelled up at me.

I ignored her. Wait for Bryan. We needed Bryan. At least Alicia had accomplished that. I took two steps down and moved to my right, away from Alicia, far enough away from everyone to watch them all, and to talk to Joseph without being overheard. Akashi gave me a withering look and started down the steps.

Was I making the right choice? I had to wait for Bryan. Was Akashi truly angry with me or did he want them to think so?

Akashi stopped about ten steps down, a third of the way, and in range if Alicia threw the ball down there. Mediating with his life. "What's happened?" he called down to the dais, suggesting immediately that he was not involved, that I was not involved. I praised him silently, and held my ground.

Joseph. "Tom's at the hospital. Dr. Debra is trying to stop him from taking Bryan. Tom is arguing."

No one had answered Akashi. "Nava," I called down. "Nava, I came to take you up on your invitation to talk. This does not appear to be a convenient time"—I glanced at the tree, at Alicia, hoping for a reasonableness I no longer expected—"but perhaps we can prove to Alicia that talk is a workable way to make change."

Nava looked trapped, her face a mask of anger and fear, her throat red with emotion. Hunter answered without looking at me. "It is difficult to negotiate in good faith under threat."

Bravado. I needed bravado. "Did you discuss my proposal? You asked me to discuss it with all of you. I'm here."

Alicia spoke to me. "Haven't you figured out yet that you can't talk to these people?"

I ignored her, just like I had ignored Ruth. Alicia was leaving if the ship left, if she lived through this little escapade. And Ruth, Ruth mattered in the long run. But Nava and Hunter mattered more.

Ruth glared up at Alicia. "No talking until Alicia stops or dies."

Meaning until they captured her or killed her. I mumbled under my breath to Joseph. "You might back the skimmer out."

"I already did. Tom still hasn't pried Bryan out of the hospital. They need a wheelchair of some kind, or someone to walk with Tom, help take Bryan's weight."

Dr. Debra was a small woman who often spoke bitterly of her days as a field surgeon during the war. She'd always acted, at best, coldly efficient with us. I whispered to Joseph, "Liam. But tell him to stay behind Alicia. Keep him out of harm's way."

I called down to the dais. "Well, we can stand here and wait to see what happens, or we can talk."

Lightning forked above us, followed closely by bone-rattling thunder.

Lyssa called up to me, her voice higher than usual, shaky. "Can you come down? We could hear you better."

"Why don't you come halfway here?" I said. I glanced at Akashi, who nodded almost imperceptibly.

Alicia said, "I don't think that's such a good idea. I'd rather hear both sides of the conversation. I don't want anyone too close."

Good. She had just publicly distanced herself from me. "That's fine, Alicia." I called to the Council, "How about a change of topic. Gianna, what's happening with the meteors?"

She took a few steps up, turning so we could all hear her. "They're a risk." Her face said not-too-risky. "Some may hit ground, maybe cause fires, damage the immediate area around them. None in this swarm are long-term weather-changers and none of the trajectories appear to put them in the middle of Artistos. Mostly by the lakes." She looked at Akashi. "Your band might be wary, though."

"Have you called them?" he asked.

Joseph in my ear, "Liam is helping Tom get Bryan. The big rock may swamp the plains with water. Models suggest it won't reach Artistos, but could drown us here. Gianna knows."

Gianna, speaking clearly, her hands wringing, her eyes on Akashi. "Yes. Mayah is watching. She didn't seem worried." Gianna glanced nervously from Nava to Alicia to me. She wasn't giving up her conversations with Joseph.

"All right, Gianna, we won't worry too much." Was Gianna truly an ally? Probably not for Alicia. Maybe for me. I shouldn't give away my own conversations with Joseph. I asked, "Nava, how long until Bryan is here? How badly is he hurt?"

Below me, Chayla crossed the dais and set her tray of sandwiches in front of the Council. No one touched it. Chayla backed away and started walking up the steps.

Nava frowned at me. "Anytime, he should show up anytime."

"And after that?" I asked her and Alicia at once.

Hunter shrugged. "That's all we've been asked to do—to bring him here."

I glanced up at Alicia. Alicia's shadow, all of our shadows, fell long on the steps and floor and walls, as if the shadows themselves felt like I did, stretched and thin. The low sun painted one side of her sharp, angular face with light, illuminating her light eyes and frosting the dark tips of her hair with reds. None of us could talk to her privately, not even Joseph. Had she thought farther ahead? A risk-taker. Jenna said we needed that, but I didn't want it, not now. What did Alicia mean to do? Just back off and head for the ship? Or would she do damage on her way out if she could? How badly did she want to hurt Ruth?

Ruth called up. "Then we'll see if she can figure out how to get away."

Lyssa made a hushing sound. "Then we let her go. We never let them come back." Her voice shook. "Isn't that enough?"

Ruth's voice dripped sarcasm at Lyssa. "They've breached our perimeters and threatened our lives. We can't keep them out, Lyssa." Ruth still held the stunner. The tree was protection, but when Alicia wanted to climb down, what then?

I stalled for time. "I like Lyssa's idea. Let them go."

Lyssa looked up at me, pleading. As if I could help her.

No one answered me.

Joseph said, "They're in the park, two minutes."

Chayla passed Akashi, neared the top of the steps, and safety.

Alicia called down, "You. Stay here."

I gritted my teeth. Alicia didn't even know Chayla, quiet Chayla who served, uncomplaining, who had helped me with child care more than once. "Let her go. She's just different, like you and me."

Alicia shifted the ball from one hand to the other. "I don't trust any of them. If you trust her so much, let her stand by you."

Chayla's eyes were wide. Her body shook. We had no

right to scare her. "Chayla," I said, "go ahead. Walk out. She won't hurt you."

Alicia shot me a quick angry glance.

I spoke, making sure my voice carried. "Alicia, you have an opportunity to show compassion here."

She squinted, silent for a long moment. She bit out her acquiescence. "Fine, Chayla. Go out. Stay nearby and suggest that others don't come in, except for Bryan and Tom."

I nodded. A small victory. My will had to stay stronger than Alicia's.

They must almost be here. I addressed Nava again. "If you won't talk to me now, I'll stay after Alicia and Bryan leave. We can talk then."

"No," Alicia hissed loud enough for me to hear. "Come with us."

"I can't." We could not all flee at once, not if Council was free to act. Liam and Kayleen wanted to stay, and there was no time to force them. No time to get Kayleen and Paloma in line and get a decision. The only way to get Bryan and Jenna and Alicia and Joseph away was to hurry. "I can't," I repeated, swallowing hard, biting back tears, my anger, even with Alicia, gone to sadness. I glanced at Akashi, at Gianna.

"Are you offering yourself as hostage?" Hunter asked. "Come on down here."

I shook my head. "After they leave. My word is good."

The scraping sound of footsteps. Tom's voice. "We're here."

My gaze flicked between Alicia and the dais. I spoke quietly. "Bryan. Come here please."

"Chelo." The pain in his voice ripped through me. I was afraid to look. The moment felt like standing on a log over a stream, balancing, barely balancing. Alicia gasped from above me in the tree, screaming out, "You had no right!" Her words echoed in the stone around us.

I heard him sidle up next to me, felt his hand on mine. I looked briefly, and my eyes teared against my will. The skin around one eye and all down one cheek was swollen and dark. Medi-tape held slashes in his skull and along one arm closed.

I didn't have time, or heart, to see more. I squeezed his hand. Only then did I notice Liam from the corner of my eye. He'd ignored me, and come in. "Liam, please wait outside."

I couldn't see him, couldn't tear my gaze fully away from the dais, or the stunner in Ruth's hand. His voice was shaky but loud enough for people to hear. "I stand with my father." He started down toward Akashi.

Akashi jumped up two steps at a time, keeping Liam near the top, farther out of danger, stopping and standing with his son, looking down. Akashi's face was a mask of anger, and he hissed, "I'm sorry, Bryan," through his teeth.

"Alicia," I said. "Hold them off. There's two hebras tied to the tree. I'm going to put Bryan on Stripes. When I come back, I want you to go down the tree and get on Lightning. Then ride. Quietly. Go to the cornfield past the hebra barn. I'll have Joseph pick you up in the skimmer."

"I'm not done here," she said.

"No, you're not. You have to hold them off until I get Bryan on Stripes." I pitched my voice low, hoping, even with the acoustics of the amphitheater, to keep the Town Council from hearing. "Akashi has a weapon. He will shoot you if you do more than hold the situation in balance."

She flinched. I didn't look at Akashi, sure he would understand, and sure he would do it.

Joseph gasped in my ear. I ignored him, too.

I leaned down and slid my own microwave gun from its leather pouch, palming it, hoping no one would recognize it from a distance. This wasn't over, and I wasn't going to lose Bryan. I looked at him more carefully. The facial injuries were matched by a taped tear on one bicep, bruises on his hands, and cracked knuckles. I glanced down. His foot was casted, heavy, and the same leg was deeply scratched. "Can you walk?" I asked.

He shook his head. "Only if you can take my weight."

Not a good strategic choice. "Liam?" I called.

Tom spoke from just above me, out of my line of sight. "I'll do it." I swayed briefly, realizing how easily he could have stunned me if he had wanted to. He came around and stood by Bryan, letting Bryan put his weight on Tom's shoulder. Bryan's hand separated from mine.

"Thank you," I said to Tom. I called down to the dais, "I'll be back," resisting asking them to wait there. Alicia would see they waited; Akashi would see she did no more than that. The urge to flippancy had to be fear—but absurdly, I felt like giggling. Momentarily.

I stood while Bryan started back away from me, leaning hard on Tom. He was so slow now! I backed out, trusting Tom to watch in front of us. I kept backing up until I lost the view of the amphitheater, although Alicia, wedged in the tree, remained clearly visible. I turned, hoping against all reason that there would be no one near the hebras.

No luck.

Stile and Julian stood watching us, Chayla next to them. Stile stepped toward us. I called out, "No, back away."

Stile stopped, looking at me, his eyes wild and confused, his stunner in his hand. He started to bring the gun up.

I raised my hand with the microwave gun. "I will use this. And then Alicia will use . . . will use what she has."

He stared at me, his mouth open.

I struggled to keep my voice from shaking, to keep my hand with the little weapon in it from shaking. "I don't want to do this, Stile." My voice shook. "If I use this, I have to leave, too, and I gave my word I wouldn't do that. Bryan won't hurt you."

Chayla stepped forward and put her good hand on Julian's arm. "Let them go," she said. "They let me go. Bryan is not the threat."

Stile looked around. No one else was close, although a few people stood a few meters away, watching. Eric was among them, back from whatever errand he had run. He looked ashamed; the others nearby looked curious and confused; not threatening.

Stile looked at Bryan, his eyes roaming Bryan's damaged face, his cast. Confusion and sorrow showed in his face. "I'm sorry, Bryan. You didn't deserve what you got. I've seen you stand still to get picked on. I would've done what you did, and sooner."

Bryan looked evenly back at Stile, his eyes glazed with physical pain. He managed a short nod and one side of his mouth quirked into a half smile, but he didn't speak.

Stile dropped the hand that held the stunner, pointing the weapon at the ground. "You two are all right." He swallowed. "Go safely."

I breathed a long sigh of relief.

The three of us continued walking, moving at Bryan's tortured pace. I hissed at Tom. "How are we going to get him up? He can't climb the mounting straps."

Tom frowned. "I don't know."

Eric must have seen the problem. His voice was slow and carefully measured as he said, "May I help you?"

I looked him over. His face was earnest, open. Eric had no stunner. I'd never seen him with a weapon, never even seen him hunt. I nodded and stood where I could watch, the microwave gun resting easily in my hand, not feeling so heavy anymore. "I'll watch from here."

Bryan turned toward me, his eyes tortured. "Where am I going?" He stared, confused, blinking. He knew nothing of the *New Making,* nothing of the skimmer or Joseph's skill. And I could not tell him here.

"Do you want to stay in Artistos?"

He shook his head. "I want to stay with you."

"It's safer if you go," I choked out, blinking back a fresh round of tears, trying to keep my eyes clear and watchful. "Trust me."

He nodded, slowly, painfully. "Where?" he asked again.

"Far away." Deep sadness filled me. "Far enough that I may never see you again."

He said, "I didn't want this to happen. I'm sorry, I let you down."

I couldn't go to him, couldn't drop my guard, so I said, "You will always be my family."

"Will you be okay?" Bryan asked.

I glanced at Tom, who smiled at me, briefly, bitterly, encouragingly. "I think so. Go."

Bryan's return look was confused, but he mumbled, "Thank you, thank you for getting me out." He turned toward

Stripes, standing resolutely, waiting to be helped onto the big beast. He hated weakness, and I knew he hated that moment. His head came almost to Stripes's tall back, taller by a foot than Tom or Eric, and wider by far than either of them. Tom made a mounting block of his hands, and Eric stood close. Bryan stepped into Tom's hands with his good foot and reached for the saddle with his damaged hand, barely getting a good grip. Eric pushed up on Bryan's casted leg, awkwardly, hands around Bryan's big thighs, and Tom squatted, putting Bryan's good knee on his shoulder, standing and thrusting. Bryan fell half across the saddle, his face twisted with pain, his eyes glazed. He didn't cry out. He slowly swung his leg over the tall saddle, and sat up.

Stripes turned to look at me quizzically. I whispered to her, "Carry him carefully."

I had to get back. "Tom, can you stay here with Bryan?"

Tom nodded. "Be careful," he said.

Helping us would cost him. My voice choked up as I said, "Thank you."

Another flash of lightning, farther away, near the High Road, followed by a long roll of thunder. No more than an hour remained until dark. This had to finish. "Joseph. I'm getting Alicia away. Bring the skimmer as soon as I say; not before. The corn—"

"I heard you." His voice flattened, carried shock. "You aren't coming."

"Not now."

"You have to." Joseph sounded lost.

Movement caught my eye. Stile, staring up at the tree branch. He raised his arm, aiming the stunner at Alicia.

I screamed and raised my hand, raised my own weapon.

The soft *click-thwack* of a stunner sounded louder than it was.

Stile crumpled.

I whirled.

Tom.

Joseph screamed in my ear. "Chelo! Are you okay?"

Tom stood with his stunner out. He waved it at me. "Go. He'll be all right."

I jerked my hand down, suddenly dizzy. "No," I answered Joseph. "No. I'm not okay. Tom stunned Stile."

Joseph-in-my-ear fell silent. I darted back to the top of the stairs. Nava and Hunter and Wei-Wei huddled together on the dais, talking so softly I couldn't hear them. Ruth stood on the edge, eyeing Alicia.

Leaves rustled. "Chelo," Alicia hissed. "Come here. Is Bryan safe?"

I sidled over, watching below, standing under the tree. "Go," I said, "go now. Tom is watching out for you. Lightning is tethered at the foot of the tree. Bryan is waiting. Ride slowly, ride like you're in control. Fool them. I'll . . . I'll do my best to give you enough of a start."

I glanced directly up at her. She looked . . . intent. Her eyes shone. Her hands rested on the tree, cupping limbs. She jackknifed down through the fork she had been watching the amphitheater through, landing on her feet, her knees bent, above the lip of the amphitheater, almost pitching forward and over. Her arms windmilled and she found her balance, standing just above me now. What if she'd fallen? Would she have killed us both?

Her hair was in disarray. She laughed, lightly, then she pulled out the ball from a knot in her shirt. "Your turn." She thrust it forward, holding it with both hands, telegraphing her intent.

Then she let go.

I caught it, an automated motion. The ball was warm from her hands.

I held a weapon in each hand.

"It's the only way you can hold them for us," she said.

Why hadn't she just kept it, backed down the tree, used it as a shield for her and Bryan? Or was she right? I cursed.

Movement. A thin figure running up the steps. Ruth.

I lifted the ball. "Stop!" All eyes turned toward me, toward the object I held in my upraised hand.

Ruth stopped, glaring at me. "I knew you were no better."

"I am better," I said. "I want peace."

Ruth laughed. She knelt down in front of me, halfway up the steps, and leveled her stunner at Alicia.

Alicia only needed to step back and run, but she leaned forward, her own microwave gun in her right hand, firing it at Ruth.

The shot was a stream of light, hitting Ruth in the torso.

Pain bloomed on Ruth's face. She yelped and fired the stunner, a wild shot. She had danced out of Alicia's beam, but her free hand clutched her stomach and she glared at Alicia and me. Her arm came up again, pointing toward Alicia, and my hand raised of its own accord, pointing my own gun at her.

Akashi's voice behind me, directed at Alicia. He, too, held up a weapon, so that Ruth's stunner and Akashi's microwave gun pointed at Alicia and my microwave gun pointed at Ruth.

"Shoot Ruth," Joseph whispered in my ear.

I kept my eyes on Ruth, speaking slowly. "Alicia. I'll shoot you myself if you don't save Bryan."

Silence. The moment stretched, everyone still, threatening or watching. My hand trembled. I braced it with my other hand.

Alicia hissed. I glanced up at her. Her face was a mask of anger and fear, crazy, disconnected.

I screamed at her. "Alicia! Get Bryan to safety!"

She turned and was gone, a flash of foot the last I saw of her.

Every eye in the amphitheater turned toward me.

"Akashi, Liam, see them safely off. Bryan's not strong enough to ride by himself." I risked a glance at them, saw Akashi nod, Liam's face full of concern and fear. "Akashi—ride behind Bryan. Help him. Bring the hebras back. Liam—run beside them." I watched Ruth glare at me.

Akashi's voice was laced with concern. "That leaves you alone."

I nodded, turning back to face Ruth. "I know. But I need to know Bryan and Liam are safe." I didn't have to say he could control Alicia, talk to her, keep her from doing anything stupid. "Go, now," I said, sure that Joseph would know the command was meant for him. He had surely listened to the whole conversation.

I heard Akashi and Liam leave.

I gestured at Ruth with the hand that held the microwave gun. "Move away, back down." I spoke louder, directing my gaze at the whole assembled Council. "Don't doubt that I will use this to be sure Bryan escapes safely."

Ruth spit out, "You will answer for letting Alicia go."

I responded immediately. "It was neither my right, nor yours, to hold her. She would not have chosen this path if she had a home here, like I do. If she had been loved as a human being, as a girl."

She stayed where she stood, too close to me. "We will hunt her down. Whatever it takes."

I didn't think so, but now wasn't the moment to say so. "Bryan's safety matters."

Gianna spoke up. "Are you . . . are they . . . going back to the plains?"

She couldn't know I knew the plains may be swamped in a day.

But she knew. Would she tell me? She swallowed, looking like she wanted to say more, but she held her tongue. Maybe she'd talk in private. Could I count on her? "It will be all right. I can guarantee Alicia won't return to Artistos. That will have to be enough."

Hunter snapped at me. "How can you guarantee that?"

"Trust me." I gestured again at Ruth. "Go, and I will follow you partway down. Don't get too close. We have time, and I intend to have that talk I came for."

"We will not talk under threat," Hunter said.

I raised the hand that held the ball. "I will give this to you when Akashi reports that Bryan is safe." I shrugged, trying to appear calm. "I don't want it."

Ruth started down, her eyes on me, hatred and pain controlling her face. She still held her stomach.

"You'll heal," I said, following her, keeping at least five meters between us. She rejoined the group on the dais, and I sat in a seat on the edge of the aisle, five rows back from the dais, close enough to talk to them. I held the ball where they could see it, could see that I was ready to throw it. If I threw it from here, I would die, too.

The ball was heavy enough to pull a little on my arm, like holding a glass of water and struggling not to spill it. I hated holding such a thing, hated sitting here.

I spoke to the whole group of them, arguing for the only hope I had left. "I want to stay . . . on Jini at least. To stay here in Artistos or with the West Band. To help." I was mad now, angry at them for ever doubting me, for putting me in this place, making me able to hurt them. My voice rose with my anger. "I've always tried to help—I have never hurt any of you!"

Hunter nodded quietly. "How do we know your intentions are good?"

I sighed, tired of this argument, my anger falling to disgust. "Maybe you have to trust. Maybe you'll have to rely on what you know of me. I don't want to die, or to live outcast like Jenna. This is *my* home. It is only since Steven and Therese died"—I glanced at Nava, who watched me with a blank face—"only since then that I have been treated badly, by a handful of people who are afraid of what I am, but refuse to see *me*. Or people who are scared of Jenna, or Alicia. Well, I'm not them." I stopped, breathing hard. "On the way in, I ran into Gary, and he wished me luck. He complimented me on how I took care of his children when I took my turn in the nursery school." I could still leave. We could all leave. "We have skills to offer if you treat us respectfully."

"Give us Alicia and we will consider it," Hunter said.

I shook my head. She was beyond my reach now anyway. "I'm past waiting for you to consider." The amphitheater fell silent. There was nothing new to say. Even the storm seemed to have passed, to have fled into the mountains for the evening. The sky between the remaining clouds shone the soft blue that heralded dusk.

About ten minutes into uncomfortable silence, light flashed over the High Road, a streak of fire, a meteor. Fire flared, filling a huge patch of cliffside instantly, almost an explosion. We all jumped. I stood, watching it, forgetting myself and my task for a moment.

"Chelo!" Gianna screamed my name.

I turned.

Ruth had taken aim at me.

"If you shoot me"—I raised the ball—"this falls. Will it go off, then? Do you want to find out?"

I tilted my head back toward the light of the forest fire. "That fire? What it represents? The challenge of living here? I'm stronger with you. And you with me, with us. All that's missing is trust." I glanced back at the fire again, although I didn't look for long this time. Even far away, and moving away from us, up the cliffs where it could burn no farther than to the lake eventually, the fire felt menacing and fast. A rock had started a kilometer of woods burning. When we went up there, we'd be able to tell where the impact was. There would be no stick left by the crater. If the meteor was even big enough to leave a recognizable crater. We'd seen it before, heard it in roamers' tales. Meteors that left only fire behind, and maybe scattered bits of rock if you could find them.

Sometimes pretty rock. Maybe I'd like roaming.

When the solar system skipped stones, we knew. I pulled my attention back. I was losing focus. Tired. I had to keep focused. But anger and loss . . . and loss . . . I stood.

I wanted to watch for the skimmer. "You're no good at talking. I'm going back near the top. But I'll be watching. Come on up if you want to discuss anything real." I stared at Ruth. "But keep some distance."

I sat at the top step, near the tree, looking toward the plains. The guild halls and town stood between me and a clear view. Neat rows, all repaired from the earthquake.

Artistos looked orderly.

I could see almost every direction, and I would certainly hear anyone that tried to sneak up. There was no one in sight now, except a group that stood far away, watching. Chayla and Eric and Julian and who knew who else.

The skimmer's lights might be visible from here. Maybe I should climb the tree. But no, that would leave me vulnerable for a few moments. I couldn't trust Ruth's honor enough for that. Now I'd never know if Alicia killed Varay or she loved him or both, or how she felt about Joseph. But she'd be in cold sleep, and then somewhere else, with nothing to fight.

Hopefully.

The war we were born for was separating us, even now, rending the last bit of family we had in two.

I wanted Joseph to stay! I forced myself away from that thought.

There was one more thing I needed to know. "Gianna—can you come closer?"

She came, easily, unafraid.

I felt grateful for that.

When she was close enough the others couldn't hear, I whispered, "When will the tsunami come?"

She looked startled, but answered quickly, "After noon. Just."

"Thank you for your help," I said.

"Joseph helped me. I don't know how, but he has much better access to data." She looked at me curiously. "What can you tell me? What can he do now? Did he really turn off the nets, and how did he do it? Does he have a machine?"

The sky was clear now over the ocean, over the plains, and getting dark. Another meteor streaked through the atmosphere, burning up before it hit the ground. "I'll tell you the story after it's over, Gianna. You'll have to wait until then. It won't be long now."

She nodded. "I can wait." She swallowed and shifted on her feet. "I hope it's a glorious story."

"Me, too."

I'd barely gotten up here in time. The engine hum was audible. It scared me still, like my memory from when I was a baby, with Chiaro. Lights flashed on the far side of town. I couldn't see the skimmer itself, but I heard it throttle down and land.

Artistos was eerily silent. "Joseph," I whispered.

Joseph spoke in my ear. "Are you still all right?"

"Do you have Bryan and Alicia?"

"They're climbing in. I'm coming to get you. Go out into the park."

I shook my head. Realizing he couldn't hear that, I said, "I can't. I think I can get you away. I can't do more. Tell Jenna to leave early."

There was a long silence. Gianna was close enough to look at me quizzically. Joseph could just be on another earset for all she knew. All she would ever know, I thought. Finally Joseph said, "Can you come tell me good-bye?"

I caught myself shaking my head again. "No," I whispered. "No, I don't think I can." I started crying, deep wracking sobs. I set the ball on the ground, in reach, and wiped at my tears. "Come back if you can."

"I'll call you when we get to the ship."

The skimmer's lights rose and circled, dipping my way. For a moment I thought he was coming here after all, and my heart rose against my resolve, but the skimmer disappeared again, toward the spaceport.

I looked down. They'd heard it, too. Recognition painted their faces. Nava's mouth hung open. Lyssa looked at the sky, as if she expected something to fly over any moment. Ruth glared at me. Hunter let out a low whistle, and he, too, looked up at me. I was too far away to read his eyes, but he had to know the game had changed, that we held more power, more of our own technology, than he'd thought.

I picked the ball up, but stayed seated, glancing back and forth between the place the skimmer's lights had last been and the group huddled on the dais. As soon as my tears slowed, I started down the steps, carrying the ball carefully, holding the microwave gun pointed down as if it were sharp scissors. Gianna followed me, near my back, keeping her own silence. It took a long time to make it down the steps.

It seemed a great emptiness had descended on me as the skimmer turned away, as if a meteor had plunged through me, burning me inside out. I was committed now, committed to Artistos, my future hanging on the next few minutes. I stopped a few meters from them, at the foot of the steps, but out of reach of the dais. Hunter watched me carefully.

I gazed back at him, my face still wet with the tears of Joseph's leaving, but my voice steady. "Are you done considering? You will not see Alicia again, or Joseph, or Bryan.

But the rest of us plan to help you." I was sure Kayleen and Liam would stay.

Ruth glared at me, as if she wished I would disappear. Her hand fondled her stunner. Hunter's face was unreadable. Nava looked conflicted, her gaze swinging from me to Hunter and back again. Her hand crept to her stunner. "Give the ball to Hunter," she said evenly, in her best command voice.

Tom called down from above us. I didn't dare look back as he said, "Let her be, Nava. The others are leaving."

"How do you know?" Nava asked.

He'd heard my conversation with Bryan, but he couldn't know about *New Making*. I did not want to reveal it to them yet. I spoke quickly. "They have a skimmer. They can take it to Islandia."

If Tom guessed something else, he didn't say.

"Our nets, our information?" Hunter demanded.

"They will come back on in the morning."

"But the meteors?" Lyssa asked.

I felt sorry for her, our only clear support on the dais, but too weak to make a difference. Too scared. I spoke gently. "They will fall anyway, Lyssa. Knowing when will not stop them."

"Give Hunter the ball," Nava repeated, drawing her stunner.

"I . . . want to know you are sorry for sundering my family. For Bryan's beating." I swallowed. I had nothing to apologize for, not for myself. But Alicia . . . "I am sorry for Alicia. Sorry I am holding this thing."

Silence.

I heard Tom's steps as he walked down and ascended to the dais to stand next to Nava. He put an arm over her shoulder, pulling her near to him. She did not resist, but kept her eyes on me. Finally she nodded. "Yes, Chelo, I'm sorry for all of it." Her voice told me she meant it, but she had not yet said how she would change anything.

I waited.

"I will see that Artistos treats you better," she said. "I'm sorry for the loss of the others. But you must guarantee that . . . that at least Alicia will never return."

I shifted on my feet, struggling for a true answer. "All I know is that she will not return for years. That is all I can do."

She took a step toward me, her face more open than I'd seen it since the day we left.

I stepped up to the foot of the dais, holding up my hand, shaking, the ball heavy and unwelcome. Hunter reached down and took it from me.

It was as if a sigh filled the auditorium. Hunter's face relaxed, Nava smiled. "You did the right thing, Chelo."

My knees felt weak and shaky, and the emptiness of the moment threatened to overwhelm me. I did not want to fall at their feet, didn't want to be here anymore. Not right now. "I'm going to wait for Akashi and Liam." I turned away from them, starting up the stairs.

Hunter spoke behind me. "Give me the other gun."

I turned to face him. "I think I'll keep it for now." I glanced at Ruth. "I hope I never need to use it."

I thought Hunter was going to argue, to insist, but after a long moment he nodded at me.

"Will you stay with us?" Tom asked.

"Not tonight. If they'll have me, I will stay with Akashi and Liam."

I turned away from them all again, leaving Nava to control Ruth. She would do it.

I looked up to see Liam standing at the top of the stairs. By the time I finished my climb, Akashi had joined him. They reached their arms out for me, supporting me. We said nothing, just walked together away from Commons Park, leading the hebras. A meteor streaked across the sky, missing Artistos, missing the High Road, landing, perhaps, near Little Lace Lake.

28

DEPARTURES

I didn't see any more meteors that night.

I made it as far as Little Lace Park before I sat, unwilling to move. Akashi tied the hebras nearby and rustled up a tent from somewhere, and they bundled me inside it just as dark enveloped the park. When I climbed under the blankets, I felt so empty, so wrung-out, and so worried that I was sure I wouldn't sleep.

That was my last conscious thought until I woke from a dream.

In my sleep, I stood alone on the cliff's edge, looking over the blackened Grass Plains (which still smoked in my dream), watching the *New Making* rise away from me. It moved slowly, every inch of its passage pulling at me, pain knifing up my spine as it rose, and rose, and rose, and I screamed inside the dream and fell, jerking, landing hard on the hard ground near the cliff's edge, staring into an empty sky that faded to green tent fabric.

I crawled outside. Dawn had just begun to paint bright spots on the dewdrops clinging to the tall fall-yellow grass stems. Akashi and Liam sat outside, bundled in blankets, one on either side of the door, looking toward town. If they slept, they didn't sleep in the tent.

I looked from Akashi to Liam, both faces grown dear to me. I swallowed hard. "Thank you for watching over me."

Liam pulled me in close and kissed my hair, speaking

softly, "You watched over me. We could have all lost, maybe even been killed, but you found a way for everyone. Even Bryan."

I snuggled into him, grateful for his warmth in the cool air. Akashi watched me closely. "He's right. I believe you can make a better future now."

I shook my head. "I didn't do this, not really. Alicia forced the issue, and Alicia freed Bryan. I just helped them leave."

"Alicia's choices would not have ended well. You helped everyone be themselves by taking advantage of people's strengths."

"Joseph." I swallowed hard. "Joseph outgrew this place in the last few weeks. He needs something more. Perhaps now he will find it."

Akashi smiled softly at me. "I'm glad you can think of it that way. Perhaps the world out there is ready for him. I suspect he will be challenged." He scraped his fingers through his hair. "What about you, Chelo?"

I didn't need a fight with Nava. Artistos might as well be empty without Joseph. "Can I go to the West Band with you?"

"Of course," Akashi said.

Liam squeezed me harder, and I wanted to stay in the warm, soft place in his arms. Pushing myself free was hard.

I swallowed, missing Joseph already, and stood up, straightening my rumpled clothes. I walked out by myself, finding the outhouse and then going to the edge of the cliff above the Lace River. The redberries had nearly all fallen from the bushes and the few that remained were shriveled and dry. Leaves crunched under my feet. The emptiness born when the skimmer flew back to the *New Making,* carrying Bryan and Joseph, had settled into my bones, my skin, my heart. I had been here, in this park, with Therese and Steven, with Joseph, on more than thirty Trading Days.

But Joseph and I would not walk to Trading Day together again.

As if he heard my thoughts, Joseph whispered in my ear, "Chelo?"

"Are you ready yet?"

"Soon."

"Paloma and Kayleen are coming back here?"

"They're almost ready to leave. Paloma is brushing Jenna's hair."

"Really?" I pictured the tangled mess of Jenna's rough one-handed twisted braid. "That'll take all day."

Joseph laughed. "Nope. She cut it off. Jenna's giggling. You should see her. She can't wait to leave."

I could picture it in my head: Jenna shorn and happy, Jenna one step closer to becoming herself again. "Tell Jenna—tell Jenna thanks. And to take care of you."

He didn't reply.

"Tell Paloma and Kayleen to bring the hebras with them, all of them. I'll meet them at the top of the trail. If the wave comes like you think, and it's dangerous, if you have to go, then go. I'll try to get there to watch you leave."

"I want to see you again," he said.

"It's too risky to bring the skimmer in here."

"We put the skimmer away." He was silent a moment, as if distracted by something on his end. "Sis? We hid the skimmer in a clearing partway up—on the same side as the First Road."

Good. "Thanks. We might need it."

"Kayleen knows where it is." A note of pride crept into his voice. "I went with them, as backup, but she flew it. She did okay."

I remembered her stumbling walk from yesterday. "Is she doing better? She was getting confused yesterday."

"She's still a little unstable, but better. Do you still have the projector?"

I felt in my pocket. I'd forgotten about it, between guns and bombs and Alicia and . . . and everything. "Yes. Tell Jenna I'll keep it safe. I have the frizzers, too, the ones she sent for Alicia and Bryan. And a microwave gun."

His voice made me imagine his face earnest and concerned. "Be careful with that stuff—don't get caught with it. I don't want to find you living in the woods like Jenna when I come back."

"I'm going with Akashi and Liam, with the West Band."

"Good." His voice shook. "I wish you could ride down." He hesitated. "I'll come back."

"I know you will." A lump filled the back of my throat.

"Jenna says it takes years to go and return," he said.

My voice choked, and my eyes stung. "I'll be here." The river and the redberry bushes and the tent trees blurred as water filled my eyes. I struggled to keep the tears from my voice. "Someone needs to wait for our parents, anyway. Now, go on, get ready. Oh . . . and turn the data back on. I promised they could have it this morning."

He laughed. "I've set it so the net restrictions all release when I leave the area. I think that's safer."

"All right. I'll call you as soon as I'm close."

His voice went silent in my ear and I cried then, hard, sobs wracking my body. I sat, my head on my arms, wishing for more time. He'd outgrown Artistos. And Artistos had rejected him for it. Perhaps he was born to leave, although I was sure our *altered* parents had imagined different circumstances.

We were what they made us, but our lives made us what we were. Our actions, our choices. My *altered* parents did not make me to stay and help Artistos, nor Joseph to flee in a nearly empty ship.

Akashi and Liam and I took Stripes and Lightning through town, heading for the cliff overlooking the Grass Plains, Akashi on Lightning and Liam and I doubled up on Stripes. We passed small groups of people on the road, walking toward the cliff. I spotted Gianna, and stopped Stripes, leaning down. "Gianna? What's happening?"

"People want to watch the wave." She grinned at me, her eyes flashing friendly conspiracy. "I told them all about the wave yesterday—I figured it would keep people from thinking too hard about you. Now, I'm sure it will happen, and that we'll be well above it, but able to see. Everyone wants to see."

"Thanks." Regardless of the dream, it seemed fitting that the *New Making*'s flight would have an audience.

"The meteor came down this morning, almost exactly on the other side of Fremont. Joseph beamed me a sat-shot of it better than any of ours. I'll show you when we get back."

"When will the wave come?" I queried her.

She shrugged. "Waves. An hour. Maybe a little more." She gazed up at me. "It's funny—they don't look like much now. But they will when they get here. They'll hop the lower cliffs as if they were a stair." She reached a hand up to take my hand. "I didn't hear the skimmer last night. Is Joseph safe yet?"

"Soon. Ride with us?" I glanced at Akashi.

He nodded and loosed his mounting rope for her. She climbed up, sitting behind him, her arms hanging loosely at her sides.

I felt glad she rode with us.

Nearer the cliff, the crowds were heavier. Some people looked at me strangely, others waved. They all moved out of our way and made room. As we neared the big winch, I spotted Lyssa and Tom and Nava and Hunter, a few feet back from the edge of the cliff, easily in sight of the trailhead. I didn't see Ruth. Hopefully she'd gone back to her band.

We dismounted and tied the hebras, and I went to stand near the Council, joined by Liam and Akashi and Gianna. Nava's gaze met mine for a long moment, and even though she didn't smile, she nodded and warmth touched her eyes. After she turned back to watch the sea, Tom grinned as if I were his own child come to stand near him.

In my dream, I had stood entirely alone as *New Making* flew away. Standing here, with everyone, felt like a symbol of hope.

I looked down the trail. A line of hebras snaked along the plains, already near the bottom of the cliff. I breathed out a sigh of relief, realizing only now that I had been afraid they would go, too. The town needed Kayleen now, needed her skills. I needed her.

Past the spaceport, the *New Making* gleamed in the late-fall sun. It had to work, to fly them safely away. It had to.

Should I wait, let Kayleen and Paloma get up here? The ocean looked calm, but the sea was surely coming. I stepped a few feet back from the edge. "Joseph? I'm here."

His voice came through high and excited. "We're ready."

I glanced at my chrono. A half hour had passed since we picked up Gianna. "Is Bryan okay?"

"He's already in cold sleep. Jenna thought that was better."

So many mysteries Joseph was seeing and I was missing. "When he wakes, tell him I miss him."

"I will."

Bryan might not hear those words for years. He might sleep in transit until they arrived at Silver's Home. I stepped back to the edge, and glanced down in time to see Kayleen's dark hair frame her face, to see her look up and wave at us. Surely she was too far away to pick me out, but they'd be able to see the crowd.

I whispered to Joseph, barely choking out the words, "Go safely."

"Blood, bone, and brain."

I laughed then, appreciating the depth of his simple childhood explanation. "Go now, before I make you stay. I love you, little brother."

"I love you, too, sis. Don't let them push you around."

"I won't."

I stood still, watching. Seconds took a long time to pass. The ship looked as silent as before, the sea as calm.

Gianna came up next to me, and took my hand. I looked past her, to Nava on the other side of Gianna. Nava whispered, "The *New Making*," understanding dawning on her face. Somehow she knew. Perhaps simply by the way I watched the ship.

It didn't matter anymore. I stood, my eyes glued to the ship, my heart beating fast.

A deep rumble began to fill the plains, growing louder quickly. White steam began to rise up below the *New Making*.

The crowd gasped.

On the horizon, the sea swelled, a smooth elongated hump, a moving hill of water.

The ship rose, gracefully, in slow motion, rising up until it was even with us, a silver arrow. I wanted the moment to take a long time, wanted *New Making* to hover gracefully in the air.

It accelerated away, leaving a white line behind it in the blue sky.

Then it was gone.

The white steamy line of its passage thinned and lost form, and then disappeared altogether. I watched the empty place in the sky where the ship had flown, not wanting to look down to the empty place on the Grass Plains where it had rested. The blue sky mesmerized me until people around me screamed, and I looked down to see the sea rise up over the low cliffs where the Grass Plains met the sea, and rumble toward the spaceport, like frothy fingers reaching for us.

"The shuttles!" Nava exclaimed.

Tom reached for her and folded her in his arms. The water rose around the hangar, the only building big enough to see well from the cliff's edge. The wave washed over the big building's roof. The building stood, just slightly askew.

Kayleen! I leaned out over the edge as the water slammed into the cliff so hard that the ground beneath my feet shuddered. Kayleen's dark hair and Paloma's golden hair shone against the gray and brown cliff, their faces bright and intent. I heard them yell, but the wave made too much noise to make out their words. They hadn't fallen.

Gianna's hand pulled me away from the edge of the cliff. I stood, shaking, images of the powerful ship, of my powerful and beautiful little brother, and the powerful wave all mixed up in my head. I looked around.

Nava looked stunned. Tom had released her from his embrace, but he still held her hand. "The shuttles might be okay. I'll check on them tomorrow."

Akashi and Liam were nearby, and as I caught Liam's eyes he smiled at me. Akashi smiled, too, then leaned up to say something to Liam.

My gaze returned to the water churning at the foot of the cliff, beginning to withdraw. Glancing out, the splashy whitecaps of the second wave climbing the low cliffs began to jump up and shine in the sun. I watched until Kayleen's head bobbed up the last bit of trail. She was leaning forward whispering to Longface, praising him for something. She looked up and saw me. Her face transformed into a wide smile and she dismounted, handing Longface's reins to the nearest by-stander, and ran toward me, toward Liam and Akashi and Gianna and Nava and Hunter and us all.

Gianna whispered, "A glorious story, indeed."

I pulled my attention away from the empty sky, the receding wave. "At least it's over."

"I suspect," she said, "I suspect it's just beginning."

Turn the page for a preview of

READING THE
WIND

BRENDA COOPER

Available now

TOR® A TOR HARDCOVER

ISBN-13: 978-0-7653-1598-4   ISBN-10: 0-7653-1598-X

PROLOG

A CONTINUATION OF THE STORY OF CHELO LEE, DATED AUGUST 3, YEAR 222, FREMONT STANDARD, AS BROUGHT TO THE ACADEMY OF NEW WORLD HISTORIANS

∽

The last story I told you was of our sundering. The long war for the wild planet Fremont ripped the seven of us apart: it sent away my brother Joseph, his sweetheart Alicia, our friend Bryan, and our best protector, damaged and broken, Jenna. The sundering sent them to the stars, aboard the silver ship, the *New Making*. It left three of us on Fremont: three genetically changed teens amongst a few thousand original humans.

I could have stayed with Kayleen in Artistos, where I grew up, but Artistos would have been full of Joseph's ghost: in our house, in the guild halls, in Commons Park, in the school.

Instead, I went with the West Band of field scientists, or roamers, to build a different life for myself. That choice was, in a way, a different and smaller sundering.

I no longer lived in my town with my friend Kayleen, but instead I roamed wild Fremont with the one other like us, Liam.

So the story I will tell you now begins after both the big sundering and the little sundering, after the ship flew away, and after I fled Artistos to become a roamer.

Two and a half years passed between the end of the last story and the beginning of this one. The first was my year of sharp pain from losing contact with Joseph. I spent the second year learning to be a roamer, and the rest becoming useful, maybe even needed, within the band. Becoming family.

By the end of these years, I was happy. I loved being a roamer, loved being able to hunt and run and be smart and be myself. The West Band gave Liam and me respect in spite of our differences and we gave them more success than they had before.

Even though Liam and I didn't promise each other a future with words, our hands warmed when we touched, and we found each other in any crowd, across nearly any distance.

I had my own little wagon—no small thing.

And every year, we got to visit Jenna's cave twice. Our cave now. We named it the Cave of Power, and there we were learning who we were.

Perhaps, in spite of the gaping hole where my brother had been, I was happier than ever.

The only shadow falling on my life was the one I saw in Kayleen's eyes when we went to town.

1

WE SPEAK

Herb-scented smoke from the early evening fires lifted my heart while drumbeats lifted my feet. Cool spring air bathed my skin. My skirt swirled, slapping my calves as I danced behind Liam. A light sheen of sweat coated his back and thighs, shining nearly gold in the last full rays of the sun.

It was the end of our semiannual visit to town, a night reserved for the two bands of roamers to feast and compete together.

Twenty-five of us from the West Band had started this stick dance. Just an hour in, ten remained.

Our bandmates chanted with the drums, helping us dance the divide from dusk to night, holding bright torches. The pace increased yet again, the drums seeking to exhaust us, the chant to buoy us. Dark-haired slender Sasha fell away next, followed by red-blond blocky-and-strong Kiara. They rolled free of our feet and took torches, joining the chant, cheering for us, for the band. Every time I began to fade, Mayah's voice wormed into the part of me that could quit, blocking it, whispering, "shuffle, two, kick, three, turn, jump, jump . . ."

As the stars winked awake, my kicks grew higher, my dip and swirl lower and faster. The drummers increased the tempo until sweat poured from them like it poured from us.

The clacking of wood on wood warned us just before long, brightly painted sticks slid under our feet, horizontal, a foot above the ground. The swirling sticks demanded precision and height from our jumps. A crowd passed the sticks back and forth, hand to hand. The watchers were all roamers, most from our band, some from the East Band, friends and a few skeptics, two judges.

More dancers fell away, feet tangling, bodies rolling.

More sticks. The East Band had danced first. They'd managed five sticks—we already danced over ten. The joy of competition tore a grin from me. And it was the band's win—normal band members danced with us when we passed the East Band's mark. No one could blame our win on Liam and me. We were free to play; it didn't matter now that we were faster and stronger.

Contest had changed to exhibition.

A few of the East Band left the circle. Not all. Just the ones who hated our differences.

Three of us remained, then two. Me and Liam, jumping, kicking, close to each other then away, a dance between us more than for the others. Fifteen sticks, and still we didn't stumble. The stick-bearers grinned and raised them so high my skirt flew up past my knees. Drummers began to call for replacements. Chanters called our names: "Liam! Chelo! Liam! Chelo!"

Liam threw his head back and laughed, and I joined him, giggling, so short of breath the laugh tore pain from my belly. Pain or not, our laughter reflected joy in moving well, joy in success, joy in being with each other and surrounded by family.

I held out my hands, palms down and he shook his head, *not yet*.

Jump, twist.

He grinned at me, his dark eyes bright with exertion.

Swoop, turn.

Faces, grinning. Kiara and River and Sky and Abyl.

Hop, high, down, just the toes, then up again over two sticks. Cheers all around us. I reached a hand to steady Liam and we leapt together as one, holding hands. We side-hopped over the seated circle of watchers, just above their heads, landing hard, almost falling. After, we stood, slick with sweat and glowing in the firelight of twenty torches.

A cheer erupted, a celebration of our prowess and, perhaps, relief that we were done. The Last Night celebration of Spring Trading was now officially over, and the rest of the evening could be given to seeing friends.

I stopped by my wagon to change from my dancing skirt into pants and a shirt, and to slip light leather sandals onto my feet. My home was small, but it was mine—a tiny kitchen and an everything-else room just longer than I was tall and half as wide; light enough to be pulled by a single hebra. I'd painted the inside pale blue with clouds and birds and, here and there, the tip of a tree. A silver space ship arced across the ceiling, for my brother, who had gone into the sky.

Dressed for a trip into Artistos, I hesitated briefly in my doorway, centering. The wagon Liam shared with his parents, Akashi and Mayah, stood close to my smaller wagon, signifying we were all in the same family group. Maps decorated both, identifying us as geographers. Light poured from the window in Akashi's wagon, illuminating the designs. My fingers caressed the paint, running across the slight ridges where mountains and lakes dotted the terrain here on Jini, the largest of the two continents on Fremont. I had hand-painted them on the side of the wagon, not sure even at the time if I was painting myself into a profession or into Akashi's family. As usual, Akashi apparently knew my feelings, even the contradictory ones. He had simply smiled and helped me get tough parts, like Islandia's Teeth, painted right.

I shook my head, pushing aside the memory. Right now, I had to find Kayleen.

Liam emerged, dressed simply in a pale green hemp tunic and brown pants. Like me, he stood a head taller than most of the original humans on Fremont. A shock of blond hair hung over dark eyes, and a long braid twisted down his back nearly to his waist. He broke into a warm grin as soon as he spotted me. My grin answered his, and I immediately felt almost as much like we were one connected being as I had in the dance.

"We did great!" He reached for my arm, his voice tinged with pride and satisfaction. "Dad said he was watching from the hill. He thought we'd dance all night."

"Well, and I thought you'd never stop," I teased. "I thought we'd just go until one of us fell."

He laughed, not like in the dance, but soft and low. "We'd have worn out the drummers."

"Or ourselves." I stepped briefly into his arms, then pushed away, unwilling to be lost inside of his embrace. "Let's find Kayleen. I'm worried about her. She seemed so . . ." I searched for a good word. ". . . so listless yesterday. She didn't get excited about the maps we found in the cave on the way down and she barely ever looked at me."

He put a hand on my shoulder and looked past me, as if lost in thought. "She's trapped here. We're free."

For just a moment I was glad that she hadn't seen the dance. Then a flash of guilt at the thought ran through me, making me shiver. "Let's go." I squeezed his hand.

We jogged side by side, heading into town from our encampment in Little Lace Park. The Lace River ran down a short cliff to our right, full with rushing winter-melt water, singing into the gathering darkness. Here, we could walk freely, without sorting every sound for the dangers that roamed or grew in the wilds.

Twintrees and lace maples and redberry bushes lined the path, reaching new spring branches across, trying, as always, to reclaim any part of Fremont we humans struggled to tame. Night birds twittered and called to each other.

Kayleen still lived with Paloma in one of the four-houses a block away from Commons Park. When I knocked on their door, Paloma opened it, smelling of spring mint and redberry. "Chelo and Liam! Come in. How are you?"

"We're fine," Liam said.

Standing in her doorway, I remembered a hundred times I'd stood here before, starting when I could barely reach the knob. This close, streaks of gray showed in her blond hair and wrinkles blossomed like flowers around her blue eyes. "Is Kayleen here?"

She shook her head. "Almost never."

"Are you all right?" I asked.

She shook her head again, short and sharp, then smiled and said, "Sure. Will you come in for tea?"

I wanted to stay and talk to her. But finding Kayleen was more important. "Do you have any idea where she is?"

"She's probably down by the hebra barns—she has a young one she's taken a fancy to, and spends much of her time there." Paloma twisted her hands together. "She goes out after work every night, and only comes home to sleep. I don't even know what or when she eats any more."

I winced. "I'm sorry."

Paloma sighed and took my hand. "The nets work well right now. We've asked less and less of her. Even Nava leaves her alone some days. Kayleen's been helping Gianna with the satellite data, and she identified the tracks of the last three good-sized meteors almost perfectly. Gianna is almost the only one she talks to anymore." Her voice dropped lower. "I'm sure she misses you."

Even though there was nothing accusing in her tone, guilt tugged at me. I looked up at Liam. "Maybe we should stay in town next winter."

Liam turned to Paloma, his voice apologetic. "We *can't* stay now. The band needs us the most in summer."

"She would like to see you more." Paloma paused. "Me, too. You can stay here if you like. I . . . I'd like your opinion about Kayleen."

"We're leaving tomorrow. We have to go; surely you understand." I glanced down at my chrono. "We should get to the barn."

Paloma smiled. "I know. Look, I'll talk to Nava and see if Kayleen can come visit you for a while this summer. Is that okay with you?"

"Of course." I returned her smile and touched her hand. Small comfort, but all I could offer. "What about this baby hebra she's adopted?"

Paloma smiled again, as if she, too, were enamored of the little beast. "She has. A young one with the prettiest green highlights in her brown striping when the sun shines on it. Kayleen's training her. She already follows Kayleen around the pasture, and she'll be ready to ride by midsummer. She named her Windy."

I smiled, picturing Kayleen with the young hebra. "I hope I meet Windy."

Liam held Paloma for a moment, kissing the top of her head, and then I embraced her. Her head came to my shoulder, and for the first time ever it struck me that I could protect and help her more than she could protect and help me. "I hope everything works out all right," I murmured.

Part way down the street, I turned to look back. Paloma stood in the door, watching. She gave us a little wave.

I held my precious sun-fed flashlight, but left it off to protect my night vision as we jogged down to the barns. Even though warm night air tickled my skin, the winter had been harsh and long, and only about half of the fields had been planted so far. We passed a few people heading home from late-night chores, exchanging polite half-waves. Already, town life seemed small.

As we neared the barns, Stripes called out a greeting to me, and two or three other hebras whickered. Their tall graceful forms made black silhouettes outlined by the soft light from the barns. Their heads swiveled toward me. I went to Stripes and buried my face in her neck fur. She'd been in the common herd once, but Akashi had bought her for me the first spring after I joined the band. As he'd offered her lead to me, his eyes had twinkled with joy. "You need someone you know you can count on."

I'd cried.

I breathed in Stripes's dusty barn smell. "We'll leave tomorrow," I whispered into the long ear she swiveled down toward me.

As if in response, she dropped her big head over my shoulder, nearly an embrace. Her hot breath trickled along the back of my neck.

I pushed away gently and looked around. I didn't see Kayleen, or any other human movement. "I don't think she's here," I whispered.

Liam called out, "Kayleen!"

No response.

Low evening lights made circles on the rush floor in the long, tall barn. The hebras each came up to be greeted, turning their long ears toward us and asking silent questions with their wide, intelligent eyes. Two or three of the females had spindly-legged spring babies beside them, but I couldn't tell if one might be Windy. They were all beautiful.

Kayleen was not with any of them.

At the end of the aisle, I called again, "Kayleen, are you here?"

Still no answer.

We stepped out the back door into the big practice ring, and I called a third time. "Kayleen?"

Liam stepped out into the corral, and leaned against the metal bars of the big practice ring. "I don't see any sign of her."

A single light bolted high on the outside of the wooden barn illuminated his face and shone on his blond hair.

I walked over near him, and clambered up on the bars, sitting on the top one. It made me taller than him by almost a meter. "Do you remember last fall, when I told you Kayleen seemed so lost—somewhere—that I could barely get her attention?"

He reached a hand up and set it over mine where it clung to the bar. "Yes, I remember."

"I'm scared for her. Maybe, like Joseph, she's become too different."

"Have you talked to Gianna?" he asked.

"Not this trip, not enough to ask about Kayleen. Besides, Gianna is so much older. It's not the same as having *friends*." A brief shock of bitterness crossed my heart. "And you know who's here. Garmin and most of the other people our age haven't changed, so there's no reason to think they're kind to Kayleen."

"I know." Liam hopped up next to me on the bars. "But it's not like the East Band loves us. Surely some of how she's treated is up to her. If she's distant with us, imagine how she must be with everyone else."

I moved closer to him, brushing thighs. "I'd still like to help her if I can. I think . . . maybe she's living too much in the nets and not enough in the real world."

"Maybe."

His profile in the half light swelled my chest. Simply looking at him made me feel I could float from the bars and land on the barn roof. "Being with us in the wild, she wouldn't be in the nets so much. You have to pay attention out there."

Liam sighed. "Well, I wonder if she's focused enough for that? I wouldn't trust her to travel by herself. Someone would have to come back for her, and we'll be way out by Rage Mountain this summer. It would be too hard."

I nodded. "I should be able to help her. She and I used to be so close. . . ."

"She has to *let* you help her." He reached an arm over my shoulder and pulled me close, unbalancing us a little so I gripped the rail harder. "You can't solve every problem."

I never could. It had always taken us all. I missed Jenna's watchful eye and weird way of helping us learn, and I missed Bryan's silent strength. I even missed willful and lost Alicia with all of her pain and anger. Most of all, I missed Joseph. He'd be able to help Kayleen in ways I couldn't—he, too, rode the wind. And more. He flew space ships. Where was he, and how different from me had he yet become?

Liam must have felt my need, because he held me close and began to hum softly, a sweet song of summer fields. I looked up at a sky full of stars gathered around Faith and Summer. I searched for a third moon, which would have been a sign of good luck, but didn't find one.

The barn light switched off.

"Why did the light go off?" Liam asked.

"Because I couldn't stand to watch you two anymore," Kayleen said. "Because I'm crazy and I do crazy things. Because I live too much in the nets and not enough in the real world." A pause. Her voice, ripped with pain, floating down from the top of the barn. "I can't be trusted to travel by myself."

I sat up. How much had she heard? "Kayleen?"

She didn't answer.

I turned on my flashlight and shone it upward, looking for her. We called her name, and Liam took my light and scrambled up onto the roof. After a while, he called, "She's not here."

He climbed back down and stood a little distance from me, his arms by his sides, the closeness between us turned awkward by her sudden absent presence. She was fast—if she wanted to ditch us here in the dark, in her place, she could. I looked up at where the light had been, and spoke, hoping she was still close enough to hear me. "Kayleen. We're just worried about you. I miss you."

The hebras stamped quietly in their stalls and a cool wind blew softly through the rafters.

Liam added, "Come out. So we can talk."

We waited, still standing a little apart, listening carefully for any sound that might be our friend, our sister. Twenty minutes passed, in which we said nothing, afraid she would hear, or that she wouldn't hear.

We walked back, side by side, not touching, not saying anything.